CHRONOS WARLOCK

SHAMI STOVALL

Published by
CS BOOKS, LLC

Cover Design: Chris McGrath
Editors: Nia Quinn, Celestian Rince

IF YOU WANT TO BE NOTIFIED WHEN SHAMI STOVALL'S NEXT BOOK RELEASES, PLEASE VISIT HER WEBSITE OR CONTACT HER DIRECTLY AT
s.adelle.s@gmail.com

To John, my soulmate.
To my patrons over on Patreon, because they're amazing.
To everyone who read an ARC copy, thank you so much!
To Drew, for being a great agent.
To Soundbooth Theater, for the amazing audio.
To my Facebook group, for all the memes.
And finally, to everyone unnamed, thank you for everything.

CONTENTS

BOOK 1 RECAP

Adair and Carter Finch were warlocks, brothers, and partners in their own magical PI agency. Throughout their years of traversing the globe to solve crimes for witches, wizards, and other magical beings, they never once failed to solve a case.

They were legendary, with few privy to the secret of their success.

Those in the know attributed Adair and Carter's remarkable abilities to a pact they had made with Chronos, the manipulator of time. Thanks to Chronos's magic, the brothers could rewind time up to twenty-four hours. This allowed them to rectify mistakes, endlessly investigate, and even daringly test risky theories, helping them solve the most complicated of murders and locate the most elusive of victims.

Unfortunately, while on a mission in France, Carter died, and Adair had failed to rewind time.

It wasn't Adair's fault—a monster claiming to be a god had the power to nullify magic, and prevented Adair from saving Carter. But Adair was never the same after that.

Adair returned to his hometown of Stockton, and for ten years, wrestled with depression that hounded him like a second shadow. He stopped taking clients, rarely used his magic, and found himself talking more to DoorDash delivery people than anyone else.

Until Bree Blackstone, a twelve-year-old girl, came pounding on his apartment door.

Bree's mother, Vera, had been murdered. And Bree had been specifically instructed to go to the Finch brothers if ever she was in trouble—they never failed to help a client, after all.

Now going by simply "Finch" after his brother's death, Adair was initially hesitant. But realizing the gravity of Bree's situation, he reluctantly took on the case.

Bree's father was the prime suspect. He had been killing cats by the dozens, and the night before Vera's death, there had been an argument between him and his wife. Even the lead detective on the case, Rhett Jenner, figured it had to be Liam Blackstone, the only person with a discernable motive.

However, as Finch investigated, someone shot Bree, attempting to silence her, the only witness to the crime.

Finch rewound time, saving Bree and restarting the day, and he became convinced the true perpetrator wasn't Bree's father, but someone or some group involved in Vera's demise.

In order to gain lockpicking abilities, Finch made a pact with Kullthantarrick, a trickster spirit. This spirit, who everyone called "Kull," said she would help only if Finch found her a human body to inhabit. Finch agreed.

Ultimately, his investigation led him to believe the police were behind the murder. When sifting through the evidence at the police station, it turned out the cops were caught up in a witches' feud, which had cost them the lives of several police officers. Because of their paranoia, the cops had forced

Liam Blackstone to kill cats and make magical items, which upset his wife. Vera attempted to tell the police to leave them alone, and was killed in the resulting struggle.

Once Finch, Bree, and Kull pieced together the events, Bree implored Finch to identify the exact officer responsible for her mother's death and put an end to the witches' feud, thereby preventing further police fatalities.

Again, Finch reluctantly agreed.

Finch ended the feud by defeating the leader who had murdered the cops, and brought her to justice. Then, just as Finch was confronting Rhett Jenner, the lead detective and actual murderer, Detective Jenner revealed himself to be a warlock.

Jenner had bonded with the magic-nullifying monster that had killed Carter—Gixmoth the Desolate.

And now Jenner had the same abilities to neutralize Finch's magic.

Without his ability to rewind time, Finch had to physically fight Jenner. In a cowardly attempt to distract Finch, Jenner turned his gun on Bree. Finch pushed her out of the way, getting shot in the process.

Kull leapt into the fray, but was crushed by Jenner's boot and killed.

And in their last moments fighting the deranged detective, Finch swore he wouldn't lose anyone else. He made sure Bree was safe before throwing himself at Jenner for the final showdown.

Fortunately, Finch won—via electrocution—and before he could die, Bree returned to give him the motivation he needed to rewind time.

And on the final day, Finch did everything perfectly. He resolved the witches' feud, gathered all the evidence to convict Jenner, and even managed to squeeze in time for a haircut.

Finch had saved Bree, her father, Kull, the police, and even a random dog. Of course, he still owed Kull a body, and Bree some lessons in magic, but those could wait for another day.

Now on to "Chronos Warlock," the second book in the series...

CHAPTER
ONE

Finch had fondled a lot of things in the past, but corpses had never made the list.

Until tonight.

He exhaled, and his breath came out as a fine mist. The temperature was set to freezing in the mortuary's body storage room. The steel doors, colder than the air, practically burned Finch whenever he touched them with his bare hands. He would've given his left leg to have a pair of gloves in that moment.

Frisbee-Bloth & Carlos Mortuary was one of the most popular in Stockton, and Finch had visited many times. He had also used their autopsy suite on several occasions, with permission from the owners, of course. Few knew the strange needs of the owners, who had to feast on dead flesh in order to stave off their magical illness. A layperson would call them *zombies*, but to those who knew anything about magic, they were known as *draugr*, people on the verge of losing themselves to the curse of the undead—unless they consumed human flesh.

Finch kept the secret to himself to have full run of the mortuary after hours.

The mortuary's storage room was built to hold forty bodies at a time. Against regulation, "longer term" residents were packed into a freezer room in the back, allowing for sixty more dead bodies. That was how the mortuary kept their prices so low—by skimping on the costs of *individual packaging*.

Uninterested in the back room, Finch rooted around the lockers. The fluorescent lights flickered overhead, creating an atmosphere perfect for any horror movie.

Finch opened a large steel door, reached inside, and yanked out the tray.

Normally, a single body was placed in each locker, positioned with their back on the tray, their toes pointed upward, covered by a modesty sheet. Unfortunately, Stockton always had a parade of people getting shot, getting hit by a vehicle, or being punched in the heart by obesity and diabetes. Mortuaries were overworked, as sad as that statement was.

Two dead men rested on the tray, each on their side. Finch pulled off the white sheet. The corpses were barely embalmed and still awkwardly malleable. Their stomach skin sagged into a disgustingly fleshy pool around their midriffs. Finch pushed one body to the side and then rolled the other onto his back, so he could get a better look at the individual.

The man's mayonnaise complexion and sunken eyes screamed *dead*.

"What about this one?" Finch asked, his voice gruff and betraying his irritation. It was well past the time he usually hit the sack.

A plump pigeon hopped around on Finch's shoulder, her eyes giant, yellow, and staring in opposite directions. She replied with a soft *coo* as she tilted her head from side to side.

Finch knew he looked like an insane hobo speaking to a flying rodent he had smuggled into a mortuary. Thankfully, he wasn't losing his mind—the pigeon was a trickster spirit by the name of *Kullthantarrick the Sneak*. She swaddled her true appearance with the forms of animals, hiding from humans in plain sight.

Kull—as her friends knew her—leapt from Finch's shoulder and landed squarely on the stomach of the dead body.

She lowered her bird head and observed the navel. "I'm not fond of outies." Then she eyed the genitals. "They looked squished up." And finally, she examined the corpse's legs. "Stubby. Not hairy enough."

Finch pinched the bridge of his nose. How did he get into situations like this?

"I don't like this one," Kull said with a dismissive *coo*. "This body is so… lumpy. I want a form with more panache."

"What does that even mean?" Finch asked.

"I want to be *memorable*. I need to be a human with something distinct! A plain body won't do. It's going to be the only body I have for the rest of my life, after all."

"This guy is fat." Finch pointed to the corpse. "That's a distinct feature."

Kull shook her head. "No. I need to be special. I need to have something that sets me apart." She spread her blue-and-gray wings. "I want to walk into a room and have everyone turn their heads to see me." She shook her largest feathers, her gaze on the ceiling, her focus clearly on images only she could see in her mind's eye. "I want everyone… to remember me afterward."

"I think I saw a tattoo on the face of this other corpse," Finch said as he rolled the first dead body back onto his side. Kull leapt off and landed on Finch's shoulder. Then Finch yanked the other body until the corpse was on his back. "That would be distinct, right?"

Kull pushed her feathers, her eyes wide. "Oh! A giant tattoo? *On his face?* Perfect!" She flapped her wings and landed on the dead man's collarbone to better examine everything.

Finch cringed.

The second body *did* have a tattoo. He hadn't seen it fully until this very moment.

It was a swastika. On the corpse's forehead. With two tiny Uzis on either side.

After a happy coo, Kull turned around to face Finch. "This one is perfect."

"*No*," Finch groaned. "Forget this one. I'm not letting you inhabit this body."

"W-Why not? I'll definitely turn heads with a crazy tattoo! No one will forget me."

Finch frowned so hard it almost hurt his face. "I swear to god, if you plant your spirit in this body, I will shoot you myself."

All Kull's enthusiasm deflated faster than a popped balloon. She leapt back onto Finch's shoulder and then drooped her wings.

Finch hastily rammed the tray back into the locker. The foot of the first man caught on the edge of the door, and the whole table *slammed* halfway into position, unable to go any further. Finch groaned as he heaved around the dead bodies, fidgeting until they were squished together enough to close the locker door.

As Finch fumbled at his task, his cellphone buzzed. He tried to ignore it as he kicked the locker door shut, but the buzzing continued. Who was calling him at two in the morning? No one who had any respect for him, obviously.

Finch walked over to the next locker.

"Can we look at the female bodies next?" Kull asked with a sad *coo*. "I think most human women get more attention than the men."

"I don't want to look at dead naked women," Finch muttered.

"But I want the option to be a female human. I'm more *female* in my actions."

Finch eyed the pigeon. "You said you were okay with any human body, regardless of age or gender."

"Well, I *am* a shapeshifter." Kull fluffed her feathers. "I've never been too attached to my physical body. I just figured, since everyone refers to me in the feminine, maybe I should be female."

Finch grabbed the next locker door, and was about to open it, when his phone beeped. Someone had probably sent him a text message. Hating the fact someone even had his phone number, Finch dug around in his coat pocket and withdrew his phone.

It was the latest and greatest Apple whatever. He despised it, but at least his phone had the DoorDash app, so he forgave it for constantly stealing his location data and purchasing trends. Without the underpaid deliverymen of his area, Finch was pretty sure he would've starved to death years ago.

Finch glanced at his phone. Sure enough, someone had texted. He also had *ten* missed calls, which was odd. When had his phone buzzed that much?

When Finch poked around in the call history, one missed call was from "Jessica Finch." He immediately deleted it. Finch didn't want to think about her.

The other nine missed calls were all from the same person—Jayson Edworth Woolsy the Fourth.

Or as everyone in Oakland knew him… Jay-W the Landlord.

Finch knew the man. He owned hundreds of buildings in

and around Oakland, along with plenty of empty plots. Jay-W was the type of person who specialized in helping people file for government assistance, so he could reap all the benefits of California's tax system. He specifically rented his apartments out to low-income families and gangsters, so he could get their monthly checks and barely do any maintenance. The residents didn't have any options to leave, which was the whole key to the scheme.

Everyone knew, actually. It wasn't a hidden operation. Some people just didn't care—so they became his tenants.

Finch had done work for the man over a decade ago. Well, Finch and his brother had done work, but after Carter died, Finch never returned any of Jay-W's calls.

Jay-W's text to Finch read:

> i kno ur back in biz u POS

Finch exhaled, but his frustrations stayed with him.

"Is a friend texting you?" Kull tilted her pigeon head, but Finch hid the screen. She bobbed her head up and down. "I didn't know you had any friends, actually. And I've been living in your apartment for weeks now. *Weeks.* Why don't you have anyone in your life?"

Finch placed his hand on Kull's bird face and practically squished her against his shoulder. "Shh."

His phone beeped again. Another text message. It read:

> i ne dur help w/sumin

> u kno i got the $$$

If there was one thing Jay-W had in excess, it was money. The man owned an entire warehouse worth of vintage cars. They all ran. They were all cleaned and waxed monthly. Jay-

W also owned several mansions. One in Oakland, one in LA, and one up near Lake Tahoe. And he also collected sports shoes by the hundreds, with famous athletes having signed most of them. Jay-W desperately wanted his face next to the word *gaudy* in the dictionary.

Finch decided he would reply this time.

He wrote:

> Thank you for your inquiry.

> A representative will get back to you within 3-5 business days.

It was sarcastic, but Finch didn't care. Why was Jay-W contacting him in the middle of the night? Finch had important work to do.

He pulled open another corpse locker. The smell from this one twisted his stomach into a tight knot. He gagged and then coughed back the pungent odor of chemicals.

Kull, unaffected, fluffed her feathers. "Why haven't I met your friends? You're not embarrassed by me, are you? I can change shape into something cute…" She curled herself on his shoulder, in a way unnatural for birds. But when she unfurled her body, Kull had transformed herself into a brown squirrel.

Kull pressed her front paws into her chubby cheeks. She moved her whole face around, her black eyes twinkling with elation. Boasting a coat of fluffiness that would give the softest pillow a run for its money, Kull puffed her tail.

She was a mischief spirit, capable of turning into the most mischievous animal of a given category. The most mischievous bird was the pigeon, according to her. And the most mischievous feline was the black cat. And now, apparently, the most mischievous rodent was a brown squirrel…

"I'm adorable," Kull said in a tiny voice. "Everyone will love me. You should definitely introduce me to your friend."

Finch's phone beeped.

The new text message read:

> this is sserisous
>
> call me
>
> ur the only warlock i trust

Finch couldn't stifle his groan. He didn't much care for Jay-W, but he also knew the man would escalate his methods of pestering Finch if he ignored this.

After coughing back more of the chemical smell, Finch glanced over at the squirrel on his shoulder. "Do you like this body?" He motioned to the decomposing lump on the table.

"No," Kull stated.

Finch slammed the locker shut. "Then I guess we'll need to check another mortuary. Some other night. Right now, let's get out of here. I need to make a phone call, anyway."

"To your best friend?" Kull asked, her tiny squirrel ears perking up.

"Jay-W isn't my best friend."

"Who is?"

Finch didn't answer that. He didn't want to think about the depressing reality of his quiet life. However, in his silence, Kull smiled wide. She placed her squirrel paws on the side of his cheek.

"Is it me?" she whispered.

Finch swatted her away. "Stop that. My *best friend* is *not* a mischief spirit."

"Is it Bree?"

"It's *not* a twelve-year-old girl, either." Finch scoffed as he stomped off toward the door. "I have plenty of other friends.

Good friends. They're just... busy. And live in other countries."

"Oh." Kull swished her puffy tail. "After you're done talking to Jay-W—who sounds super fun, by the way—can we call your other friends? To let them know you're doing better than you were before."

Finch pushed open the doors out of the mortuary, his patience of the evening dying. As soon as his business with Jay-W was over, he was going to sleep for thirteen whole hours.

CHAPTER
TWO

inch stood next to his car in the middle of the empty *Frisbee-Bloth & Carlos Mortuary* parking lot. Kull sat on his shoulder, her puffy squirrel body rather adorable, though Finch would never admit that aloud. It was a dry evening—all California was devoid of moisture—and he quickly called Jay-W back from his contacts list.

It only took one ring.

"Finally answerin' my calls, huh?" Jay-W answered, his voice gruff, his accent strange. He spoke with some mix of *Southern twang* and *West Coast casual*.

"What're you doing calling me at two in the morning?" Finch growled. He paced around his vehicle—a Toyota Celica that had seen better days.

"You're awake, ain'tcha? Now listen—I need you to get over here as fast as possible."

"Where is *here*?" Finch sarcastically asked.

"Oakland, fool. I'm back home to get business done. My two pukes for sons can't handle nothin'."

Finch made a full circuit of his vehicle. If he weren't tired, he would come up with an excuse to get out of this, but as it stood, his mind stalled out.

"What's the job?" Finch asked with a groan.

Jay-W snorted. "I'm not tellin' you the details over the got-damn phone. Someone will hear, and this is for your ears only. Got it?"

"You don't need me specifically. Get a local warlock or hire a witch's coven."

Jay-W could make a mountain out of a ditch with any situation. It was a manipulative trick he often used to get people to work faster than they normally would.

"You don't understand," Jay-W said, his voice practically a whisper. "This is different. I need *the best.*"

He always needed "the best."

Finch rolled his eyes. "Can you at least tell me how long you think this is going to take?"

"No. *Now get over here, Adair.* And get your brother, too, huh? I tried callin' him, but some old woman just kept answerin' and tellin' me she didn't know who Carter was."

"Carter died," Finch quickly said, though the statement didn't sting as much as it had before. It was just a fact now, and no longer a festering splinter lodged in his heart.

"Carter? *Died?*" Jay-W huffed out a laugh only a lifelong smoker could muster. "Damn. I didn't think anyone could kill you two."

Finch didn't reply.

"Whatever. I only need one of you, anyway. Just get your ass over here."

Jay-W ended the call before Finch could say another word. That was fine—Finch preferred that. As a matter of fact, Finch preferred Jay-W's style of communication, even if Finch disliked the man. Jay-W hadn't started their phone conversation with a greeting or any small talk, nor had he even bothered to say goodbye. Jay-W said what he wanted. That was it. Wham-bam-thank-you-ma'am.

That was Finch's style.

"Jay-W sounds aggressive for a human," Kull said. She placed her squirrel paws on Finch's cheek. "Why did you let him talk to you like that? Normally you get grumpy."

Finch unlocked his Toyota and took the driver's seat. He placed Kull on the center console. "Jay-W was one of our first clients." Finch started his car and pulled out of the quiet parking lot. "He used to give Carter and me all kinds of work. Once we were a little more experienced, we started taking on clients from all over the world, but we always remembered it was Jay-W who got us our startup capital."

"Aww... So he *is* a good friend!"

Finch gave her a sardonic glance. "No. He's not. I'm just a chump for nostalgia."

"From my research, *all* humans are chumps for nostalgia."

"Research?"

"Yeah!" Kull snickered. "All the movies and TV shows I watched. And all the social media. Bree was even showing me all the newest YouTubers and celebrities. I know all about humans."

Finch doubted that. Spirits rarely interacted with humans directly, including Kull, despite her fascination with them. Could someone learn human nature by just watching TV and doomscrolling through the internet?

After a long sigh, Finch turned down the street and headed for his apartment. Even though Jay-W wanted him in Oakland right away, Finch was going to sleep first. He'd deal with everyone's lunacy in the morning.

———

Finch awoke to banging on his apartment door. He rolled over, marked the time, and then glanced at his phone. It was difficult to see the clock on his lock screen past all the notifications of missed calls and text messages. Jay-W obviously hadn't slept last night—he had been too busy pestering Finch.

Groggy and confused, Finch zipped through the messages, reading one out of every three words. Something about *taking too long* and *this is important* all mixed together with a dozen swear words.

Jay-W was panicked.

That worried Finch. Normally, Jay-W wasn't *this* insane. Could there be an honest-to-goodness problem this time?

In the cold darkness of his messy bedroom, Finch heard his apartment door unlock and then open. There were only two people in the world who had a key to his front door…

His bedroom door slammed open a second later, the living room light streaming in and practically burning Finch's eyes. With a groan, he sat up.

"Adair!"

Bree Blackstone leapt into his bedroom, a twelve-year-old girl with the energy and vibrance of a cocaine-addled parrot. She had dark brown hair that went past her shoulders, and blue eyes so striking, it was hard to see much else on her otherwise plain face.

Without another word of greeting, she jumped onto the foot of Finch's bed, all smiles.

But her happiness died the instant Bree laid eyes on Finch's bare chest.

"Are you okay?" Bree lifted her hand to point. "What happened?"

Finch grabbed at the old scar on his right side. It was massive, spanning from his collarbone to the inside of his armpit and across his upper ribs. And it never looked right—

the edges remained red, even though he had been injured more than a decade prior.

He hated whenever anyone noticed it.

"Nothing happened," Finch stated matter-of-factly. "Forget you ever saw anything."

"It looks painful," Bree said, her brow furrowed.

"I don't feel a thing."

"Maybe we should get it looked at. Papa is here with me, we can drive you. We know a witch and—"

Finch narrowed his eyes. "I'm *fine*."

"But you really don't take care of yourself." Bree smiled again as she slid off his bed. "Don't worry. Papa and I will help you."

"I don't want help." He shot her a glare. "I'm a grown-ass man. I can take care of myself."

Bree waggled her finger and then pointed at the scar again. "That looks gross. You're in trouble. We're helping you. End of discussion, mister."

Out of sheer laziness—because Finch just wanted out of the conversation—he activated his magic. Everything froze in place, even Bree, mid-sentence. The colors drained from the world, melting to the floor and then vanishing. Then all the objects around him disappeared in the same manner, crumbling away until there was nothing but a white void.

And then there was nothing.

Finch blinked. When he opened his eyes, he was back in his cold, dark bedroom, knocking echoing through his apartment.

Chronos, a powerful manipulator of time, had made a pact with Finch. Now, Finch could rewind time to a point he had marked, up to twenty-four hours. In this case, he rewound time to a few minutes before Bree had barged into his room.

Instead of reading through his text messages like he had

done before, Finch swung his legs off his bed, grabbed the clothes he had worn yesterday, and tugged them on. A T-shirt, jeans, a coat, and black socks were all he needed. Once Finch was fully dressed, he picked up his phone and poked through all the notifications.

His bedroom door swung open, and in leapt Bree, exactly as before.

"Adair!"

"Good morning," Finch grumbled, never glancing up from his screen.

The girl leapt onto the foot of his bed and bounced up and down, smiling bright. "Papa and I are here because we have good news. Aren't you excited?" Bree stared at him for a moment and then crossed her arms. "Hey! Did you know we were coming?"

No one ever felt when Finch rewound time—they sensed nothing, unaware of the world rearranging itself because of his power—not unless Finch had given them the *Mark of Chronos* before he activated his magic. Bree knew Finch had Chronos's magic, but ever since her mark had worn off, she wasn't aware of whenever Finch rewound time. Now Bree just guessed.

"I had no idea you were coming over," Finch muttered, still scrolling through the spastic text messages. "What news did you want to tell me?"

"Oh, you knew we were coming." Bree squinted at him. "I bet you already know what I'm going to tell you, too."

"Nope." Finch found the last text message from Jay-W and sighed. It was nothing but a demand to get to Oakland, but this time punctuated by a water gun emoji—whatever that meant.

Bree crawled over his wrinkly blankets. "But did you know I was going to do *this?*" She whacked him in the back of his head with his own pillow.

Finch, taking in a long breath, gave serious thought to rewinding time *again* just to catch the pillow before she struck him, but he opted against it. He smoothed his coppery hair and then stood. "Okay. *Get out.*"

With a giggle, Bree tossed his pillow onto the bed and then hopped off. "Okay, maybe you didn't know we were coming. But hurry! We have really great news, and we have to do everything before school starts." She dashed from the room before Finch could say a peep in response.

Finch continued to poke around on his phone, his thoughts on Oakland, and the last time he had visited that godforsaken city.

A panicked yell pierced the silence of the apartment, removing the last of Finch's grogginess. He leapt from his bed, stormed out of his bedroom, and stood at the edge of the living room, taking in all the details.

Finch had a living room that bled into the kitchen, with some tile flooring, but not much. Bree stood by Finch's four-chair table, her smile still squarely in place. Her father, Liam Blackstone, protectively held one of his arms in front of her, pushing her back and away.

A strawberry poison dart frog sat on the back of Finch's shabby couch, the frog's bright red skin, blue legs, and giant shiny eyes hard to miss, even if the apartment was gloomy. All the blinds were drawn, and only the fluorescent lighting illuminated the space.

"Adair," Liam said, his voice laced with relief. "Watch out. I don't know where that came from, but it's poisonous." He pointed a shaky finger at the frog.

The amphibian licked one of its eyes with its long tongue.

"*Kull,*" Finch snapped. He strode to the couch and glared at the poisonous creature. In a low voice, he growled, "What did I tell you about scaring Bree's father?"

The frog responded with a tiny *ribbit* and then a snicker.

Kull leapt from the couch and landed on the carpet, but in the short time it took her to sail through the air, she transformed herself into a lustrous black cat with shiny fur unlike any other.

"I was just having a bit of fun," Kull said with a laugh. "Bree enjoyed it."

The girl happily nodded once.

Her father, Liam, glanced back at her with a frown. "You knew?"

Bree responded with an innocent shrug.

"Ah... I see."

Liam was the type of man who could be easily mistaken for a lamp post. He had no spare body fat, his face was narrow, and his nose was large—and crooked—enough that one *could* hang a hat on it, if they wanted.

He wore brown slacks, a white button-up shirt, and thick-rimmed glasses. His dark hair and blue eyes were clearly where Bree got hers.

After straightening his glasses, Liam faced Finch. "I took the liberty of grabbing you breakfast." He motioned to a cup of coffee and two donuts on the table. "I hope you don't mind."

Finch grumbled a mild protest, but he didn't put enough effort into it to even form words. He ambled over to the table, plucked a donut off the plate, and then took a bite.

Sugary.

Despite Finch's many attempts to get Liam to leave him alone, the man continued to pester him. Apparently, Liam felt indebted to Finch for everything he had done to save him and his daughter. Finch didn't care—he didn't want any praise or any thanks. He wanted to be left alone.

"How are you today?" Liam asked, his words stilted, betraying the fact he didn't know what to say.

"No, Papa, I told you what to say," Bree harshly whispered

to her father. She tugged his sleeve and dramatically rolled her eyes. "Remember? All the YouTube videos I showed you?"

Liam's ears pinkened, and he nodded once. "Right. You did show me. Let me try again." This time, when he faced Finch, his awkwardness radiated from him like a stink. "Adair, is everything *Gucci* with you?"

Bree giggled, clearly delighted with her father's modern slang.

"Everything is Goodwill at best," Finch quipped. After he finished his donut, he grabbed his tepid cup of coffee. "So why are you two here? Just to force small talk on me? Or was there a goal behind all this?"

Kull leapt onto the table and nibbled the other donut. "Are you here to spend the day with us? We're going to Oakland."

"Oh, goodness no," Liam muttered. He shook his head. "We're here because Adair said he wanted to lease out an office and start up his PI business again. Bree scoured the internet, and we found the perfect place."

CHAPTER
THREE

Nestled in a prime location, near the cleanest McDonald's in all Stockton, and only two blocks from the courthouse, was a vacant office space trying too hard to be *hip* and *cool*.

Finch stood out front, his gaze lingering on the large window walls and the glass door. The sign out front had a phone number and the picture of some smug realtor who had clearly gone through two hours of makeup before having their photo taken.

The floor-to-ceiling windows offered an impressive view of the bustling city outside, ensuring a dynamic backdrop to any workday. There were gigantic wide-open spaces with plenty of room to roll a chair around. And the office space boasted polished concrete floors that contrasted nicely with the soft neutral tones of the walls, which Finch appreciated.

He crossed his arms as he panned his gaze over the rest of the office.

Integrated open-plan workstations, constructed with sleek metal and warm wood finishes, were strategically positioned to, no doubt, foster "collaboration." A high-end kitchenette with stainless steel appliances and matte-finished cabinetry sat in one corner, perfect for those midday coffee breaks.

This office space literally had everything. And it was on the ground floor, with plenty of parking in the back. Damn near unheard of for downtown Stockton.

"What do you think?" Bree bounced around the front door, as bright as the morning sun that shone all around them. "I found it online, and even though it's the most expensive option, I think it's the best and it's so awesome. All the other PIs will be jealous."

Kull wandered along the glass windows, peering inside with her large cat eyes. She purred, then flicked her tail. "I like it. This is the kind of place you would see in fancy cities. Or on a TV show. Or on the news."

"I hate it," Finch stated, no emotion in his voice.

Bree deflated, her frown so prominent it could be seen from space. Her father hurried to her side and gently patted her shoulder. Then he fixed his glasses and glanced over his shoulder at Finch.

"Really?" Liam asked. "You haven't even looked inside. You could at least give it a chance."

"I can already tell—it's not right for me," Finch said.

"You could at least," Liam repeated, drawing out his words in a harsher tone, *"give it a chance."* Then he subtly nodded to Bree, who had turned her attention to the inside, still frowning.

Finch motioned to the office space. "There are pre-built cubicles in there for fifteen people." He sarcastically pointed at himself. "Do *I* look like fifteen people to you?"

Bree's joy returned just as quickly as it had left her. "Wait, no! This is the good part. You have room to expand and hire people." She placed her hands on the glass windows, gesturing to the workstations. "See, you can go there, and a secretary could go over there. And that'll be *my* desk there, because it's close to the window. And Papa will be back there."

Finch pinched the bridge of his nose. "You're not going to work for me."

"But I'm your apprentice."

That was technically true. Finch *had* promised to train Bree in the ways of being a warlock, though he regretted that promise. Bree had the potential to be a witch, but for some reason, she refused to learn anything about her natural magic. She wanted to be like Finch himself—and someday make a pact with Chronos.

Liam, like Finch, was a warlock, but unlike Finch, Liam specialized in crafting magical items. That held no interest for Bree, apparently.

"You need to go to school," Finch said. "Normal, human middle school. You don't have time to work in a PI office."

"Some of my friends have part-time jobs." Bree grabbed her father's arm. "You don't mind, right, Papa?"

Liam stared down at his little girl, his eyes searching hers, his brow dappled with sweat. Ever since the death of Vera, Bree's mother, it seemed Liam couldn't deny his daughter anything. He sighed as he said, "I'm sure we can make it work if that's what you want."

"But *I* don't want it," Finch interjected. "And remember that I'm the PI, since clearly everyone has forgotten that fact."

Kull sauntered over with natural cat-like swagger. She rubbed against the side of Finch's leg, purring as she went. "You know," she said, "warlocks keep their promises. That's the very cornerstone of their magic, after all. Well, *good* warlocks, at least. *Bad* warlocks break their promises. And usually die horrible deaths."

That was true. Warlocks didn't have magic of their own— they borrowed it from other magical creatures, but only after they made a pact. And *pact* was just an old-timey word for *promise*.

Still, Finch rolled his eyes. Why were they all determined to guilt him into renting this office space?

His phone buzzed again. Jay-W had woken up, it seemed.

"I'll think about it," Finch snapped. He pulled out his phone and dismissed the notifications about fifteen missed text messages.

"I took the liberty of printing out the lease agreement for you to review," Liam said matter-of-factly. "I left the paperwork at your apartment. It's all on the counter next to the fridge."

Finch stopped messing with his phone. He sardonically glanced up to meet Liam's gaze. "You already printed off the lease agreement?"

"I like to be prepared." Liam straightened his already straight and ironed shirt. "It makes life infinitely easier."

Bree clapped her hands once. "You'll read it over, won't you, Adair? This is a really nice place. Can't you imagine growing your business? I can. It'll be amazing."

Finch glanced back at the empty office space. When he had run a PI firm with his brother, it had just been the two of them. They hadn't even bothered with a secretary. They had preferred to do things at their own speed, and their own way.

But when Carter died, everything had fallen apart. No one was around to help pick up the pieces.

"I said I'll think about it," Finch muttered. He tore his attention away from the office. "How much is this place, anyway?"

"Only six thousand a month," Bree said, smiling.

Finch exhaled for a solid three seconds. "You clearly haven't taken any finance classes in school yet, have you?"

After a forced cough, Liam placed a hand on Finch's shoulder and turned him slightly away from Bree. In a hushed tone, he said, "Bree spent a lot of time on this. Please just consider it."

"Fine," Finch growled. He stepped away from Liam and sighed. "Listen, I'll deal with all this once I get back from Oakland." He pointed at Bree. "At least bring me a list of your top five offices. Got it, kid? Give me options."

Bree nodded once, and then gave him a salute. "Yes, sir. I'll definitely do that. We'll get all the lease agreements and all the details."

"Fantastic."

———

On paper, the drive to Oakland was only an hour and a half. In reality, it was a four-hour endeavor that typically involved stop-and-go traffic, three car accidents, two homeless men crossing the freeway, and a partridge in a pear tree.

Before Finch left Stockton, he marked the time, just in case anything happened along the way. He didn't want to run up to the time limit of his rewind ability. He could only go twenty-four hours from wherever he placed his mark, and allowing it to go to the limit was the reason his brother had died.

So Finch made sure he had a little extra time before he met Jay-W.

He drove through Concord, hoping to miss most of the traffic that plagued the highways of California. Kull sat in the passenger seat of his vehicle, humming most of the trip since Finch kept the radio off. Occasionally, Kull shouted and pointed, and when Finch needlessly swerved, she snickered.

"You could be the death of us," he growled as he straightened his vehicle and stayed on the road.

"I get really bored if I'm not causing some mischief," she playfully said.

As they neared Berkeley, the sun was setting, painting the sky with dark oranges and pale shades of purple. The Pacific Ocean glittered wondrously, and Finch understood why people called California the *golden state*.

Finch drove along the northern edge of the city. He could get into Oakland proper if he took a major highway, but they were always crowded. The city roads were easier. His phone had buzzed the entire way, though. Jay-W never relented. The man wanted what the man wanted, and he never took no for an answer.

An irritating trait.

"What's that?" Kull muttered as she placed her paws up on the dashboard. "Traffic? Out in this area of town?"

"Damn traffic follows me everywhere."

Finch glared at the cars stopped in the middle of the road. This wasn't traffic. He pulled up behind them and counted a total of five cars all parked in the way. None of them were damaged—no fender scratched—yet everyone was outside their vehicle and milling about.

After a long sigh, Finch parked his Toyota on the side of the road.

He then rummaged through his glove compartment until he found a permanent marker. He yanked Kull over onto his lap. "Hold still."

She purred as he marked her fur with the point of the pen. Finch drew three straight lines, and then a fourth going through them, so they were a line of lowercase *Ts*. Her black fur hid the pen's ink perfectly, but that didn't matter—Kull now carried the *Mark of Chronos*. If Finch rewound time, Kull would know it happened and also remember everything that had occurred.

Unlike the rest of the world.

"Is something wrong?" Kull asked.

"Wait here." Finch opened his car door. "I'm going to ask these lunatics what they're doing."

Kull took a seat on the center console and tilted her head. Finch exited the vehicle, slammed the door shut, and stomped forward.

The road was mostly deserted, and obviously neglected. Potholes riddled both lanes, and the lines had faded almost completely from the concrete. On one side of the road was a large fence that bordered the backyards of a dozen homes. On the opposite side was a scrubland forest, the kind that grew around the regional parks—the ones where forest fires often started because no one ever tended to them.

Finch shoved his hands into his coat pockets as he reached an elderly man standing on the side of the road. The man wore overalls, a baseball cap, and thick boots. If Finch had to guess, he would say this was some sort of handyman. Why was he here?

"What's going on?" Finch snapped as he drew near. He motioned to the congested road. "Why is everyone stopped? I have places to be, dammit."

The handyman frowned. "Oh, sorry about that." He pointed to the woods. "A car was parked here for a long time, so some folks came to investigate. They heard screams. Apparently, a girl and her boyfriend went into the park, and only the boy came out."

CHAPTER
FOUR

"A girl is missing and no one has gone to search for her?" Finch asked.

The handyman shook his head. "It's dark. A couple called the police. An officer said he would be here, but that was thirty minutes ago. Everyone is gettin' worried."

The dying light of the sunset offered little in the way of illumination. Finch rolled his eyes, his thoughts wavering between getting back in his car or searching the woods. Then his mind played a dark trick on him—and he imagined Bree lost in the woods.

Cursing under his breath, Finch turned toward the trees and stomped forward.

"What're you doing?" the handyman called out.

"I work for the police," Finch replied. "I'll have a look."

"Bless you!"

The undergrowth crunched beneath Finch's shoes as he slid down a steep incline. The smell of damp leaves and fresh vegetation hung in the air like a mist. Finch shoved his hands into his coat pockets, fighting back the chill. The harsh shadows provided plenty of places to hide, and Finch wasn't even entirely sure what he was looking for. How old was the girl? What was her name?

"What's wrong with me?" Finch grumbled to himself. Asking basic questions would've made his life easier.

The creak of a branch caused Finch to whirl around on his heel, his heart hammering. Heat blazed within him, and Finch had to force himself to calm down, lest his flames ignite the woods by accident.

Kull, as a graceful black cat, sat on the branch of a nearby oak tree. She swished her long tail, her sleek fur beautiful in the reddish glow of sunset.

"I thought I told you to wait in the car," he said.

Kull leapt from the branch to Finch's shoulder. She landed gracefully, barely disturbing him. She was a spirit first, and an animal second. If she wanted to be silent and nearly weightless, she could be.

"I couldn't let you have all the fun." Kull purred as she hunkered down onto his shoulder. "I overheard everything. We need to find a girl before it's too late."

With a roll of his eyes, Finch resumed his forward march. In order to fully search a wooded area as large as this, a whole search team was often required. People would hold hands, walk in a straight line, scouring every inch of land. As a lone person, Finch was at a terrible disadvantage.

Good thing he had an infinite amount of time.

And a little flashlight on his phone.

———

After three hours of searching, Finch found nothing. The darkness was his enemy, and the frigid evening clearly wanted him dead. Finch shivered back the terrible discomfort as he sifted through shrubs and detritus, his phone battery nearly depleted.

But still, there was no trace of any girl.

More surprising, Finch never heard the cops arrive. He knew Oakland's police policy about missing persons—the cops typically waited twenty-four hours before starting a full-blown investigation, just in case the person showed back up on their own. However, the cops typically took the time to investigate potential domestic abuse cases. If a boy and girl entered the woods, and only a boy left, that was a red flag.

Despite that, there were no cops.

"We're having a rough time of this," Kull muttered. "Maybe we should split up?"

"No."

Finch definitely did not want a mischief spirit out messing with potential evidence in the woods. But just as he was about to suggest rewinding time and starting over, he heard the faint sounds of growls and wet, fleshy tearing.

He straightened his posture and shone his light in the direction of the strange noises. With cautious steps, he made his way between the trees, careful not to trip on the exposed roots or piles of dead leaves.

Not too far from his location was a group of eight coyotes. They swarmed around a fresh kill, their muzzles bloody, their heads all shoved together to get most of the flesh. The smell of copper and wet dog replaced the natural odor of the woods.

"Oh, there's our girl," Kull said, which took Finch by surprise.

He flashed the light over the "kill" and realized there were a pair of human legs sticking out between the gnashing maws of the ravenous coyotes.

Finch snapped his fingers, and embers flared from his hand. All eight coyotes flinched. When Finch waved his flames in front of his body, the canines grimaced and ran off into the darkness of the woods, leaving the girl behind.

The girl…

There was no point in examining her closely. Even from ten feet away, with his faint flashlight, Finch could tell this was futile. The coyotes had chewed through too much of her skin and muscle for anyone to properly identify her.

"Do coyotes usually kill humans?" Kull asked with a tilt of her head.

"No," Finch intoned. "They're scavengers. Which means the girl was dead before that lot stumbled upon her."

There was no pool of blood around her. It was mostly jelly—coagulated blood. It took six to nine hours for the blood to congeal like that, so the girl had likely died before Finch even started his drive to Oakland.

That also meant whoever had left the girl in the woods had likely killed her. Perhaps they were even banking on the coyotes to cover up most of the evidence.

"Well, do we have to stay here?" Kull batted at Finch's ear. "I don't like this. It makes me… not mischievous. And I don't like that feeling, thank you very much."

Finch rewound time.

Everything within the gloomy forest came to a standstill. The wind, the owls, and even the swish of the leaves—they stopped, frozen. Then the colors drained, leaving the area a mess of black. Lastly, the environment melted away into a white void.

Finch was back in his car, just outside his apartment. He sighed, because he didn't want to have to make the whole trip back to Oakland, but here he was. Perhaps, if he was fast enough, he might be able to find some evidence left at the scene of the crime—or at least, beat the coyotes.

———

Finch drove like he had a pregnant lady in the back and she was already eight centimeters dilated.

He flew through the streets of Concord, and then Berkeley, even getting honked at a few times as he dangerously cut off a few individuals in his haste to return to the shabby road. Once Finch arrived, he noticed the handyman and the couple parked by the side of the road, all three of them looking agitated.

After all that effort, Finch had only arrived thirty minutes earlier. They had likely just called the police.

Finch took a deep breath and glanced up at the beautiful sunset that was just starting to develop on the horizon. The light would soon fade, but this time, Finch knew exactly where to look to find the girl's body.

"Let's go," Finch said.

He drew the mark on Kull a second time. She purred the whole way through.

Once out of the vehicle, and with Kull on his shoulder, Finch stomped over to the handyman. "I'm here to help look for the girl." Without waiting for a response, Finch walked around the man and headed into the woods.

"O-Oh—are you with the Oakland PD?" the handyman called out. "You're here already? That's an amazing response time."

"We live to serve," Finch shouted back.

"Is that a *cat*? Shouldn't you have a search dog?"

"This is police business, old man. Just stay on the road."

Determined to get to the girl's body before the coyotes, Finch dashed through the trees, trying to determine the best route to get to the girl. He made his way between thick tree trunks, and pushed aside several bushes, creating a shortcut. Thankfully, his memory was rather reliable—they made it to the girl's body long before any scavengers.

And in the fading light of the sunset, she didn't actually look that bad.

The "girl" appeared to be a woman in her early twenties. She wore a sleeveless lime green dress that went to the midpoint of her thigh and hugged her body as tightly as shrink wrap. Her outfit complemented her blazing red hair, which was long enough to be tangled in the twigs and leaves. Her skin was unnaturally pale—and obviously cold.

She had been dead for at least a couple hours.

Finch slowly approached the body, his chest twisted with equal amounts of disgust and rage. Who killed a young woman and then dumped her body out in the woods?

If he had gotten here earlier, he would've driven by and never known anything had gone wrong.

Finch knelt next to the woman, and Kull leapt off his shoulder. She landed on the leaves and examined the body alongside Finch.

There was a ring of redness around the woman's throat. She had likely been strangled.

"Oh, Finch." Kull arched her back in classic Halloween black cat fashion. "Look!"

Finch tensed and glanced around. "What? Where?"

"Here on the body! Right here. Do you see? The tattoo?"

On the woman's left shoulder was a small black tattoo of a fox's face and a handgun. It was rather distinct—but Finch had never seen anything like it. Was it a symbol for something? Perhaps an organization?

"I don't understand," Finch muttered.

"Are you serious?" Kull leapt onto his shoulder and purred so loud, Finch almost couldn't hear himself think. "Her red hair? Her puffy lips? That signature dress? This is *Fox-Pistol!*"

Kull might as well have been speaking a foreign language.

Finch ran a hand down his face. "What is a fox pistol?"

"*What?* How do you not know?" Kull, obviously filled to the brim with excitement, leapt down again and trotted around the body. "Fox-Pistol is a Twitch and Instagram star! She's a smokin' hot gamer girl who also does a bunch of modeling."

The information settled over Finch like a wet blanket. He really didn't care about any of that. "Why would I know who she is?"

"Haven't you ever seen the girl who plays her video games in a hot tub? That's Fox-Pistol! C'mon, everyone knows her, even most fae courts."

"I have never heard the words *video games* and *hot tub* uttered in the same sentence before. Why would anyone do that?"

Kull chuckled. She continued to circle the girl, as though she were a predator, but the tone in her voice betrayed all her joy.

"Why play games in a hot tub? To show off your bikini, of course!" Kull lifted her feline head and smiled. "And also, so all her viewers can pretend they're relaxing in the hot tub with her. Fox-Pistol is one of the most attractive human women ever. Some witches claim she had to use magic to look that good."

"*Was* one of the most attractive human women ever," Finch morbidly quipped.

"She has over fifty million followers." Kull glared up at Finch. "You must know her."

"I have literally never heard of her until right now."

Although with that information, Finch suspected he knew why Fox-Pistol was targeted. She probably had a lot of admirers—some of whom might not be entirely stable.

"When did she get famous?" Finch asked, his thoughts on Fox-Pistol's murderer.

"Two years ago."

"Hm."

Finch glanced around the area. He didn't see any footprints, or any signs of a struggle. Fox-Pistol wasn't even wearing any shoes. Finch suspected the killer had brought her here after their tussle, though he wasn't sure why. Was it because of the coyotes? Or had the crowds on the street scared the killer halfway through some sort of plan?

Kull sat down and sighed. "I still can't believe you haven't heard of Fox-Pistol. I'm a mischief spirit and I know all about her. What's your excuse as a human?"

"I don't have time to watch bimbos in hot tubs," Finch muttered as he flashed his light around the clearing. The sunset wasn't helping him search.

"I think your human biases have blinded you."

"What does that mean?"

"Foolish humans equate beauty with ditziness. But Fox-Pistol runs her own business and makes millions of dollars. She's strategic. Look at her videos!"

"*Was* strategic," Finch absentmindedly replied. The longer he glanced around, the more he became convinced there was nothing of interest. He stood and brushed himself off. "All right—let's get out of here. We need to inform the authorities of the location of her body." He exhaled. "Actually, we should probably wait here until the cops arrive. We don't want our coyotes to mess up the corpse like they did last time."

Silence grew between them. The hoot of a far-off owl echoed through the woods. Finch shoved his free hand back into his coat pocket.

"Wait," Kull whispered.

"What is it?"

There was a long moment of cold quiet. Then Finch realized what Kull was about to say.

"No," he said as firmly as he could.

"*Please?*" Kull leapt for his shoe and then clawed at his

pants. "This is perfect. She's dead! I could use her body. And I would be *so memorable* if I was Fox-Pistol!"

"*No.*"

"Why not?"

Finch sighed. "Because she's famous. You can't—"

"I can! This way, no one has to be sad about her death. And if the boy who killed her finds out Fox-Pistol is still alive, he'll probably come back to finish the job. We can catch him then! Right?"

"That is the worst idea I've ever heard," Finch said with a groan.

"Please? *Please?*" Kull's pupils grew circular and huge, until all the yellow in her eyes was eclipsed by black.

Finch glanced down at the lifeless body in the middle of the woods. It was a shame someone so young had to die in such a terrible manner.

Catching the killer would help bring more justice to the world...

Finch took a deep breath and then sighed for a full thirty seconds. "Fine. *Fine.* We'll do it your way."

CHAPTER
FIVE

Kull purred as she took a seat directly in front of
Finch, her back to the corpse. "Well, then... That
means our pact is now complete."

With a huff and roll of his eyes, Finch nodded. Spirits and
fae were always so formal. Once he completed their pacts,
they always wanted to formally acknowledge it, as though
they were getting legal documents notarized.

As a black cat, Kull bowed her head until her fur touched
the dirt. "I, Kullthantarrick the Sneak, recognize that you
have completed your end of the bargain. Thank you,
warlock."

"No problem."

A sense of release flooded Finch's mind. Kull's hold over
him was lifted, yet her magic remained. Every magicless
human had the capacity to make a total of five pacts at once
—one tethered to each of an individual's *cores*.

The five cores were the crown, the eyes, the heart, the
soul, and the loins, and Finch had three of them bonded with
different magics. Chronos, the greatest manipulator of time,
was tethered to his crown. Ke-Koh the Ifrit of Rebellion, was

tied to his heart. And Kull, the little mischief spirit, had claimed his eyes.

Normally, warlocks couldn't untether any of the magic attached to their cores—only the creature they made a pact with could do that. However, once the pact was complete, the warlock would retain the magic until they voluntarily gave it up. But once they had given it up, it was gone forever.

Currently, Kull's magic prevented Finch from being caught on camera—or any electronic device. It was as if he were invisible. Her magic also allowed him to undo any lock, mundane or mechanical.

Finch decided to keep hold of her magic for now. It was useful, and he could ditch it if something pressing came up. Besides, he considered it smart to have utility powers. There had been one too many times Finch needed to avoid cameras to do his job properly.

He still had the pacts to complete with Chronos and Ke-Koh, however... But Finch knew he'd deal with those another day.

Kull stood and then turned to face the corpse of Fox-Pistol. After a prolonged moment of silence, she glanced over her shoulder and stared up at Finch with her feline eyes practically glowing.

"Adair," she whispered.

"What?" Finch didn't like where this was going. "I'm not going to touch the body."

"I have a favor to ask of you."

"I just said I wasn't touching the damn body."

Kull twitched her whiskers. "I want you to mark the time once I've... become human."

After a full minute of mulling over the statement, Finch finally asked, "Why?"

"Because it would be disrespectful to Fox-Pistol—and to my decision to leave my spirit form behind—if I simply took her body for a test drive, as a human would say. I shouldn't wear her skin as a suit, and then later revert to a spirit, perhaps even to change my mind when I had the opportunity."

"You don't have to change your mind."

Kull shook her head. "I don't even want the option. This should be permanent. It's a once in a lifetime experience that would only be cheapened and made sad if I did it over and over. *Being born* should only happen once. And this will be my birth."

She sounded different. Serious. No mischief and mirth in her tone.

That was different. Finch hadn't heard a mischief spirit get so contemplative before. Then again, he didn't associate much with spirits outside of pacts. This was the first time he had known one for so long. He knew spirits had a wider range of emotions than the ones they claimed as their source of power, but seeing it was still surprising.

"You know, if you do this, you'll die," Finch said. "You'll be giving up your immortality. And humans are fragile. You might die early. And then it'll be over."

"I understand. But it will all be worth it if…" Kull's ears twitched. "If I find people who remember me. Love me. I've never experienced those things before, and I've lived so long… with the humans I love forgetting me. I want things I can't have as a spirit. Like a family."

Kull had once fallen in love with a human. Her reward? He, and his family, had forgotten about her. Nothing had ever hurt as much, apparently, and now she wanted to find someone who would cherish her like she desired.

"All right," Finch said. "I'll mark the time once you're done."

"Thank you, warlock." She fidgeted with her paws. "I have one more favor to ask."

After a short sigh, Finch crossed his arms. "What is it?"

"Will you help me? Be a human, I mean? I know our pact is over now, and there's no reason for you to help me, but... you're one of the few humans I trust. Can I count on you? At least until I'm confident on my own?"

That was a much larger ask than marking the time.

But Finch wasn't going anywhere. He had already figured he would need to help Kull navigate her way through the human world. He wasn't about to abandon her now.

"I'll help you," he said. "You have my word."

"Thank you... Adair, my human friend."

The little mischief spirit stepped close to the dead body. Finch just waited. The night air rushed over them, as though it, too, wanted to watch everything taking place.

Kull leapt onto the woman's chest. She sat down, but her body sank further than it should, slowly disappearing into the corpse. Kull shimmered and became semi-transparent as she melded with her new form. Right before her feline head disappeared, it became wispy, ghost-like, and undeniably ethereal.

She vanished.

And then, the body took a deep breath.

Finch wondered if the process had hurt. Did the spirit feel loss? He decided not to ask. It seemed personal, at least to Kull.

As the woman's body regained color, the cold crept closer, filling the area with a harsh chill.

Finch marked the time just as Kull sat up in her new body.

5:29 p.m.

She was a woman with fiery red hair, puffy lips, a heart-shaped face, and a petite nose that upturned slightly at the tip. She had a lean frame, and when she stood, Finch understood why Fox-Pistol was a social media star.

Everything about her either screamed *cute* or *sexy*, sometimes a combination of both. Photoshop would have nothing to correct, even though she was currently smeared with mud on her sleeveless green dress, arms, hips, and knees.

With shaky hands, Kull reached up to touch her face. Her slender fingers grazed her cheeks, and then chin. She patted her neck, and continued to her collarbones.

"I'm alive," Kull whispered, her voice different from before, yet strangely close to her tone as a spirit.

"Is it everything you ever dreamed of?" Finch sarcastically asked.

"Better." Kull stared at him with her new human eyes. They were as blue-gray as the morning waves across the Pacific beaches. "I can feel myself breathing. It's so amazing."

"If you're excited about that, get ready for the delight of *constantly needing to use the bathroom*," Finch quipped.

Kull, with genuine earnestness in her voice, said, "I can't wait. Perhaps we should go right now?"

"Do you need to?"

"I don't know. Do I?" Kull giggled, her face lighting up at the mere thought.

"Oh my god." Finch pinched the bridge of his nose and exhaled.

It was going to be a long night, he could already tell.

Finch glanced at the clock on his phone. It was 5:30 p.m. The sun set so early now—it felt later than it really was.

Kull stepped forward, grimacing the whole time. "Ow," she muttered. "Ow. Ouch." She glanced down at her bare feet and frowned. "The twigs are poking me. Does this happen to all humans? Does nature hate us?"

"That's why we wear boots and make sidewalks." Finch glanced around, hoping her shoes would be nearby, but they weren't. "Don't walk around. I'll carry you back to the car."

He stepped close and then scooped Kull into his arms.

She was lightweight, and Finch had little difficulty holding her, but she squirmed for a moment, clearly confused and awkward. As he turned to walk out of the woodlands, Kull wrapped her arms around his neck and snickered.

"What is it?" Finch asked.

"You touched the body," Kull playfully whispered.

He sighed as he stomped through the undergrowth and headed in the direction of the road. It was darker now, and twice a low-hanging branch whapped him in the face as he marched through the gloom. Finch gave serious thought to summoning a shadow spirit just so he could see through the darkness.

As he walked, his phone buzzed in his coat pocket. Jay-W. The man was persistent.

"We're going to need to stop to get you shoes," Finch said, trying to ignore the vibrations.

Kull excitedly sucked in her breath. "And a clean outfit?"

"Sure, whatever."

Finally, Finch stalked uphill toward the road and exited the woods. The handyman and the handful of concerned locals were still there. Once they saw Kull in Finch's arms, a few of them clapped.

"The officer found her!" one person shouted.

Finch stepped onto the road, and the handyman hurried over. With a smile, he muttered, "I'm so glad the girl is okay. I was mighty worried."

"She got lost," Finch said. "I'm going to take her to the hospital."

"Good idea."

Finch placed Kull down and brushed himself off. He cleared away leaves and twigs while Kull did the same. Then she ran her hand over her sides, smoothing her dress.

A man across the street, standing next to his POS vehicle, nodded toward Kull. "Hey! Are you hurt?"

She shook her head. "No. Thank you, though! So kind of you to ask."

"Right. Well, I'm going to leave then." He got into his car and drove off. The other looky-loos did the same, one by one driving off now that the drama was over.

Not the handyman, however. He seemed concerned enough to stay until the bitter end.

"Where is the boy who was with you?" he asked Kull.

"I don't know. I got lost, and he just left." She patted her upper leg and then frowned. "Adair…"

"Yeah?" Finch walked over to his car and opened the passenger-side door.

"I don't have any panties."

The older handyman clearly hadn't expected that. His eyebrows shot for his receding hairline, and his eyes doubled in size.

"Maybe I lost them in the woods," Kull muttered. She glanced over her shoulder. "Should we look for them? I hope they aren't dirty."

Finch, his face growing hot, quickly walked over and took her by the shoulder. "No," he replied, curt. "We aren't going to search the side of the road for your damn underwear. Let's get into the car." He leaned in close. "*Less talking.* More moving."

He steered her away from the balking handyman and hurried her straight to his Toyota. With a forceful push, Finch loaded Kull into the car and then slammed the door shut. He leapt over his hood to get to the driver's side, intent on leaving as soon as possible.

"Is that young woman going to be okay?" The handyman rubbed his red cheeks. "She was probably assaulted and can't remember. Poor thing."

"The Oakland PD will handle it," Finch said as he took a seat. "Thank you for your assistance."

He slammed the door just as his phone started to ring for the hundredth time. Finch glanced over at Kull. She sat in her seat with a wide smile, her eyes conveying her earnest joy. They practically sparkled.

"I'm a human," she whispered, as if she still couldn't believe it. "Your chair feels crusty under my new skin."

Finch ran his hand down his face. He couldn't believe this was happening. His normal evenings had long since disappeared. Now he had to deal with pantie-less spirits in human bodies, complaining about the scratchiness of his upholstery.

"Can we shop at a Walmart?" Kull tilted her head in a cat-like fashion.

Finch gave her the most disbelieving narrow-eyed squint. "Why?"

"That's a very human experience. Everyone shops at a Walmart, don't they? I need to experience this as well."

Finch's phone buzzed again. In order to escape the lunacy of the conversation, he decided to answer it this time. He poked the screen of his phone and held it to his ear. "Finch here."

"You motherfucker," Jay-W growled. "Stop ignorin' my calls."

Finch hung up.

He glanced back at Kull. "You know what else is very human? Buckling your seat belt."

With a giggle, Kull grabbed her seatbelt and carefully secured it across her shoulder and lap. "I remember when cars didn't have seatbelts," she proudly stated. "I also remember when humans used to say cars wouldn't replace horses, because horses were so much more reliable and affordable."

Once again, Finch's phone buzzed. This time it felt

angrier than before. That was probably his imagination, though. He answered it again.

"Finch here," he said, calm and borderline sarcastic, as though he didn't know who was on the other end.

"You better not hang up on me again," Jay-W said, his voice almost the same tone as Finch's, just with a hint more seething. "Where are you? Why aren't you at my place? You should've been here *yesterday*."

"Stop calling me. I'm on my way."

"Aren't we going to Walmart?" Kull asked. "We could stop there first."

"Don't worry, we'll stop there," Finch murmured.

Jay-W ground his teeth so loudly, the sound came through the phone. "You are testin' my got-damn patience, Adair."

"I'll get there when I get there." Finch ended the call before Jay-W would say another word. Then he glanced over at Kull. "Okay, so, when I'm on the phone, no talking. That's just good manners."

Kull nodded, her smile never fading. "Yes. I need to learn all the human manners I can. I don't want to be the goofball everyone laughs at."

"I've got bad news," Finch muttered. Then he pulled a pen out from his glove compartment. "Also, hand me your arm. I need to draw the Mark of Chronos on it."

"So that I remember everything once you reset the time?"

"As quick as a whip, you are."

CHAPTER
SIX

There were two Walmarts in Oakland—three, if you counted the one in Union City, just south of Oakland's city line. And they were the worst Walmarts of all time.

Unfortunately for Jay-W, Finch had to drive by his home to head south, where all the Walmarts were located. Once inside one of the infamous Walmarts, Finch regretted all the decisions that had brought him there.

Entering the Oakland Walmart was like stepping into a parallel universe where the laws of decency had been flung out the window. The entire store was best described as "the aftermath of a discount apocalypse." Clothes everywhere. Towers of boxes set up like a mid-match Jenga game. Lights flickering overhead.

Finch traveled through the superstore with his hands in his coat pocket, his gaze straight ahead. It was 6:02 p.m., and the place was packed.

The floor, a mosaic of unidentifiable stains, crunched underfoot.

But despite the disgusting bargain-bin jungle, Kull

practically skipped alongside him, her eyes big. She giggled a few times when her eyes landed on SALE signs.

"You never went into a Walmart as a mischief spirit?" Finch asked.

Kull, still barefoot, took careful steps across the questionable tile floor. "I've been inside a Walmart before, but that isn't the point. Now I'm human. Now I can experience what everyone else experiences here."

"Losing your sanity?"

Kull shook her head. Then she flung her arms wide, smiling wider than ever. "I get to purchase things!"

Her cheery declaration was silly, even for 2024. People glanced over, frowning. Finch shot them cold glares. The other customers left them alone.

"You don't seem happy," Kull said with a slight tilt of her head. "Don't humans enjoy Walmarts? They're everywhere!"

"I dislike *this* Walmart." Finch sighed. "Something terrible always happens. Somehow, it usually ends in a fistfight."

"Really? That's so exciting." Then Kull gasped and grabbed Finch's arm, jerking him from the tiled walkway onto a stale carpeted portion of the store. "Look, Adair!" She dragged him into the swimwear section. "We found bathing suits!"

"We don't need a bathing suit," Finch grumbled.

"But what if I need to be in a hot tub?"

Finch pinched the bridge of his nose. "We aren't going to any hot tubs. We're going to focus on whatever Jay-W needs, and then we're going to look for the man who left you in the woods. That's our current plan. Nothing extra."

With her attention completely on the swimsuits, Kull giggled. Had she heard anything Finch said? He didn't know. However, her sheer unmitigated delight dulled his irritation. At least she was having fun during her first hour of being a human.

"This looks similar to something Fox-Pistol would wear." Kull grabbed a pink bikini with glittering sequins and hugged it close. "I can't wait to show it off for all my followers on Twitch!"

"*Keep your voice down*," Finch growled through clenched teeth. He nervously glanced over his shoulder, hoping no one was paying attention to them. "Do you see any other humans shouting out their every action? No. Because that's not normal."

Kull nodded along with his words. Then she stopped and snatched an even skimpier bikini from one of the display shelves. It was a comically tiny thing—mostly string, with a single metal buckle over the front. It shone under the fluorescent lighting.

"This is even better," Kull whispered in awe as she held up the floss-thin bathing suit. "And I can use the bottom as panties. Isn't that great, Adair?"

Finch smacked her arms down and held back a tirade. With his face growing red, he glared down at her. "For the love of all that is holy," he whispered, his tone heated. "*Please*. Keep your commentary to yourself."

"Can I get this?"

"Fine. Sure. *Whatever*." Finch ran his hand down his face, trying to rid himself of the building embarrassment. "Now that you have... a bathing suit... let's go get you shoes."

Kull held her new clothing close. The tag said the bikini —which was less cloth than a hand towel—was somehow forty dollars. And while Finch thought that was highway robbery, he didn't comment. He didn't want to be in the bathing suit section any longer. Sixty seconds was sixty seconds too long.

They headed deeper into the Walmart, away from the glorious escape of the front doors. The farther in they traveled, the more the place had its own distinct smell.

Fortunately, the shoe section masked that pungent odor with the scent of new leather, which was quite pleasant.

"Look at all these shoes!" Kull hopped over to the first display and fingered every pair. "I always wondered why humans amassed objects in a single location, but now I think I understand. Which will fit? I can't change the shape of my body anymore. I need something just for me!"

An older lady, who was sitting on a bench and trying on a pair of sneakers, glanced up after Kull's commentary, her brow furrowed in confusion.

Finch stepped between her and Kull. In a harsh whisper, he said, "*Keep. It. Down.*" He doubted anyone would figure out their situation from Kull's bizarre comments, but Finch preferred not to speak to anyone. He dreaded the questions.

The older lady picked up her shoes and moved herself to another bench—one much farther away.

"I'm going to look for something Fox-Pistol would like." Kull hurried deeper into the section, giggling the entire way.

Again, Finch found his irritation draining when he realized how happy she was. At least one good thing had come of this trip.

Finch refused to go deeper into the shoe section, however. He awkwardly waited at an endcap, staring at a pair of sneakers with lights flashing at the bottom. He had thought they were meant for a child, but they were sized for an adult and on an adult mannequin.

"When did the world get so weird?" he murmured to himself.

Something shifted under the closest bench, and Finch stiffened. The older lady was far away, and at first, Finch thought it was something she had left behind, but he quickly realized that wasn't the case.

The something under the bench was magical in nature.

A pair of yellow eyes opened in the shadows under the

bench. The pupils were slits, reptilian, but much too intelligent to be an animal. The eyes glanced up at Finch, but he couldn't make out the shape of the creature's body. The shadows around it were supernaturally dark.

"*Warlock*," the something under the bench whispered.

Finch sighed. "Yes?"

"Are you here to make a pact?"

"No."

"Wait… You're Adair Finch, aren't you, warlock? I've heard the legends of your exploits. You must be here because of the killings."

Finch shifted his weight and turned to fully face the bench. "Killings?"

The yellow eyes narrowed. "Don't play dumb. You catch killers, don't you? Supernatural threats. Haven't you come to the Land of Oak to find one? The monster who targets women…"

"I didn't know there was a killer here." Finch held back an exhale. He should've known the moment they found a body off the side of the road. Something terrible was going on here.

Perhaps Jay-W really did have a need for him after all…

"My magic can help you, warlock. Make a pact with me."

Occasionally, spirits, demons, and other sorts of creatures *wanted* to make pacts with warlocks. In those instances, it was because they wanted something specific—and they wanted them desperately. Finch disliked dealing with creatures then, because they often pestered their way into his life over and over again.

"Who are you?" Finch asked.

"My name is *Festallenius the Revenge*." The yellow eyes moved through the darkness as the creature snickered. "I'm a spirit of jealousy, at your service."

Finch absolutely hated working with spirits who derived

their power from destructive forces. Sure, the pollution spirits were strong, but they were grimy in every sense of the word. A spirit of jealousy was no doubt heinous and probably wanted something sinister for its magic.

Then again, magic based on *wanting things from others* would likely be interesting.

"Make a pact with me," Festallenius repeated. "Do it. *Do it.*"

"I'm busy," Finch stated.

"With the spirit who gave up her eternal form to masquerade as a human? Bah." Festallenius snorted. "Pathetic."

Finch rolled his eyes. When he glanced over at the far corner of the shoe section, he realized Kull had gathered up ten pairs and was haphazardly trying them on. "What do you know about this killer?" Finch asked, his mind divided.

"I'll tell you everything I know." The spirit snickered. "If you make a pact with me."

"That's not how this works. How about you tell me what you know, and then I *consider* helping you."

Festallenius hissed. Then his yellow eyes vanished, and the darkness under the bench returned to the normal levels.

Why was a spirit of jealousy inside of a Walmart? Normally, spirits were only found near areas that truly exemplified the core of their magics. Spirits of life were typically found in a hospital nursery, whereas spirits of grieving were found in a graveyard.

Perhaps Festallenius had come here in search of a warlock—or perhaps the Walmart really brought out the worst in people.

Kull came skipping back, only four pairs of shoes in her arms. They were all the tallest heels available, each a shade of green that only slightly matched her dress. "Look, Adair. I found these. Help me."

"*Help you?*" Finch repeated. "What're you talking about?"

"I don't understand how to walk in them."

Kull sat on the bench, slipped a pair of six-inch heels on, and then attempted to stand. She swung her arms around in great circles, but ultimately fell forward. Finch caught her before she hit the dirty linoleum floor.

"What are you doing?" Finch growled as he helped her stand straight.

Kull smiled. "Fox-Pistol always wears shoes like this. Help me understand. Do I… balance in them? How do they work?"

"I have no idea. Just wear normal shoes."

"I can't do that. I'm Fox-Pistol now. Fox-Pistol always wears shoes like these." Kull sat back down on the bench and fiddled with the footwear, like she could somehow find the exact right position on her feet that would make walking easier. Then she stiffened, her expression melting into something neutral. "Was there a spirit here? Just now?"

Finch nodded. "One of jealousy."

"I can smell it. I think it's still nearby."

"How long are you going to retain your magic?" Finch knew some spirits inhabited bodies, but he had never associated with them. From his understanding, their magic faded, and they eventually died, like normal human beings. Unlike normal human beings, spirits who took bodies just ceased to be once their vessel had perished.

"The five cores of Fox-Pistol's corpse were empty," Kull said, her voice monotone. "In order to inhabit this body as a human, I filled the soul core with my spirit, and then I tethered myself by filling another core with my consciousness. I attached myself to the corpse's eyes, and by doing so, I've permanently weakened myself. The last three cores of this body are shallow, but they retain parts of my magic… just not all of it."

"Will you always be able to sense other spirits, then?"

"I'll always have some of my magic, yes. And other spirits will know me for what I am—an impostor." Kull's smile slowly returned. *"But* now I can feel things. The whole range of emotions, not just a keen sense of mischief. My new soul core—the one infused in this body—is something *more* than a spirit. I'm like a half-human!"

Most spirits thought it disgusting to give up their eternal life for the short-lived one of a human, but it seemed Kull didn't have that regret. At least, not yet. Finch was grateful for that.

"I'll find some other shoes… One moment!" She bounded deeper into the shoe section.

Then a hand slammed down onto Finch's shoulder and turned him around.

Finch—in an extremely rare occurrence—had to look *up* to meet the gaze of the person. A corn-fed bundle of testosterone and muscle shaped like a man, stood before him. The man's bald head shone with the overhead lights, his pupils so small it was as if he saw the world through pinholes.

He smelled of sulfur, and Finch felt the demonic essence of someone who had *infernal bloodlines* somewhere in their family tree.

"You're Adair Finch, aren't ya?" The man's gravelly voice was as rough as sandpaper.

Finch's eyebrows went for his hairline. "You're… one of Jay-W's thugs."

The man grabbed the collar of Finch's coat and yanked him close. "Unless you want to pick your teeth up off the floor with broken fingers, you're coming with me."

CHAPTER
SEVEN

Finch pulled himself out of the thug's grasp. "Watch yourself. I'm not like other warlocks you might know." He brushed off his coat, his nose wrinkling in disgust as the smell of sulfur grew stronger.

"And I'm not like most men you know," the thug said, his breath as sweet as brimstone.

He wore an ill-fitting three-piece suit with a red tie that was too short. His muscles were barely contained, and he wore his clothing like he was punishing it for existing.

"I told Jay-W I would get to him when I was ready," Finch said. "Beat it."

The thug narrowed his eyes, his hands clenching into tight fists. "I had specific instructions to bring you back—no matter what."

"I'm busy, asshole. I'll get there when I get there."

In Finch's imaginings, the man would return to Jay-W, tell him to wait, and everything would be fine. Unfortunately, the real world wasn't as rational as Finch's imagination. The thug exhaled and then threw a right hook.

Finch got punched so hard he forgot cursive.

A few moments later, Finch opened his eyes, his mind fuzzy, his vision blurred. He knew, from the leathery odor, and the crust on the floor, he was still in the Oakland Walmart, but it took him several seconds to remember everything that had just transpired.

"Ugh, not again," he muttered with a groan as he slowly got himself to his feet. He pushed up on his own knee in order to stand, his jaw throbbing.

Heat surged through his chest, and he exhaled embers as he turned his glare to the thug. If Finch wasn't careful, his fire could destroy the whole building, but if this thug wanted to fight, he would get a fight.

Either way, Finch was about to teach this loser what it meant to mess with a warlock who had zero fucks to give.

The other customers in the shabby Walmart fled the area. They knew what was coming, probably from the look on Finch's face. And no employees bothered to show their faces. This was California—you didn't get involved in active crimes that were taking place. You just let them happen.

"Wow, you got into a fist fight so fast," Kull said, standing in the aisle of the shoe section. She softly clapped a few times, her smile genuine. "Now we've had a full experience here at the Walmart. Hurray!"

The thug turned his attention to Kull and then froze. His eyes grew wide, and he sucked in his breath. "Wait," he said. "Are you *Fox-Pistol? The* Fox-Pistol?"

Kull took one step forward in her new heels. She giggled, held two fingers up like a peace sign, and then held them close to the side of her head in a cutesy pose. "That's right! It's me, Fox-Pistol."

"Fuckin' A." The man patted his coat, and then the pockets of his slacks. He pulled out a cellphone and then a marker. "Can you sign this?" He offered her the phone. "And then can I get a picture? M-My name is Lloyd, by the way."

Lloyd's entire tone and demeanor had shifted. Now, he sounded more like an excited schoolgirl ready to squee, his beef with Finch completely forgotten. As Finch rubbed his sore jaw, he watched the exchange in mild disbelief.

"Aren't we in the middle of a damn fight, asshole?" Finch asked as flames formed in one of his hands.

Lloyd sheepishly waved away the comment. "C'mon, man. I'm sorry. This is Fox-Pistol. *The* Fox-Pistol. I wouldn't have thrown nothin' if I knew she was here."

Finch could hardly believe his ears. His fire died as his bewilderment grew.

He supposed the fight was over. For some reason.

Kull scribbled her name on Lloyd's phone and then passed it back with a smile. The huge thug awkwardly stepped close to her and then held up his phone to take a selfie. He had to point it low to get Kull in the photo, and Finch was certain the angle of the camera saw far too much down the front of Kull's green dress, but he didn't say anything. Finch was still caught up in the bizarreness of the situation.

After snapping a few pictures, Lloyd stepped away. He scrolled through his new collection, a smirk on his wide face. "Nice." After a few moments, Lloyd glanced up, his brow furrowed in realization. "Wait, are you here with Adair Finch?"

"That's right." Kull wobbled on her legs and awkwardly took two steps closer to Finch. She didn't fall, but her ankle shook something fierce. "I was *attacked*. And Adair is going to help me catch the guy." She patted Finch on the shoulder. "He's a great warlock, and my best human friend."

Lloyd narrowed his eyes at the last statement, but his suspicion clearly didn't last long. He returned his attention to Finch. "This is why you've been late?"

Although this wasn't the reason, Finch half-shrugged and nodded.

"You're popular if both Jay-W *and* Fox-Pistol hired you?"

"A lot of people want my time," Finch said with a sigh.

"Jay-W is real mad, though. *Big mad.*" He turned to Kull like she would get what he was saying.

She giggled and gave him the thumbs up. Finch had no idea what was going on.

"I can't believe you're here, of all places," Lloyd said, speaking directly to Kull. "I've been watchin' your *Call of Duty* gameplay videos for over a year now. You deserve more subs."

"Thank you." Kull placed a hand on her cheek. "It means so much to me that you know who I am."

"Of course. Everyone knows about you. You're smokin' hot. *Smokin.*"

Finch finished rubbing his chin and then rolled his eyes. *Everyone* knew her? He doubted it.

"Well, I need to stay close to Adair while we track down my attacker," Kull said. "As long as I'm with him, we can head over to Jay-W's. Oh! But after I get clothes, because these are dirty, dirty, dirty."

Lloyd nodded once. "Wait. Let me call Jimmy. He drives one of Jay-W's limos. He can come pick us up, and I can take you over to *The Boutique.*" He quickly poked his cellphone, sending out a flurry of messages, his giant fingers struggling to tap all the correct letters.

"I'll take care of her," Finch stated.

Lloyd growled a curse under his breath. Then he shot Finch a glare. "You took Fox-Pistol shoppin' in a dump like this? The girl deserves somethin' fine for a body like hers. Jimmy and I will treat her right."

Kull clapped at these statements, which probably came

across like *brain damage* more than it did *genuine happiness*. Finch wasn't sure what to do about that, though.

"All right, all right," Lloyd said as he tucked his phone back into his coat. "Jimmy's on the way with the limo. Let's get out of this dump and into a real store."

"I can't wait!" Kull kicked off her heels. "To real shopping!"

Finch glanced at his phone.

6:21 p.m.

———

The back of the limo was dark. LED lights lit up most of the floor, giving it a red and blue vibe that made Finch think of the police. There were special shot glasses with the word WOOLSY on the side. Jay-W's last name. The man was obsessed with himself.

Kull sat on the bench seat next to him. She bounced in time with the soft music playing from the limo's impressive sound system. She wore a new blue dress that matched her eyes, and fine heels she could walk in, and it had all been picked out for her by the woman who ran the boutique.

Now, she looked *stunning*. Even without much else—no makeup, no perfume, no styling of her hair—Kull's new body had a natural beauty that practically oozed from every invisible pore.

Lloyd, the bruiser, awkwardly sat on a separate bench seat, the leather straining under his massive weight, his head tilted so he didn't touch the roof. The limo stank of sulfur.

No one spoke.

Finch glanced at his phone.

7:13 p.m.

"Are we almost there?" Kull asked, her cheery tone completely out of place for the dark limo.

Lloyd nodded. "Yeah. Jay-W's place is by the docks."

"Oh, wow. And is Jay-W also a warlock, like Adair?"

The thug lifted an eyebrow as he slowly shifted in his seat to face her. "No, Jay-W isn't. But... I didn't know you were... in on all this." He motioned to their surroundings. "You know warlocks and wizards and witches?"

"I know plenty of them," Kull said with a shrug. "And you... You're infernal, aren't you? Just a little bit." Kull pinched her forefinger and her thumb. "You smell as though you're related to a powerful demon. A duke, maybe?"

Again, Lloyd became excited. He shifted to the edge of his seat. "Yeah, that's right. They say my great-great grandma had a thing with Valefar." He cocked his head. "How'd you know?"

"Fancy demons have a special scent." Kull tapped the side of her nose.

"Watching your videos and live streams... You never seemed to indicate you knew anything about this. You never mentioned magic or the realms beyond or spoke about the importance of the moon phases."

"Oh, well, that's because I just recently found out." Kull pressed a hand on her cheek. "Um, I have *awakened*. I see the true world beyond the veil and delirium that keeps mortal humans ignorant. What's the word humans use?" She snapped her fingers. "I'm *woke* now."

"That's not it," Finch said, monotone and sarcastic.

Ignoring Finch's commentary, Lloyd asked, "And even though you know what I am, you're not afraid? Most everyone won't deal with an infernal. Only Jay-W was willing to give me a job."

Kull waved away his comment. "Of course I'm not afraid of you. I have Adair with me."

That statement chilled the man's excitement.

Lloyd glanced over at Finch as though this were an

elaborate prank. But then he sat back in his seat and visibly mulled it all over. "I suppose... Jay-W does say he's the best."

The limo drove into an underground garage, ending the conversation. Once the vehicle came to a complete halt, Finch once again glanced at the time.

7:20 p.m.

Lloyd stepped out and held the door open. Finch and Kull slipped out of the vehicle into the massive underground garage. At least fifteen cars were parked within, including two other limousines. Each was shinier and more expensive than the last, but Finch had seen them before.

Jimmy stepped out of the limo. He was one part man, one part coat rack—thin, tall, and draped in fancy clothes. He smiled wide, his yellow teeth the most notable feature of his appearance.

"Okay, I drove you, do I get a picture now?" he asked, motioning to Kull.

She smiled and nodded. "Of course! Anything for my fans."

Jimmy walked over and held his phone up for a selfie-style photo. Finch sighed and wondered why no one ever asked him to take the picture, but he suspected the men preferred to be close to Kull when they snapped a shot.

And sure enough, Jimmy wrapped his arm around Kull's waist, his hand sliding lower and lower, until he had crossed the line of decency. He took a picture right at that moment, snickering as he did so.

Finch, barely holding his anger back, grabbed Jimmy's suit coat from behind and shoved him away from Kull. "Keep your hands to yourself," he growled.

"What was that?" Jimmy shot him a glare and then reached for something held in a well-concealed shoulder holster.

"It's okay." Kull patted Finch's shoulder. "He just likes me and thinks I'm *smokin hot*."

Finch gave her a sidelong glance. "You shouldn't let them touch you like that," he whispered.

"Why?" she whispered back. "I want them to like me."

At a loss for words, and unsure how to tell her that this *wouldn't get them to like her more*, Finch decided to drop it. If Kull wanted to be human, she could learn about how disgusting humanity could be the hard way.

"Over here," Lloyd said. He gestured to the elevator door at the end of the garage. It was ornate, with white and silver fixtures. "Jay-W is already in a mood. We better not keep him waiting any longer."

CHAPTER
EIGHT

Jay-W's abode was everything Finch remembered.

Finch strolled into the living room from the garage elevator, his hands in his coat pocket, unimpressed with the opulent surroundings.

The living room was a cozy nook, if the definition of "nook" included enough space to host a royal ball. Floor-to-ceiling windows offered a view of Oakland's port, which was a far nicer view than the city itself.

Famous artwork hung on the walls and over the massive fireplace. Each piece was worth the GDP of a small country, but that wasn't why Jay-W had them. Anyone who knew anything about art dealing knew it was a massive front for money laundering. Since the "art world" typically accommodated those who wanted to anonymously buy high-dollar paintings, and since the industry regularly allowed large cash deals, it was perfect for avoiding taxes and paper trails.

And if Jay-W loved anything, it was avoiding taxes.

The massive thug, Lloyd, hurried across the living room.

"C'mon, this way," he said, as though Finch hadn't been here a dozen times before.

Kull wobbled on her feet, clearly unaccustomed to her heels. That didn't stop her from smiling, though. She marveled at the windows, grazed her fingers over the plush seats, and even admired the money-laundering artwork.

"What an interesting home," she said in a dreamy tone. "It's similar to Fox-Pistol's. Hers is pinker, though."

Finch casually walked by her, his interest solely on the far door. "Just stick close to me. You wouldn't want to get lost in all this lavishness."

When Kull attempted to rush to Finch's side, her heels caught on a rug. She fell forward, but Finch rushed over in time to catch her. Kull held onto his arm, nervously chuckling.

"I'll get the hang of it." She stood straight. "I promise."

Finch said nothing. He waited until she was back on her feet before turning around. Lloyd had already disappeared into the main hallway. Clearly, the lumbering stack of muscles wasn't the most observant.

Kull shuffled her way forward, slower than normal. Finch also slowed his pace to make sure he was close, in case anything happened. Once she was near the wall, Kull placed a hand on it for stability.

"Why aren't you more concerned?" Kull asked with a tilt of her head.

"Concerned about what?" Finch walked to the hallway and stopped. He waited as Kull made walked over.

"Concerned about Jay-W. He's been calling you for days. Don't you think this is serious? Shouldn't you run to him so you can hear what he needs?"

Finch rolled his eyes. "It's not serious. I'm willing to bet my life on it. He's the epitome of drama, and thinks every tiny problem in his life is the biggest concern in everyone else's."

"Oh, interesting."

Despite Finch's statements, he had a tiny niggle of a worry that Jay-W might have an actual serious problem. Finch had found a dead girl on the side of the road, and a jealousy spirit in Walmart had claimed there was a killer on the loose who specifically targeted women. Perhaps Jay-W was concerned about this threat and had been trying to get Finch's help this whole time.

Finch and Kull walked down the hallway. It stretched longer than a marathon, and passed a kitchen with marble countertops so shiny, they were blinding.

Once they made it to the end, Lloyd stood next to a large wooden door and motioned them close. He opened it and then silently gestured for them to enter.

Finch went in first, with Kull hopping in after him, her energy knowing no bounds. Lloyd shut the door without following, leaving them with the man who was already at his desk.

Jay-W.

He was as corpulent as he was demanding, and he sat behind his grandiose desk with a look on his face like Mufasa had just told him he owned everything the light touched.

In one hand, Jay-W held a glass of brandy. Finch wasn't absolutely positive, but he was confident that it was the finest, oldest, and most ludicrously expensive brandy one could find in California. Because it wasn't just a drink—it was a statement.

And in the other hand, Jay-W held a cigar. It was probably fancy in some way, hand rolled or something equally dumb, but Finch was done caring. The smell irritated him.

Of course, all those signs of wealth were designed to detract from the fact that Jay-W was *not* a good-looking man.

He wasn't even good-looking compared to a dumpster—he was the type of person you didn't want to stare at too long because of the lingering acne pockmarks, the thin hair, and the yellow-stained teeth too large for his mouth.

His eyes, though…

Jay-W had eyes so icy blue, they bordered on white. Magic radiated from them, different than the kind that sprang from spirits or permeated the undead.

"I finally got you here," Jay-W said as he leaned back in his chair, his slimy smile growing.

"You had to send your thugs for me?" Finch shook his head. "What is it you want that is so important?"

Jay-W's beady eyes flicked over to Kull. "Who's the broad?"

As if she had been waiting for a cue, Kull giggled, smiled wide, and then made the same pose with her fingers in a little peace sign. "I'm Fox-Pistol! You might've seen my channel on Twitch, or all my modeling photos on Instagram. Millions of people have! Remember to like and subscribe because I'm filled with rizz!"

It was as if Kull was mashing together several of Fox-Pistol's slogans into one bizarre introduction speech.

Jay-W, clearly baffled, his large face sweaty, slowly returned his attention to Finch. Without actually speaking, he mouthed the words, *"Did she just say she was filled with jizz?"*

After a short sigh, Finch stepped between Kull and Jay-W. He ran a hand down his face, trying and failing to tamp down his embarrassment. "No. She's just… using internet lingo. I think."

Jay-W shook his head and frowned. "What the hell are kids sayin' these days? Nothin' makes me feel old like *internet lingo.*"

"Never mind that. Just ignore her. She has to stick close to me."

"I help Adair with his work," Kull said, peeking over Finch's shoulder. "We make a great team."

Jay-W waved a fat hand through the air, his cigar smoke swirling around. "I don't care. She's your assistant? Fine." Then he eyed Finch. "You replaced your brother quick, huh?"

Finch narrowed his eyes. "Carter died over ten years ago."

"Oh. My mistake. You were in no damn hurry to replace him. Heh." Then Jay-W lifted an eyebrow. "Who did it? Who got Carter? And did you get your revenge?"

"I…" Finch hesitated to answer. He only just recently learned who the killer was, and the only reason he hadn't left to go hunt down the witches and the magic-eating monster was because he didn't have a way to deal with them. How was he supposed to counter their tricks? He needed more time. "I'll get my revenge," was all Finch finally said.

Jay-W shrugged. "Fine. You don't want to talk, fair. But now we have to talk serious. I have work for you."

"What work?" Finch demanded. "What's so important that you needed the greatest warlock to look into it for you?"

Jay-W leaned onto his desk, his eyes narrowing. "My wife."

That was all he said.

My wife.

Finch waited, hoping for some elaboration, but it never came.

"What about her?" he finally prompted.

Jay-W reclined in his large, leather chair. "She's cheatin' on me. And I want you to find out with who."

There was a brief moment where Finch gave serious consideration to leaving. Just… rewinding time, and exiting the situation so thoroughly that no one would ever know he had been here.

"*Anyone* could trail your wife," Finch said through clenched teeth. "A normal PI you pay by the hour. Maybe even an Uber driver who wants money under the table. Literally anyone. You don't need me—or my skills—to find out who your wife is seeing on the side."

"Yeah, wise guy? Well, it might surprise you to know I already did all that." Jay-W took a puff on his cigar and then blew out a long line of smoke. "I hired a PI, a photographer, some shady-lookin' chicks who say they find cheatin' spouses all the time for celebrities—they couldn't find anythin'."

"What makes you think your wife is cheating, then?"

Jay-W pounded his hand on his desk. His brandy sloshed around in the glass. "She disappears every weekend and comes back on Monday smellin' odd. She says she's just out with her girlfriends, but she's usin' *magic* to hide from me. *Magic*, Adair. She fuckin' hired some witch to make a brew that makes her difficult to spot on cameras, and maybe she's invisible, I don't know."

"That doesn't mean she's cheating on you."

Jay-W pointed at him with his cigar. "No one goes to that length to hide if they're innocent. She's doin' somethin' she doesn't want me to know about—and it's another man. You got me? Find her. *Find her and bring her back, with proof she's been with some other guy.*"

Finch sighed. He didn't even try to conceal it—he sighed just loud enough that it filled the room. "So, this has nothing to do with the killer running wild in Oakland?"

"Killer? What killer?" Jay-W took another drag on his cigar. As he spoke, smoke wafted from his mouth. "There were more than a hundred dead bodies found last year in the city. All homicides, not some heart attack bullshit. Which killer are you talkin' about?"

"Forget I mentioned it," Finch muttered.

Oakland had the third-highest crime rate in all California, behind only Stockton—Finch's hometown—and San Bernardino, which had connections to a cartel. Bodies piled up in Oakland like leaves in autumn, and it didn't surprise Finch that Jay-W had no idea what was going on.

"Okay, well, where do you think your wife is?" Finch asked, mentally resigning himself to the assignment.

"She's definitely at the waterfront. Do you know where Jack London Square is? There's a fancy nightclub that opened there—*Level 22*, they call it. The first couple floors have fancy drinks, and near the top there's a secret casino, but it's not open to the public."

Jay-W reached into a desk drawer and pulled out something that resembled a metal credit card. He slid it across the top of the desk, and it came to a stop right at the edge. Finch walked over and scooped it up.

The little metal card read: *You have reached Level 22.* The letters were done in a beautiful font, and shimmered silver.

It was a nice card. Too nice. And it felt cold to the touch.

"What is this?" Finch asked as he turned it over.

"Level 22 is owned by some werewolf," Jay-W said with a shrug. "And he hates the fae or something. All his cards are made from a special type of iron, and it hurts their skin, apparently. I don't give a shit."

Kull's eyes went wide. She slipped around Finch and snatched the metal card from his grasp. "Oh, wow. This is *boreal iron*. So fancy. If anything will burn the fae—it's this."

Finch took the card back and tucked it into his pocket.

Jay-W gave Kull a second glance, as though he were actually seeing her for the first time. "You can tell it's boreal iron? Humans can barely tell the difference between types of bread. How's a girl like you know any of that?"

Kull clapped her hand, and paused, after each word as she said, "I'm, Adair's, assistant."

Finch pinched the bridge of his nose. He didn't want to tell Jay-W about how he had found a dead body on the side of the road, and how a spirit of mischief had taken it over.

Then it occurred to Finch—was Kull acting this way *specifically* to agitate him? That would be very... mischievous. He gave her the side-eye. Kull just smiled in response.

This was going to be a long night.

Finch patted his coat pocket. "Right. Well, I have the card. I guess I'll go ask around at the club. What's your wife's name?"

"Charlotte Woolsy. Sometimes people call her *Charlie*. Ask for both."

"All right."

"Good." Jay-W took a longer drag on his cigar before adding, "And Adair—if you find my wife, and get proof she's been messin' around, I'll pay you a hundred grand."

That was a ridiculous amount of money for how simple a job this was, but Finch wasn't going to complain. He sarcastically saluted with the card in his hand.

"Aye, aye," he muttered.

With a hundred grand, he could easily rent out the office space Bree wanted. Finch told himself that was his reason for doing this—to make her easier to cope with.

"What if we find your wife, and she's *not* cheating?" Kull asked while holding up a finger.

Jay-W frowned. "Hmpf. If ya find her, and she's innocent, at least get me all the details about the magic keepin' her hidden from me, and I'll still pay you a hundred grand. I hate bein' kept in the dark."

Mimicking Finch's movements, Kull also saluted as she said, "Aye, aye!"

CHAPTER
NINE

As Kull and Finch rode the elevator down into the private parking garage, Finch glanced at the clock on his phone.

7:32 p.m.

"So, what do you think about this case?" Kull asked, rubbing her chin with an over-the-top quality. "Is the wife innocent? Or sus?"

"She's cheating on him." That was the case nine times out of ten whenever a woman started disappearing for long periods of time. Plus, Jay-W *looked* like the type of man a woman would cheat on. If Finch had a gun pressed to the side of his head, he would confidently say that Jay-W had the right idea.

"But why? He obviously loves her."

"*Obviously*?" Finch asked, curious as to how she came to that conclusion.

"Yeah. Look at how worried he is about her! Obsessively following her every movement, and upset when he doesn't know where she is... He wants to be with her. It's making him sad that she's so far away. That's love. It has to be."

Finch ran a hand down his face. He would call this *stalking* or *controlling*, and definitely not *love*, but what did he know? He decided to drop the conversation. The mischief spirit clearly derived her understanding of human emotions from TV, YouTube, and Hollywood movies. It would be hard to explain reality to her.

Plus, what was Finch supposed to say? Kull was enjoying her new life. Was he supposed to tell her some things were just dour and terrible?

No.

Finch's brother, Carter, had always told him: never take something you can't replace. And Finch couldn't replace Kull's optimism and joy with anything meaningful. Why depress her? The world would do that all on its own, without his help.

The elevator doors opened, and Kull confidently walked out. She even motioned to her heels as she did so—no more stumbling and bumbling. "Well? Do you like?"

"Like *what*?" Finch asked with a groan.

"My walking. Don't you think I picked up on this fast? I'm drip." Kull tossed back some of her fiery red hair as she said the last word.

Sus? Drip? Rizz? Finch was starting to lose track of all the made-up words Kull was using.

Finch slowed his walking and turned to face her. "What's wrong with you? Why are you talking like that all of a sudden? You're acting like you're five when you're actually five *hundred*."

"W-Well, Fox-Pistol uses these phrases… So I should, too, right?"

Since Finch already had his phone in his hand, he unlocked it, and then offered it to Kull. "Here. Show me one of her videos. Until I see what this Fox-Pistol is like, I feel like I'm never going to understand what you're trying to be."

Kull smiled wide as she snatched his phone from his hands. With shaky fingers, Kull tapped on the apps. She bit her lip and narrowed her gaze, fidgeting as she ambled her way through everything.

"You don't think this is weird?" she whispered.

"What's weird? Social media stars? Because I *do* think those are bizarre."

"I meant—me. Acting like Fox-Pistol. I'm not really a human. I'm just in her body now, assuming her life. As a human yourself, don't you find that... odd?"

Finch did think Kull's whole future was about to be one long *Weekend at Bernie's* skit, but that reference was as dated as he was, so he didn't make it. Instead, he shrugged. "I've seen a lot of weird things in my life. A spirit inhabiting an empty body is hardly at the top of the list. Stop overthinking everything."

The corners of Kull's lips twitched upward in a small smile. "Thank you."

"What's taking so long?" Finch asked.

Kull nervously laughed. "Uh, well, I just realized that *I'm* using a phone! I was trying not to shout or clap or get too excited, since I'm trying to be serious right now, but it's so exciting. Look! I'm poking the screen with human fingers!"

Finch sighed. He glanced around, hoping no one was watching this awkward exchange between them. Fortunately, the limo and its driver were nowhere to be found. Obviously, Jimmy'd had to drive off to help one of Jay-W's sons or something.

"Okay, here it is," Kull said as she handed his phone back. "This is the YouTube app, by the way. I had to download it."

"Fantastic," Finch grumbled.

"She posts all her streams from Twitch over here, and she also makes fun little videos. See this one? It's her most recent! Apparently, she made it yesterday. It already has four hundred and forty-two thousand views. That's nearly half a million."

Finch pressed the play button, ignoring the urge to make a sarcastic comment.

The video started up with a beautiful woman facing the camera. She wore a pair of designer sunglasses, even though she was indoors, and seductively licked her lips before she began speaking.

"Hello, ding-dongs. It's me, Fox-Pistol."

The rest of her outfit was nothing more than a skintight, strapless black dress. Her room was grotesquely pink, and she even wore bright rosy headphones with a pair of fox ears designed into the headband.

"Today we're watching a video about a dad who can't afford to buy his kids soccer equipment." Fox-Pistol winked to the camera. "Grab a drinky-drink or a snacky-snack and let's watch."

"I thought you said this woman played video games while in a hot tub?" Finch asked, already tired of the video. Everything about Fox-Pistol was exhausting.

Kull tilted her head. "You *want* to watch her in a hot tub? Didn't you say that was dumb?"

"I-I don't want to watch her in a hot tub. This just doesn't fit with what you said would be happening."

The video continued to play on the phone, while Finch's face heated and he tried to think of a way out of the situation.

At first, he thought this would be a video about how Fox-Pistol would find a father struggling to pay for sporting equipment, and then she would pay for it herself. Finch had stumbled across those kinds of heartwarming viral videos in the past. He enjoyed those.

Instead, Fox-Pistol was playing a video game—some sort of military shooter that he assumed was *Call of Duty*—and then next to her was a video *inside of her video*. What was this? A reaction thing?

In the smaller video, a father didn't have enough money to buy the nice soccer ball, so he reached for a cheap ball. It was the last one in the whole store. Another man rushed over and took the ball out of the bin before the father had it in his hands.

Fox-Pistol, while playing *Call of Duty*, frowned at the video. "So, this guy said no one wants this ball, and this other guy just *spawns* and comes to take it? Pretty sus if you ask me."

"See? *See?*" Kull tapped the side of his phone. "She says these things. I need to say the same things now. Like *drinky-drinks* and *snacky-snacks.*"

The father in the video turned to his children and shook his head. He couldn't buy the ball. Now they had to leave the store without anything.

Then Fox-Pistol laughed. "Wow, how pathetic is that? If my father couldn't buy me a soccer ball for school, I'd die of embarrassment! What is it? Like ten bucks? Anyone can afford a ten-dollar ball, you cheapskate dad."

Finch frowned.

He hated this video.

"What is this?" he growled.

Kull glanced up and smiled. "Fox-Pistol makes humans laugh by making fun of these videos. She says she's *poking fun at the poors*. And she does it while being an awesome gamer with skills! Aren't you amused? I just thought all humans enjoyed things like this."

"Most of us don't," Finch muttered under his breath. "Everything about this was awful. And these were my good video-watching eyes."

Kull tapped at his phone screen and swiped the video to the very end. "This is the part where she talks about her upcoming release schedule, and when to see her stream next. I should, uh, probably know this… Since I'll need to upload something."

Finch just stared at her with his eyes half-lidded. "*You're* going to make a video? You might want to wait until you've had some more practice blending in. Currently, you're about as convincingly human as a singing animatronic found inside a Chuck-E-Cheese."

On the phone, Fox-Pistol winked at the camera, her pink lips practically shining in the expertly positioned lighting. "*Anyways*, that's all for today! I hope you guys enjoyed this video. If you did, make sure to hit that like button!" She jutted her thumbs in the air as she made her last statement.

Finch was ready to delete the whole app, but Kull motioned him to continue watching.

"And just in case you're wondering," Fox-Pistol said with a coy smile, "this weekend I'll be celebrating my boyfriend's birthday." She winked again and stuck out her tongue. "So no videos until Monday. Don't worry, my fellow foxes and vixens—I'll have a fun compilation of all the crazy stuff we'll be getting up to at the clubs. We're even attending a private concert. I know you're all jealous!"

Then the video ended.

Finch wasn't entirely sure what to make of that.

Fox-Pistol's body had been found on the side of the road. According to the witnesses, a man had accompanied her out, and then left alone. Had that been Fox-Pistol's boyfriend? His birthday gift to himself was murdering her?

"Maybe you *should* make a video right now," Finch whispered, his eyes narrowing until he was glaring at his screen.

Kull's expression brightened in an instant. "Really? You think so? What should it be about? Should I watch someone else's video and make fun of it? Or should I splash around in a pool? Play some *Call of Duty*?"

"Anything. Just let the killer know Fox-Pistol is alive. Maybe even mention we'll be going to the Jack London area on the docks."

Kull pointed to the elevator. "Oh! Let's film inside Jay-W's house. That's the kind of location Fox-Pistol uses all the time."

"Weird men's mansions?"

"No. Just bougie. Fox-Pistol loves bougie things."

Again, Finch found himself on the wrong side of the lingo divide. He had never *been hip to the jive* with the kids, and he figured he never would be—unless spelling kids with a 'z' was still considered cool. Finch could manage that.

"Whatever," Finch said with a groan.

He tapped the elevator button, and the two of them rode it up. Finch had concocted an entire elaborate lie for why they were returning—to explain himself to the bodyguards—but when the elevator opened, the living room was empty. No Lloyd. No Jimmy. No Jay-W.

It was just them.

Finch held up his phone. "Okay. So, I film you? And then we leave?"

"I should do a live stream," Kull said. She golf-clapped her hands. "Fox-Pistol always does surprise live streams. I'm sure her fans—well, *my* fans—are totally expecting one. So many people will see it!"

"How are you going to do this? Do you even know how to log into Fox-Pistol's accounts?"

Kull took Finch's phone and poked around on his apps. With a smirk, she said, "Have you already forgotten that I'm a mischief spirit *first* and a human *second*? I still have some of my magic... Like the ability to get past pesky things like passwords. Look here. I'll be into her account in no time."

As Kull poked around on the phone, Finch decided to creep into the long hallway. He stayed close to the wall, and glanced up and down, looking for anyone. He heard talking from Jay-W's room, and Finch listened hard to see what was going on.

"Got-damn I've gotten fat," Jay-W said with a grunt. "I don't even recognize myself in the mirror anymore."

"You could always work out," someone replied. Lloyd. His voice was distinct. Clearly, he had been called in to entertain the lonely Jay-W. Or perhaps lift things.

"*Alexa*, remind me to go to the gym," Jay-W shouted.

"I've added *gin* to your shopping list," a feminine voice replied.

"Eh… Close enough."

Convinced Jay-W and his thug wouldn't be walking into the living room anytime soon, Finch crept back to Kull. She was still poking at his phone, but she smiled when he drew near.

"I have one of her accounts," Kull confidently stated. "Her Instagram." She flashed the screen over to Finch. "See? My mischief magic still works!"

"Why don't you have access to all her accounts?"

"Oh… uh…" Kull nervously played with her red hair. "It turns out, some of these programs have more security than I thought." With a forced chuckle, she added, "But one is enough, right? We're fine."

"Sure. How do we do this?"

"Well, since it's Instagram, maybe we shouldn't go live. I don't think that's popular there. Instead, just film me, and I'll make it a reel."

Finch didn't know what the difference was between streaming, a video, a reel, or a live stream, so he just let Kull handle everything. She glanced around the room, ran over to the one of the gigantic couches, and threw herself on the cushions.

"Okay, film me here," she said.

Finch held up the camera and hit the record button. "Okay. We're filming."

"Hello, ding-dongs," Kull said. "It's me! Fox-Pistol." She laughed and then stretched out on the couch, arching her back in an exaggerated fashion. The dress threatened to reveal her bikini bottom, but it never actually shirked its duty.

"I'm here having a wonderful time in Oakland." She winked. "My boyfriend's birthday is going to be crazy, and I'm about to head over to the Jack London area of the Oakland docks to celebrate, because that's what us humans do."

Finch rolled his eyes and held back a groan.

The video had started strong, and now it was meandering into weird.

Kull lifted her hand. Then she traced the edges of her lips with her pointer finger, and without warning, slid that finger into her open mouth. Her tongue played around the length of her digit, and she moved deeper and deeper.

"What're you doing?" Finch asked, louder than he wanted. And although he was flustered, he managed to turn off the video as he walked over to the couch.

Kull stopped her seductive act and tilted her head. "Hm? Fox-Pistol does that sometimes on her streams. Don't humans consider it sexy?"

"You're verging on pornographic." Finch found it difficult to find the right words. He wasn't even sure what sucking her finger on camera was supposed to accomplish. He was so baffled, and conflicted, he was silent for a full thirty seconds. "Maybe some people find it sexy," he finally said, "but *why* would you do it?"

"Do *you* find it sexy?" Kull asked.

Finch, who was already bordering on crimson, somehow grew redder. He turned away rubbed his hot face, and stared at the floor. "Okay. New plan. I just set up the camera on a chair, and you film whatever you need to without me."

"Wait!" Kull hopped off the couch and held out her hand. "Let me see the video! We don't need to do another one. I'll, uh, try to upload what we have. I think I know what to do. I've seen humans do it in the past. It doesn't seem hard."

After a long sigh, he handed over his phone. "All right. Once you're done, let's get out of here."

CHAPTER
TEN

Since Finch and Kull had taken a limo to Jay-W's, they had to take an Uber back to Finch's vehicle in the Walmart parking lot. The entire drive, Kull used Finch's phone to edit her video until it met her approval. Then she uploaded it to Fox-Pistol's social media at 7:58 p.m.

Once they arrived at Finch's car, they both slid inside and fastened their seat belts.

But Kull was quiet. Too quiet.

She glanced over, her hand shaking, her expression haunted.

"I have a problem," she whispered.

"What is it?" Finch asked as he started up his Toyota.

"I'm... I'm dying."

Finch snapped his attention to her, his brow furrowed. "*What?*"

Kull solemnly nodded. "I'm so sorry, Adair. I thought all these feelings would go away, but that's just not the case. They keep getting worse." She motioned to her face. "My mouth won't stop watering." She grabbed her stomach. "My tummy keeps clenching." With a frown, Kull returned her attention to Finch. "At first, I just had dull aches, but now it's so *painful*. My head is throbbing."

All the information swirled in Finch's mind until he wanted to laugh. He relaxed in his seat, taking a deep breath. Kull had almost killed him with her wild declaration of dying.

"I can't believe I messed up being a human so badly." Kull grabbed her long, red hair and twisted her fingers into her locks, pulling hard. "I'm so sorry. I should've taken better care of my body. Now look what happened!"

"Calm down," Finch said with a chuckle. "You're just hungry. We'll swing by a burger joint on the way to Level 22. You'll feel better after that."

"R-Really?" Kull let go of her hair and perked up in her seat. "Everything will be okay?"

"Yeah. Everything will be fine."

"But why am I hurting? I don't understand."

"It's just your body's way of telling you that you need something," Finch muttered as he pulled his vehicle out of its parking spot. "It's an urge. A signal. Whatever. Just listen to the signs and you'll be fine."

Kull clapped her hands, her eyes bright with life once more. "Oh, excellent! I knew you would be a great human teacher. Thank you, Adair!"

Finch rolled his eyes.

Now... if only he could remember the place that had the best milkshakes...

―――

8:10 p.m.

Finch and Kull sat in a booth at *Grill Thrill Burgers*. The interior's red, white, and blue theme was as patriotic as it was garish. American flags hung on the walls. Pictures of people who had consumed a three-pound burger were on their "champion leaderboard," and the restaurant's mascot was, appropriately, a jolly fat man next to a charcoal grill.

Kull sat across from Finch, inhaling her burger like she hadn't eaten in a week.

It was a monster of a sandwich. Kull had insisted on ordering the double-bacon western because, according to her, "All humans love bacon!"

Finch ordered the same thing, since it was easy, and he lazily chewed through his meal while watching Kull practically make a meme of herself.

With BBQ sauce slathered across one cheek, she glanced up and smiled at Finch. "This is the best thing humans ever invented."

"Wait until you try the milkshakes."

"Are they bacon-flavored milkshakes?" Kull pulled a strip of bacon from the burger and ate it all on its own. "I never knew food was this satisfying. No wonder humans are eating all the time—it hurts them when they get hungry. I thought three times a day was silly, but if it makes their tummy feel better, why aren't they doing it *five times* a day? Six times?"

Finch sipped his water and lifted an eyebrow. "Some do."

"Wow. Lucky!" Kull took another huge bite of her burger. She seemed feral.

A man with a tray of food walked by the booth and gave Kull the once over. He wore tight jeans and a cowboy hat, like he had just come from a dude ranch. The man smirked. "You're lookin' good."

Kull happily smiled back at him. "Thank you," she said with a mouth full of food.

"You here eatin' with your father? Why not come sit with me, baby girl?"

Finch shot the cowboy a glare. "I'm only thirty-seven."

Then he did some quick mental math, and his chest twisted in dread.

Damn, he thought. *I could* be her father. Finch pinched the bridge of his nose and groaned. *Goddammit.* For a warlock with time powers, time had a way of continually sneaking up on him.

He consoled himself with the fact he couldn't be Kull's father—she was a spirit who was centuries old. But Fox-Pistol? How old was she? Twenty? Finch hated this realization.

"I'm twenty-one," Kull said matter-of-factly, and then gave Finch a wink, no skill at subterfuge whatsoever.

"Right," the cowboy awkwardly muttered. "You wanna sit with me?"

Kull shook her head. Then she swallowed the last of the food in her mouth. "No. I have a murderer following me, and Adair has to find Jay-W's wife so we can prove she's not cheating on him. It's going to be a busy evening."

The cowboy seemed to contemplate this and think it so bizarre he didn't dignify her statements with a response. He simply walked off with his tray of food. Finch preferred this outcome.

Kull set her burger down and burped. Several other patrons glanced over and stifled giggles. Kull didn't seem to mind their stares. She waved to a few of them.

"Are you done eating?" Finch asked.

She nodded. "Yup. It's, uh, actually starting to hurt in the opposite direction. Like maybe I ate *too* much."

Finch set his burger down. "All right. Let's get a milkshake and then go. We've already wasted enough time as it is."

———

At night, the Oakland docks had a life of their own. Everything was lit up with yellow, red, and white lights, creating a bubble of illumination so bright, it turned the dark sky above it a lighter shade of blue.

Construction cranes dominated the edge of the docks, while skyscrapers sat just behind them, many filled with restaurants, bars, and exclusive clubs.

Cargo ships rested in the waters just beyond the nightlife, and the lights of the city reflected off the constant ripples, giving the whole area a pulse that invigorated Finch.

He parked his car in the cheapest spot—which still cost him thirty bucks for five hours—and then headed for Jack London Square. Kull matched his pace, her gaze up on the lights, her mouth constantly in an *O* of awe and wonder.

The logo for Level 22 was cleverly hidden inside the billboard design for the nightclub called *Oasis*. The palm trees were tilted and twisted in the shape of the word *Level* and the number *22* was bolded in the billboard's directions for how to get to Oasis.

That was how it was for most businesses owned by the supernatural. They were in plain sight, if you knew where to look. Most humans only saw the sign for Oasis, and a helpful set of directions for getting there.

The Oakland docks had a load of ambient magic, unfortunately. It was difficult for Finch to pick out one thing. Several fae were here, that he knew, but the stench of werewolf was also thick in the air.

He kept his hands in his pockets as he headed straight for his destination. A warlock like him could be considered trespassing on some supernatural creature's turf if he wasn't careful.

"I love this place," Kull said as she pointed to a bright set of signs with a glittering advertisement on them. "Look at how wonderful this is. Humans are amazing."

"Amazing?"

"They do all this without magic? How is that not amazing?"

Finch hadn't thought of it that way.

Instead, he kept his sights on the road. It only took a few minutes of walking for him to reach his destination: a tall building filled to the brim with parties, nightclubs, and liquor. The Oasis had a sign done in gold, and it shimmered as Finch and Kull walked under it to get to the front door.

8:33 p.m.

The lobby was filled with individuals on their way to the ground floor bar and dance floor. Each flashed their ID to the building's security before making their way inside. Everyone seemed young to Finch—twenty-somethings, and all looking for a hookup. They wore sexy outfits, or slick suits, and were already in a jovial mood.

When Finch reached one of the bouncers, he flashed his iron Level 22 card. The muscled man gestured to the elevator, away from the magicless bar and festivities taking place in the Oasis.

Before he reached the elevator, Kull tugged on his coat sleeve. "Adair?"

"Yeah?"

"Can I stay down here while you do all your questioning?"

He glanced over, his eyes squinted. "Why?"

"I really want to go in to the Oasis." Kull pointed as the doors opened to reveal a dimly lit bar and dancefloor. The multicolored lights flashed throughout the area as waitresses walked around with cocktails. It was a hip joint if Finch ever saw one.

"I thought you told that cowboy we were busy?" he asked.

"But places like this are where humans find true love." She smiled up at Finch. "I've seen it all the time in movies."

Finch held back a laugh. He wanted to tell her that was all nonsense, but he couldn't bring himself to crush her dreams. Besides, there was a small chance someone could find true love in a bar or nightclub. Very small. But still a chance.

"Did you forget a murderer is probably after you?" Finch rubbed his temple.

Kull frowned. "But this is a public place. I won't leave! I promise. And you're *Adair Finch*. If anything happens, you'll make it right with your magic, right? Everything will be okay for just a little bit."

Although Finch thought this whole thing was silly, he shrugged and gestured for her to go into Oasis. He would be right back—as soon as he finished searching out Level 22. Kull probably wouldn't get into too much trouble.

Probably.

Kull giggled, gave Finch a hug, and then hurried over to the bouncers. She didn't have an ID, but the moment they got a good look at her, they motioned her straight in. Pretty girls got all the special treatment, it seemed.

Finch entered the elevator and rode it up to the top floor. The doors opened to reveal a small hallway with yet another muscled man in a suit. When Finch flashed his card *this* time, the man smiled wide enough to show off teeth that seemed just a little too sharp.

Not vampire fangs—but the wild teeth of someone who had been a werewolf for most of their life and disliked being in their human form.

Finch nodded once to the man before stepping into Level 22.

He quickly understood why Jay-W's wife might be attracted to the place.

The luxury nightclub was stunningly beautiful. The chandeliers wept crystals, lush black rugs were made of some of the softest material Finch had ever stepped on, and the gentle golden lighting gave everything an expensive feel. Soft jazz music played from speakers in the ceiling, rounding out the ambience.

It was a place so fancy, even the perfectly spherical ice cubes in everyone's drinks had pedigrees.

The clientele was also in a league of its own. The moment Finch took in a deep breath, he knew everyone here was supernatural in some way. While some looked completely human, magic radiated from them like heat off a heat lamp.

Plus, there was a werewolf behind the bar.

Not like the bouncer outside, who had to remain in human form. No, this bartender was a full-blown anthropomorphic wolf. He stood on two legs, his black fur lustrous over a body made of pure muscle. He wore a suit tailored for his lycanthrope body, his little vest a shade of gray that complemented his ebony fur.

He even had a tail hole in his pants, so his large and bushy tail could wag around, unhindered.

And the bar had clearly been built to accommodate a beast nearly eight feet tall. It was larger, more spacious, and made of material that wouldn't easily be scratched by the man's claws.

His long muzzle and pointed ears really gave him the silhouette of a wolf, but his dark eyes were alight with human intelligence. And having dark eyes was a good thing —only werewolves with red eyes could spread the lycanthrope disease. If this wolf lost his temper and bit everyone here, there was no chance of a werewolf outbreak. Oakland had had too many of those already.

The wolf's ears shifted in Finch's direction as Finch walked over. The beast turned to greet him with a fang-filled smile.

"Good evening," the werewolf said, his voice rich and confident. "You seem familiar, but I don't think I've seen many warlocks in these parts. Take a seat. I'll pour you something smooth."

There were three other customers at the bar, all women. Even from ten feet away, Finch knew they were full moon witches—the most powerful kind. Magic had a scent similar to gunpowder, and full moon witches wore their magic like musky perfume.

The witches all sat close together, laughing over drinks. Finch leaned away from them as he took a seat at the bar.

"I'm Enzo, the evening bartender." The wolf man held out a clawed hand. "Let me see your card."

Finch handed it over as he glanced around. There was a game of poker in the back, played on a large, solid-wood table. Next to that was a roulette wheel, but it seemed a white rabbit was the one manning it. A moon rabbit? It stood on the table that supported the wheel, its ears perked high. Moon rabbit spirits were rare, and often tried to trick humans by offering immortality in exchange for precious objects. Why was one running part of the casino?

It probably wasn't a normal game of roulette, that was for sure.

Enzo examined Finch's iron card. Then he brought it to his canine nose and inhaled deeply. "Wait a minute," Enzo growled. "This smell... It's Jay-W. *He* gave you his card?"

Finch nodded once.

The fur on the back of the werewolf's neck stood on end, his lips curling back as he growled. "*Get out.* I told that fat waste of space he wasn't welcome here anymore. *And that includes his stooges.*"

CHAPTER
ELEVEN

F inch didn't get out of his seat. Instead, he just held up a hand. "I can explain."

Enzo hooked his claws into Finch's coat collar and then yanked him forward. Finch was practically on top of the bar, the werewolf's hot breath on his face.

"Did I stutter?" Enzo snarled.

Finch was at his limit for the evening. He had been sucker punched, ridiculed, belittled, and now threatened? There was no more patience to pass around, and Finch was going to get his answers one way or another.

He grabbed the werewolf's wrist and tightened his grip. "Put me down," Finch said, quiet and icy calm. "Or else."

Werewolves weren't known for their tranquility. The lycanthrope illness often involved rage issues, and it was always made worse while they were in wolf form. Some werewolves kept themselves in control, but Enzo seemed thrilled to offer Finch a threatening smile.

"Or else what, *warlock?* I'm about to send you to Jay-W in an ambulance."

"An ambulance wouldn't take me to a person's house, genius."

That insult was obviously too much for the werewolf's limited self-control.

Enzo hauled Finch fully up onto the bar counter, but the werewolf clearly hadn't been expecting flames. Finch unleashed a burst of fire so intense, it scorched Enzo's wrist, arm, and shoulder, burning through fur, flesh, and suit alike. The smell of smoke, burnt hair, and cooking meat filled Level 22 as the flames swirled behind the counter.

Finch's fire came from Ke-Koh, the Ifrit of Rebellion. Ke-Koh's fire was more intense whenever Finch was held against his will—which had somewhat happened in this situation. Ke-Koh's magic was also tied to Finch's heart core, meaning it would be empowered whenever Finch felt strong emotion —which had *definitely* happened here.

Enzo howled in agony and released Finch's coat. There was a reason Finch held his wrist—to immediately incapacitate one arm.

Despite the injury, Enzo flashed his fangs and then leapt over the bar. He slammed Finch onto the floor, his massive three-hundred-pound body landing on Finch's chest, the claws of his good hand digging into Finch's left shoulder.

Winded, Finch gritted his teeth, ignored his tunneling vision, and placed his other hand on Enzo's muscled chest. A second torrent of flames washed over the werewolf. Enzo roared as he leapt away, his clothing eighty percent ashes, and his furless flesh blistering. In spite of all that, his eyes were wild, his claws extended, his fangs still bared.

Finch barely had time to get his feet when the werewolf lunged. Fortunately, Finch had the presence of mind to sidestep the attack. He slammed into a nearby table, embers and heat wafting from his whole person. Half *Finch's* clothes were nothing but ash on the floor of Level 22.

Beeping shrieked throughout the establishment, and then water burst from the ceiling, spraying the bar, the counter, and the main sitting area.

A few patrons shouted in surprise, and everyone moved to the corners of the room. Except the individuals playing poker, who didn't stop their game. They only occasionally glanced over to see the ruckus. Neither the smoke nor the sprinkles seemed to disturb them.

"Kill him!" the moon rabbit shouted with gleeful joy. "Rip him up, Enzo!"

The three witches watched the brawl, their eyes glittering with interest.

"*Fight, fight, fight,*" one shouted, clearly inebriated.

Finch took a deep breath. When Enzo wheeled around to face him, Finch exhaled. The fire he breathed was white. It filled the whole casino nightclub with blinding light and heat so intense, most people had to shield their frail eyes. Steam filled Level 22 as well, as the emergency sprinklers were no match for Finch's magic.

The key to mastering magic tied to one's heart was channeling and controlling emotions. Finch wanted this conflict *over*, and he focused his anger on that one task alone to get the fire so concentrated.

Enzo crumpled to his knees. Finch stopped his attack, white smoke wafting from his body, spits of flame shooting from his mouth with each exhale.

Werewolves were much tougher, stronger, and faster in their anthropomorphic wolf form. While masquerading as humans, they were just as susceptible to damage as the next chump. But maintaining a were-form required discipline and dedication.

Obviously too injured to maintain such a form, Enzo reverted into a human. His injuries mostly knitted themselves closed—a benefit of the form reversion—but Enzo was still rather seared.

What remained of Enzo's clothes didn't fit him. He was a muscular man, but still a man. He was also only six feet tall, which meant he had lost a good two feet. His skin was as dark as his werewolf fur, and his eyes the same shade as before, but now dulled with agony. He kept his head shaved, which revealed a white tattoo of a crescent moon behind one ear.

"Detective Harris?" Finch asked, his question practically a gasp as realization hit him.

He knew this man.

His name wasn't *Enzo* at all—but when Finch had known Harris, he hadn't been a werewolf, either. Elijah Harris had been an admirable police detective.

The half-charred man on the floor couldn't seem to push himself off his knees. He glanced up, some burnt skin flaking off his charbroiled shoulder. It took him a pained moment, but "Enzo" came to his own realization.

"Adair?" Harris asked. "I thought I recognized you, but... aren't you dead?"

"That was my brother. I just took a break. From life. I'm back now."

Finch went to Harris and knelt, but he didn't touch him. Harris was too cooked.

"I'm so sorry," Finch muttered. "I didn't know it was you."

When Harris laughed, he huffed. Then he grimaced and tightly wrapped his arms over his injured chest. "You did a number on me. *Damn.*"

"Finish him," one of the drunk witches called out. She ended her dark statement with a tipsy *woo.*

"Enzo, bite him!" the other joined in. "*Bite him!*"

"Or make out! That'd be even better!"

"With the moon as my witness, do somethin', dammit!"

Finch glanced around. Half the luxury casino and nightclub was more a smoldering wreckage now, complete with a postapocalyptic smell of burnt meat and plastic. Well, mostly behind the bar and the empty sitting area. The poker table was unharmed, and everyone continued their game, despite the mayhem only a few feet away. One man even delicately played a card. "I'm all in," he whispered.

The fight clearly wasn't the most unusual thing that had ever happened here. The supernatural had a way of attracting conflict, and some were just dulled to it.

"I'm sorry," Finch said with a groan. "I'll make this right."

Harris snorted and then glared at him, his eyebrows completely burned off. "Are you touched in the head? What're you gonna do to make this right?"

Finch activated his magic granted to him by Chronos.

Time halted. Everything stopped moving—even the embers floating through the air. Then the colors drained from the world, slipping out of every object. It left Level 22 as a still frame from a black-and-white movie, devoid of life.

Lastly, all the shapes melted from Finch's view, disappearing into a white void.

Then Finch took a sudden breath, and he was back in the woods just outside of Oakland. Fox-Pistol's body was on the ground in front of him.

Once again, it was 5:29 p.m.

Kull sat up and then glanced around with her human eyes. Fox-Pistol was beautiful, even while covered in leaves, missing her shoes, and generally dirty. Her red hair shimmered, and her eyes twinkled.

"What happened?" Kull asked.

"I got into a fight with a werewolf," Finch muttered with a sigh.

Kull giggled. "And you were telling *me* to be careful.

Maybe you should take some of your own advice." Her mirth faded as she asked, "But why did you get into a fight?"

Finch held out his hand to help Kull stand. "It was actually an old buddy of mine. Detective Elijah Harris. He used to work for the Oakland PD. I don't know when he became infected with lycanthropy."

Once Kull was on her feet, she frowned. The twigs underfoot were clearly bothering her. Finch scooped her up into his arms.

Kull wrapped her arms around Finch's neck and smiled up at him. "If he's your friend, why were you fighting?"

"I don't know." Finch rolled his eyes as he walked through the dark woods back to the road with his parked car. "I just wanted to fight something. It's been one of those evenings."

"You *want* to fight things?"

"It was just a stupid impulse decision."

"Like a human urge? Like hunger?"

Finch huffed a laugh. "Something like that."

Kull tilted her head to the side. "Humans just get urges for all kinds of things?"

"That's how it works."

"When I was just a spirit, I mostly obsessed about mischief and tricks." Kull tightened her arms around Finch, her gaze distant. "It's more complicated being a human than I thought." Then she snapped her attention to Finch and smiled. "You have the urge to fight all the time?"

"Just occasionally." Finch shot her a glower. "I was sucker punched in a Walmart earlier this night. All that pent up aggression had to go somewhere."

As they walked through the woods, Kull kept her eyes on Finch's face. He glanced down, his eyebrows knitting in irritation. "Is something wrong?"

"I think I have an urge right now," she whispered.

"What is it?"

To his surprise, Kull touched his forehead. "Are you okay, Adair? Is your friend a full-blown werewolf? Did he have red eyes?"

"No, he wasn't a contagious werewolf." Finch leaned away. "You don't have to worry about me."

"Well, my urge to keep you safe is rising." Kull hugged him tight.

Finch stomped through the undergrowth, the road not too far now. "I'm perfectly capable of looking after myself."

Kull remained silent as Finch walked out of the woods onto the pavement of the road. All the people from before were there, including the handyman who had first spotted Fox-Pistol heading off into the woods with a man. A few people clapped.

"The officer found her!" one person shouted.

As Finch strode over to his vehicle, the older handyman in overalls hurried to his side. "I'm so glad the girl is okay," the handyman said. "I was mighty worried."

"She got lost," Finch said, no emotion in his voice as he stepped around the man. "I'm going to take her to the hospital."

"Good idea."

Both Finch and Kull said nothing to the others. He set her down in the passenger seat and then went around to the driver's side. Once situated, he drew the Mark of Chronos on her forearm again, to make sure she would remember everything when he inevitably reset the time.

"I was about to talk to someone inside Oasis," Kull said with a longing sigh. "But you reset time too fast. I want more time, Adair. I want to go back so I can finish my conversation."

Finch gave her a long stare as he finished drawing her mark. "You didn't get that out of your system?"

"I was barely there."

A buzz from Finch's pocket told him that Jay-W was calling again. After a powerful exhale, Finch answered.

"Finch here."

"You motherfucker," Jay-W growled. "Stop ignorin' my calls."

"Calm your man-tits," Finch snapped back. "I'll find out who your wife is sleeping with."

Jay-W was shocked into silence—which was quite rare. It only took him a moment to recover, though. "You know why I've been callin' you?"

"I'll swing by to pick up your Level 22 membership card. Just leave it out."

"Are you…"

Finch had never told Jay-W about his time powers. Back when his brother was alive, Finch had kept it rather secretive. Only spirits, gods, and some of the fae knew who Finch was bonded to. Well, plus Bree and her father.

"Are you *sleeping with my wife?*" Jay-W demanded.

"*What?*" Finch knitted his eyebrows. "No. I've never even met your wife."

"How do you know she's cheatin' on me? How do you know about Level 22? Are you a *dog,* Adair? Have you been with my wife, talkin' about me? *Is that it?*"

His volume was rising and rising, like a teapot that hit boiling and just wouldn't stop screaming.

"I'll kill you, Adair! They'll *never* find your body."

Finch smacked himself in the face and dragged his hand down past his chin. Why did he do this to himself? Jay-W continued his accusing tirade, his vocabulary more colorful by the second.

"Wow, he sounds perturbed," Kull said, both her eyebrows high. "And see? He *really* loves his wife, because he definitely doesn't want you anywhere near her."

Finch hung up on Jay-W, who was midsentence into yet another threat.

Then Finch reset time again. Everything stopped. The colors faded. And then the world melted away.

When Finch took a breath, he inhaled the musky odor of the woods on the side of the road. Kull sat up in her new body, her beautiful, red hair tangled with leaves and twigs.

Again—it was 5:29 p.m.

"Wow, you rewound time just to exit that conversation?" Kull asked.

"I do it more often than you know," Finch quipped.

He scooped Kull up into his arms and headed for the road. This time, he would just ignore Jay-W's call, take Kull to get some clothes, and then swing by Jay-W's to pick up the card and pretend to be informed on the whole matter.

That was obviously the easiest and fastest solution.

CHAPTER
TWELVE

Finch didn't answer any more of Jay-W's calls. Instead, he drew the mark on Kull, drove to a random clothing store, got Kull some things, and then went straight for Jay-W's house.

It was 7:00 p.m. when they arrived, a good twenty minutes earlier than before.

Finch parked his car in the underground garage and found Lloyd the part-infernal thug standing watch by the elevator door. Lloyd straightened himself and reached for a weapon inside his coat as Finch approached.

"It's me," Finch muttered as he waved a hand. "Adair Finch. To see Jay-W."

Lloyd was about to comment, but his eyes grew huge when he spotted Kull. "W-Wait. Is that—"

"Fox-Pistol? Yes. She's my assistant. Or whatever."

Kull bounded up to Finch's side, her tall high heels giving her little trouble, even when she did bizarre things, like skip. "I'll sign your phone, if you want."

Lloyd quickly pulled out of his cellphone and handed it over, his giddy expression bordering on the lewd. Finch rolled his eyes during the entire exchange, and then took Kull into the house once they were done. Lloyd waited at the elevator entrance, completely starstruck.

As they traveled upward, Kull smiled. "I like that man. His demon smell is unique. I think he likes me too…" She glanced over, her mirth fading. "Adair, how do you know when you're in love?"

"How the hell should I know?" he quipped.

"You've never experienced it?"

Finch didn't reply. The elevator door opened, and they walked—in silence—through the living room, down the hallway, and all the way to Jay-W's office. Finch opened the door to find Jay-W ready for them, already positioned behind his massive desk.

Lloyd must've told him about their arrival.

Jay-W sipped his cognac and then puffed on his cigar. He stared at Finch with his icy blue eyes. "I finally got you here." He leaned back in his chair—exactly like before.

"Yup," Finch said, less enthusiastic this time.

"Who's the broad?"

Before Kull could answer, Finch said, "She's my assistant. No further questions." Kull deflated a bit, her time to shine clearly robbed from her. Finch continued. "You needed me for something?"

Jay-W gave Kull an odd glance before returning his attention to Finch. "It's my wife."

"She's cheating on you?" Finch quickly asked.

Jay-W's splotchy face grew red. "You guessed that awfully fast, fuck-face."

After making a mental note about how he should handle this conversation the next time, Finch shrugged. "Was she murdered? This is Oakland, after all."

After a long drag on his cigar, and with a piercing glare, Jay-

W replied, "Nah, you had it right the first time. She's cheatin' on me. I just don't need it rubbed in my face by some washed-up warlock." He exhaled a cloud of smoke. "I want to know who my wife is bangin'. Find out for me. You've never failed me before."

Not wanting to waste time in Jay-W's smoke-filled office, Finch cut to the chase, his tone emotionless. "Where do you think your wife is?"

"She's definitely at the waterfront. Do you know where Jack London Square is? There's a fancy nightclub that opened there—*Level 22*, they call it. The first couple floors have fancy drinks, and near the top there's a secret casino, but it's not open to the public."

Just like before, Jay-W reached into a desk drawer and pulled out his exclusive club card for Level 22. The boreal iron was cold to the touch as Finch took it from the man. Without wasting time on questions about it, Finch pocketed the card.

"Is there any reason why you might not be welcome there?" Finch asked. He was curious as to why Harris had gotten so angry once he learned of Jay-W's involvement.

Jay-W cracked half a smile. "I may, or may not, have won too much money playin' at their poker table." He gestured to his blatantly magical eyes. "Some magics just trump others, if ya get what I'm sayin'."

Finch knew.

Few magics beat Chronos's ability to control time. It was an utter and overwhelming advantage against most.

"That's all I need," Finch said as he turned to leave.

Kull stepped forward, her hand out. "Wait!"

Both Finch and Jay-W turned their attention to her. She had practically shouted her word, to the point there was a mild echo. Finch dreaded whatever inane thing she was about to say.

"Mr. Jay-W, do you mind if I ask you a few questions?" Kull rubbed her chin in a questioning manner. Too much.

Jay-W either didn't notice or didn't care. "I suppose."

"Do you love your wife?"

"Of course I do, what kind of stupid question is that?" Jay-W motioned to Kull, then glared at Finch, like this was all his fault, somehow.

Before Finch could interject, Kull got her next question in.

"How did you know you were in love with her?"

The question grated on Finch. He knew why Kull was so obsessed with it. Back in 1842, Kull had met a human painter by the name of James Hershaw and became obsessed with him and his art. When his whole family forgot about her—it had obviously left a scar that never healed, which was rare for spirits.

Spirits didn't typically make connections like that.

And now she wanted someone to think about her like she had thought about James.

"I want to know how to tell if *I'm* in love," Kull said, breaking Finch out of his train of thought. "Because I don't know what to look for."

Jay-W set his cigar down and gave Kull a pensive stare. "Love is special. It's when someone knows you, *accepts you*, believes in you—even when no one else did, or no one else will. It's a new kind of emotion... It'll feel like a twinge in your chest whenever you hear their name." He picked his cigar back up and took a short drag. "And when someone you love betrays you, it's the worst fuckin' thing that could ever happen. You'll hurt for the rest of your life. You got me?"

Kull nodded once, a serious edge to her expression. "Oh, I know that part already. I just... wanted to know more about how humans feel it." Her smile returned as she said, "Thank you, Mr. Jay-W! That was really helpful."

She walked over to Finch. Together, they exited the office and headed down the long marathon hallway. Kull stared at the rug underfoot as they went, the cogs of her mind visibly turning.

Finch didn't say anything to her. He just allowed her to mull over the situation and the bizarre advice.

Jay-W's words were almost poetic. Up until the end. It made Finch wonder if Jay-W really had loved his wife once upon a time, and hadn't always been a controlling lunatic. How long had they been married? Finch assumed only a short while, but he honestly didn't know.

Once they reached the living room, Kull threw herself onto the couch. Then she posed, one knee up, the other leg down. "Are you ready?"

Finch stood rooted in place, bewildered into silence.

"For my video, silly." Kull giggled. "Remember? We filmed one last time. We need to do it again!"

"Oh. Right." Finch pulled out his phone. "But this time, don't put your finger anywhere near your mouth, understand me?"

"Okay, but shouldn't I do *something* sexy?"

There was a long moment of strained silence between them. Kull leaned forward on the couch and squinted at Finch.

"What?" he barked.

"What do you think I should do?" she asked.

"Keep a healthy amount of clothes on," Finch quipped.

Kull frowned. "*That's* what you think is sexy?"

"I didn't say it was sexy—I said that's what I think you should do."

Kull crossed her arms and playfully glared. "That's not what Fox-Pistol would do. She would be fun and flirty."

After a long sigh that barely captured Finch's desire to jettison himself from the conversation, he said, "Listen, I'm not someone who should be directing a Fox-Pistol video. Just… do whatever you think she would do." Then he pointed at her. "But also keep your clothes on."

"Hmm. Okay. Start filming!"

———

They stopped at the same burger joint, only this time, they ate there at 8:02 p.m., and Finch was feeling proud of the fact they had done everything slightly faster than before.

Once finished, they went straight to the Oasis. Kull practically skipped up to the door, her eyes glittering. Finch had to touch her shoulder to even get her attention.

"Don't leave the nightclub, all right?" Finch said. "Remember. A murderer might be here."

She nodded as she said, "I know. I'll be here. I just can't wait to test out all my new knowledge." Kull smacked Finch on the shoulder. "Good luck with your werewolf buddy. Don't reset time too early, okay?"

Finch sighed as he left her to her nightclub shenanigans. The short elevator ride up to Level 22 had him forgetting all about that, though. The last time he had seen Detective Elijah Harris was more than eleven years ago, when Carter had still been alive. Working with Harris had been enjoyable. What had happened since then?

When the elevator door opened, Finch flashed his card to the human-form werewolf and then strolled inside. The soft jazz music greeted him first. The place was as Finch remembered it. Classy. Atmospheric. The moon rabbit sat alone, on top of the table that held the roulette wheel. The poker players were deep in their game.

And the three drunken witches were at the bar.

The werewolf behind the bar turned his ears toward Finch before he turned his body. It was Harris, his wolf form just as intimidating as ever. Eight feet tall, wearing a fancy suit with a vest, muscles barely contained by the lustrous black fur...

"Good evening," Harris said, his voice rich and confident. "You seem familiar, but I don't think I've seen many warlocks in these parts. Take a seat. I'll pour you somethin' smooth."

Adair walked over and took a seat. He stared the wolf in the eyes. "What happened, Harris? When did you get infected?"

The werewolf froze, his face shifting from *hospitable* to *tense*. He rested both his hands on the bar counter, his claws visible. "And you are?"

"It's me. Adair Finch." After a long sigh, Finch added, "I didn't die. That was my brother."

"Adair? Seriously?"

Finch was about to give a short account of what had happened to Carter, and why he'd had to take a break from the world, but he didn't get a chance. Harris grabbed him and pulled him into an awkward hug with the counter between them. The werewolf's large padded hand slapped him on the back a few times.

"I can't believe it!" Harris broke the embrace. "You aren't trickin' me? This is real?"

Finch nodded once. For the first time during the whole night, he genuinely smiled. "Yeah. It's me. I can't believe I've found you in a dump like this."

They both laughed as they glanced around at the opulence that hung from every fixture. Then Harris hardened himself once more.

"I'm Enzo now," he said, no hint of sarcasm. "Elijah Harris is officially dead. That's what all the reports say—what my tombstone will confirm. After I got lycanthropy, I... I had to. For my wife and daughter."

"What?" Finch leaned in close. "Why?"

"I wasn't myself." Enzo turned his glare to the bar counter. He tapped his razor-sharp claws on the wood. "For years. I was violent. Unpredictable. Savage. And I was too late to get the cure. You know how it goes. Better I die a human—a hero cop—and my wife get the benefits, than me stay in her life as a beast, am I right?"

Finch held his breath.

If a police officer died in the line of duty, their family was compensated. A spouse could collect a monthly paycheck forever, basically, and children under the age of eighteen would get something as well.

"When did this all happen?" Finch whispered. The jazz music almost covered his words.

"Eight years ago," Enzo replied, his wolf-ears twitching. He glanced up, his expression impossible to read. "I've been job hoppin' around ever since. I finally found a job here in Oakland, but to be honest, this city isn't what it used to be." He reached under the bar and grabbed a clean glass. "What brings you here, Adair? When did your brother die?"

"Carter died over ten years ago." Finch sighed. "And I'm here for a lot of reasons."

Enzo grabbed a bottle of Hennessy and poured Finch a drink. Then he slid it over. "Well? Start with one. I don't got all damn night."

"We need refills," one of the full moon witches called out. "Our sexy wolf needs to tend to us."

Finch could tell Enzo held back a groan. That almost made Finch laugh—almost.

Enzo poured the ladies some more liquor, all smiles, his fangs a brilliant white that contrasted well with his fur. Once he was done, he slid back down to Finch. "Well? You gonna tell me anything? What brought you here? And why do you stink of Jay-W?"

"That's the thing—I was on my way to Oakland when I

stumbled across a dead girl." Finch threw back his Hennessy, enjoyed the flavor for half a second and then exhaled. "Some spirit of jealousy tells me it's been happening a lot lately."

"Damn straight," Enzo growled. "Two regulars died a couple months back. Both strangled, even though they were powerful witches in their own right."

The information gave Finch pause. He glanced up and met Enzo's eyes. "Strangled?"

"Did I stutter?"

Finch snorted back a laugh. That was how Fox-Pistol had died. Perhaps it wasn't her boyfriend after all…

"What does this have to do with Jay-W?" Enzo asked.

"Well, when I got here, he wanted me to help find his wife." Finch traced his finger over the rim of his glass, his expression hardened. "He said I could find her here, but now I'm a little worried." Finch met his friend's gaze once more. "Do you know where Charlotte Woolsy is? I'd hate to find another dead body."

CHAPTER
THIRTEEN

"**D**o you think Charlie is actually in danger?" Enzo asked.

"It's a possibility. The girl I found dead in the woods had been strangled. There might be a connection."

Finch wasn't being entirely truthful. He didn't think Jay-W's wife was a target of the woman-killer, but it was a lot more legitimate a reason to search for her than attempting to catch her with another man. Finch got the impression Enzo wouldn't help if infidelity was the only potential crime on the table.

Plus, Finch was becoming more and more concerned about this madman. What if Kull was in *serious* trouble? If the serial killer could kill two powerful witches, what hope did a half-spirit human have?

Sure, Finch could rewind time, but he didn't actually want her to experience the terror of death now that she was human.

The werewolf twitched his ears, his gaze distant. Then he returned his attention to Adair. "I still have friends in the Oakland PD. I spoke to them after my two regulars went missing and then were found dead. I know there have been more homicides—all strangulation. All women."

"I thought you said you were officially dead? Why are you still talking to old coworkers?"

Enzo growled, his fur standing on end. The tension grew as the witches at the other end of the bar glanced over. They smiled and twittered among themselves, their hopeful expressions telling Finch they wanted a conflict, if only for the amusement.

"I'm dead to Uncle Sam, my family, and normies who know nothing about magic," Enzo said, clearly attempting to control his anger. He took a breath and then continued, "The chief and the supernatural division of the PD know I'm alive, but they can't risk having a goddamn werewolf on the force. *Too unpredictable and violent*, they all claim."

Finch and Enzo didn't say anything for a few moments.

Finally, Enzo exhaled, his anger gone and replaced with a woebegone tone and expression. "They're right. But still."

"So, how many women have died via strangulation?" Finch asked. "In cases where the police think the killer is linked?"

"As far as I know, thirteen," Enzo replied.

"Across how long a time period is that?"

"The last seven months. Every couple of weeks I hear about another."

Finch leaned onto the bar. "Okay. So, where's Charlotte Woolsy?"

Enzo snorted. With a tilt of his head, he smiled, revealing polished, white fangs. "*Charlie* doesn't like strangers following her lately. She comes in here on Friday, plays a bit of poker to win some cash, and then leaves. I don't see her for the rest of the weekend."

Winning cash at the Level 22 casino would give her money Jay-W couldn't track, which was a clever move on her part. Finch wondered if it really would be difficult to find her.

Finch sighed. "Where does she go?"

"I don't know," Enzo stated.

"No idea?"

"Probably to a hotel on the docks. But there are plenty around."

"Hmm."

That was mildly convenient. Even if Finch had to reset time multiple times to check every hotel bar and exclusive nightclub, he could. It would be tedious, though. Looking for a better lead was his top priority.

The full moon witches waved to Enzo a second time. The werewolf walked over, refilled their drinks, chuckled a few times at their whispered comments and then made his way back over to Finch.

Enzo's mirth vanished as he leaned onto the bar and whispered, "I fake laugh at this job so much I've forgotten how my real one sounds."

Finch glanced over at the women. They eyed Enzo hungrily, and obviously wanted him to return. "Are you worried they'll complain to the owner if you're not attentive?"

Enzo snorted. "The owner doesn't actually do anything— he's like the *Elf on the Shelf*. And he's a wolf, like me. We stick together. I just need to avoid angering the witches so we don't have to deal with their foul curses."

"I see."

After clicking his impressive claws on the bar counter, Enzo said, "The killer only goes after attractive women."

"Interesting."

Finch wondered why. He also wondered about Enzo. The longing in his voice reminded Finch how much Enzo had enjoyed being a detective.

"Where were the dead bodies found?" Finch asked. "The ones who were strangled?" Fox-Pistol had been out in the woods. Was that part of the killer's regular operating procedure?

Enzo snorted. "One body was found in the water, not far from here. The other was found at the dump, just on a pile of trash."

Both outside. Just like Fox-Pistol.

But Finch knew he was making a big leap in logic. Strangulation was a common cause of death in homicides—and anyone could do it. If the cause of death had been exsanguination, he at least could've narrowed the killer down to some sort of vampire, but Finch wasn't that lucky.

Plus, Fox-Pistol had enough fame that any number of people could want her dead. And Finch still couldn't rule out her boyfriend. There was still a good chance Fox-Pistol's death had nothing to do with the recent string of murders in Oakland.

It was better to just gather information rather than conclude anything—at least for the time being.

Unfortunately, Fox-Pistol's death aligned with all the other killings in this serial murderer case, meaning he needed to be extra observant when with Kull.

"The spirit of jealousy told me that the killer was magical in nature—some sort of supernatural being." Finch eyed Enzo. "Is that what you've heard as well?"

Enzo nodded. "Yeah. Traces of magic were found on the bodies of the victims. Our warlock in blue said the source of the magic was more akin to a curse, so the killer likely isn't a spirit or a wizard."

The excitement in Enzo's voice took Finch back to twelve years ago, when they had teamed up to find a kidnapper. They had worked tirelessly together, all for the safety of a little girl. Enzo had said that nothing made him prouder than the moment they busted in the door to the old apartment room and found her.

Pushing those thoughts aside, Finch mulled over the other murders. Magic was like gunpowder—when a gun was fired, residue was left behind. Same with magic. Technically skilled individuals could determine the type of magic, which easily narrowed the potential source. Infernal, cursed, spiritual, divine—there were many kinds of magic, and knowing the category was helpful.

With his tail wagging slightly, Enzo continued, "If I had to guess, I'd say it's a human who has been transformed. Most of those insane transformations are because of a curse."

"Like werewolves?" Finch quipped.

Enzo's tail instantly stopped. "Yes. Like werewolves. But that wouldn't be my first guess for the murderer in this case. Us wolves tend to rip our victims apart, not strangle them."

"And a vampire would've drained their blood."

"That's right."

Finch stood from the barstool, his mind swirling with all the new facts. He was hoping the Oakland killer was, in fact, the one who had killed Fox-Pistol. If they were one and the same, it would make everything easier.

He glanced at his phone.

8:30 p.m.

Finch rolled his eyes. It was fine. If he wanted to do things faster, he would need to rearrange the order he did them in. As long as he didn't answer Jay-W's phone calls, perhaps he could swing by his house last—with his wife in Finch's arms—to do everything else earlier.

"I need to go," Finch muttered. He tapped his knuckles on the bar countertop. "Thank you. For the help."

Enzo nodded once. "You're gonna handle this murderer, is that it?"

"Yeah, probably."

"Without your brother?"

Tense, Finch offered him a glare. "Someone's got to do it."

"Feh. There's so much darkness around that everyone's overwhelmed. I'm glad there are still men like you who are willin' to clean it up. I'd be there too if…"

But Enzo didn't finish his sentence.

The longing in his tone wasn't lost on Finch. Being a bartender wasn't Enzo's calling in life, that much was obvious.

Perhaps…

Finch pinched the bridge of his nose. "Listen, I'm opening an agency again. I've been looking at office buildings and all that boring crap. I'm going to need some help, though. Do you think you'd be up to it? Joining my agency, I mean? Helping me with the darkness and all that."

"Bullshit," Enzo growled.

Finch waited.

"Wait, are you serious?" Enzo leaned onto the bar, his canine expression still intimidating, even when he was smiling. "There's a reason not too many fools hire wolves."

"How does a hundred grand for the first year sound?" Finch asked.

Jay-W's prize money for finding his wife was a good start for someone of Enzo's caliber. Plus, Finch *could* rent Bree's favorite office by just using money in his savings. Or he could get it another way.

"You didn't answer me." Enzo flexed his hand, his claws extending and retracting. "Everyone knows wolves deal with a lot of rage. You're not worried that I'll lose my grip on sanity and go for your throat?"

Finch recalled how Enzo had leapt over the bar in an attempt to gut him in the middle of Level 22—all over a simple insult. And while that was concerning, Finch always had a trump card. No werewolf had control over time itself.

"I'll be fine," Finch said.

"Ya know, you and your brother were like this all the time. Secretive about your magics. You never told anyone how you knew so many things, and found evidence so damn fast."

Finch held his breath.

If Enzo joined his agency, he'd have to tell him what was going on, but he wasn't going to reveal his secrets ahead of time. This whole night could be a test for Enzo, really. Finch could take him on a trek around the city, hunting down the killer, rewinding time as much as needed...

And if Enzo handled it brilliantly, Finch would be true to his word. If Enzo couldn't handle it, or he really was a rage-oholic who couldn't control his temper, Finch would forget to draw the Mark of Chronos on Enzo when he rewound time for the final instance... And then Enzo would never remember anything that had happened. Enzo could go back to life as a bartender in an upscale casino and bar.

There was no downside for Finch.

He shrugged. "You want the job or not? I told you I can handle it. When did I ever lie to you?"

The werewolf didn't need much time to mull it over. Enzo huffed a laugh and then flashed a frighteningly fanged smile. "You and Carter were always the best—the only warlocks who never failed at anything. I suppose you could handle one wolf on your team. But only because it's *me* we're talking about."

"As cocky as ever," Finch quipped.

Enzo effortlessly leapt over the bar counter and slammed his padded feet onto the floor on the other side. With a feral smirk, he headed for a door at the far end of Level 22, beyond the poker table and the mysterious moon rabbit roulette.

"I'll break the news to my boss and grab my things. Wait here. It'll just take a minute."

Finch glanced at his phone.

8:35 p.m.

He wondered if Kull was okay, but exhaled when he realized they still had plenty of time. The next step was to find Jay-W's wife. Which hotel had she gone to? In the meantime, they'd just have to keep their eyes peeled for Fox-Pistol's killer.

———

Twelve minutes later, at 8:47 p.m., Enzo came out of the back room. looking completely different. He no longer wore the fur of a wolf, but the skin of a man.

Actually, he was more muscle than man—the type of guy with shoulders so broad, they could moonlight as landing pads for small aircraft. Clearly, Enzo had filled the holes in his life with weightlifting.

Enzo also had a head so bald, the dazzling chandelier lights reflected off his skin. His eyes were just as intense as his wolf form, though. The type of gaze that betrayed the fact he was a cop—and he thought most people around him were criminals.

Enzo had never worked as an undercover detective—he didn't have the demeanor for it.

And currently, he wasn't dressed in a nice suit, like he had been when he was a bartender. Instead, Enzo wore a white tank top, which contrasted nicely with his dark skin, and a pair of gray sweatpants, which completed his hobo-chic outfit.

Well, the flipflops *really* completed his outfit. They gave him the California vibe he had been lacking.

Finch shook his head. "You quit your job and immediately let yourself go."

"Ha, ha," Enzo growled. "You work as a comedian for a while after your brother died?"

The patrons of Level 22 also took interest in Enzo's new outfit. The full moon witches seemed particularly disappointed.

"Do you just not own any nice clothes?" Finch asked. "Or is there a practical reason for this getup?"

Enzo tugged on his loose tank top, and then pulled on the elastic waistband of his comfortable sweatpants. "These stretch and expand. When I *wolf out*, I don't have to worry about ruining them. That way I won't be committing indecent exposure along with all the battery I'll likely be engaged in."

"When you wolf out, does everything get enhanced?"

Enzo snorted back a laugh. "Jealous?"

"Just curious. You're the one who brought up indecent exposure."

"Heh." Enzo rubbed the back of his neck. "Well, everything gets enhanced, yeah, but I hate the loss of control. The anger I feel is like a second person inside of me— someone constantly trying to take the steering wheel. Nothing is worth that."

One of the witches held up a finger. "Oh, Enzo. My drink is running low."

"I'm off the clock forever," he quickly replied. "Someone new will be comin' out to offer you service. Just sit back and relax."

Enzo had a tone of restrained irritation. The witches didn't seem to like that. All three of them frowned, their fingers curling around their empty glasses.

"It'll only take you a second to get us refills," one of them said with a slight slur.

"I said *no*."

The witch curled her lip into a sneer. "I'd like to speak to your manager."

"And I'd like to speak to your *mother*," Enzo growled. "Tell her she should be embarrassed because she raised someone to act like an infant in public."

The witch's eyes went wide, and she touched her collarbones like she was literally clutching her pearls.

Finch immediately leapt between them and ushered Enzo toward the door. "Sorry about that, ladies. We have to go." He nodded in their direction, hoping they were all too drunk to think of using their magic to escalate the confrontation.

As they headed toward the door, Finch thought back to his time working with Enzo. Detective Elijah Harris never drank and never touched any controlled substances.

"Have you been drinking?" Finch asked under his breath. "I thought you didn't want to anger those witches."

"I've never had a drink, not once," Enzo said, ice in his tone. "I told you—I hate the thought of losing control. But anger… It comes to me so easily sometimes. I told them I was off the clock *forever*. What did they think that meant?"

Not wanting to discuss this further, Finch opened the door. "You sure your boss didn't care you quit?"

"He thinks I'm going to come crawling back to him." Enzo stormed through the door out of Level 22. "He says my job will be waiting when I'm done playing detective. What a jackass."

Together, they walked down the short hallway away from Level 22. The security guard wolf gave Enzo an odd stare as they passed.

"See ya later, Dennis," Enzo said, never glancing backward.

"See ya," the man replied in confusion.

Once in the elevator, and heading for the ground floor,

Finch asked, "Do you think the Oakland PD has more leads they're just not telling you?"

"No," Enzo stated. "Ever since the last police chief was appointed by that corrupt as fuck mayor, the police have been failing harder than the infrastructure of Libya."

Finch honestly chuckled. "Now who's the comedian?"

"Did I say somethin' funny?" Enzo growled. "It's an actual shame, Adair. And people wonder why Oakland is an active dumpster fire."

"Fine. If the detectives can't give us any leads, we'll start by asking around." As the elevator came to a halt, Finch held up his hand. "But first, we need to fetch my assistant."

"Your assistant?" Enzo narrowed his eyes. "Since when did you have an *assistant*?"

"It's a long story. You'll have to promise me that you'll be nice."

The elevator doors opened, and Enzo just frowned.

Finch was a bit worried his "assistant" wouldn't mesh well with his new coworker, but now wasn't the time to start regretting his decisions. Maybe they would get along.

CHAPTER
FOURTEEN

Finch and Enzo crossed the large and luxurious lobby over to the giant set of double doors—the entrance to Oasis. The thump of music was so loud it pulsed through the floor. As Finch pushed open one of the doors, a blast of music assaulted his ears. He gritted his teeth and fought through the auditory assault to enter the establishment.

It was like stepping into a glossy magazine ad, where the lighting was just dim enough to make everyone seem mysteriously attractive and the furniture seem brand new.

The U-shaped counter was manned by a bartender in a suit and a top hat. He smiled as he put on a show, pouring drinks from ridiculous heights and tossing ice cubes behind his back. Finch wondered if the man was once a ringmaster —his showboat skills were a little *too* impressive.

Finch didn't want to enter too far. Everyone here was clearly wrapped up in the game of "hooking up as fast as possible," and Finch wasn't in the mood for any of that.

He scanned the nightclub, searching for his fiery-haired

assistant. The *thump-thump-thump* of the music threatened to steal his hearing.

The dress code for Oasis was nothing short of ostentatious. It made Kull a little easier to pick out, since her green dress and cheap shoes weren't really the height of fashion.

There she was.

Kull sat in a corner booth with a man who could pass as an albino. He had blond hair, skin so pale it practically glowed, and teeth so ivory Finch could see them sparkle from his location by the door.

When Kull glanced his way, Finch motioned for her to leave. She smiled, nodded once, and then held up a finger. Satisfied she had gotten the message, Finch exited the nightclub. His ears thanked him, once the door was shut and the electronic music was contained within Oasis.

Enzo stood near the elevator. He just looked... out of place. Like a hobo who had wandered off the road and into a fancy establishment. Everyone entering the lobby gave him strange glances before veering away.

"She's on her way," Finch said as he approached his werewolf buddy.

"So, you said you found a dead body in Oakland." Enzo glanced over and lifted an eyebrow. "When did that happen?"

"Just a couple hours ago."

Enzo straightened his posture. "*What*? What're you doin' here, then? Did you report this to the police? Have you done anything to investigate?"

"Relax. It's complicated. I'll explain once we're in the car, but rest assured I have it under control."

"Don't tell me you're a drunkard now." Enzo narrowed his eyes into an intense glare. "Is that why your *assistant* is in a nightclub? Grabbin' you some booze?"

"No, that's not why she's here."

The door to Oasis flew open. Kull sprang out with a smile as bright as the sun. To Finch's bewilderment, Kull spun in a little circle and hummed to herself before slowly making her way over to Finch and Enzo.

Her red hair fluttered as she walked, her dress hugged her body tight, and every head in the lobby whipped around to get a better look at the social media star in their midst.

"Oh, Jesus Christ," Enzo muttered the moment he laid eyes on Kull. He rubbed his eyes and shook his head. "Now I understand why she's your assistant."

Finch shot him a glower. "*It's not what you think.*"

"She's half your age, for fuck's sake. I know you must miss your brother, but this is just pathetic."

Kull quickened her step until she was at Finch's side. With her signature smile, she said, in an overtly cheerful tone, "Oh, Adair! It was so magical. Listen to this! They were playing games, and they drank all this alcohol, and they were competing to speak with me, and whoever drank the most was the winner, only I got to pick their drinks, so I picked something called a *blue mischief maker*, and I think it was fate —the winner—and I'm so, so glad I was there, and I need to tell you the best part."

She didn't even take a breath as she yammered through her confusing explanation. Finch nodded once or twice, trying to follow the story, but it was obvious Kull was speeding it along to get the part she was the most excited about.

"Oh, wait!" Kull's eyes grew wide. "I-I'll be right back! I forgot something, and it's so important!"

She whirled on her heel and hurried back to the Oasis doors. To her credit, she never tripped or stumbled. She really was a fast learner with difficult footwear.

After a prolonged moment of silence, Enzo placed a hand

on Finch's chest. They locked gazes, and Enzo's eyes drilled into Finch's.

"Be straight with me," Enzo said, his voice low. "Is that girl mentally challenged?"

Finch jerked away from the other man. "N-No, goddammit." Then he stepped close and whispered, "She's a spirit. Or... she *was* a spirit. She inhabited the body of the *dead girl*. The one I told you about. She's just learning to be human."

Relief, and a little bit of confusion, visibly washed over Enzo. He crossed his arms, his expression halfway between scolding and bewilderment. "You... Wait, so..."

"Yes," Finch said. "That's why I was going to explain it in the car. It's *complicated*. She's my assistant because she's a spirit I had made a pact with. Now she's a human, and it would be great if you helped her be more human, because I don't think I'm doing a very good job, to be frank."

Enzo clicked his tongue in disapproval. "Tsk. I've seen spirits who inhabit bodies."

"You have?"

"Yeah. There's two of them who live in a tent under the overpass. They're hobos who never learned how to integrate into human society. I think they occasionally lend their minor magical powers to the other bums who live in that camp city—that's how they survive."

Finch pinched the bridge of his nose. He absolutely hated the thought of Kull living in a homeless encampment. "Okay, well, my goal is to make sure that never happens. Kull doesn't deserve that."

"Kull?" Enzo asked. "Her name is *Kull*? What a dead giveaway that she's not human."

As if being summoned by her bizarre name, Kull dashed back out of the Oasis. She hurried over to Finch, her unmitigated joy radiating from her every pore.

"I had the most amazing time," she said.

Finch exhaled. "I'm glad." Then he jutted his thumb over his shoulder at Enzo. "This is my wolf friend. You can call him Enzo."

"Oh." Kull smiled as she held out her hand toward Enzo. "I'm so happy you two didn't get into a fight this time!"

Enzo hesitantly shook her hand, his face screwed up in utter confusion. He clearly had no idea what she was talking about.

Finch took Kull by the shoulder. "Listen," he muttered. "Let's get to the car and tell Enzo everything there, all right? Away from prying eyes and random eavesdroppers."

"Then can I tell you everything that happened in the Oasis?" She grabbed Finch's coat sleeve. "It was so amazing."

"Sure. Yeah. Whatever. But after we get Enzo up to speed."

———

With his car idling, Finch explained the events of the evening, starting long before Kull got her new body. He sat in the driver's seat, his hands over the air vents, soaking in the warm air as it rushed into the cab.

Enzo sat in the front passenger's seat, his arms folded over his chest. He leaned most of his weight on the door, facing Finch as much as he could in the small Toyota seat.

Kull sat in the back seat, smack dab in the middle, so she could easily glance between the two men. She bounced up and down in her seat so much, she was practically a helium molecule. Her smile never waned, her energy never drained —she listened to Finch's words, patiently awaiting her time to speak.

"—and then Jay-W gave me his member card for Level 22," Finch said as he reached for the glove compartment. He withdrew his Sharpie and then sat back in the driver's seat. "That's when I met you for the first time."

"The first time?" Enzo asked.

"Yeah." Finch gestured to his arm. When Enzo held it out, Finch uncapped his pen and drew a single line on Enzo's forearm. "Ya see, I can go back in time. Because I made a pact with Chronos."

"Bullshit," Enzo said. He didn't pull away his arm, though. He allowed Finch to continue the drawing. One more line. Then another. "Isn't Chronos one of the Titans?"

"The *Teen Titans*?" Kull interjected with a playful smile.

"No, not the damn comic book Teen Titans—I mean the Greek proto-gods." Enzo shook his head. "They're all dead. The Titans died when Tartarus was destroyed. You *can't* be bonded to Chronos."

Finch finished drawing his mark. He ignored Enzo's statements as he continued with, "This is the Mark of Chronos. Now that you have this mark, you'll remember everything, even after I rewind time, just like Kull and me. Those who *don't* have this mark, won't be aware of the time shifting. Remind me to draw this, because if I don't, you'll forget everything. Got it?"

Enzo growled as he jerked his arm away from Finch. He rubbed his skin, glared at the marker lines, and then shot Finch a glower. "You can't manipulate time. No one can do that."

Finch didn't respond.

After a full thirty seconds of no one speaking, where the only noise was the howl of the hot air gushing out of the vents, Enzo's expression shifted. He leaned forward in his seat, his eyes locked on Finch's. "You can really rewind time?"

"Yes," Finch replied matter-of-factly.

"Then rewind time. Rewind it so I'm not a werewolf

anymore." He glared. "Get your brother back. What the fuck are you doing here?"

"I can only rewind it up to twenty-four hours." Finch sighed as he settled himself into his seat. "And I have to mark the time I'll return to. Like… a save point in a video game. I can't just go back as far as I want. I'm sorry."

A small part of Finch thought his old friend might take this news poorly. To his surprise, Enzo just exhaled. His shoulders relaxed, and his attention slowly drifted to the ceiling of the car.

"Figures," Enzo muttered. "Magic always has some bizarre limitations." Then he snorted out a laugh. With a smirk, he glanced back over at Finch. "Is *this* how you helped the Oakland PD? It is, isn't it? And it's why you and your brother were so damn good at solving everything."

Finch nodded. "Yeah."

"You weasel. Why didn't you tell us?" Enzo playfully punched Finch's shoulder. "If we had known, we could've—"

"No one can know," Finch stated, cutting the other man off. "Don't go around telling anyone, all right? Just know that… You need the Mark of Chronos if you want to remember anything about this investigation."

Enzo snorted. "Fine."

Kull bounced in her seat faster. Both Finch and Enzo turned to face her. Somehow, her face-splitting smile grew wider.

"Kull?" Finch asked. "You want to tell us what happened in Oasis?"

"I met someone." Kull grabbed the back of both the front seats. She scooted to the very edge of the back seat. "And we fell in love. Isn't that amazing, Adair?" With a squeal of pure delight, she added, "Now we just need to get married and grow old together!"

CHAPTER
FIFTEEN

"That was fast," Enzo quipped.

Kull nodded. "I wanted to become a human so people would remember me, and so I could find love, and a family, of my own." She motioned to her body, and then fluffed her hair. "Thanks to Fox-Pistol, and assuming her identity, I have tons of people who remember me, admire me, and never want to forget me." Kull clapped her hands together once. "And now that I've fallen in love with a man, I only have one more goal before I've completed everything I've ever wanted to accomplish."

Enzo lifted both his eyebrows, his suspicion obviously rising.

"Even *Adair* hasn't fallen in love yet, so I'm clearly a better human than even he is." Kull wistfully sighed. "This is all so magical. I'm practically speedrunning all my goals."

Finch held back a long and pain-filled exhale. "Just tell us what happened in Oasis. Start from the beginning."

"A man approached me, and everything that happened afterward was fate." Kull took a more serious tone as she recounted her tale. "We played a game that involved drinking a *blue mischief maker*. A man played next to me—his name is Caleb—and he won. I told him mischief was my specialty, so we started talking. Mostly about alcohol, but when I said I wanted to talk about other subjects, he said, *If stars were thoughts, my sky would be lit by you, for every shimmering light is a wish to know the universe in your eyes.*"

Enzo snorted a laugh. He caught himself halfway through and choked the rest of it back, turning his amusement into a wheeze.

Either Kull didn't notice, or she didn't care. She rubbed her face, her smile never fading. "My heart felt like it flipped in my chest. No one has ever said something so nice to me. Not ever. Those are the kinds of words in love songs—the kind I see humans say in all their movies."

Finch sardonically wondered which movie or song Caleb had gotten his pickup line from.

Small tears ran down Kull's cheeks. She kept rubbing her face, trying to clear them away. "I'm so happy that all my emotions keep spilling out of my eyes." She laughed at her own statement, her tone raw.

Enzo clearly had to stifle yet another laugh. Finch shot him a glare, and the man fell silent. Despite her smile, Kull continued to cry, her hands trembling as she wiped away the waterfall of emotion.

"I told Caleb I wanted to have a relationship, and he said that was what he wanted, too." Kull's face was rosy, and she continued with, "He was just so nice. Every time he spoke, that heart-flipping feeling happened all over again. It must be love. It must be."

Enzo glanced between Kull and Finch. He said nothing, just observing, his expression unreadable.

After a few more tears fell from Kull's eyes, Finch exhaled. "Why didn't you bring him out of the club to meet us?" he asked.

"I suggested he come meet you, but he said he'd rather wait, because of all the drinks he had consumed." Kull wiped her face again. "So, I figured we'd all go see him once we found Jay-W's wife. It would be better this way—that way he's never in any danger. I... I couldn't stand that."

"Maybe you should step out of the car and get some air." Finch pointed to the night sky. "Admire the stars. Calm down. Then we can talk about our next move."

"Right." Kull slid across the seat and opened the door. "I need to pull myself together. Tonight is such a good night—I don't want to ruin it." Then she stepped out of the Toyota and shut the door behind herself.

Once she had gone, Enzo glanced over at Finch.

"Why didn't you tell her Caleb is just a douche-canoe?" Enzo asked. "He's clearly a fuck-boy trying to pick up ladies at a nightclub. If we went back to Oasis right now, and planted a gun in that man's temple, fifty bucks says he wouldn't be able to remember her name."

Finch narrowed his eyes at the other man. "Didn't you hear her? She's so happy *it's spilling out of her eyes*. You want me to tell her she's wrong? And her new love is fake?"

Enzo shrugged and nodded at the same time. "Better than her makin' a mistake."

"That's one of the perks of manipulating time," Finch muttered. He glanced out the car window, watching Kull as she stared up at the night sky. "Kull can make as many mistakes as she wants. I'll just undo them. Why not let her have her fun while she still can? You only get to be that optimistic once."

Finch remembered when he loved going to nightclubs, exploring the world, and talking to new people. Back when Carter was still around, they would go to every new place just for the experience of it. Everything was fun. Everything was fresh.

Back when certain locations weren't tainted with bad memories, and thinking about specific people didn't cause his thoughts to run black and painful.

Those were the good ol' days.

Finch suspected life just had a way of slowly losing its magic for everyone. He didn't need to hurry that process along for Kull.

"So you really can rewind time?" Enzo asked again, his tone filled with disbelief.

"Yeah."

Then Kull opened the car down and sat back down. Her happy tears were gone. Instead, she had a look of gleeful determination. "Okay. I'm ready. What's next?"

"We should figure out what hotel Charlotte Woolsy went to after she left Level 22." Finch tapped his fingers on the steering wheel. "We'll start here at the docks, and work our way outward if needed."

"We'll just ask around for her?"

"Until we run across some opposition."

Enzo huffed. "That'll take forever. Charlie clearly wanted a place to spend some cash. I suggest we hit the hotels that have expensive events or casinos, and I sniff around." He tapped the side of his nose. "Wolves are good at picking up people's distinct odors. And I know Charlie's."

"Oh, excellent!" Kull scooted to the edge of her seat. "I like this! And once we've found Charlotte, and caught this murderer, we need to head back to Oasis so we can pick up Caleb—once the drinks have gone through his system. Okay? I really want you to meet him, Adair!"

———

There weren't many fancy hotels in Oakland. Most of them were private resorts that kept out the riffraff—or "the poors" as Fox-Pistol would say in her old videos. Even places like the Hilton weren't actually inside Oakland's city limits—the closest Hilton was nestled in the airport.

No one wanted to be *in* Oakland.

And of those hotels within the actual city, there were only a handful that accommodated the supernatural, and even of those, there were only so many positioned around the docks.

Fortunately, that narrowed down the places Charlotte would likely visit to three hotels.

There was the *Lake Merritt Grand Hotel*, bustling with both human celebrities and the fae—specifically, the redwood elves. Of all the supernatural races and peoples, redwood elves loved luxury and drama the most, and they were *only* found in California and Oregon. Upper-end hotels, fine dining, and especially gambling—redwood elves desired and cultivated it all. They were even the ones who had supposedly started Hollywood.

That was why there was *wood* in the title, though most humans had no idea.

Then there was also the *Oakland Waterview Plaza*. It was more a resort with private ballrooms, poker tables, massage parlors, and boating games. From the looks of it, the place was likely run by a *different* group of fae—naiads. They were fae who presided over bodies of water, and it was clear a whole nest of them had formed under the docks of Oakland.

And lastly, there was the *Golden Gate Manor*, which appeared to be a place for individuals to detox—especially from magical substances, like witches' brews. The hotel was a bunch of upscale rooms with only a few places for events or group activities. Finch put it on the bottom of the probable list for Charlotte.

As they drove around the busy and dirty streets of Oakland, Enzo rolled down his window. He inhaled the air as they went. All Finch could smell was human waste and smoke, but Enzo seemed to have a keener nose than most, even while in his human form.

Wolves were just better at finding people in general.

The moment Enzo pointed them down one of the major roads, Finch was glad he had hired the man. Eventually, they came to the Lake Merritt Grand Hotel. Which was perfect, because it lined up with all Finch's theories. It was the most likely destination of someone with a lot of cash to spend, and big enough that it would be easy to hide from a stalker husband.

"She's probably here," Enzo muttered.

"You can smell her?" Kull asked.

"Jay-W has a specific scent, and Charlie reeks of it." Enzo glanced back at her. "Then again, so do all his thugs, so maybe we're chasing the wrong trail."

"I don't smell normal physical things as well—my spirit self identifies with magic, so I smell that the best," Kull said matter-of-factly. "This place smells of... fae. Redwood elves, to be specific."

Enzo groaned as he returned his attention to the outside of the vehicle. "Elves hate werewolves. Especially in this town."

Finch parked the car in a spot that cost him thirty dollars, but before he stepped out of the vehicle, he glanced into the back. "Stay close to me while we're here, got it?"

Kull gave him a thumbs up. "Because the killer could be here?"

"You made a video announcing you'd be at the docks—this is a place Fox-Pistol would stay at, isn't it?"

Kull leaned forward to get a better look at the outside of the building.

The pathway to the front doors was covered by a red carpet lined with meticulously manicured hedges that seemed to stand at attention, honoring each guest's arrival.

The entrance itself was grand enough to have an archway, and several bellhops and valets stood at the ready.

"Oh, yes," Kull said with a nod. "This is *definitely* the kind of place Fox-Pistol would stay. Very bougie."

Finch, Enzo, and Kull all slipped out of the Toyota and headed for the entrance. The air smelled of blossoming flowers and sea salt from the nearby water—a pleasant mix that woke Finch up.

As they entered, all the bellhops and valets turned their heads. They didn't look at Finch, no. All their gazes were on Kull and Enzo, who both stood out in their own unique ways.

Kull because of her beauty, and Enzo because he was cosplaying as a hobo.

"Welcome to the Lake Merritt Grand Hotel," one of the bellhops said with a falsely cheery tone.

Finch barely managed a wave as he strode into the building. The doors opened automatically, and once they were in the vast space of the welcome lobby, he glanced over to Enzo. "Can you smell her better in here?"

"Yeah." Enzo sniffed the air. "The scent is definitely stronger here. I'd bet my life Charlie is somewhere here."

Finch wanted to get straight to the investigation, but as he headed for the front desk, something strange happened. A whole gaggle of twenty-something-year-old individuals came hurrying over. Behind them was a team of muscled individuals, most of whom were wearing holsters under their suit jackets.

Finch froze, and so did Enzo, their attention on the concealed weapons.

Kull, on the other hand, continued forward, oblivious to the fact Finch and Enzo had stopped—and oblivious to the group of people descending upon her.

"There you are!" a man shouted.

The man held a smartphone in his hand like it was a sword as he rushed straight over to Kull. His perfectly coiffed blond hair didn't move, even as he picked up his pace into a run. The man was as thin as a broom, and wore a suit as expensive as the hotel.

Kull turned just as he dramatically pulled her into a hug.

"Oh, we've been so worried," the man said.

"You have?" Kull awkwardly returned the embrace.

A woman flew from the group and yanked Kull from the man's grip. She examined every inch of Kull, especially with the dirt smears on her dress.

"Oh my god, Samantha," the girl breathed. *"What happened?"*

This twenty-something-year-old girl had hair as black as midnight, and as shiny as wet ink. She wore a little red dress that complemented Kull's green one, and she was nearly as beautiful—and currently much cleaner.

The rest of the crowd, at least ten other people, swarmed around Kull.

"Fox-Pistol! There you are!"

"We've been worried sick!"

"What happened? Tell us everything!"

Finch and Enzo were shoved to the side by the muscled men packing heat. Finch rubbed his chest as he gritted his teeth, his anger slowly growing over Kull's ever-escalating shenanigans.

"What's going on?" Finch growled at the nearest bodyguard.

The man wore sunglasses, even inside. He adjusted them as he said, "Stand back. We're protection for the talent."

CHAPTER
SIXTEEN

The woman with the red dress and inky hair was the next to throw her arms around Kull in a tight hug. "Samantha, I was so worried." She released Kull and frowned. "Why didn't you answer your phone?"

"I think I lost it," Kull said as she patted her body.

"You *lost it*? How?" The woman grabbed Kull's shoulders. "You have to tell me everything. Let's get up in the suite."

Finch wanted to protest, but the bodyguards wouldn't let him through. He tried to step forward, only to get a forceful shove to the chest, knocking him a few steps backward. He rubbed the spot he had been hit and glared.

"That's technically a misdemeanor battery, asshole," Enzo said, his final word more of a growl. "You better watch yourself."

"No one gets near the talent," the man said, his words slow and threatening.

The crowd of beautiful individuals all streamed toward the elevators. They fawned over Kull, asking her about the dirt on her dress and the shoes she wore. It was obvious Kull couldn't handle all the questions being thrown her way—it was a bombardment worse than an inquisition.

"I, uh, was out in the woods," she said.

"In the woods?" someone asked, practically gasping.

Another woman shouted, "This is the craziest night!"

Halfway to the elevator doors, Kull dug her heels into the glistening marble floor. "*Wait*. I can't go without Adair and Enzo." She turned around so fast, her radiant red hair fluttered around her. "Adair, aren't you two coming?"

Everyone stopped.

The people around Kull held their breath. The bodyguards trying to stop Finch didn't move. All eyes were on Finch and Enzo, their collective confusion enough that Finch almost felt uncomfortable.

They all clearly thought he shouldn't be here.

Or perhaps it was just Enzo's hobo-chic that was bothering them.

Either way, the tension grew with each silent second that passed.

"Fox-Pistol hired us," Finch said off the cuff. "As bodyguards. For the weekend." He shrugged, as though this was no big deal.

The black-hair woman protectively wrapped an arm around Kull. "And who are you?"

"This is Enzo, uh, *Franks*." Finch motioned to Enzo, hating that he didn't know the man's fake last name. Then he gestured to himself. "And I'm Adair Finch."

None of the beautiful people recognized his name—but the man working the front desk of the hotel completely froze. He glanced over, his eyes wide, and then hastily grabbed the telephone on the front desk and called someone.

Clearly, the fae at the front desk knew who he was...

"I don't want your actual name," the woman said with a

sneer. "When I said, *who are you*, I meant, *who do you work for?* What security company?"

"I'm a freelance individual who mostly works as a private detective," Finch stated. Which was completely truthful.

"A private investigator?" The man with the styled hair patted his blond locks. They barely moved. "I didn't even know private investigators still existed. I thought that was, like, a 1930s job."

Enzo stepped forward. "And who are you? Why are you touching Fox-Pistol like that?"

The man silently gasped, his mouth opening into a dramatic O as though his whole family had been insulted. "Are you *serious*? I'm Louis Dion, thank you very much. I'm Fox-Pistol's manager and social media director."

Louis, the offended social media manager, spoke with the slightest of French accents. Finch suspected the man had moved to the United States from Lyon—that French city had a distinct dialect that Finch had always appreciated.

"I'm Harper," the woman with the inky black hair and red dress said. She held Kull even tighter and offered Enzo a glower. "I'm Samantha's best friend and content manager. And here's a hint—most bodyguards stay *silent*. We're here to have a bombastic weekend, not get interrogated by some wannabe cops."

"Oh, Adair is better than a cop," Kull said. The moment she spoke, everyone else was quiet. She smiled wide as she added, "He's been helping me ever since I woke up in the woods."

Her last statement chilled all excitement in the room. Finch almost wished she hadn't said anything, because now the partygoers were whispering.

"You know what? Everyone, go back to your rooms." Harper snapped her fingers several times. "Go. Go. We'll party tomorrow." When everyone dragged their feet, she glared. "I said *go*. Samantha clearly needs some space right now, and you all need to respect that."

The large group dispersed, most of them heading for the front door of the building. The only people who remained were Louis, Harper, Kull, and the ten bodyguards. The others had all been groupies, apparently, though Finch wasn't sure if that was the official term or not.

He wasn't very social media savvy.

Harper pointed at Finch, and then gestured to Enzo. "If Samantha hired you to protect her, you stay with us." She snapped her fingers and then pointed at the elevator. "Let's go."

Enzo snorted.

Then, as a group of fifteen people, they entered the massive elevator and hit the button for the highest floor—the forty-fourth. That was impressive, considering that less than five other skyscrapers in Oakland had more than thirty floors. *This* was the tallest place around. Finch suspected the redwood elves had given out favors, or paid a steep price, for such a privilege.

It took a few moments for the elevator to speed to the top.

Finch glanced at the elevator's inspection record. According to California law, all elevators had to be inspected every year, and the inspection record had to be posted inside the elevator itself.

The last inspection for this elevator had been in 2020, nearly five years ago. It was most definitely expired.

But that didn't mean the elevator was malfunctioning. No, the exact opposite. The elevator zipped along, smooth and quiet.

All this told Finch was that the redwood elves who ran

the hotel were likely paying off the Oakland city officials. No one came to inspect this place on the regular. The elves could do whatever they wanted—and since elves were focused on keeping guests happy, they likely kept everything smooth and functioning out of sheer pride. They just didn't want any silly human city officials all up in their business.

Once they reached floor forty-four, the elevator door opened with a *whoosh* akin to a contented sigh.

Everyone—all fifteen individuals—funneled out into the hallway. This hotel was too large to have a single penthouse suite. Instead, it had four gigantic suites, one for each cardinal direction, on the topmost floor.

Louis and Harper led Kull to the first door.

"She's on this floor," Enzo whispered to Finch. "One of the other rooms."

"Charlie?" Finch asked.

"Yeah."

As everyone entered the nearest suite, Finch slowed his pace to get a good look at his new surroundings. He also glanced at the time.

9:32 p.m.

"This is a single suite?" Enzo asked under his breath, his tone bordering on awe.

The suite was huge. Too huge.

Finch already hated it.

The living room was so vast, a person might need a map and a compass to navigate from the sofa to the minibar. Most places had a single couch and a TV, but this one had three of each, and one TV was mounted in the ceiling... for some reason.

One whole wall of the living room was made up of floor-to-ceiling windows. The view they offered probably justified whatever price the hotel charged per night. The entire city of

Oakland was on display, as though it were their personal kingdom.

The gorgeous black and gold decorations had obviously been crafted for this hotel. Lake Merritt-themed silhouettes were stamped across everything.

The dim lighting reminded Finch of the Oasis nightclub. The soft lights left a lot to the imagination. It made everything more beautiful and also more mysterious.

"Do you see this?" Enzo elbowed Finch and then motioned to the balcony.

A custom-made stone-based swimming pool was built straight into the hotel. The water went all the way to the edge, and Finch imagined that if they swam in it, they would feel like they were swimming into the distant horizon.

"Finally," Harper said with a sigh. She combed her fingers through her silky black hair and smiled.

Then she pulled Kull over to the trinity of couches, each pointed to the center of the room, creating a semi-open triangle with one giant coffee table between them. The black leather appeared velvety, even from where Finch stood by the door.

Kull and Harper took a seat. Louis practically pranced over with his phone still glued to his palm. He sat on the other side of Kull.

The other bodyguards gathered around the bar and kitchen. They didn't pour any drinks—that was probably against their contract—but they did start making small talk like this was normal operating procedure. Finch didn't bother paying much attention to them.

He walked into the living room, making his way closer to the luxury couches.

Louis turned to Kull. "Okay. Spill the tea. Where's Waylon? Did you two get into a fight?"

"Who is Waylon?" Kull asked in response.

Everyone in the room, except for Finch and Enzo, chuckled.

"Don't mess with us, Samantha." Harper crossed one leg over the other. "Tell us everything. You and Waylon drove into town on your own, but you haven't texted or messaged anyone. I thought you were having a *romantic evening*, but that's clearly not the case."

"As your manager, I need to know everything," Louis said, scooting closer. "About everything. Who you date, where you go. We've talked about this."

"Right," Kull muttered.

"So why did you upload that gross video?"

"Huh?"

Louis held up his phone and poked at the screen. Kull's video filmed in Jay-W's house played, though it was on silent. "We've discussed this a hundred times. You can't upload videos without my approval. I have editors who will make them shine."

"R-Right," Kull said.

"You look awful here, Fox—you've added ten years to your age using this shit camera."

"O-Oh." Kull forced a chuckle. "Sorry about that. I'll try to remember." She tapped the side of her head and stuck the tip of her tongue out. "I haven't been remembering much since, uh, I crashed in the woods!"

Harper and Louis both gasped.

"Are you serious?" Harper asked.

"No cap?" Louis asked at the same time.

With renewed interest, Harper searched all of Kull's body, touching and poking at her shoulders and then her hips. "You don't look like you've been in a car accident. You just look like you rolled around in the dirt."

"I'm fine," Kull said. "Just, uh, forgetful." With a shrug, she added, "I don't remember Waylon."

"Your boyfriend?" Harper stared at her for a long, baffled moment. "You were going to celebrate his birthday this weekend, remember? You've been dating him for six months. It's your half-year anniversary."

Finch found it odd anyone would celebrate their six-month anniversary, but he pushed that from his mind. Instead, he focused on the fact no one knew where *Waylon* was. Fox-Pistol's boyfriend was missing.

In Finch's experience, he probably *was* the killer. An angry or jealous boyfriend killing their significant other wasn't uncommon, and they typically tried to leave town right after the incident. Sometimes, they acted like nothing happened, but those idiots were always caught. The ones who fled didn't fare any better, but they at least avoided incarceration longer.

"Waylon wasn't in the woods with me," Kull finally muttered. "I don't know where he is."

Harper snapped her fingers and pointed at Louis. "Call him."

"Already on it, girl," Louis quickly replied.

He tapped his phone, and it went straight to speaker mode. The ringing blared from the phone's speaker. Once. Twice. Three times. Finch figured the man wouldn't answer, but then the ringing ended.

There was a static click, and then a rough huff of breath on the other end.

But no words.

"Waylon?" Louis asked, sass in his tone. "What're you doing? Where are you?"

No one answered. The breathing stopped. More clicking. When Finch closed his eyes, his imagination filled in the blanks. Was that the sound of teeth gnashing? Was that Waylon being irritated? Or something else?

Then the phone call ended.

Finch opened his eyes, and everyone in the living room was awkwardly silent.

"What the fuck was that?" Harper demanded.

Louis shrugged. "I'll call him back."

Once again on speaker, he held up the phone so Kull or Harper could speak. But this time, there was no ringing. The call immediately went to voicemail.

"The voice mailbox of the person you're trying to reach is currently full," said a cheery robotic voice. "Please try calling again later."

Waylon must've turned his phone off.

Louis ended the call. He smoothed his fancy suit, but he clutched his phone close, as though it would comfort him in this trying time.

"Is Waylon just out doing his own thing?" Harper asked.

Louis shrugged. "Seems like it. A little awkward, if you ask me." He waved a hand through the air. "Don't let this get out. We will have drama for *days*."

"Right…"

But they went silent after that.

No one seemed to know what to do with all the new information. While Harper and Louis exchanged baffled glances, Finch sat on the couch. Enzo sauntered over and took a seat next to him. Once he was fully settled, Harper glowered at them.

"What're you two doing?" she asked in a small, but angry, voice.

"It's okay." Kull placed a hand on her bare shoulder. "I like having Adair close. He's a great bodyguard. You'll see."

Louis rubbed his chin as he blatantly appraised Finch, and then Enzo. "They both give me serious daddy vibes. I can see why you'd keep them around."

Enzo sneered. "As an actual father, I take offense to the

term *daddy*." He spoke the last word like it was rotten and he needed to spit it out as quickly as possible.

Louis replied with a lifted eyebrow and a wink. "Oh. A man with strong muscles *and* opinions? I like that."

Enzo sardonically turned to face Finch. "I thought I would avoid this crap now that I wasn't a bartender."

"I thought you'd avoid it now that you're dressed like a bum," Finch quipped.

"Hm." Louis motioned to all of Enzo. "There's no hiding this physique. You could easily be an Instagram bodybuilder. Maybe sell some supplements." Louis scooted to the edge of the leather couch. "I could make this happen, and I would only charge eight percent of the revenue. Then I won't be the only one calling you daddy."

With barely restrained rage, Enzo crossed his arms over his chest. "Call me *daddy* one more time, I dare you."

The social media manager clearly didn't think the threat was serious. He waved away the comment with a smile. But when Louis turned his attention to Finch, all mirth disappeared.

"You're just a charisma black hole," Louis said, deadpan.

Finch didn't dignify that statement with a response.

"You hold yourself like you're both the most powerful person in the room, and also the most disinterested." Louis chuckled through every word as he said, "*And you wouldn't be that smug if you saw Samantha's bank account, trust me.*"

"Adair *is* the most powerful person in the room," Kull said, genuine and cheerful.

But that only seemed to irritate both her social media manager and her good friend.

"Isn't he a PI?" Louis leaned back in his seat, poked at his phone, and then huffed. "Google says the average PI makes about fifty-two thousand a year." Again, laughing his way through the sentence, he said, *"That's just embarrassing and pathetic."*

"Wait." Harper's eyes widened. She glanced over at Kull. "Is that why you hired a private detective? To find Waylon?"

Kull slowly nodded. "Uh, yes. Right. For Waylon."

"Listen, if that fuck boy left you, let him go." Harper placed a hand on Kull's shoulder and looked her dead in the eyes. "Instead of celebrating his birthday, we'll just have a crazy *breakup party*. It'll be amazing."

"You want to celebrate… breaking up?" Kull actually frowned. "That seems counterproductive to what I hope to accomplish."

"What? Why?"

"And since when do you use the word *counterproductive*?" Louis whispered.

"If I break up with someone, doesn't that mean I won't find love?" Kull asked the question slowly, as though solving a difficult math problem.

Harper waited. When no one else spoke, Harper laughed once. "What the fuck is wrong with you? Did Waylon get you high? Is that it? Is that why you crashed in the woods?" She ground her teeth and growled out a curse. "I told you he was worthless. What a dick."

"So, I didn't love him?" Kull asked. She tapped the side of her head. "My memory is fuzzy."

"No, you didn't love him. What have I told you? The moment you say you love someone, you're just giving them control over you. Don't ever tell one of these fuck boys you love them. Keep them guessing. Say you really like their company, but remind them that you like hanging out with other people, too."

Kull nodded once. She glanced over to Finch, who silently shook his head. When Kull returned her attention to Harper, she whispered, "Well, I *think* I love someone…"

Harper cupped Kull's cheek with a hand. They stared into each other's eyes. "Samantha. You're clearly loopy, girl. Love isn't real. We've had this talk."

The color drained from Kull's face. "It's not real?" she asked in a tiny voice.

"Remember? Trying to find true love is like searching for a place that doesn't exist. It might as well be Santa Claus. It's what stupid Disney-girls chase, and then they get knocked up and live a middle-class life. That's not you."

Kull nervously laughed. "But, uh, Caleb said—"

"Why don't we talk in private?" Harper hooked one of her arms around Kull's. When she stood, she took Kull with her. "But first, let's get you lookin' good. C'mon. Then you can tell me everything that happened from the woods until you arrived here."

"Um, okay."

Kull shot Finch a glance. She seemed hesitant and uncertain. About everything. Finch almost intervened on her behalf—wanting to tell everyone in the suite to stop messing with her head—but this was the first time Kull was actually speaking with another woman. Maybe Harper had some good insights Finch couldn't offer.

Maybe Harper's warnings about "fuck boys" would help Kull spot them.

This could be a learning experience.

Hopefully.

Finch prayed this wasn't a terrible idea.

Kull nervously smiled as Harper led her straight to one of the bedrooms.

"I need to do a bit of work." Louis smiled, stood from the couch, and then hurried over to the balcony doors. He poked around on his phone the entire time, obviously consumed with whatever was on the screen.

Finch and Enzo, basically alone in the middle of the

massive suite, glanced over at one another. Finch tensed when he realized Enzo was trembling. Parts of Enzo's shoulder had fur, and the tips of claws were poking from the ends of his fingers.

"What's wrong?" Finch whispered.

"There's fresh blood," Enzo muttered. "Somewhere on this floor. I just now caught a whiff of it."

CHAPTER
SEVENTEEN

Finch stared at his phone.

9:40 p.m.

"Let's go look," Finch said.

Enzo motioned to the bedroom. "You don't want to wait for our social media princess? You seemed concerned somethin' might happen to her." Enzo glanced at the door where Kull had disappeared. "Hell, *I'm* worried about her. Did you hear that lady? She sounds like one of those lunatics who gets married specifically to divorce a man and take half his money."

Finch *was* concerned, but not for those reasons.

Now that Fox-Pistol's boyfriend was missing in action, Finch had more to think about. Was he still out there? Would he come back to finish off Fox-Pistol? But blood in the hotel was a big red flag. And Jay-W's wife was on this floor—what if she was in trouble?

His decision about leaving was momentarily put on hold when someone knocked on the suite door.

One of the bodyguards ambled over and opened it. Standing in the hallway was none other than one of the fae—

a female redwood elf. She wore a tight pencil skirt suit that hugged her slender body.

The human bodyguard, who clearly knew nothing about the supernatural, stared for a long moment.

"I'm the hotel manager," the elf said with a forced smile.

Louis flew across the room and went straight for the door. No matter what he did, his phone remained planted firmly in his dominant hand. "Excuse me, excuse me. I'm the one who booked this room. Is something the matter?"

The bodyguard shifted out of the way, but didn't actually remove his hand from the door.

"I would like to speak with Adair Finch, if he's available." The elf maintained the same smile and tone through every word. It was almost creepy.

"You came here to speak to... the sad cop?" Louis narrowed his eyes. When the woman didn't deny anything, he slowly whirled on his heel. "Did you hear that? You're wanted at the door, PI."

Finch and Enzo both stood. Together, they made their way across the gigantic living room, and then out the door of the suite into the hallway with the elf. As Finch walked by Louis, the social media whiz gave him a long and thorough stare, like he was trying to discern if Finch really was important.

The bodyguard shut the door, leaving just Finch, Enzo, and the woman alone in the corridor.

The elf was stunning up close—they always were.

Her skin was reddish in complexion, and her hair black with slight dark green highlights. The redwood elves loved their trees so much, they often infused their flesh with fresh branches, giving them their distinct coloration. Most humans would've said the woman was of Native American descent, but Finch knew better.

The woman's black hair was coiled tightly into a bun, the

tips of her pointed ears hidden within layers of her inky locks. She also sported a pair of small, silver glasses. They were perched perfectly on her pointed nose, almost at the very tip.

"My name is Liligale Vi'Thamis, Head of the Pacific Court," the woman said with a grace that betrayed her love of etiquette.

Finch knew the drill. The fae—especially the ones who aligned themselves with any sort of court—wanted everyone to follow protocol. "I'm Warlock Adair Finch," he said, no emotion in his voice. "And this is my associate, Enzo, uh, *Bond*." Or whatever his fake last name was.

Liligale turned her dark eyes to Enzo. "It is quite the insult that you brought your *dog* to this establishment."

"Don't let her rile you," Finch quickly stated, hoping her words wouldn't cause any transformations.

"Heh." Enzo shrugged. "I might've been more offended if her insult wasn't so creatively bankrupt."

Liligale held up a delicate hand to the bottom of her pointed chin. Every feature about her was angular, as though sculpted. The dark green strands of hair shone between the black ones, and fae magic pulsed throughout the hallway.

"I can get more creative with my insults," Liligale said, her voice practically reverberating off the floor and walls. "For the fact of the matter is—we don't tolerate the cursed here. It's an insult to bring your filth into a friend's home. That's what you've done here today, Adair Finch. And I don't appreciate it."

The word *filth* obviously irritated Enzo much more than the dog comment.

He had already been primed to transform after he caught the scent of blood in the building, and now Enzo was digging his claws into his skin just to keep himself in human form.

Finch glared at her. "Did you come up all the way to the top floor just to chide me?"

"I came here to ask what you were doing in *my* hotel." Liligale's magic remained in the area, soaking into the carpet, seeping into the lights and tinting them slightly green. "You didn't even come to introduce yourself to me before heading to one of our suites. Most would consider your presence here a trespass—but I'm being gracious. I'll allow you to explain before I do anything further."

"I'm here because I'm looking for Charlotte Woolsy," Finch stated.

The *instant* he said her name, the lights in the hallway flickered. The elf's magic had fluctuated with her shock, and she caught her breath as though she had been slapped.

"You know about Charlotte?" the woman whispered, her lip twitching.

That was an odd way to word that question.

"Is there something you want to tell me?" Finch asked.

Liligale hesitated. She stepped back as her magic swelled and once again took hold of the area. With a sweet smile— more sinister than anything else—she motioned to the elevator. "Please. Come with me to my office. I think we should discuss Charlotte's presence here."

With the elegance of a trained dancer, she spun on her high heel and headed for the elevator. Every step she took, her hips swayed, playing up her enchanting beauty.

"She's on this floor, isn't she?" Finch whispered.

Enzo snorted. In an equally quiet voice, he replied, "I think her suite is the last in this hall."

"I suspect the elves know everything that happens inside this hotel."

"Probably. They're nosy fucks. And I told you they hate wolves."

Finch darkly chuckled. "Yeah, I got that the moment she opened her mouth."

Liligale stopped at the elevator and turned to face them. Her expression hadn't really changed, but the anger in her eyes had doubled. Finch knew he was pushing his luck. He would rather head to Charlotte's suite, but he decided to hear out the elves first. Perhaps they could answer all his questions and clear up some of this mess.

"You still smell the blood?" Finch whispered as they walked down the hall.

Enzo nodded once.

They both entered the elevator. Enzo stepped around Liligale, and the fae wrinkled her nose in apparent disgust.

"Touch me, and I'll have your pelt made into a coat," she said, calm and icy.

Enzo moved to the corner, his teeth sharper than normal, his claws clearly visible.

The elevator lowered, and Finch positioned himself between Enzo and the elf. He glanced over and met the woman's gaze. "Is there a reason you've got a problem with wolves?"

"The lycanthropy curse is vile," Liligale said matter-of-factly. "If one of our caretakers gets infected, all the trees they've bonded to will wither and die."

That made sense to Finch.

Lycanthropy—along with most curses—infested the heart and soul cores of an individual. Magical plants, like the special redwoods the elves cultivated, always drew their magic from a caretaker's soul. If the soul was cursed, or otherwise tainted, the plants would suffer.

"So, you don't like vampires, either?" Finch asked. "Or draugr?"

"We've actively tried to purge both of them from the area,"

Liligale said, a hint of pride in her tone. "They're like rats, though. A few are still skulking about Oakland. They keep their undead hidden with red gemstones that house the hearts of fae."

"I see…"

The elevator door opened on the fortieth floor. Liligale stepped out, followed by Finch and Enzo. This was a floor with conference rooms and gigantic offices. Pictures of the nearby lake hung on the hallway wall, many so giant, someone could drive a car through them.

A large wooden door at the end of the corridor opened as soon as Liligale drew near. Finch felt the pulse of magic in the area, and sensed the undeniable might of the fae. However, it was all so overwhelming, it was difficult to sense anything else. It was like the fae magic was smoke—he couldn't possibly detect anything else when his nose was burning and his eyes watering.

The massive office had a large redwood desk and several chairs.

The room was a curious mix of nature and urban sophistication. One wall was entirely glass, offering a breathtaking view of the cityscape, while another was a living tapestry of moss and vines.

The furniture was sleek and minimalist, a nod to human design, but each piece was inlaid with delicate elvish carvings, whispering tales of old forests and starlit skies.

And there were also four male elves in suits. All waiting.

Finch tensed when he noticed the men. They were all positioned around the edge of the room, each wearing clothing specifically tailored for their tall and lean bodies. How long had they been waiting? Or did they just stand around in the office when they weren't needed?

What was going on?

Enzo was clearly just as unnerved because the man took

cautious steps toward a seat. "What is this?" he demanded. "If you want to talk to me, there's no need for this. You don't need to bring out goons."

Liligale replied with a dismissive huff. "These are my associates here at the hotel, and knights of my court." She sauntered her way around the desk and then sat with such grace, she never made a sound. "I want them here while we discuss Charlotte Woolsy."

All this intrigued Finch. He hadn't expected the elves to get involved with anything Jay-W was doing.

"Okay." He sat near the desk. "I'm listening."

"How much is Jay-W paying you?" Liligale leaned back in her extravagant office chair. "We'll double it for you to just leave Oakland."

Finch held his breath while he mulled over her offer. "Why?" he finally asked.

"We don't want you involved."

But Liligale offered no other explanation. That worried Finch almost as much as the random killer on the loose.

"Why?" he asked again, this time with a laugh.

"Your reputation precedes you," Liligale stated. "And we don't need someone of your caliber interrupting our plans here in Oakland. You see, Charlotte owes us quite a bit of money."

Enzo chuckled. "Damn, Charlie. What were you thinkin'?"

Liligale ignored Enzo and continued. "She comes here often and racks up a debt, gambling away at the poker table. We've been allowing her to keep a running tab, since we know she's good for it. Or perhaps I should say... since Jay-W is good for it. But lately, it's becoming too much."

"How much does she owe?" Finch asked.

"She owes us about five million, currently."

Finch held back a curse. That would probably upset Jay-W. But would it upset him more than Charlotte cheating on him?

"Let me guess—you don't want me helping Jay-W *specifically*," Finch whispered as everything clicked in his mind. "This isn't really about his wife. She's just a pawn."

Jay-W owned a lot of property around Oakland. The elves, no doubt, wanted it. Perhaps Jay-W would be forced to unload some of his land in order to cover his wife's substantial debt. That was probably why the elves had allowed it to get so bad…

Liligale pointed at Finch. Then she tapped the tip of her nose. "Very smart. Now, how much was Jay-W paying you?"

That meant the elves here *wanted* to get into a confrontation with Jay-W. But why? To run him out of town? No one really liked the man. He was gross, ugly, rude, and human—fae hated all those things.

Finch held up a hand. "Before I agree to anything, I want to speak to Charlotte."

"That's not possible."

"Why not?" Finch slowly asked.

Liligale didn't reply. She stared at him, her face carefully set in a neutral expression that betrayed nothing. Finch hated it. She was hiding something.

"I'm not agreeing to anything until I speak with her," Finch stated, each word a promise.

"That's unfortunate to hear."

Someone pressed the barrel of a handgun against the back of Finch's head, the steel digging into his scalp. One of the four male elves had silently crossed the room behind him —Finch hadn't noticed. The air was too thick with fae magic. It was a little disorienting.

"What is this?" Finch whispered.

Liligale shook her head and smiled. "You really only have two options, Adair. You can take my money and leave Oakland. Or you can die. Either works for my purposes, really."

CHAPTER
EIGHTEEN

With the handgun pressed firmly against the back of his head, Finch mulled over his options. If the elf fired, Finch would be dead in an instant—and if he was dead, he couldn't rewind time. It would be all over.

On the other hand, Finch knew they didn't actually want to kill him. The redwood elves ran a luxury hotel, and having a warlock murdered on their premises would be a stain on their reputation they'd likely never recover from.

But they were clearly desperate.

Liligale watched him with fire in her eyes—a type of desperation that was bizarre, if only because Finch didn't understand why.

They were afraid of him speaking to Charlotte. They wanted him to leave without seeing her. Which probably meant something about this whole situation was contrived, or forced, or maybe even fabricated. And Finch would likely figure it all out.

That was why they were afraid.

Finch *had* to speak to Charlotte. He knew she was here,

and just a few floors up. Rewinding time was a possibility. Then he could come back earlier and speak with her.

"Well?" Liligale asked, her voice stressed. "What will it be, warlock?"

Two of the gun-wielding elves circled close to Enzo. They were fidgety, obviously filled with nervous anxiety. They didn't like being close to a werewolf, that was for certain.

"*Don't touch me,*" Enzo growled, his words guttural and disturbing.

Finch glanced over, surprised to see his friend was already in the beginning stages of transformation. Enzo's ears were shifting, his fur rippling across his skin, and his irises growing to the point they swallowed up the white of his scleras.

"You need to calm down," Finch muttered under his breath.

But before Enzo could do that—or Finch could call off the elves—one pressed a gun into Enzo's temple. And that was too much for the werewolf.

In an explosive outburst of cursed magics, Enzo's body changed shape, his bones cracking and reforming, his muscles tighter, and his whole skull expanding into its canine form. The entire transformation was less than two seconds and rather horrifying to see close up.

Startled, and obviously afraid, two of the elves opened fire on Enzo. The bullets ripped into his werewolf form, but they weren't enough to stop him.

Liligale shouted something—probably for help—but her words were cut off halfway because Enzo leapt from his seat, flew over the desk, and slammed into her chest. They collided with the floor in front of the gigantic window with Enzo pinning the redwood elf.

With all the feral power of a rabid animal, Enzo dug his claws and fangs into Liligale's flesh.

"Kill the beast!" one of the male elves shouted.

The man holding Finch hostage forgot all about Finch's presence. The elven knights all rushed around the desk, some opening fire.

While they were distracted, Finch grabbed one by the back of the collar, yanked him around, and then punched him across the jaw. The man stumbled backward. Then Finch reached into his pocket and withdrew the Level 22 member card.

It was made of boreal iron—and all fae burned whenever they touched iron.

Using it like a knife, Finch slashed the redwood elf across his gun hand.

The man yelled. The iron card had effortlessly sliced through his flesh, and the injury was growing, as though a fire had started in his skin, and was spreading. The elf dropped his firearm, his eyes wide.

Finch dove for the weapon, stood, and then fired on the elf, striking him in the chest twice.

The man collapsed to the floor, bleeding out onto the carpet.

Enzo leapt off Liligale and savaged the next closest knight. Enzo crunched his fangs on the man's neck and shook his head around like a dog ripping meat from the bone.

There were at least twelve gunshots, all in rapid succession.

The good thing about werewolves—or perhaps bad, if you were fighting one—was that they were difficult to kill while in their wolf forms. Unless someone was using silver, the injuries to the werewolf wouldn't be fatal. Instead, the injuries would tear away at the cursed magic. Only once a werewolf had sustained enough damage would they revert to their human form.

And in human form, they could be killed like any other chump.

The redwood elves were clearly just trying to riddle Enzo with so many bullets that he would be forced to change back.

But until then, their bullets were just causing him to get angrier and angrier. And since Enzo's lycanthropy was tied to his *heart core*, the cursed magic grew stronger and stronger with intense and volatile emotions.

Some of the bullets weren't even penetrating Enzo's flesh. His cursed magic was becoming that powerful.

When Finch had seen Enzo in Level 22, he had appeared to be a sophisticated werewolf. He had worn a suit, and upheld intelligent conversation. His black fur had been groomed, and his fangs, while sharp, not too menacing.

The Enzo tearing the elves apart wasn't anything like the Enzo from Level 22.

This Enzo was monstrous.

The cursed magics had warped his body. Enzo's fangs were more prominent, his claws long and hook-like. When Enzo glanced around, his eyes darted from one person to the next, barely seeing anything—his intelligence replaced with pure rage. With each inhale and exhale, he was growling and snarling, his saliva tainted with fae blood.

The vines and plants on the wall suddenly exploded outward. They were like the tentacles of a creature, and they reached for Enzo. Under the power of fae magic, they attempted to hold the werewolf in place, the leaves and vines growing and becoming thicker with each passing moment.

Finch held up a hand. Fire erupted from his palm. The blaze incinerated the wall, scouring the plants so thoroughly, he thought he heard a scream of magic as they died. The vines attempting to hold Enzo went limp.

No sprinklers activated, even as the smell of charred vegetation filled the air.

One of the elf knights turned his gun on Finch.

Fortunately, Finch was just a little faster. He shot the man, twice in the chest and once in the neck. The man crumpled to the floor, grasping at his injuries.

By the time Finch turned back to Enzo, the werewolf was drenched in elf blood, his tank top and sweatpants a dark shade of crimson that only existed in horror movies, massacres, and nightmares.

Once the elf in his mouth was dead, Enzo stood to his full height—eight feet tall—his ears erect, his eyes wide. He took deep breaths, his nostrils flaring. When his gaze settled on Finch, there was a moment of cold dread.

"Harris," Finch whispered. "It's me. Adair Finch." He didn't dare take a step backward. The wolf in Enzo would love to chase something.

A low growl filled the room.

Enzo stalked forward, his hackles raised.

Finch stayed rooted in place. "What would your wife think if she saw you right now?" he asked, practically shouting.

Enzo stopped. A flicker of intelligence came back to his eyes.

"What would your daughter think?" Finch added in a whisper.

Clearly shaken, Enzo slowly turned his attention to his hands. He turned them over, so he could stare at the padded palms. Blood matted his fur and coated his claws. With each passing second, his rage faded, the magic weakening.

The heart core was difficult to master. Any magic tied to it was enhanced—and weakened—by the state of one's emotions. Enzo took shallow breaths, his anger melting into deep regret. Regret always lessened the power of the magic. It was an emotion that drained an individual and removed purpose.

"Adair," Enzo said, his voice rusty. "I…"

Finch stepped closer, one hand up. "It's okay. Everything is fine. You have to stay calm."

Enzo didn't reply. He just stared at his bloody palms. They shook.

With each breath, Enzo's werewolf form became a little tamer. His claws became less hooked, his fangs shorter, his eyes once again filled with intelligence.

"I… killed…" Enzo clenched his jaws, seemingly unable to complete his sentence.

"It's okay. I can rewind time. Everything is fine."

Finch wasn't entirely sure if Enzo was hearing him. That didn't matter, though. This wasn't permanent.

Finch cautiously made his way to the office door and then peered out into the long hall. No one was there. The gunshots hadn't been quiet, though, and Finch knew someone would come to investigate. Probably sooner rather than later.

But he didn't want to restart time yet.

He needed to speak with Charlotte, even for just a few minutes. And now that the redwood elves weren't blocking his way, this was a perfect opportunity.

"C'mon," Finch said. He swung the door open wide. "Let's get back to the top floor."

Enzo, still in his werewolf form, hesitantly glanced up. His shallow breaths were ragged now, his ears low.

"You don't have to worry," Finch said. "I'm telling you—this is basically a dream. It's not even real. Don't worry about it." Again, he motioned Enzo to the door. "Let's hurry, so I can gather some info before it gets to be too difficult."

Narrowing his eyes in confusion, Enzo stomped to the door. He said nothing as he stepped into the hall, but his gaze fell to his crimson clothing. Red droplets stained the floor with every step. The dog footprints he left behind could be considered cute if they had been made with red paint instead of blood.

"Can you become human?" Finch asked.

Enzo didn't reply.

He also didn't transform.

"It's fine," Finch said. "Don't worry. We'll just head to the top floor, and once I rewind time, you'll be back to your normal self."

He wanted to pat Enzo on the shoulder, but Finch thought better of it. Enzo clearly didn't want to be touched. Or speak.

Together, they walked down the long corridor and made it to the elevators. They summoned one, and thankfully, no one was inside when the doors slid open. Finch stepped in, Enzo close by, and then he hit the button for the forty-fourth floor.

Soft music played inside the elevator as they traveled.

Finch glanced over. Enzo stared a hole into the ceiling, his thoughts elsewhere. His clawed hands hadn't stopped shaking. It seemed Finch's reassurances weren't having any effect.

They reached their destination, and the doors slid open.

The suites were just as they had left them. Four doors for each of the best rooms in the hotel. Enzo had said Charlotte's scent was coming from the last door, so Finch went straight there. He passed Kull's suite on the way, and he decided not to stop. If any of the Fox-Pistol gang saw Enzo in his wolf form, they would all cause problems. Finch didn't want to have to deal with that.

When he reached Charlotte's room, he pounded on the door.

"Charlie?" he called out.

No answer.

Enzo walked up behind him, stinking of so much blood,

Finch tasted copper. After a long sigh, Finch placed his hand on the door. He still had access to Kull's mischief magic. Her magic was tied to his *eye core*, which meant he had to visualize the magic in order to use it.

Thankfully, her magic was perfect for unlocking doors and slipping by security. Finch visualized the door unlocking, and then the mischief spirit magic did the rest.

With a soft *click* the suite door opened without the need for a key card.

"Come inside, but wait by the door," Finch whispered to Enzo. "It'll be difficult to explain why you're covered in gore. I just need to ask Charlotte a few questions, and then we're gone."

Again, Enzo said nothing.

Finch stepped into the suite.

It was nearly identical to Fox-Pistol's room, complete with three colossal couches, TVs, and a pool built into the balcony. The lights were just as dim, and the minibar stocked with just as many boozes.

Finch stepped in, glancing around as he went. Was Charlotte already sleeping?

No.

He spotted a woman. She was in the middle of the suite, on the floor, surrounded by her own blood. The sharp corner of the stone coffee table had a chunk of her scalp, and a little bit of her hair.

No one else was here.

Finch made his way to the body. There were no signs of breathing. Just a pale corpse.

Dead.

"Goddammit," he whispered to himself. Then Finch glanced at his phone.

10:01 p.m.

Enzo had smelled blood at 9:40 p.m. which meant Charlotte had probably died around that time.

Now Finch knew why Liligale hadn't wanted him to see Charlotte, not even for a moment. She was dead. And Finch had the feeling the redwood elves had been in the process of covering it all up when Finch mysteriously showed up on their doorstep.

This explained a lot.

After a long exhale, Finch turned to face the entrance. Enzo loomed in the doorway, hunched over so he could fit, one clawed foot in the suite, one foot in the hall.

"Charlie's dead," Finch stated. "I'm going to rewind time. Just… wait in Level 22 until I come to see you again, okay?"

Then Finch activated Chronos's magic.

Everything stopped. Color drained from the world until it was just black and white. And then, everything melted away.

When Finch blinked, he was back in the woods. Kull was on the ground, her red hair tangled with twigs and leaves.

It was 5:29 p.m. once again.

CHAPTER
NINETEEN

"What happened?" Kull asked as she sat up.

"Enzo and I got into a fight with the redwood elves." Finch rubbed his face, mulling over the situation.

"You got into *another* fight?" Kull snorted out a laugh. "I can't let you go anywhere without me, obviously. You always get into a scuffle with something."

Finch exhaled as he walked over and then scooped Kull up into his arms. She held on to his neck, her smile there, but not as beaming as usual.

"Are we going to go get Enzo?" she asked.

"I…"

Finch carried her through the woods, his thoughts a mire of negativity. Enzo wasn't in control of his rage. Few werewolves were—it wasn't his fault—but he still lost himself at the smallest of provocations. That would make everything difficult.

Everything.

"I'm giving serious thought to just rewinding time and

allowing him to forget," Finch whispered to himself more than Kull.

But Kull's eyes widened, and she tightened her grip around his neck. "What? You can't do that. Well, you *could*. But you shouldn't."

"Why not?" he growled.

"Why would you? He's your friend. And I haven't seen you with many friends before. You seemed happy. You both were constantly giving each other looks—laughing about the same things."

"He's not in control of his rage. He'll cause more fights than I ever could."

Kull shook her head. "So help him."

Finch held his breath as he stepped over a broken branch. It was easier said than done. Werewolves were under a curse, after all.

But…

If his brother were still around—if Carter were here to weigh in on the conversation—he would've advocated for Enzo to stay as well. Carter always went out of his way for others. No path was too difficult. As long as things weren't impossible, Carter would do it.

And Finch *hadn't* seen many of his friends in years. Enzo had been a great detective for the Oakland PD, and a great man to work with back in the day. Perhaps Finch could help him get his lycanthropy under control.

"All right," he muttered. "We'll go get Enzo."

Kull playfully kicked her legs back and forth in excitement. "Yes! Perfect. I think this is the best course of action."

When Finch stepped onto the road, all the people waiting cheered. The handyman—as always—hurried over.

"The officer found her!" one person shouted.

"I'm so glad the girl is okay," the handyman said as he neared Finch. "I was mighty worried."

"She got lost," Finch said, practically tripping over his words in his haste to speak. "I'm going to take her to the hospital."

"Good idea."

Both Finch and Kull said nothing as they headed to Finch's vehicle. He set her down in the passenger seat and then went around to the driver's side. Then Finch quickly drew the Mark of Chronos on her arm, to ensure Kull would remember everything once he rewound time again.

As he started the engine, the corners of Kull's lips twitched and her smile faded. "Adair?" she whispered. "Can I talk to you about something serious?"

Finch drove his vehicle away from the crowd of people and headed straight into Oakland. "Of course. What is it?"

"Is love real?"

"Yes," he quickly replied. "It's real."

"How do you know? Since you've never been in love yourself?"

Finch held back a powerful sigh. "I've seen it. I know it exists."

"Oh, thank the good stars," Kull said with a chuckle. She comically wiped sweat from her forehead, her smile slowly returning. "But I have something else I want to discuss."

"What is it?"

"Harper said men don't *want* to fall in love. All they want is pussy."

Finch cringed and inadvertently slammed on the brakes as he approached a stop sign. The whole car shook, his seat belt digging into his body. Even Kull was knocked around a little bit. She pulled her knees up to her chest and stared at him.

"Don't ever say that word again," Finch muttered. He kept

the car stopped at the four-way intersection, his discomfort with the situation mounting.

"Which word?" Kull asked.

"You know damn well what word I'm talking about."

Kull giggled. Then she leaned her head onto her knees. "Why not? Is it because it's a secret?" She smiled a coy smile. "Do humans not generally know? Have I discovered something super hidden?"

Finch took a deep breath, and then turned to face her. "No. Everyone knows."

"Everyone?" Kull sat straight again and frowned. "Everyone knows men just want p—"

"Don't," Finch hissed. "Yes. Every adult human knows that. That's why they say *sex sells."* He pointed at her. "And I said don't say that word anymore."

Kull's gaze fell to the floorboard. "Oh. So, everyone knew —but me."

"Basically."

She glanced over at him. "And all men just want... They just want the *p-word*?"

Finch pinched the bridge of his nose. After mulling over the words, he sighed. *"Most* men want that."

"And women have the p-word?"

"Yes."

"And men want it more than love?"

"Some men," Finch muttered. "Other men are looking for love. Some don't want any of it—and some men want other men."

Kull nodded along with his words. "Oh. That seems complicated. More complicated than I thought."

"It can sometimes be difficult to tell the difference when you first meet a man. That's why people date. It can take a long while to understand someone."

Finch left the intersection, his grip tight on the steering

wheel. He hated the topic of the conversation, but perhaps he couldn't avoid it any longer.

Kull tapped her fingers on the tops of her knees. She stared at Finch while he made his way through the busy streets of Oakland. After a few minutes, she asked, "Why can Harper say the p-word, but I can't?"

"Because it makes me uncomfortable."

"But I've seen you fight people. And kill people. And, also, totally use fire to burn away a whole house." She tapped her bottom lip. "And *that* word makes you uncomfortable? Not any of that other stuff?"

Finch groaned out a long exhale. "Yes."

"Wow. It must be a really powerful word if it gets under *your* skin, Adair." Kull pretended to pocket the information, making the hand gesture of stuffing it away in a pocket—even though her dress had none. "I'll keep this information safe. Don't worry. Your enemies will never find out."

Finch wanted to be mad, but he snorted out a laugh. "My only weakness," he quipped. "You found it."

After a genuine laugh, Kull fell silent. They drove into Oakland, and instead of heading to the Walmart, or the burger joint, he decided to head straight to Level 22. Once they had Enzo, they could all figure out what to do next together.

By the time Finch made it to the parking lot just outside the Oasis, it was already 6:02 p.m. The traffic was terrible everywhere in Oakland.

Finch killed the engine.

"Adair," Kull said. "I need to go inside."

"Why?" He turned to her, his eyes narrowed. "You should just wait here until I get back."

"I… I want to speak with Caleb. He said such wonderful things to me. I repeated them to myself over and over when

Harper said love wasn't real. That's how I knew—in my heart —she was wrong."

Finch almost regretted asking, "What did Caleb say? I know you told me—tell me again."

Kull sat up straight and smiled. In a dreamy voice, she said, "If stars were thoughts, my sky would be lit by you, for every shimmering light is a wish to know the universe in your eyes."

He was impressed Kull could remember the line verbatim. She clearly thought it was special and wonderful and magical. That made everything awkward.

"And what do you want to do?" Finch asked, dreading everything she was about to suggest.

"Can we both go into Oasis and speak to Caleb?" Kull plucked a leaf out of her fiery hair. "I'm fairly confident he's my truest of loves. Or at least... I want to make sure by talking to him again. I'll know once I hear his voice and feel that heart-flip sensation I had before."

"All right. Fine. But we're in and out."

Kull held up a finger and frowned. "I don't have any panties. Again. Do you think that'll be a problem? Will anyone notice?"

Finch slowly removed his coat and then passed it over to her. "Just tie this around your waist. You'll be fine until we go shopping."

She did as instructed, which made her look more like a drunken college student than a famous social media star. As they walked into the glitzy building, and headed for the ground floor nightclub, Finch shoved his hands into his pants pockets and sighed. He wanted to get this over with as quickly as possible.

They entered Oasis, and the music assaulted his ears. Finch stayed close to Kull as they moved across the large room, weaving between people standing around or half dancing.

The place smelled of sugary booze.

They approached a half-circle booth, and Kull touched Finch's elbow and pointed at a man with a pink polo shirt, frosty blond hair, and a nose ring.

Obviously eager to get to her love, Kull practically shoved her way over to the booth. Unfortunately, Caleb sat almost in the dead center of the semi-circle, making it difficult to reach him.

Kull placed her hand on the table, but Caleb had his back to the room, his eyes on the woman next to him. Kull waved, but it didn't get his attention. She glanced over at Finch, her smile still in place, even if her eyes betrayed her uncertainty. "Huh. He's busy, I guess."

Finch moved her closer to the booth, so they were almost up against the end of the table. "We can wait."

Caleb was facing a beautiful young woman with a petite frame, short black hair, and so much goth makeup on her face, she could've been part raccoon and no one would've noticed. She swirled a colorful drink and eyed Caleb as he slid closer to her.

"I want to get to know you more," Caleb said, shouting in order to have a conversation.

"Why?" the woman shouted back.

"Because if stars were thoughts, my sky would be lit by you," Caleb replied in a poetic fashion, "for every shimmering light is a wish to know the universe in your eyes."

The exact same line he had said to Kull.

Finch almost laughed.

"Eh. Gross." The woman rolled her eyes and turned away.

"Wait, let me buy you another drink!"

"No, thanks."

Caleb inched closer, trying to get more of her attention. And while he was busy, Kull gently tugged on Finch's shirt, and then guided him a few feet away from the booth.

He leaned close to her so he could ask, "Are you okay?"

"He said the same thing to that other woman," Kull said, her voice almost lost to the *thump, thump, thump* of the music.

Then she said nothing else. Kull stared at the floor between them, her hands shaky, even as she wrung them. Finch had never seen Kull this distressed. He placed a hand on her shoulder.

"Say the word, and I'll burn this place to the ground," he said.

Kull's smile briefly flickered back across her face. "No. I just want to leave."

He nodded.

Together, they made their way across the dance floor, and then past the bar. Once they exited Oasis, the volume level of the world was back to reasonable. Finch rubbed his ears and then rotated his shoulders.

They stood in the building lobby, near the elevators that led up to Level 22. An occasional person walked by to enter Oasis, the music blaring whenever the door was opened.

It was mostly quiet otherwise.

Kull ran both her hands into her red hair. She sank her fingernails into her scalp and scrunched her eyes closed.

"Oh, no," she whispered to herself. "Oh, no, no, no. I've made a mistake."

Finch exhaled. Then he awkwardly reached out and gently patted her shoulder. "You don't need to worry about it. There's more fish in the sea, and—"

"But why?" Kull interjected. She shook her head and ground her teeth. "*Why*? Why did Caleb say the same thing to someone else? Was he just... confused? Did he think she was me? They didn't even connect over something silly and fun."

"Caleb probably says it to everyone," Finch muttered with a sigh.

Kull opened her eyes and snapped her gaze to Finch's. "Everyone? It wasn't for me? It wasn't... special?" She knitted her eyebrows. "But why? I don't understand."

"We just had this discussion. You know why."

"Is it... the p-word?"

"Yes." Finch crossed his arms. "That's what nightclubs are mostly for. It's not about finding love—it's about hooking up. Or whatever the kids say nowadays."

"But why lie to me?" Kull stepped closer to Finch, her voice rising like she was interrogating him. "Why not just tell me he wanted to *hook up*?"

Finch exhaled. He wasn't entirely certain a spirit-turned-human would understand, so he tried to come up with the best analogy possible.

"Remember when you were hungry? And you felt that *urge* to *eat*? Do you remember what it felt like after you ate that hamburger? How you were satisfied and felt better?"

Kull stared into his eyes and nodded.

"Men sometimes have that urge. An urge to... to hook up." Finch tried not to cringe, but in his soul, he wanted to roll into a ditch to escape this conversation. "And once they do *hook up*, the hunger goes away. At least for a while."

Something he said clearly resonated with Kull. Her eyes widened with understanding, and she stood a little straighter.

"So, I'm just *a hamburger?*" Kull practically shouted the last word, and someone walking by gave her a quizzical glance.

"A metaphorical hamburger, yes."

Kull took a step away from Finch and rubbed her arms. "Oh. I see."

And then she said nothing. Her eyes became distant, and her fingers tightly gripped her biceps.

"You don't need to feel bad," Finch said.

No response.

"This happens a lot—where someone might exaggerate their feelings in order to hook up. It's nothing."

"I don't want to talk about it," Kull quickly replied, her voice small.

And then again, silence.

No smile. No jokes. No mischief. Kull stared at the floor, unseeing. Finch didn't know what to say to her, or even what angle to take to make her feel better. He didn't understand—it wasn't her fault this had happened. It was Caleb's. In a perfect world, he would've been upfront with what he wanted. But the world was far from perfect.

"Enzo is probably waiting for us," Finch said as he awkwardly rubbed the back of his neck.

Kull nodded.

Together, with no words between them, they went to the elevator and traveled up to the floor with Level 22. Finch patted his pants pocket and realized he didn't have a member card. They hadn't gone and seen Jay-W since he reset time.

When the elevator door opened, Finch stepped out into the hallway and spotted the werewolf door guard.

He strolled over. "Dennis—I'm here to see Enzo."

The man—Dennis—stared at Finch for a long time, clearly baffled. He obviously didn't understand how Finch knew his name. But after a moment, he held up a finger. "I'll go say something to Enzo, one moment."

Dennis walked in and out rather quickly.

Enzo came out a few moments later, once again wearing his tank top and sweats. Like Kull, he had a pensive expression—like he was lost in his thoughts.

"You ready?" Finch asked.

"No one remembers," Enzo murmured. He turned his attention to Finch, meeting the man's gaze. "Absolutely no one remembers. Not my boss. Not anyone in the club. It's like… everything we did wasn't real."

Dennis, who stood just a few feet away, glanced over, both eyebrows high. He didn't say anything, though. He seemed content to just listen and be confused.

Finch took Enzo by the shoulder and guided him toward the elevator doors, away from the ears of those who wouldn't understand.

"You really can rewind time," Enzo said, his tone filled with awe.

Finch nodded once. "Yeah. So, you don't have to worry. Like I said—think of it like a dream."

"No one should be that powerful. This is too much."

"You're just reeling because it's new. Everything is fine, I promise."

Enzo pointed at him. "I had the same damn conversation with my boss the last time I quit. Word for word. Nothin' had changed."

"It happens," Finch said with a groan. "I repeat a lot of conversations."

"It's just… wild."

"It's nothing."

Enzo took shallow breaths, and even folded his arms as they all entered the elevator. Right as Finch pushed the lobby button, Kull's stomach gurgled so loud, it eclipsed the elevator music.

He turned to face her.

"We didn't get any hamburgers this time," Kull whispered. She stared at the floor as she said, "But even though my stomach made noises, I don't really feel hungry. I feel… not happy."

"My apartment is nearby," Enzo muttered. "I've plenty of food. And I can grab a few things before we head out."

Kull glanced over at Finch. "I'd like that."

"All right," Finch said. "If you both want to, we'll do that. Lead the way, Enzo."

CHAPTER
TWENTY

Enzo's apartment reminded Finch that the man was now a bachelor.

Enzo had a single couch in the living room, set up in front of a TV resting on the simplest of TV stands one could purchase at IKEA. There were no photos on the walls, or plants on the windowsills, or any decorations of real note other than the half-empty bookshelf filled with DVDs and video games.

The place was tidy, and didn't smell of yesterday's food, which was a step up from the usual bachelor life.

Enzo led them inside, and then locked the apartment door once they were in.

"I've got chairs in the kitchen," he said.

After crossing the barren living room, they made it into the kitchen. There was a well-loved microwave, a huge stack of take-out menus, and a decent set of pots and pans hanging on a rack above the stove.

The four-person table was positioned near the kitchen window, and was the nicest thing in the whole apartment. The surface was clean, and the chairs cushioned.

Nothing screamed *I used to be a police officer* more than the tidy interior of the refrigerator. Enzo opened the door to reveal everything was properly labeled and stored in their appropriate spaces. Vegetables in the crisper tray, butter on the door slot—it was like Enzo couldn't get rid of his training for evidence lockers.

"Your apartment reminds me of Adair's," Kull said as she took a seat. "But it's way cleaner."

Finch sat next to her. "I've been better about cleaning it."

Ignoring their commentary, Enzo removed some ground beef from the fridge. "What do you two want?"

"I've only ever eaten hamburgers." Kull frowned. "And I kinda never want to eat them ever again, if I'm being honest. I mean, they're *great*, but…"

Enzo glared at Finch. "You've only ever fed her *hamburgers?*"

"Don't look at me like that—she just became a human. Hamburgers were easy."

"Tsk." Enzo pulled out an onion. "I'll make us something my ma used to make."

Kull glanced around, but with nothing interesting for her attention to land on, she asked, "Do you have many friends over?"

"No," Enzo curtly replied.

"Neither does Adair."

Although Finch wished she wouldn't go around talking about that, it dawned on him that Enzo was, in fact, quite lonely. Finch could see the signs—because he exhibited them all as well.

When he glanced over at Kull, she offered him a sly little smile. Her innocent comment hadn't been innocent at all. She had specifically made the pointed comment, and Finch held back his sarcastic commentary. She just liked getting under his skin a bit—as all mischief creatures did.

Forty-five minutes later, Enzo pulled a pan out of the oven.

Finch glanced at his phone: 7:20 p.m.

With some swagger in his step, Enzo brought the pan over to the table. "I know what you're thinking," he said with a smirk. "*Oh, Enzo, you're so funny and charming and attractive and extremely humble. Surely, you can't also cook. That's too much for one person!*"

Kull giggled, her smile returning in full force.

"Boom." Enzo set the pan on top of an oven mitt, directly in the middle of everyone. "That meat didn't loaf itself."

After a quiet golf clap from Kull, Enzo grabbed three plates from the cabinet and placed them around in front of everyone. Then he grabbed some broccoli he had steamed on the stove and doled out a healthy helping to everyone.

As though imitating the showmanship of Chef Gordon Ramsay, Enzo served the meatloaf. There was a fine saucy layer of tomatoes on top, and the red sauce dripped onto the table in a few places. With a frown, Enzo cleaned it up once everyone had their food.

Kull took a bite of her meatloaf and practically melted in her seat. She quickly chewed, swallowed, and then went for an even bigger bite. "So good," she said between bites. "I love this. Humans are so skilled at making food."

Then she ate a piece of broccoli.

Finch thought she might hate it, but he was completely wrong. Kull smiled wider and gobbled down the vegetables as well.

"These remind me of a field I used to visit," she said, chewing. "That field was always filled with so many other mischief spirits, especially at night." After swallowing the last of the broccoli, Kull added, "Did you know werewolves are weak to silver?"

"I was aware," Enzo said, irritation in his tone. He stabbed a piece of meatloaf and ate without chewing much.

"Well, before *everyone* knew, it was actually a secret." Kull laughed as she said, "You see, the first werewolf ever tried to keep it hidden. Let me tell you the story!"

"Okay?"

"There was this woman and man who loved each other, but then the woman wanted to be with someone else, but she also didn't want to be unfaithful, so she cursed her lover to become a wolf."

Enzo opened his mouth like he was about to say something, but he held back any commentary. Instead, he listened intently and chewed his food slower.

"The wolf was so angry that he decided to challenge the woman's new lover to a duel." Kull held up a finger. "But the wolf was tricksy! He actually enlisted the help of a *mischief spirit* to spread the rumor around that his only weakness was wolfsbane, which is a type of flower people used to brew into poison."

"Wolfsbane doesn't harm werewolves?" Finch asked, genuinely curious.

Kull shook her head. "Nope. But it sounds like it should, right? That was all part of the ruse!" She chuckled as she added, "So during the duel, the man had all his weapons coated in wolfsbane, thinking he would have the advantage."

"What happened?" Enzo asked.

Kull cut herself another slice of meatloaf, and then dramatically stabbed it over and over again with her butter knife. "The man was killed by the wolf, obviously. But the story doesn't end there!" She stopped mutilating her food. "The woman was so angry this happened, she attacked the wolf herself."

Finch, who had never heard any of this, tried to think of

famous witches who might've been responsible for the curse. Or maybe it was a warlock? He wasn't certain.

"The wolf, much to his eternal sadness, killed the woman." Kull held a piece of meatloaf high with her fork. "But when he did, part of the curse broke! He could once again become a human... But whenever his anger flared, the wolf would rise. You see, the curse was forever tied to his heart and soul, for his love for the woman lasted beyond her death."

Then Kull dramatically slammed the fork down on the plate.

Enzo and Finch were silent.

"Mischief spirits all know this tale," Kull said with a giggle. "Spirits are weak—one of the weakest of magical beings—but we have influenced a few notable things throughout history." She ate the meatloaf, cleaning her plate. "This loaf of meat and all the grass on the side really helped me remember that."

"Grass?" Enzo whispered.

"Do you know why silver harms werewolves?" Finch asked. He knew the answer, but he was curious to see if spirits did.

Kull nodded. "Of course. When Khonsu, the moon god, gave his moonlight to mortals, it transformed into silver. And since Khonsu hates curses so much, his magic breaks them apart with ease." She waved her fork in the air as she spoke.

Finch nodded. "That's right."

Then Kull's eyes widened. "Wait. I want to try *all* the human foods."

Finch raised an eyebrow. "All of them?"

She turned to face him, her expression more serious than ever before. "All of them. We should... go right now. I want the flavor of human chefs in my mouth."

"That's some weird phrasing." Enzo sat forward. "And aren't you full now that you've had some meatloaf? Maybe we should wait."

"Adair can rewind time, and then I'll be hungry again." Kull grabbed Finch's arm. "Let's just take a little while and try some foods. We can all go together. It'll be a celebration! For Enzo joining the PI agency."

Enzo turned away, his expression shifting back to something neutral. "Listen, about that." He stood from his chair, gathered everyone's plates, and then brought them over to his sink. "I've been giving this a lot of thought."

"About how fun it'll be to work with us?" Kull asked.

"No. About why I quit being a cop in the first place." Enzo practically slammed his dishes down. He clenched his hands into fists. "I was with Adair for less than four hours and I lost my cool. *Four hours.* I know you can rewind time—and apparently my outburst didn't actually happen—but the memories of killing all those people are still there. It's my nightmare."

Finch stood, but he said nothing.

"I don't think I can work with you," Enzo whispered. "I mean, seeing you is fine. Having dinner was fun. But... I can't handle those intense situations anymore. I'm going to lose it. I'm going to wolf out and kill people. And I don't want that. That's why I faked my death. That's why I don't ever visit my wife and daughter. *That's why I can't be around normal people.*"

His hands were clenched so tightly, blood dripped from his palms. The droplets fell and hit the white tile of the kitchen, a darker red than the tomatoes.

Kull also stood up. She furrowed her brow as she turned her attention to Finch.

"*Say something,*" she mouthed, not actually uttering a word. "*He's your friend.*"

After a short sigh, Finch walked around the table and

approached Enzo. "Remember when you asked me why I didn't just tell Kull what to do, or tell her Caleb might be a douche?"

Enzo glanced over, his eyes narrowed. "Yeah."

"Remember how I said she can make as many mistakes as she wants? Because I'll be there to correct them all?"

"What're you gettin' at?"

"Werewolves rarely master their anger since one slipup is disastrous. They can't learn from their mistakes—because one mistake means people will die." Finch leaned against the kitchen counter and met Enzo's harsh gaze. "But *you* can. You can make as many mistakes as you want. You can use this opportunity to master your rage."

Enzo's gaze fell to the sink filled with dishes. "Even if that's true, I still remember everything that happens."

"I remember everything," Finch stated.

His words lingered, the kitchen silent. It was clear the others had to give that sentence thought.

"I'm not going to force you to do anything," Finch eventually said. "But if you can come to terms with the fact some things aren't real—like what happened to those redwood elves—I think I can help you."

Enzo took deep breaths. When he unclenched his hands, he stared down at his bloody palms.

"Could you make me forget?" he whispered.

"I could. But then you wouldn't learn how to control anything. It would just be *me* learning how to control *you*."

That last statement seemed to stir something within Enzo. He nodded once. Then he wiped his hands on his kitchen towel, staining it with streaks of crimson.

"All right," he said, more determined than ever. "I got this. I'll try—I'll see if I can wrap my head around this *fake reality* bullshit and master this curse." Enzo flashed Finch a smile. "Let's go have some celebration food, then. Pizza first."

———

After Finch drew the Mark of Chronos on Enzo, he rewound time.

He was back in the woods, with Kull, but not for long. They quickly left, got Kull clothing, and then met Enzo outside Oasis. Without wasting much time, they went to the best pizza joint in Oakland.

Yo Momma's Pie.

It looked cheap, with its plastic tablecloths, dirty cups, and forks so chipped they hurt to eat from, but the pizza was second to none. Perfectly cooked crust, plenty of cheese, flavorful sauce, and fresh toppings placed with care—it was a spark of passion in an otherwise gloomy parlor.

"This place is so good," Kull said as she dove into a second cheesy slice. With a smile, she chewed.

"I come here every Tuesday," Enzo casually said as he leaned back in his chair. Half the pizza was piled high with meat, and Enzo had already demolished most of it.

Finch nibbled on his third slice. Pizza was good, it just wasn't his favorite.

"Oh my god, is that Fox-Pistol?" someone shouted.

A teenage boy, maybe sixteen or seventeen, came hurrying over. His eyes were as big as the plates in the pizzeria. His face was marked with blackheads, and his hair was greasy. Despite that, his smile was genuine, and when he got close, he maintained a respectful distance.

"Are you really Fox-Pistol?" He half laughed, clearly nervous. "Samantha Garson, right? I-I hope it's not weird I know your real name. It's on your Wiki."

Kull stopped eating and gave him her full attention. "I don't mind. Do you want a picture with me? I can sign your phone if you want, too."

"Oh, really?" The boy was breathless. "That would be amazing!"

He wore a black shirt with white text across it. The boy fumbled for a moment, and then smoothed his shirt so the writing could be read. It said: *I HAVE TWO MOODS—(1) HELLO, (2) I'LL CUT YOU.*

"I'm even wearing your merch," he said. Then the teenage boy reached into the pocket of his jeans and pulled out his phone, his hands trembling. "No one at school is going to believe I saw you. No one."

"You'll have this picture," Kull said as she moved close to the boy. She even wrapped an arm around his back, and the boy's face went bright red. "That's proof, right?"

The teenager slowly turned his attention up to the ceiling, as though everywhere else he would look would get him in trouble. "Uh, yeah. They might think I deep faked it, though."

The boy snapped a couple pictures with his phone, desperately trying to keep the angle steady, and not too high. When he was done, Kull signed the back of his phone case.

"Oh my god, this is so cool," the boy said. "My name is Max. It was so awesome to meet you. I watch all your videos."

Kull sat back down. "Aw! Thank you so much."

"You're way nicer in person than I thought you'd be."

"Oh." Kull mulled that comment over. "Maybe I should be meaner?"

Max laughed once, almost in surprise, and then settled into an earnest chuckle. "Yeah. Good one. Uh, I'll leave you alone. Sorry for bothering you." He hurried away, leaving the table but constantly glancing back.

Once he was out of earshot, Kull turned to Finch. "So... was this a *hamburger situation?*"

Finch shook his head. "No. He was honest and upfront. Rather respectful."

"Will you tell me if a hamburger man shows up?" Kull tilted her head to the side. "I want help determining who they are."

"Sure. I'll point out any hamburgers."

Kull smiled as she picked up her pizza again and started eating. Enzo, clearly baffled, just stared at Finch for a long time.

"Hamburger man?" he whispered.

"It's a long story," Finch muttered. "Don't worry about it. Instead, let's finish this and go to the next restaurant. We can talk about Charlie while we sample some more food."

CHAPTER
TWENTY-ONE

inch, Enzo, and Kull stood in the lobby of *The Apex*, one of the finest restaurants Oakland had to offer. It had a Michelin Star and was rated as a top experience by several travel blogs.

Finch had never heard of the place.

Inside, it was neon red and the darkest, blackest of velvets. It felt luxe in a way no place previous had. There was a small crowd of people waiting to get inside, and one by one, the groups were turned away. No one had been allowed inside, which made Finch afraid they would also be turned away.

"This place might be too fancy for us," he whispered.

"But this is the best human food?" Kull's eyes widened. "We. Must. *Try it.*"

Enzo shrugged. "If they tell us to leave, I know a crab shack that's probably just as good."

When the maître d' finally motioned for Finch and the others to step forward, he greeted everyone with a bright smile. "Ah. I see we have Samantha Garson in your party this evening. We were expecting her tomorrow night, for the ten top, but if you're early—or just want to eat here tonight as well—that suits us just fine."

The man wore the fanciest of suits. When he bowed slightly, it was done while maintaining the polite smile.

"You already knew I was coming?" Kull asked with a tilt of her head.

"That's correct. We received your reservation last week, and we've been eagerly looking forward to your visit."

"Oh, wow. I have great taste."

The maître d' honestly chortled. Then he led them all into the restaurant. The place was gigantic, and even had a mezzanine balcony sitting area where people could overlook the entire kitchen. The man led them straight to a table near the wall, and two more waiters rushed forward to pull out all the seats at once so Finch, Enzo, and Kull could sit down at the same time.

"Thank you," Kull said.

The maître d' half bowed a second time and then reached into his suit jacket. He produced three small seasonal menus.

Finch held up a hand. "Do you have a tasting menu? We, uh, just want to try everything you have."

"Three tastings? Even the desserts?" Once Finch nodded, the maître d' tucked the menus away. "I'll tell the kitchen at once." He turned and hurried off.

Enzo leaned forward. "Did you see the prices on the damn menu?" He huffed and then rolled his eyes. "It'll cost us over *eight hundred dollars* for the three of us to have a tasting."

"It's fine." Finch shrugged. "It's not real, remember? Well, the experience will be real, but not the money."

Enzo relaxed back into his seat. It was cushioned, and he wiggled a moment until he was fully comfortable. "Huh. I hadn't thought of it like that." Then he crossed his arms over his chest and glanced over at Kull. "So, you're famous-famous?"

"Fox-Pistol is so super popular," Kull said as she nodded her head.

"I've literally never heard of her until I met you."

"Do you like to watch people play *Call of Duty*?"

"Video games are for nerds," Enzo stated.

Kull pointed at him. "They're a form of entertainment that not only stimulates your deep cognitive functions, but also your imagination." She snapped her fingers. "And also smokin' hot ladies play them now, so they're super cool. At least, according to the comment section under all Fox-Pistol's videos."

Enzo only replied with a huff.

"Playing video games for social media got her enough money to pay for this and a luxury suite," Finch said matter-of-factly.

For a short while, Enzo seemed to mull that over, as though there was something to this "nerd stuff" after all. But he didn't comment.

"We should discuss Charlie, though." Finch sighed. "She was as dead as they get when we saw her."

Kull's eyes went wider. "Jay-W's wife is dead?" She made the statement so loud that several people within The Apex glanced over.

"*Keep it down,*" Finch hissed. He scooted his chair closer to the table. "She *was* dead. She died around 9:40 p.m., but Enzo and I didn't get to her until a little after 10 p.m."

Enzo shrugged. "She looked like she had died by falling and hitting the edge of her coffee table. But I didn't get to look long. Plus, I was a bit preoccupied."

"The redwood elves knew she was dead. That was why they wanted me to leave immediately. And from the way they were acting, I suspect they had something to do with Charlie's fall."

"We could go see her tonight," Kull said. "But that reminds me…"

Then she tapped her lower lip with her pointer finger. Several men snuck glances in her direction, and Finch prayed to whoever was listening that she wouldn't attempt to be sexy in the middle of a classy restaurant.

While a waitress was walking by, Kull held up a hand. The waitress stopped and gave Kull her full attention. "Yes, miss?"

"Do you know what *love* is?" Kull leaned most of her weight onto the table and stared directly into the woman's eyes. "The last lady I asked said it wasn't real. Is that how you feel, too? As a woman, I mean."

"Uh…" The waitress held her *uh* for at least three seconds as her mind processed everything being said. Finally, she answered with, "Love is an emotion." A lame, but accurate, response. Finch was almost impressed.

"Yes, but how do you know you love someone? Is there a way to know for sure?"

"I'm just a waitress," she said with a chuckle.

"But you're also a woman, right? I'm a little confused right now. I thought you could help."

The waitress bit her lower lip. Then she said, "Uh, well, love is like when you have a best friend, but more." She offered a weak shrug. "It's when you think of that other person as the one you'll always trust. And if you really, truly love that person, you never grow tired of them."

Kull slowly nodded along with the waitress's words. "Oh. Okay."

"Is that everything, miss?"

"Yes. Thank you so much."

The waitress hurried away, like she never wanted to be put on the spot like that ever again. Kull then glanced over at Finch.

"Everyone always gives me a different answer," Kull whispered. "No one seems to really know what love is."

Before Finch could respond, three waiters made their way to the table. They placed several plates on top of the crisp white tablecloth and then arranged a set of sparkling glassware in front of everyone. A fourth waiter walked around pouring everyone a glass of white wine. The polished silverware glinted in the dim atmospheric lighting as a *fifth* waiter placed it on the table next to the plates.

"We would like to present you the amuse-bouche," the wine-pouring waiter said as he finished pouring Kull's glass. "These are bite-sized glimpses into the chef's artistry—a blend of seasonal flavors and textures to tantalize your palate."

"Wow, I've never had an amuse-bouche before." Kull eagerly glanced down at her plate, obviously unaware of the bizarre look the waiter gave her.

The waiter nervously laughed away the comment and then pointed to the three small portions of food on the plate. The other four waiters vanished without a word, leaving them with everything they would need to enjoy a wonderful meal.

"This first tasting sample is a seared scallop resting atop a truffle-infused cauliflower puree. The second is a carpaccio of wagyu beef with aged parmesan. The third—"

But Kull wasn't waiting for the entire presentation. She picked up her silver fork and skewered the scallop. It had been elegantly presented—practically a work of art—but when she poked it, the scallop rolled through the white puree and squished a bit. She shoved the whole thing into her mouth, even though it seemed like an ordeal to do so.

The waiter stared at her, aghast.

A moment later, Kull gagged. She barely held back a *harf* and immediately reached for the satin napkin sitting next to her plate. With all the grace of a picky four-year-old, she spit the half-chewed scallop onto the napkin.

Enzo couldn't stop himself from laughing. He tried—he obviously tried—but his attempts to stifle his amusement only made it seem like he was coughing and laughing at the same time.

Half the patrons at nearby tables were all facing their direction. Some people whispered and pointed.

Finch's face grew red, but in his heart, he wasn't surprised by this turn of events at all. He hated seafood, especially scallops, and he didn't blame Kull for having the reaction she did.

"Wow." Kull rubbed the top of her tongue and frowned. "*This* is the best human food?" She turned and stared up at the waiter. "Have you *tried* pizza? This is just gross. And it felt slimy. It wasn't good at all."

The waiter was at a loss for words. "Was it cooked improperly?"

"Well, you should only eat creatures that have a spine. Everyone knows that." She held up a finger. "The creatures without spines draw their life from a different source, so no matter how you cook it, there just won't be the same magic there, ya know?"

"Why did you eat the scallop, then?" Finch asked. "If you knew it didn't have a spine?"

"I didn't know that until I tasted it! But as soon as I chewed… I knew. The source of its life was different—and I was horrified."

So was the waiter. He looked as though he wanted to flee the establishment.

Someone at the neighboring table was filming the whole thing with his phone.

"Did you want to keep trying the other things?" Finch asked.

Kull pushed her whole plate away. "No. I don't even want to eat anymore. I don't feel good."

Finch understood. The spine was what connected all five cores of someone's magical essence. The crown, eyes, heart, soul, and loins were all interconnected, but creatures without spines—such as jellyfish and scallops—could never carry the same types of magics. That was why their life force couldn't be used to make magical items, and why they sometimes harbored curses from cosmic sources.

As a half-spirit, Kull was still very in tune with all things magical, and cosmic creatures never mixed well with vertebrates. Finch wasn't as in tune with magic. As a warlock, he couldn't taste the difference—he didn't like scallops because he just didn't like seafood.

But a normal human wouldn't understand any of that.

And the waiter was clearly a normal human.

"Can we go?" Kull sighed.

Finch stood from his chair, and so did Enzo. The waiter wrung his hands, baffled into silence. It was probably a rare occurrence for a famous guest to take a single bite, spit it out, and declare the whole restaurant gross.

"I'll still pay," Finch told the man. "But I have places to be, so make it quick."

———

Enzo laughed the entire time in the car. And when it seemed like he finally got his mirth under control, he would just start chuckling all over again.

He sat in the back, practically rolling around on the seats. Kull sat up front, smiling the entire drive. Instead of eating anything crazy, Finch had stopped to grab smoothies. Now Kull sipped on an *Orange Dream Cream*, much happier than she had been at The Apex.

Finch parked down the block from the Lake Merritt Grand Hotel. Then he glanced at his phone.

9:45 p.m.

Perfect.

He drew the Mark of Chronos on both Enzo and Kull and then pointed to the building.

"All right, let's head into the hotel, go to Charlie's room, and investigate. If we don't find anything concrete, I'll just rewind the day, and we'll show up *before* she dies."

"What will we do before she dies?" Kull asked.

Enzo continued to chortle.

"We'll probably just wait in her room, out of sight, and watch her death take place." He opened his car door. "That assumes we're not caught, though. Hiding out in the room is the riskiest route—because the elves are clearly gun happy. We'll want to stay away from them as much as possible."

"What about all my friends?" Kull opened her door. "Will we visit them, too?"

"No," Finch said with a groan.

"Will we visit them again when you rewind time?"

"Maybe. If my patience comes back enough to tolerate them."

Kull stepped outside and tilted her head. "I thought they were awesome. Plus, they said they wanted to party hard. Doesn't that sound fun?"

"About as much fun as taking a bullet to the head."

Enzo stepped out, and together, they headed for the hotel. Finch kept his hands tucked into his coat pockets, but halfway there, the wind picked up, and Kull shivered. And just kept shivering, with a red nose, and goosebumps across her skin. Finch wondered if she would be all right.

He removed his coat and offered it up.

Kull stared at it a long time. Then she looked up at him. "You give me your coat a lot."

"Just take it," he said with a sigh. "You need it more than I do."

"Thank you, Adair." Kull gently took it and slipped her arms into the sleeves. Then she offered him a small smile. "I wish I had a coat I could hand you."

He waved away the comment. "Forget it. This is nothing. Let's just get this evening over with."

CHAPTER
TWENTY-TWO

Once again, Finch, Enzo, and Kull entered the luxurious lobby of the *Lake Merritt Grand Hotel*. The staff at the front desk glanced over at Finch as he headed for the elevator, but he ignored them in favor of getting straight to Charlotte. It seemed as though the employee was about to motion over security, but the moment he laid eyes on Kull, he stopped.

Fox-Pistol was supposed to be here, after all.

Once on the elevator, Finch hit the button for the top floor. Kull hummed along with the milquetoast music playing softly over the speakers. Enzo scratched his arms, growling slightly whenever the elevator jostled. The instant they reached the top floor and the elevator doors slid open, Enzo stood a little straighter.

"Blood," he whispered.

Kull audibly sniffed the air, her nose scrunching afterward. "Hm. I smell a lot of fae magic, but that's it."

Finch motioned them toward the hall. They had to walk by Fox-Pistol's massive suite in order to reach Charlotte's, and as they went by, the *thump thump thump* of a massive bass playing dance music practically shook the floor.

Kull smiled and clapped her hands twice. "Wow. They really do know how to party. It's like my room is the dance floor at Oasis."

Enzo glared at the door and then shrugged. "They don't seem worried you're missin'."

"That's because they *don't* know I'm missing," Kull said matter-of-factly. "This time around we didn't make an Instagram video, so they don't know I'm not with Waylon yet. They still think I'm on a—" she giggled as she finished, "—*romantic date* out in the woods with my boyfriend."

Finch nodded once. "That's right. No one has any reason to suspect Fox-Pistol isn't just having fun somewhere."

"Looping the day is already confusing," Enzo mused.

They reached Charlotte's room, and Finch placed his hand on the door. Using Kull's mischief magic, he visualized the lock undoing itself. With a soft *click* the suite door opened. He stepped inside and then quickly motioned for the others to join him.

He knew the redwood elves would soon come looking for him. They were obviously keeping a sharp eye on the property, but this time around, no one had said Finch's name in the lobby, so he figured they had just a little more time than before.

The room was just like it had been the first time Finch saw it. Mostly black and high-class, with three massive couches in a U shape in front of a TV, with a bar, another TV behind the bar, a pool built into the balcony, and doors that led off to various bedrooms.

The stone coffee table, positioned in the middle of the couches, had crimson splatters staining one of its corners, along with a chunk of flesh and hair. A woman was on the floor next to it, her own blood pooling around her.

Besides the stink of alcohol on the air, there was nothing else in the room. The TVs were off and silent, and there was no music playing across the speakers. It was as quiet as the corpse in the middle of the room.

Enzo growled as he wandered over to the body. He didn't touch her. Instead, he knelt a foot away and sniffed deeply. Then he shook his head.

"She's dead, all right. And inebriated. Not too much, but still." Enzo glanced over at Finch. "What do you think? She accidentally killed herself?"

Finch shoved his hands into his pocket and stared at the coffee table. Then he glanced at the body. Finch had never met Charlotte, and he was surprised once he started studying her features.

She looked in her late thirties, with curly brown hair, each of the curls small enough to barely wrap around his pinky. She was lean, and athletic, and wore enough makeup to be noticeable, but nothing too garish, but her gold necklace was the size of an actual bike lock. Her outfit was tasteful—a simple sleeveless blouse and skirt that went to her knees—and her skin was naturally tanned, not the kind purchased on a tanning bed.

Finch had been expecting her to be nineteen, or something equally cringy, and as vapid as reality TV. When had Jay-W married this woman? Finch didn't know, but he was starting to suspect they had been together a lot longer than a few months.

Charlotte's wedding ring was still blatantly on her left hand, the rock large enough to choke on.

The fact that it was still here lent more credibility to the theory she had died by accident. If someone had killed her, wouldn't they have also taken the quick influx of cash?

Unless the killer had done it for personal reasons. Or also by accident.

"Can you tell what she was drinking?" Finch asked.

Enzo sniffed. He was about to answer when Kull cut him off.

"Red wine," she said.

Both Finch and Enzo turned. Kull was by the minibar, smiling wide. She pointed to a bottle that was half empty and sitting on the edge of the sink. It was a bottle of *Diamond Valley Red*, an artsy wine bottled in California.

Kull sniffed the top of the bottle and recoiled with a frown. "Ew. There's something wrong with this."

"It's just alcohol," Finch muttered. "They all smell that way."

"Oh. No. I didn't mean the normal smell. There's something *magical* with this. Something... slimy."

Magical?

Finch raced across the giant suite and went straight for the bottle. Enzo was close on his heels. They reached the minibar together, and then they took turns sniffing at the bottle. Finch shook his head. All he smelled was wine. Enzo snorted.

"I'm not pickin' up anything magical," Enzo muttered. "But alcohol always covers that shit up. Magical substances are always difficult to detect when mixed with something alcoholic."

"It's definitely there," Kull stated. She tapped the tip of her little nose. "Trust me. As a half-spirit, I know."

"What kind of magic is it?" Finch asked.

"Fae."

Which made sense, and Finch almost rolled his eyes at himself. Of course it was fae magic. The real questions now were: *Why? And what does it do?*

Kull wandered over to the body of Charlotte. She examined the woman for a moment, her smile fading into a deep frown.

"This is sad," she whispered. Then Kull glanced away. "And she smells like the magic, too. She was probably drinking it all night."

"What does this unknown fae substance do?" Enzo asked.

"I don't know." Kull mulled over the question for a bit, and then her smile returned as she said, "Maybe *we* should drink it and find out."

"Never."

"It's probably the fastest way."

Finch shook his head. "No. We don't need to do this like we're incompetent boobs. We can get someone to analyze this for us. There are warlocks, witches, and all sorts of individuals who will take magical substances and reverse engineer their purpose."

"Oh, like the Occultist? The lady in Stockton?" Kull leapt to Finch's side. "I remember her! She can definitely identify this."

Finch glanced at his phone.

10:02 p.m.

She was likely sleeping, and would demand something in return for the identification. Finch sighed as he slid his phone back into his pocket. He could rewind time afterward, so the cost wasn't an issue, but he had a feeling—since the Occultist was so formal—that getting the substance identified would strain his patience. She would demand to do it in the morning, or have them wait, or have him do something for her *before* she did the identification.

"Liam could probably identify this," Finch whispered.

"Bree's father?" Kull nodded after she asked her question. "Oh, definitely! He makes little magical items all the time. What's that called? An artificer? Bree told me all about it."

And Liam was in Finch's debt, since Finch had saved his life. And Bree's life. And he had caught the killer of Liam's wife.

Liam would more than happily identify the substance at any hour of the night. Unfortunately, he, too, was in Stockton. That was a long drive.

But worth it.

"Grab the wine bottle," Finch stated. "We're going to take it for a drive and see what we can figure out."

———

The drive was easier at night than during the day. Sure, there were no beautiful vistas in the evening, and it was difficult to see the Pacific Ocean, but the peaceful roads, and soft lights from the many cities, made for a tranquil drive.

Still over two hours, however.

During the drive, Finch kept the radio on a station that played music without any lyrics. It helped him focus.

"I don't normally leave the Oakland area," Enzo muttered. He sat in the back seat, on the passenger side, his gaze locked on something beyond the window. "Werewolves aren't welcome in a lot of places. We get chased out immediately, even if we're not contagious."

"No one will bother you if you're with me," Finch said. He kept his attention on the road, his mind mostly on the case, but now a bit on Enzo's words.

"Remember when we busted those werewolves who were smuggling in all sorts of coke?" Enzo leaned his forehead against the glass of the window. "Remember how we got rid of the whole pack because we didn't want to take risks?"

"They were violent criminals," Finch muttered.

"Still."

Tightening his grip on the steering wheel, Finch let out an exhale. "You know what?" He sat a little straighter. "Why don't we work on something to help with your wolf situation?"

Kull swiveled her head over with a smile, her eyes glittering with enthusiasm. She clearly liked this idea.

"What're we gonna do?" Enzo asked with an edge of sarcasm. "*Meditate?*"

"That's a great idea," Kull practically shouted.

"Feh. That's ridiculous. Tons of wolves have tried it—nothin' helps."

"But have *you* tried it?"

Enzo snorted back a laugh. "No. But it doesn't matter. Who's gonna teach us? Do you even know the first thing about meditation, spirit?"

"Well… no."

Finch had never tried meditation, either. He had thought about it for some time—since it was supposed to help with one's mental fortitude—but he had never actually committed to learning it.

"We can ask the internet," Kull said, her voice high-pitched and cheery.

"The internet is full of *bunk*," Finch snapped.

"That's not true! It's super helpful."

After another long exhale, Finch reached into his pocket, glanced at the time, and then handed it to Kull. It was currently 11:45 p.m., and they were almost to Stockton. Taking the last leg of the trip to meditate wouldn't hurt anyone, even if they used a stupid internet guide saying how to do so.

Enzo moved away from the window and scooted to the center of the back seat. Kull quickly flipped through the phone, brought up the internet and did a little search.

"Okay, I found something," she said, practically giggling in excitement. "It's a sort of *How Wiki* that explains the steps to the perfect meditation."

"I seriously doubt it's a professional guide," Finch muttered.

Kull waggled her finger. "You should trust more! I'm sure it'll be great."

"Fine. Hit us with the steps."

"Wait," Enzo muttered.

Finch glanced into the rearview mirror. Enzo concentrated, and while drawing on his *heart core* managed to transform into his lycanthrope form. Just like when he was a bartender, Enzo had shiny black fur and bright eyes. He grew larger—almost too large for Finch's little Toyota—and took up the whole back seat with his bushy tail, clawed hands, and padded feet.

His hobo clothing now fit perfectly, the tank top and sweatpants never ripping.

It was risky to drive around with a werewolf, but it was so dark out, and there was no one on the road, that Finch wasn't as worried.

Enzo shifted his left ear to face Kull. "All right. I'm ready."

"Okay, okay." Kull stared at the phone. "*Step one... Close your eyes.*"

Finch wasn't about to follow along with that, since he still had to drive. He glanced in the rearview mirror and noticed Enzo had closed his eyes exactly as instructed. Kull smiled as she scrolled down the list.

"*Step two... Take even breaths.*"

Enzo complied. He inhaled and exhaled at even rates, the whiskers on his long canine snout twitching.

"*Step three... Imagine a peaceful green field, and that you're standing in the center, far from whatever is troubling you.*"

Finch kept his eyes on the road, but he imagined the green grass. For some reason, his mind drifted to the grass fields of New Zealand. He had been there once, with Carter, and their time had been wonderful.

It was far, far from his troubles in Oakland.

"Huh," Kull said as she squinted at the list. "I don't

understand this. *Step four... Remember that Jeffrey Epstein didn't kill himself."*

Finch snatched his phone out of Kull's hand while cursing under his breath. "What did I tell you? Punks on the internet think they're goddamn comedians. This wiki was bunk."

To his surprise, Enzo was chuckling in the back. The man leaned forward on the front seats of the car, his laughing growing a little louder. "Damn," he said between chortles, "I almost thought that was a real guide. They got me."

Finch tucked his phone into his pocket and half smiled. Enzo's laughing was infectious. *He* had almost been fooled by the list. It seemed legit for the first three, at least.

"Let me find another list!" Kull held out her hand. "Please! I'm sure there's a real one there, hidden in all the comedy lists. Or maybe I can look up a video! One with nice music."

Finch was about to deny her request when Enzo patted him on the shoulder with the back of his hand. "C'mon," Enzo said, still half chuckling. "Let's hear it. Maybe one of them will work."

"Or maybe she'll accidentally follow a link to Pornhub," Finch quipped.

"That would be funny, too."

Finch snorted back a laugh. He hadn't felt this carefree in a while. He almost felt younger, and the thought of stumbling upon a *Pornhub's Guide to Meditation* did make him chuckle.

"All right," Finch said.

Kull clapped as she reached for his phone, and Enzo smacked his shoulder again.

They'd be at Liam's house soon, so Finch enjoyed what little time they spent on the ridiculous meditation lists.

"Oh! Look at this one. It recommends pretending to be a cat to meditate. It says we should meow and everything, which will be hilarious with Enzo looking like *this*."

CHAPTER
TWENTY-THREE

At 12:12 a.m., Finch walked up to Liam's apartment door.

Since the death of his wife, Vera, Liam and his daughter, Bree, had stayed in the *Orange Grove Apartment* complex. Their house had been the scene of a murder, after all, and until the kitchen was completely remodeled, Liam didn't want to go anywhere near the place.

Finch tried the handle, but it was locked. Fortunately, he still had Kull's mischief magic. He visualized the lock opening, and with a soft *click*, he was able to open the door. When he stepped inside, he kept the mostly empty wine bottle close to his chest. He was certain this was all Liam needed to identify the magic.

"This is technically *breaking and entering*," Enzo growled as he stepped inside. He had reverted to his human form before exiting the car, which Finch appreciated. "You sure this warlock will be okay with us entering his apartment uninvited?"

"Definitely," Finch muttered.

Kull bounded into the front room. It was dark—no lights

on anywhere—but that didn't stop her from being the ray of sunshine needed to liven up the place. She turned on her heel and touched her bottom lip.

"Hm." Kull squinted at Enzo. "Doesn't *breaking and entering* mean that something was broken for us to get inside? My magic doesn't break anything, thank you very much."

Enzo shook his head. "It just means you used *force* to get into someone's building without authorization. The slightest force, including pushing open a door, is all that's required for you to get charged."

"Wow. Interesting." Kull covered her mouth as she chuckled. "Because we break *so many laws* when we're investigating. Just… so many."

"We won't break any laws on the final day of this shitshow parade." Finch pointed to the front door. "Wait here. I'll speak to Liam."

Enzo nodded.

Kull, on the other hand, pouted. "But I wanted to see Bree."

"She's sleeping. We'll see her later."

Kull didn't argue with that. She waited next to Enzo while Finch crept through the apartment, making his way to the back bedroom doors. Using his phone's light, he shone it down the hall and instantly knew which room was Liam's. Bree's door had a little sign stuck to the front that read: **WARLOCK IN TRAINING.**

Finch let himself into Liam's room and used his phone light to navigate over to the man's bed. The whole room was completely barren of any personal effects, and all the man's clothing was neatly stored away in the closet or dresser. If Finch didn't know any better, he would say no one lived here if all he was given was a passing glance.

Once next to Liam's bed, Finch shone his light on the

man's face. When that didn't work, he shoved the man's shoulder.

Liam jolted up, his eyes wide. He gulped down air and nearly threw himself to the other side of his twin-size bed the moment he spotted Finch.

"Oh, Lord have mercy," he whispered as he placed a hand on his bare chest. Liam did a double take, glancing at Finch again and then closing his eyes for a deep inhale. "It's not an intruder. It's just... Adair?" He snapped his eyes open again and stared. "What're you doing in my room? *What time is it?*"

Finch held up the mostly empty wine bottle. "I need you to identify something for me."

He might as well have slapped Liam across the face with a trout, for all the understanding dawning in Liam's eyes.

"You're crazier than a soup sandwich," Liam whispered, obviously trying to grapple with the situation and failing to make any sense of it. "This couldn't have waited until morning? You had to break into my room?" Liam grabbed the blankets and lifted them higher on his body, frowning deeply as he did so.

"There's a magical substance in this bottle," Finch said, completely ignoring all Liam's outbursts. "Someone has been drugging a woman, and she dies because of it. I need help identifying what it is."

"A woman dies?" Liam tightened his grip on his blankets, his gaze falling to the foot of his bed. The room was still mostly dark, and his eyes remained unfocused, but only for a short moment. "All right. Um. Let me get dressed. I'll... I'll see what I can do."

"Thank you." Finch stepped away from the side of Liam's bed. "I'll be waiting in the kitchen."

———

Liam's kitchen was just as barren as his bedroom. There was a table, three chairs, and a whole lot of sadness. Finch wondered if he needed to intervene in Liam's life, but he put that on the backburner as *tomorrow's* activity. Tonight, he had to fix everything wrong in Oakland, including getting Charlie out of debt, and finding a serial murderer of women.

One problem at a time.

Kull sat at the table, humming to herself as she poked around on Finch's phone. She had wanted to search the internet, so he had handed it over, but it was already taking a toll on his mental wellbeing. Finch liked to check the time, and he couldn't do that while Kull played around on social media, or whatever it was she was doing.

The overhead light had a dimmer switch, so Finch kept the room mostly shrouded in darkness, in the hopes of not waking Bree with their intrusion. While he waited, Finch paced near the stove, wondering what could be in the wine.

Enzo stood by the window, staring out into the night. Occasionally, he closed his eyes and took deep breaths, and Finch wondered if the man was practicing some of the bizarre meditation tricks they had "discovered" on the car ride over.

A few moments later, Liam stumbled into the kitchen. He wore a pair of black slacks and a plain white button-up shirt. He was so thin that he almost looked like a cardboard cutout of a man wearing the clothing, his glasses barely hanging on to his nose.

Liam's eyes went wide as he turned his attention to Enzo. "Oh, no," he breathed. He backed away a few steps, his hands shaky. "Finch, you... you brought a murderous werewolf into my apartment?"

Enzo glared over at the man, but he didn't leave his spot by the window. He said nothing.

"Everything is fine," Finch said as he walked away from

the stove and stood near the tiny kitchen table. "The wine is on the counter. If you could just—"

"Bree is here." Liam fixed his glasses and shook his head. "I can't believe you would put her in this much danger."

"Bree's not in any danger," Finch growled.

Before anyone else could argue, Kull stood up from the table. She did it so fast, her chair fell backward and hit the kitchen tile with a *clack*. "Whoa, whoa! Calm down." She threw back her fiery red hair and then dramatically leaned against the side of the table as though posing for a photo shoot. "My name is Fox-Pistol, and I'm coming at you live from your very own kitchen to tell you that Enzo isn't dangerous. Bree is perfectly safe. Perfectly."

The silence that followed was just as awkward as her declarations.

Kull smoothed her slinky green dress, a coy smile on her face as though she had succeeded. At what, Finch had no idea.

"What… is going on?" Liam motioned to Kull. Then, in a tiny whisper, he asked Finch, "Is she a hooker? What is this?"

Finch took him by the shoulder and turned him to face the kitchen counter. "Liam. Focus. As soon as you identify the substance, we'll all leave. This is no more than a weird, and slightly confusing, dream."

After a deep inhale, and holding his breath for a prolonged moment, Liam nodded once and slowly shuffled his way to the counter. As he walked by Enzo, he looked the werewolf up and down, not bothering to hide his frown.

Liam was only a third the size of Enzo. The difference in their physique was drastically obvious when they stood so close.

"Are you in some sort of *fitness* protection program?" Enzo asked with a dark chuckle.

"I won't be intimidated by the likes of you," Liam stated.

With a huff, and after fidgeting with his glasses like he had no idea what to do with his hands, he said, "There's nothing you can say to me that I haven't said to myself six inches from a mirror."

Finch shoved Liam toward the counter. "You really got him with that zing, tough guy. Now, please—for the love of all that's holy—just focus on the wine bottle."

They walked over together, and Liam reached for the cupboards. Inside, there were glass bottles containing liquids of nearly every color. Witch's brews. Clearly, Liam had decided to store them in his apartment rather than his home while it underwent renovations. The brews contained distilled magics from witches, and no doubt one or two of them could help with identifying odd substances of unknown origin.

Liam's hands shook as he grabbed a brew. He clinked it against the side of the wine bottle as he set it on the counter.

His blatant unease bothered Finch, but only for a moment —until Finch thought over the situation.

Liam's wife had been killed in the middle of the night, by a more powerful warlock. He had lost a lot that night, and from the resulting fallout, including his job. Having a bunch of individuals in his home, in the middle of the night, one of whom was a werewolf, was probably scarier for a man who had just gone through so much.

As Liam examined the bottle, still shaken, Finch placed a hand on his shoulder.

"The werewolf is an old cop buddy of mine," Finch said, as calmly and as reassuring as he could muster. It wasn't particularly convincing, but he tried. "He worked for the Oakland PD as a detective. And the woman is actually Kull."

"S-She can turn into a human now?" Liam asked, his eyebrows knitted.

"No. She took over a body. That's her from now on."

"Oh…"

"I won't let anything happen to you or Bree," Finch stated —his tone now more aggressive, but he hoped it got his point across. "And you can trust Enzo and Kull. I… should've been forthcoming with information when I barged into your apartment."

Finch hated being forthcoming with information. From his perspective, there was a chance he would have to repeat this exact moment over and over again, and he wanted it to go as quickly as possible. Additionally, if everyone just *listened to him*, there would be no need for any of this, but he knew it was unreasonable to expect everyone's compliance.

He should've been more thoughtful when interacting with a man like Liam.

"*D'aww*," Kull said as she leaned onto the table and smiled at them. "You're good friends now? That's adorable. I'm so proud of you, Adair."

Finch rolled his eyes.

"Oh, it really is Kull," Liam whispered. "I… I should've known."

After he chuckled to himself, Liam poured the brew into the wine bottle and swirled the liquid around. His hands weren't as shaky, so Finch moved his hand off the man's shoulder and gave him room enough to work.

Liam poured the liquid onto the counter itself. Everything was wine-red. Then Liam grabbed a second brew and splashed it over the wine, adding to the mess on the counter. Some of the liquid even dripped onto the tile floor. Liam didn't seem to care, his attention solely on the concoction in front of him.

The red liquid shifted to a blue coloration, and then to white.

Liam ran his finger through the middle and then licked it.

Finch frowned.

"This is a mix of redwood elf magic and… a spirit's." Liam sighed. He closed his eyes and smacked his lips. "A delusion spirit, to be precise."

"Oh!" Kull stood straight, her eyes wide. "Really?"

"I think whatever was in this wine was meant to cause slight delusions." Liam opened his eyes and met Finch's gaze. "Or more like hallucinations? They wouldn't see reality properly, but only slightly. The redwood elf magic makes it seem as though… they wouldn't see specific things properly. If that makes sense."

"I suppose," Finch muttered, dwelling on the situation.

He had thought the wine would've put Charlie to sleep—like a subtler roofie. But instead, it had made her see things? Delusions? Specific delusions?

"I would need more of this wine if you want more details," Liam said. "Or maybe the spirit who provided some of its magic. The fae magic is making this potent, whereas the spirit magic is controlling what you see."

"Thank you, Liam," Finch stated. "I really appreciate your help."

Liam pushed his glasses higher onto the bridge of his nose and then nodded—ironically, allowing the glasses to fall right back into place. Then he glanced over at Enzo. "I apologize for my rudeness earlier. I, uh, haven't met any werewolves that were *not* highly aggressive."

"It's fine," Enzo said as he stepped away from the window. "If I were as small as you, I'd be pretty afraid, too."

Finch eyed him.

Enzo huffed and added, "But I really appreciate you helpin' us. Thank you, warlock."

Kull clapped her hands. "Okay! Now that we know the elves were giving Charlie delusions, what're we going to do?"

"We're going to see how she died," Finch said as he rewound time.

Everything froze. The color drained from the apartment. And then shapes melted away until there was nothing.

When Finch opened his eyes again, he was in the woods where Fox-Pistol had been murdered, just outside Oakland.

It was 5:29 p.m.

CHAPTER
TWENTY-FOUR

Kull sat up, her red hair full of twigs. She patted herself clean as much as possible.

"I'm really glad you can just rewind time like this," Kull said. "You saved us a drive back."

Finch walked over, scooped Kull up into his arms, and grunted as he straightened his posture. "Yeah. Woo. Really saving time."

Together, they returned to Finch's vehicle. The worried onlookers, and handyman, all gathered close, but Finch reassured them he had everything handled before placing Kull in the vehicle and then getting into the driver's seat. Once he started driving, Kull offered him a smile.

"Wasn't it great to have a friend like Liam to call on in the middle of the night?" she asked.

Finch sighed. "Where are you going with this?"

"I just think Bree's idea about having your own office, and coworkers, would be good. For everyone. But especially you."

"Oh, yeah? You're an expert on human relations now?"

Kull waggled her hand back and forth. "Maybe." Then she pointed at Finch. "Ever since I started following you around, you've been really distant—and you never spend time with anyone. But now we've met a bunch of your old friends, and you have people you can count on to help you."

"I'm just doing my job," Finch muttered.

"*And having a good time,*" Kull said in a singsong tone. "Don't deny it."

Finch rolled his eyes and remained quiet. He didn't want to think about opening a PI business, or running an office. He just wanted to focus on what the redwood elves were doing to Charlie. Clearly, something was going on, and the faster he understood their motives, the better.

When Finch arrived at the building that housed both the Oasis and Level 22, Enzo was already outside waiting for them. He already had his hobo outfit on, and the moment Enzo spotted Finch's car, he jogged over and threw open the back door.

"Finally," Enzo said as he took a seat. He leaned forward and held out his arm. "You said you needed to draw the Mark of Chronos on me every time you reset things, right? Let's do that first, before we forget."

Finch pulled out his pen and drew the mark on both Kull and Enzo. Then he turned the vehicle and headed for the Lake Merritt Grand Hotel.

"Okay, so what's our game plan?" Enzo asked. He leaned forward, an arm draped around each front seat so he was practically leaning over the center console. "We're going to force some elves to talk? If we're busting skulls, maybe I can practice some of that meditation."

Finch shook his head. "We're going inside, finding Charlie, watching her for a bit, and then going up to her suite before she gets there. Since she dies near her coffee table, we can just watch what happens while hidden in one of the rooms."

"Why?" Enzo glanced over. "You can rewind time, right?

Why not just blow in there and get the answers through force?"

"I don't do that," Finch stated. "Carter and I made rules. Unless it's absolutely necessary, I try to avoid ultra violence —or treating people like *things*."

Enzo was technically correct. Finch *could* bust into the hotel, punch a few elves in the face, and force the answers out of them. Then he could rewind time, and none of the elves would remember anything. But Finch would remember. And right now, the thought of torturing people still bothered him. He never wanted that to change, but he knew if he started doing it on the regular, it would get easier and easier.

Until he did it all the time.

Enzo stared at Finch for a long time. Once they found a spot in the middle of a packed parking lot, Kull dramatically leapt from the vehicle, still smiling. Enzo grabbed Finch's arm and stopped him from leaving.

"You mean what you said?" Enzo asked. "You really take this time-rewind thing seriously?"

Finch narrowed his eyes. "Of course I do."

"Heh." Enzo relaxed. "I remember you and Carter— always a class act, the pair of you. I'm glad that's still true."

Then Enzo stepped out of the vehicle.

Finch quickly followed him.

When Kull hopped over to his side, her smile brightening the whole parking lot, Finch removed his coat and handed it over. This was faster than getting her new clothing every night, and her skin was already covered in goosebumps.

"Thank you, Adair." She pulled the coat on this time. It was large for her, and covered all of her green dress. "Are we ready to solve a murder mystery?"

"No one has been murdered yet," Finch stated.

"But *soon*," Kull said with a giggle.

A random man a few cars down in the packed parking lot lifted his head, his brow furrowed, his expression set to *incredulous*.

Finch ignored the man. Time would be rewound eventually.

Together, they walked into the Lake Merritt Grand Hotel. Once again, the bellhops gave Finch and Enzo side-eye, but the moment they spotted Kull, their suspicions were put to rest. Fox-Pistol and her personal bodyguards—that was how everyone saw them.

As they entered the lobby, Finch veered toward the elevator, and the other two followed along. Finch pressed the fourth-floor button. The guide above the buttons stated the fourth floor was for 'Games,' and Finch knew if Charlie was gambling, that was where she'd be.

When the elevator door slid open, a man stood waiting on the other side. It was a redwood elf—one of the knights that Liligale kept close. The wiry man wore an impeccable suit and offered a gracious smile.

"Good evening." The elf turned his attention to Fox-Pistol. "Ah, Samantha Garson. Our guest of honor for the weekend. I'm so pleased to meet you."

Kull stepped forward and smiled. "I can't wait to see what games are going on."

The elf motioned to the floor. There were dozens of card tables, some more exclusive than others. Signs were placed near each one that indicated the minimum amount of money bet in order to join. It ranged from ten dollars, all the way to ten thousand. Finch figured there was a private room somewhere, because Charlie hadn't slowly racked up millions of dollars of debt by playing the ten grand table.

"Tonight, we're offering a wide array of games," the elf said. He pointed to the tables as he listed them off. "We have games of Pai Gow Poker, Texas Hold'em, Seven Card Stud, and Omaha Hi-Lo Split. Would you like to join a table? Or would you like us to show you a private venue for you and your associates?"

At first, Finch thought he would need to take over the conversation, but to his surprise, Kull gently touched the elf man's arm.

"I was hoping we could play at a table that would accommodate people like me." Kull fluttered her lashes. "I'm sure you have something like that?"

It was easy to determine if someone was magical once in contact with them. The elf's expression shifted when he realized Kull was a spirit—or a *half-spirit*, really—and he nodded once in reply.

"Oh, forgive me. Our internal briefing didn't mention... this. I'll take you to our back room." The elf bowed his head and then strode out across the gambling hall.

Kull waved Finch and Enzo along, practically laughing as she hurried after the knight. The mortals playing cards barely looked up from their games, most of them focused. Finch took note of the scantily clad women serving drinks. They offered champagne, wine, and tall glasses of beer.

He leaned close to Kull. "Can you still smell the magic here?"

"It's mostly fae magic," Kull whispered to him. "But I smell the delusion spirit... Its magic's in all the drinks. Cleverly hidden."

Finch leaned over to Enzo. "Do you smell anything?"

"Just the alcohol and the elves," he replied. Enzo shoved his hands into his sweatpants pockets, his shoulders tense. "Some smoke. And cleaner. I think they're specifically making it difficult to determine if there's magic in the drinks."

"Probably," Finch muttered.

The knight led them to a black door and opened it with

his key card. Inside was a luxurious space, complete with a small bar, lounge chairs, a large TV, and three card tables, each manned by a dealer. The whole room was done in black and gold, except for one wall, which was covered in ivy, creating a burst of green that made the place feel alive. Smaller potted plants, some of which looked like small redwoods, filled every corner.

It all added to the expensive atmosphere.

Only one card table was in use. It had two players—a man and a woman—and then there was a redwood elf dealer, a small woman with short black hair tinged green like all the others. Four empty chairs were waiting for additional players, and the knight motioned to one.

"Right this way, Miss Garson," the elf said, ignoring both Enzo and Finch.

That was fine. Finch was more than happy to play the role of silent bodyguard. He didn't want to drink or gamble anyway.

Kull stood still for a moment, her eyes on the cards. Then she stiffened. "Oh, wait, he's talking to me," she murmured. "Right. Yes. Thank you so much." She took a seat at the table, her smile somehow growing wider.

"We have a new player," the woman dealer said. She gathered up the cards, switched them out for a new deck, and then nodded to Kull. "Pleased to see you, Miss Garson. I didn't realize you'd be coming to the back room this evening."

"I'm full of surprises," Kull said. Then she turned her attention to the other players. "And you are?"

"You can call me Charlie," the woman at the far end of the table said.

Finch immediately turned his attention to her. Now that she was alive, Finch understood why Jay-W had fallen for her.

Charlie had probably been a bombshell in the '00s. She was in her late thirties or early forties now, no doubt in Finch's mind, but she still retained most of her innate beauty. Charlie wore her dark brown hair up in curls, each one defying gravity with its own unique bounce and vitality. The lights in the chandeliers overhead seemed to play favorites, because they caught certain strands of hair and made them glow.

Charlie's skin, kissed by California beach sunlight, was radiant, even inside, at the very heart of a casino. She wore a chunky gold necklace that rested against her collarbone, complementing the simple sophistication of her sleeveless blouse and black skirt.

She also wore the same wedding ring Finch had seen on her lifeless body.

How did Charlie go from being perfectly alive and alert to dead in her hotel room?

Finch glanced at his clock.

6:10 p.m.

She would be dead in a little over three hours. They just had to wait and see how.

"You can call me Rad," the man at the card table said.

Rad was an odd name, but Finch didn't say anything.

He was obviously partially fae, with shimmering black hair that was just a little *too* lustrous. He wore a snappy button-up shirt and fitted pair of jeans, and clearly was here to play cards—and nothing else. He impatiently tapped his fingers on the felt of the table.

"You both can call me Fox-Pistol," Kull said, placing a hand on her chest. "And I'm here to gamble." She glanced over her shoulder at Finch, as though trying to ask if that was okay.

He nodded once, but then backed away to the corner of

the room. Enzo followed, and the two of them watched from afar, acting more like lamps than people.

"The starting bet is a hundred," the dealer said in a sweet tone.

"One hundred dollars?" Kull tilted her head.

"Uh, no. A hundred *thousand* dollars, Miss Garson."

"Oh!" Kull sat a little straighter. "Can I... charge it to my room?" She asked the question as though she didn't know what it truly meant. Like someone repeating the line from a movie, hoping it worked in real life.

"You absolutely can," the dealer replied with a smile. "We'll keep track of the numbers, and if you have any questions, you can speak with the croupier."

Kull softly clapped her hands. "Oh, yay! Excellent."

"You should also know we keep a soothsayer in our employ." The dealer motioned to a woman behind the small bar. Finch hadn't noticed her until this moment—she was small, and blended with the shadows well.

Kull waved to the woman. "A soothsayer? You mean a half moon witch who uses her powers to detect magic. And see dreams? I'm, uh, not very familiar with soothsayers."

"She makes sure no one is actively using magic during the game," the dealer said matter-of-factly. "If you're found to be manipulating any magics, or using any sort of tricks, you'll be in trouble with all the fae here on the Pacific. Do you understand?"

"That makes a lot of sense," Kull stated.

"What game do you want to play, Fox-Pistol?" Charlie asked.

Kull tapped her chin. "Can we play the card game that's on the computer? You know. The one every computer has?"

"Are you talking about *solitaire?*" Rad asked, almost flabbergasted.

"*No,*" Kull dramatically said. She nervously continued

with, "I meant… *the other one.*" But it was obvious to Finch she had meant solitaire. He held back his own chuckle, if only because Kull was pretty hilarious as a human.

If she had her own TV show, he'd watch it.

"Why don't we start with blackjack?" the dealer suggested. "And if we want, we can move on to something more complicated."

CHAPTER
TWENTY-FIVE

"Okay, so how much have I won?" Kull asked.

"After that last, brilliantly played hand, you currently owe the house nine hundred thousand dollars," the dealer replied.

Kull nodded along with the statement. Then she bit her lip. "Hm. That's a lot of dollars."

"Indeed. You're always welcome to stop at any time to get your finances in order."

Kull shook her head. "No, no. I haven't even shouted *double or nothing* yet, and everyone in a movie or a TV show does that when they're gambling, so it's on my bucket list."

But Finch barely paid attention to that. He crept around the edge of the room, under the guise of "patrolling," and instead watched as the elves brought complimentary drinks and hors d'oeuvres. The wine was the same as the wine in Charlie's room, and it was poured into glasses with fancy silver stems, likely made from crystal in the depths of France or some shit.

Kull refused the food and drink, which Finch was thankful for, but both Charlie and Rad accepted.

However, whenever Finch tried to get closer to the table, one of the redwood elves would step between him and the table, and calmly state it was only for players, to better ensure there was no cheating.

That was fine—Finch already knew the wine had some sort of delusion properties, thanks to Liam's analysis. And sure enough, the longer the night went on, the more Charlie and Rad lost.

Kull also lost frequently. Just… too much. Finch was glad he could rewind time, because if he couldn't, he knew there were going to be some problems down the road.

After several hours of observation, Enzo motioned to the door with a tilt of his head. Finch walked over, and the two of them stepped outside, much to the suspicion of the elves in the room. They didn't follow Finch and Enzo out, though.

"What is it?" Finch whispered.

"Did you see that?" Enzo grabbed Finch by the shoulder. "The cards. Did you see them?"

"They were too far away for me to see anything."

Enzo tapped his face near his eye. "Wolves have better sight than humans. I saw. I saw everything."

Finch crossed his arms. "Okay. What happened? Why are you so bothered?"

"There were times Charlie made plays that didn't even make sense. Asking for more when it was obvious she should've stayed."

After a quick shrug, Finch said, "People make mistakes. Especially if they've been drinking."

"No. You don't understand. I watched Charlie make good calls. Then she started making *bizarre* calls. The point of the game is to hit twenty-one without going over, right? So if you had twenty in your hand, why would you ever ask for more?"

Finch mulled it over. He had watched the players steadily

lose more and more, but that could be attributed to a fair number of things. When he glanced up toward the ceiling, he spotted three cameras, all built into the corners of the hallway. No doubt, there were more—he just couldn't see them. And if the casino had hundreds of cameras, to prevent cheating, they would have footage of their own dealers.

If Finch wanted, he could watch the tapes to corroborate Enzo's statements, but what was the point? Enzo wouldn't lie about this. What they needed to figure out was how the elves were pulling off their tricks.

"Wait," Finch whispered.

Enzo lifted an eyebrow. "Yeah?"

"Do you remember the cards Charlie was holding? The specific cards?"

Enzo nodded. "I took years of training specifically to remember minute details. You never know when those bastard lawyers will throw in a curveball question about the color of someone's shoes just to prove you weren't observant. I remember all her damn cards."

"When she made mistakes—did her cards have similar suits?"

Liam had said the delusion magic in the wine made certain things appear like others. If Charlie were just seeing *random illusions*, she would know she was drugged. She'd probably start freaking out, and wouldn't continue playing a game of cards.

But what if…

"She always had spades in her hand when she made horrendous calls," Enzo stated. His eyes narrowed, and he obviously came to the same conclusion as Finch. "She's probably not seeing the number on the spades correctly."

Finch pointed at him. "Yeah. She's seeing something different."

"The elves are cheating. Just… subtly."

To get Charlie to fail. Probably men like Rad, too. And it was so muted as to be undetectable by most. Especially since not even a werewolf could detect the magic in the wine—it took a half-spirit, Kull, to even know something was wrong with the drink. And since the elves prevented anyone from using magic of their own, *and* had a soothsayer to make sure no one activated any magical abilities, this was a game that appeared legit on the surface.

Before Finch could do anything else, the door opened and Kull slipped out. She smiled, half waved, and then hopped to Finch's side.

"I quit playing," she said. "I hit one million dollars!"

"Owed?" Enzo asked.

Kull nodded. "That's right. I know the point of card games is to win, but I was having so much fun just learning the game." She rubbed the tips of her fingers together. "And also, the wax on the cards felt weird. I liked it—all textured—and it was amazing just to hold them."

Which confirmed everything Finch suspected. The spade cards were rigged.

"Let's go," Finch stated. He glanced at his clock.

8:34 p.m.

"We have plenty of time to scope out the murder scene before it happens." Charlie wasn't set to perish until around 9:40 p.m., and Finch wanted to make sure he could see it when it happened.

———

Finch, Enzo, and Kull made it to the top floor, and then walked right by Fox-Pistol's suite. The party inside was raging, but Finch didn't want to stop by and speak with anyone there—Charlie's impending murder was far more important.

He unlocked the door with Kull's mischief magic and then let the others inside. The room was just how it had been before—multiple large couches, a bar, doors that led to private bedrooms, and even a balcony with a built-in pool.

The coffee table was between the couches, and this time, it wasn't stained with blood. It was a normal stone coffee table, perfectly in its place.

"Do you think the redwood elves know we're in here?" Kull asked.

"I think, if they wanted, they could figure it out," Finch muttered. He headed for the bar and immediately began rummaging through the wine bottles. "But since you belong here—and belong on this floor—I doubt they have much reason to be suspicious."

"What if one of them recognized you?"

Finch glanced over his shoulder and huffed. "Unless I say my name, no one here is likely to know who I am. I'm not friends with any redwood elves, and I haven't been to Oakland in over a decade."

Enzo joined him at the bar. He carefully grazed his fingertips over some of the countertops and searched for dust or other signs of disturbance. However, since the hotel was immaculate, there wasn't a speck of dust. Enzo snorted and then counted the number of glasses, as though making sure nothing was out of place or disturbed.

"I think we should investigate the closets, especially in the bathrooms, and then move on to the ceilings in the closets of the bedrooms," Enzo stated. "Most of those areas have hidden service hatches or entryways, and perhaps we can learn something."

Kull bounded over to the bar. "You both sound like you know what you're doing."

"After you've investigated a dozen or so hotels, you start to see the patterns." Enzo tapped the side of his head. "What we should do is just make sure we're not surprised by someone coming in from a random location. Then we find a place that's reasonably hidden, and we wait for the show to begin."

Finch smirked. "You sound like you're comfortable with what's going to happen. Already used to my time powers, are you?"

"Your magic is simple enough to grasp," Enzo said, dismissively waving his hand. "It's not rocket science."

"You're just as cocky as ever."

Enzo placed a hand on his chest. "Before I left the force, I was given both a Medal of Merit and a Silver Star Medal for my efforts in making the city a better place. I was a damn good police officer, and certainly smart enough to solve this case."

"I knew you'd bring those damn medals up at some point." Finch chuckled as he walked out of the bar. "No one cares about your glorified smiley-face stickers."

Enzo placed one hand on the bar counter and then effortlessly leapt straight over. He gracefully landed and then jogged to Finch's side. "Hey. Carter appreciated my medals. Most people do. Don't get jealous."

"Can I see your medals?" Kull asked. She grabbed a bottle of wine and sniffed the glass exterior. "I think it's amazing you earned some! They sound awesome."

But Enzo grew quiet. He shoved his hands into his sweatpants. "I left them with my wife. I was hoping she'd give them to my daughter one day. Ya know—so she had something to remember her father by."

His tone had lost all emotion. Every word he said might as well have been read by an AI chat program.

Finch took a deep breath. Then he said, in a slow tone, "You know, since I can rewind time, we could go visit—"

"We should be focusing on the task at hand," Enzo growled.

He motioned to the room with an angry flick of his wrist. "Let's get this over with. Time is running out."

"Right," Finch muttered. "Right."

———

No service hatches.

No secret ways into the hotel room.

Once they had secured everything, Finch opened a cabinet in the bar and found it to be spacious enough for a full-grown adult man to lie down inside. And since the bar was attached to the living room, and facing the coffee table, he figured he could make a hole through the wood paneling —a small hole to see through, but not large enough to be immediately noticeable—and view the entirety of the murder.

However, since he wasn't carrying power tools, Finch needed a way to drill through the wood.

Which was where Enzo came in.

The man tapped into his lycanthrope power and transformed. Just like when he was a bartender, Enzo shifted his form so he was half wolf, half man. He still wore his tank top and sweatpants, and they fit his muscled form a little more snugly as a werewolf, but they weren't restrictive in any way.

Enzo's black fur was lustrous, and his ears stood tall.

With claws at the tips of his fingers, he was able to whittle a small hole in the bar without much trouble.

Kull watched intently the whole time, smiling wide. "Wow, it's aces that you can do this," she said. "And it's really amazing you can transform whenever you want."

"I practiced that a lot," Enzo muttered as he finished up. When he stood, he needed to wipe small bits of wood particles from his long snout. "But it doesn't matter. If I get too angry—especially in this form—I'll just lose control."

Kull inhaled and then exhaled. "You have to remember to chillax."

Enzo's ear twitched and turned to face the door of the hotel room. He tensed, the black fur on the back of his neck standing on end.

"Someone's headin' this way," he whispered.

Finch pointed to one of the bedroom doors. "You two hide in there. Hurry."

"But—" Kull said.

"Go," Finch commanded.

Enzo nodded, and Kull hesitantly followed. As they headed for the bedroom, Finch pulled out his phone and glanced at the time.

9:02 p.m.

Charlie was returning to her room early. Finch wondered if it was because Kull had joined Charlie's card game, whereas that hadn't happened in the previous iterations of the day. But whatever the reason, she was here now.

He slid into the cabinet and lay down on his back. It wasn't comfortable, but it wasn't the worst spot he had ever been in. Finch began to close the cabinet door, but someone grabbed it.

Finch tensed, ready to use magical flames, but then he recognized Kull. She quickly slid into his hiding spot with him. Unfortunately, the cabinet wasn't roomy enough for two fully-grown adults, and Kull had to clamber her way on top of Finch.

"*What are you doing?*" he hissed, practically fighting with her the whole time. "Are you insane?"

Kull clung to his clothing like a barnacle on the side of a ship. "I'm scared," she breathed, her voice distant.

"What?" Finch barked out between clenched teeth. "There's nothing to be afraid of. We're—"

"I just feel safer with you!" Kull blurted. She tensed and somehow clung even harder. "I don't want to watch someone die. I don't want to be reminded that now *I'll* someday die. What if I don't do all the things I wanted to do before then? I just... I'm scared, Adair."

The suite door opened with a beep and a click.

Finch pulled Kull all the way into their cramped place and shut the cabinet door as quietly as possible. He was on his back, one arm awkwardly around Kull's waist, and she was bunched up on top of him, all her weight practically on his stomach and chest, making breathing a chore. There was no moving left or right. There wasn't even much light—only a small trickle through the hole Enzo had created.

Kull rested her head on Finch's collarbone. "I'm sorry, Adair," she whispered.

"Shh."

Someone stumbled into the room.

Followed closely by two others.

CHAPTER
TWENTY-SIX

"I told you I'd get you the money!" Charlie shouted. The sound of her stomping filled the vast living room of her suite.

Finch, stuffed in the cabinet, his shoulder blades pressed against the unforgiving wood, just lay there, listening. He couldn't see anything yet, and instead stared up into the darkness of his hiding spot.

Atop him, Kull took deep breaths, the telltale signs of panic setting in.

"We had an agreement," a woman said, her voice proper and lyrical.

Liligale. The Head of the Pacific Court. She was here to speak to Charlie personally, it seemed. She walked into the suite with footfalls Finch could barely hear. The same for the person following her. He figured it was Liligale's knight.

"Your due date for the money is this Friday, Mrs. Woolsy," Liligale said. "If you don't have it by then, I'll be forced to send a courier out to your husband. I'm sure he can find a way to settle your debts just fine."

Someone slammed into the bar. Finch tensed as the

whole cabinet shook, and the rattle of wineglasses echoed throughout the space. Someone grabbed a wine bottle, dragging the heavy glass object across the bar, no care in their movements. Then they poured themselves a drink and slammed the bottle down on the countertop.

"This has nothin' to do with Jay-W," Charlie snapped, her voice next to the cabinet. She was the one downing the wine —Finch pictured it all in his mind's eye.

"You're his wife, Mrs. Woolsy. By law—both mortal and magical—he can be called upon to fulfill your debts."

"Don't you *dare* fuckin' talk to my husband! D-Don't even talk *about* him. I don't need no... no... prissy bitch fae to tell me what I got to do."

Charlie's slurred speech betrayed how inebriated she was.

"Mrs. Woolsy—"

"*Stop calling me that*. I can handle my own debts. I'll get you the goddamn money." Charlie stomped her way over to the couch.

Kull's breathing intensified. She trembled, and tensed, and Finch could only assume it was because Charlie was close to her moment of death. He awkwardly moved one arm around until he could gently rub Kull's shoulder.

"Don't listen," Finch whispered. "I'll rewind time in just a moment."

It only took a few seconds, but Kull stopped her shaking. She wrapped her arms over her head, blocking out the world. Finch continued to provide a comforting presence—even if she was restricting some of his air and agitating his back. She was lithe, and didn't actually weigh much, but still. Their positioning was not optimal, and a little *too* close. Finch kept his mind squarely on the drama unfolding in the living room.

"My husband doesn't have millions of dollars just lying around! He owns things. Land. Businesses. Stocks. He doesn't have the cash, so don't even bother. *I'll get it.*"

Charlie's voice rose with each sentence, but since there was a party just down the hall, and these were gigantic suites, Finch figured no one would hear.

"We're quite accustomed to people trading deeds in order to pay off their debts, Mrs. Woolsy," Liligale stated. "It's happened many a time. And Jay-W just so happens to own some of the waterfront property around here, so…"

"You're a bunch of leeches," Charlie snapped.

"It isn't our fault you have a problem with gambling. We offer facilities, and those who want to participate are welcome. You could've stopped long before now."

Charlie didn't have a comeback for that.

But Finch knew what was really going on. If Jay-W's wife started gambling, and couldn't read the cards correctly, she'd quickly start owing the elves some cash.

What Finch *didn't* know was why she kept coming back— or why she hadn't gone to Jay-W sooner. Why was Charlie hiding all this from her husband?

"Get out of my fuckin' face," Charlie shouted. "*Get out.* This is my room still, isn't it? I have t-till Friday? Get out!"

Her shouting bordered on the hysterical. When Finch glanced through the small hole in the cabinet, he spotted Charlie pacing around the coffee table, her movements uncoordinated. She waved her wineglass around, sloshing the red liquid out and spilling it across the floor.

"That's quite enough," Liligale stated. "This is your final warning."

It was difficult to see much—given the tiny hole—but Finch clearly saw Charlie hurl wine at the elf. Normally, in fae courts, such disrespect would never be tolerated. Thankfully, they weren't physically in the court, or else Charlie would've been executed right here and now. Out in the mortal realm, the fae were a little more forgiving.

Unfortunately, they weren't *completely* forgiving.

The knight stepped forward, grabbed Charlie by the shoulder, and attempted to pull her toward the door. An awkward struggle ensued. Charlie ripped her body out of the elf's hands but then stumbled backward. She gasped as she fell, neck-first, into the corner of the stone coffee table.

The resulting *crack* and *thump* were both disturbing and unmistakable. Charlie's death was, in fact, an accident. The fae hadn't *wanted* her dead. They *wanted* her husband to fork over land to pay Charlie's debt. And her dead body would complicate matters.

No wonder they had been distressed the first time Finch arrived. They had been dealing with *this* situation.

"Forgive me," the knight whispered.

Then he said something in the tongue of the fae—words of magic. Finch didn't understand them. Kull would probably understand, but since her head was in her arms, and firmly pressed against his chest, he doubted she heard anything.

"Quickly," Liligale hissed. "We must leave. Tell Rinfandall. Get him to handle this. No one is to find out we were here, do you understand me?" Liligale was simple and firm with her instructions. She wasn't fazed by the death, nor did she seem particularly sad.

"I'll see to it at once," her knight said.

And then the two of them hurried from the room, their steps soft.

Finch didn't need to see anything else. He knew what had happened. The only remaining piece of the puzzle was Charlie's motivations, and even then, they weren't particularly important.

The redwood elves had set Charlie up—and their real goal was to take property from Jay-W. Charlie, for some reason unknown to Finch, had been racking up this debt in secret. Her husband, unaware of her location or activities, just assumed she was having an affair. When Jay-W learned the truth, he would surely be both relieved and enraged.

And now that Finch knew all that, he rewound time.

The dark cabinet faded, and everything turned to white.

When Finch blinked his eyes, he found himself in the woodlands just outside Oakland. The time? 5:29 p.m., just as before.

Kull, on the ground, sat up with twigs in her fiery red hair. Her green dress was dirty, and pale skin smudged with mud. After a few pats, and carefully removing the leaves from her locks, Kull offered Finch a hesitant smile.

"I'm sorry, Adair." She smiled as she continued, "I don't know what came over me." She playfully smacked the side of her head. "I was just being silly."

Finch crunched through the undergrowth until he was at Kull's side. He knelt, scooped her into his arms, and then headed for the road, his mind half on Charlie, and half on Kull's bizarre crisis.

"I really am okay," she said.

"I believe you," Finch muttered.

"We were playing card games," Kull elaborated, despite the fact Finch hadn't asked. "Charlie seemed *nice*. And she was talking about all the things she was planning on doing, like traveling. Then I remembered she was going to die, and that thought just kept... hurting. In my chest. Whenever I thought about it."

"Why didn't you say anything?" Finch asked. "You could've voiced that concern at any time before jumping into the cabinet with me. We could've talked about it."

"I thought—maybe this is normal for humans. Like hunger. I thought I was dying when I was hungry, but I was just overreacting. Maybe my chest hurting was just me *overreacting again*." Kull wrapped her arms around Finch's neck and held him tightly. "But I'm totally fine. One hundred percent. Everything is good."

She didn't sound *good*.

But Finch wasn't sure what to say.

"What's the plan now?" Kull asked.

As Finch stepped over a downed branch, he replied, "We go get Charlie. We talk to her, bring her to Jay-W, and explain everything that's happened."

"What about the elves? Aren't they doing something bad? Shouldn't we stop them?"

Finch sighed and rolled his eyes. "It's not my job to solve every damn problem that comes along."

"But I thought you and Enzo said they were cheating? Or something? I don't think I got all the details. Shouldn't you stop that so they can't cheat other people?"

As Finch stepped out onto the street and dealt with the handyman and all the onlookers, he quietly mulled over the situation. What was he going to do? Pay off Charlie's debt? Call the elves on their theft? Point out the trick with their playing cards?

They were likely to try to kill him for spilling the beans.

And it was obvious to Finch that Liligale was more than willing to cover up a murder in furtherance of her goals.

As Finch set Kull on the passenger-side seat, she chuckled. "I, uh, don't want to think they're going to hurt—or kill—other humans, Adair. My chest hurts when I imagine those things."

After a long and pained exhale, Finch said, *"Fine*. We'll figure it out. We'll bring down the redwood elves and their whole operation."

"Really?" Kull perked up. "You promise?"

"I promise."

He shut her door and then walked around his vehicle. When he sat in the driver's seat, Kull was just staring at him.

He clicked his seat belt on, and her eyes practically drilled through his body.

"What is it?" Finch asked, irritation slipping into his speech.

"Do you think I'm terrible at being a human? For freaking out back there?"

Finch started his Toyota. "No. You're not terrible at being a human. Everyone has moments like that."

"Do you?" Kull whispered.

But Finch didn't reply to that. As he drove the car toward the rendezvous with Enzo, he said, "You have a lot to learn about being human, so don't worry if things seem strange or off. If you have questions, just ask me. Don't hide anything."

"Because I can trust you? *Always* trust you?"

"Of course you can trust me." Finch shot her a sideways glare. "I said I'd help you be a human, and that's what I'll do."

Kull nodded once, her gaze falling to her lap. Her smile stayed with her, but it was more melancholy than before. Or perhaps more pensive. Finch wasn't entirely sure, and he didn't want to waste any more time dwelling on it.

The drive through Oakland was starting to become second nature. He was outside the Oasis club within no time, and Enzo—quick to pick up on the routine—was already there, waiting. Dressed in his sweats and tank top, he hopped into the back seat and relaxed.

"I saw everything," Enzo said as soon as the door was shut. "I kept the door cracked just a bit, and listened to the whole damn conversation. Those redwood elves *obviously* set up Jay-W's wife so they can get their grubby hands on his property."

Finch pulled the car away from the curb and started back toward the hotel.

"We're going to stop the redwood elves from ever doing that again," Kull said matter-of-factly.

Enzo laughed and punched the back of Finch's seat. "Is that right? Just for the fun of it we're gonna stop their whole operation? Or is someone payin' you to do this?"

After a sigh, Finch replied, "Just for the fun of it."

Kull pointed to herself. "I convinced him."

"I like this." Enzo rubbed his hands together. "Nothin' gets me fired up like takin' down scumbag criminals. They think they're so smart, but they're not gonna see *us* comin'." Then he snorted back a laugh and turned his attention to Kull. "What happened back there? You just fled and ran straight to Adair. You could've gotten us caught."

"It doesn't matter," Finch immediately interjected. "I can rewind time. We could've *all* gotten caught and just tried as many times as we wanted."

"Yeah, well, it was weird behavior."

"We don't need to discuss it," Finch said, an edge of finality to his tone. "Kull and I talked it over, and she'll be more prepared in the future. Isn't that right?" He glanced over at her.

She slowly nodded. "Yes. It won't happen again."

But before they got more than two blocks, Enzo pointed to the glove compartment. "Remember to draw the Mark of Chronos on us. Don't want to forget before we get into the thick of it."

And then Finch suddenly had a thought. "Wait... Enzo, didn't you say there were other half-spirits here in Oakland? People like Kull?"

"Yeah. Why?"

"Is one of them a spirit of delusion?"

The same thought obviously struck Enzo. His eyes widened. "Yeah..."

"Then I think—if we want to stop these elves for good—we should go have a chat with this half-spirit..."

CHAPTER
TWENTY-SEVEN

Enzo directed Finch through the bad part of Oakland —to where there were more homeless encampments than people in the entire state of Kentucky.

Decades ago, California had shut down all its mental health institutions due to the overwhelming corruption and abuse happening within, but instead of sending the patients to other locations, they were all released onto the streets. That, combined with the rise of meth's popularity, resulted in California having a problem it could never recover from.

In an attempt to give the homeless a place to live, California made it easier for them to build encampments. Tents, tarps, and moveable chain-link fences were erected in every major city to house the addicts and those considered unstable.

When Finch parked his car outside the largest encampment in Oakland, he made sure to roll down all his windows first. If he didn't, someone would surely smash them to search the inside. This way, they would just search the inside, find nothing, and leave his vehicle alone.

They wouldn't steal the car—no, that would be too much effort, and the cops would actually do something about grand theft auto. The cops wouldn't stop petty theft, though. They had bigger problems to worry about.

Enzo stepped out of the vehicle first. After he inhaled, he smiled. "See this? We're in the right place."

"Oh, I see it," Finch muttered as he got out of the car. He immediately took off his coat and handed it to Kull as she hurried around. She tied it around her waist, but then glanced down at the ground.

"I don't have any shoes," she whispered.

And this wasn't the kind of place to go barefoot.

Finch sighed again. He kicked off his shoes and pushed them over. "They're going to be too big, but just wear them, all right? As soon as we learn everything we need to here, we'll get you some shoes."

He glanced at his phone.

6:30 p.m. exactly.

If they spoke to the half-spirit quick enough, they could still get Charlie and question her before she was murdered.

Kull slipped on his large shoes and walked with high steps. Finch, mentally preparing to step on glass or needles, pinched the bridge of his nose. It would all be over soon. He just had to deal with this a little bit longer.

"Come on," Enzo said, waving them forward. "I've spoken to a lot of the guys here. Just stay close to me, and I don't think we'll have much trouble."

The homeless encampment was positioned on a plot of undeveloped land not too far from the freeway. The roar of trucks and cars made a constant melody in the background. The sun set in the distance, lighting up the sky with dumpster-fire reds. It completely set the mood.

A chain-link fence surrounded the little "town," forcing them to enter through the "front gate."

While the night sky was strewn with the glitter of distant stars, here on the Earth, a different constellation sprawled out before them—one made of a hundred twinkling campfires, most of which were contained in oil barrels. A handful of people stood around each one, warming a can of food or lighting a new cigarette.

Finch ignored most of their stares.

"Wow," Kull said, glancing around. "So many people live here! They must all be one big happy family."

She drew the most attention, and for good reason. Several of the individuals living in the tents had a bad case of *meth mouth*—where their teeth were mostly black, and their gums actively red. It dragged their appearance to new lows. Kull, on the other hand, was a supermodel of legendary status.

Enzo deftly navigated the sea of blue tarps and cardboard, sidestepping the many sleeping bags dotting the walkway. The air was fragrant with the aroma of human urine—and the city's neglect.

The symphony of coughs and muttered curses was all Finch could hear of the men and women around him. He half expected someone to ask him for change, but for the most part, the people stayed far away.

Kull tugged on Finch's elbow. "I smell them," she whispered, her eyebrows raised.

"Yeah, I smell them, too," Finch quipped.

"No. Not the humans. The spirits inside bodies. They're close."

Enzo nodded, motioned them over, and then pointed to a green tent tucked into the corner of the encampment. Unlike some of the other homes, this one looked more permanent. It had stakes in the ground, cardboard around the sides to create sturdier walls, and even a bucket and old house gutter set up to collect rainwater.

When Enzo entered, Finch and Kull followed.

They stepped into what Finch could only describe as a *double-wide tent.*

It was spacious, but in a cramped way. There were "rooms" inside the tent, but the ceiling was low, and the bug-net windows made it easy to see outside and provided little privacy in turn.

There was a wooden chess board with four legs in the middle of the tent that acted like a table, and there were two sleeping bags set up on top of mountains of old newspapers.

The tent also came with two folding lawn chairs, both so worn, they were on the verge of disintegrating.

A man sat in one. He was younger than Finch had imagined—perhaps in his mid-twenties?—and he wore a pair of blue swim trunks and a white T-shirt. Nothing else.

He had disheveled chestnut hair that reached his shoulders, normal white teeth, and a complexion so pale, it was as though he hadn't seen the sun in a decade. Most notable, however, were his eyes: one blue, one brown.

The man was reclined as far back as possible, and didn't move much when Enzo, Finch, and Kull all entered. He took a swig from a bottle of beer held lazily in one hand, but otherwise had no reaction.

There was also a woman in the tent—a lady who had to be in her forties—with the frizziest blonde hair Finch had ever seen. She looked as though she had been electrocuted one too many times, and then perhaps hit by a bus. She was unhealthily thin, her brown eyes disturbingly watery, her skin sallow and nearly transparent.

She stood in the back corner of the tent, shaking and rubbing her hands together.

"W-Who are you people?" she asked. "Oh, no. You brought dirt inside." She reached into the mountain of old newspaper and withdrew a hand broom. "*Dirty, dirty, dirty,*" she whispered, more insane than coherent.

Then the woman rushed over and swept up the area just behind Finch, clearing away the dirt and pushing it outside.

The tent, for the most part, was organized, but Finch wouldn't have classified it as *clean*.

"Well, well, well," the man in the lawn chair said. "A werewolf, a warlock, and a mischief spirit all come walking into my tent. To what do I owe the pleasure of everyone's company?"

"Cut the bullshit," Enzo said. He tried to stand straight, but the ceiling of the tent was just too low. Whenever he attempted to have good posture, his bald head collided with the tent canvas. "We're here to talk to *you*." Enzo pointed at him.

The man took another swig of his beer. After a burp, he asked, "Are you sure? I think you might have the wrong guy."

Kull stepped forward, interrupting the whole conversation. "Oh, my goodness! You're *Garinmirgorthan the Error*! I know you. You're the spirit of delusion I met over a century ago."

"That's right." The man lifted his bottle. "I am Error. Nice to meet you. But most humans call me *Garret*. That's what my body was named."

Finch ran a hand down his face. Why did spirits always have such bizarre names?

The woman with the frizzy hair finished her sweeping and then tucked the hand broom away into the newspapers. She fidgeted with her hands, and it was only then that Finch realized she was wearing a black jogging outfit. It was remarkably free of stains, but not of mud.

Kull motioned to her. "And you're *Whisptenthera the Disquiet*! You're a spirit of anxiety."

"P-People just call me Whisp," the woman said. "I, uh, don't like when humans mispronounce my name." She scratched the back of her hands until her knuckles grew red. "But Whisp is good. Easy."

Garret tilted his head back. He stared at Kull for a long moment. "You're... *Kullthantarrick the Sneak*."

Kull immediately clapped. "Yes! That's right. You remembered!"

The noise clearly bothered Whisp, who tucked herself further into the corner.

"Why are you two here?" Finch asked, because he couldn't help himself. "You both inhabited dead bodies? Is that it?"

Garret pointed at Finch and then tapped his nose. "I found this body in the river. Whisp over there found her body in one of these very tents. Lucky finds, if you ask me."

"Why did you inhabit bodies?"

As far as Finch knew, most spirits didn't want to give up their immortality to become humans. Their magic became limited as well. What was the benefit, outside of becoming human?

"Don't you know?" Garret lifted an eyebrow. "Spirits don't feel emotions the same way humans do. And let's be real—they're looked down on by most people. Spirits don't grow and evolve—they're the same forever. But now that I have a body..."

Garret gestured to himself and smiled.

"I'm amazing."

He looked like a drunk frat boy.

"You're obviously delusional," Finch muttered.

Enzo waved his hand, cutting his way into the conversation. "No more distractions. Garret—do you have any delusion magic just sittin' around? Potions or brews or something?"

The man reached under his lawn chair and then lifted up a plastic bag. He handed it over to Enzo, the contents clinking around.

After glancing inside, Enzo frowned. "This is just a bag of booze."

Garret replied with two finger guns, and even made a *click, click* sound with his tongue.

"Goddammit," Enzo said with a sigh. He tossed the bag onto the empty chair. "Don't play games with me, spirit. We're here because we think you're selling your magic to the redwood elves."

"Oh."

"*Are you?*" Enzo demanded.

"Well, yeah," Garret replied with a chuckle. "They pay good money. Whisp and I need to eat thanks to our dumb, fleshy bodies."

"But food is so good," Kull said. She stepped close to Garret's chair and knelt. "And there's so much of it! Don't you enjoy it?"

Garret shrugged. "Sex is better. And so much more expensive."

"Really?" Kull asked with a thoughtful look in her eye.

Finch ran his hand down his face a second time, his cheeks burning. "Why do things like this happen to me?" He glanced up and frowned. "What would it take for you to *stop* selling your magic to the redwood elves?"

"What?" Garret narrowed his eyes. "That's, like, our only source of income." He chuckled, took another swig of his beer, and then shrugged. "I'm amazing. Utterly and truly. But humans don't see that, man. They don't want to work with me. All they want is meth, and I'm *real bad* at cookin' meth. I exploded a whole house once."

Enzo ground his teeth but said nothing.

Nothing angered the Oakland PD like all the meth heads. There had been more than a dozen explosions within the city limits in the last year alone.

"Us s-spirits don't really blend well," Whisp said from the

corner of the tent. "Everyone thinks I'm like this because I'm an addict, and then they h-hate me. I can't stand their looks. I get too flustered." She stared at the floor, her shoulders bunched at the base of her neck.

Enzo took Finch by the shoulder and then turned him away from the others. He leaned in close and whispered, "If we call the local precinct, I can tell them they were moving product. A few beat cops will come down here and arrest these two idiots. Bam. Problem solved."

Finch hesitated. When he glanced over his shoulder, he noticed Kull happily whispering with Garret. Whisp also walked over, drawn to Kull's smiling and laughing.

What would Kull think if they just sent the two half-spirits to jail?

And even then—that wouldn't stop the redwood elves forever.

"They're basically just criminals," Enzo muttered.

Finch sighed. He already knew the answer, he just didn't want to say it out loud…

CHAPTER
TWENTY-EIGHT

Finch turned around. He gave the double-wide tent one more glance. "The elves don't even pay you enough to buy a house?"

"Ha! Have you seen the price of homes?" Garret waved away the comment. "The only way to own a house nowadays is to patiently wait for Mr. Beast to give you one. The elves barely pay us enough to eat. They know we have no other options."

"That's what I thought," Finch said with a groan. He crossed his arms and then locked eyes with Garret. "How about you two stop working for the fae, and come work for me instead? I'm opening a PI firm, and—"

"Aren't you *Adair Finch*?" Whisp interjected with a frown. "Every spirit kn-knows about you, and your control over time." She wrung her hands. "You do everything! No task too big, no crime too small. You don't need anyone to assist you."

"That was… before my brother died," Finch said, his words cold, but not like ice—they were cold like how a rock was cold. He didn't like talking about it, even if he had come to terms with the situation. "So, now that I don't have him, maybe I could use a *little* help."

"You can't be serious." Enzo grabbed Finch's shoulder. "They're criminals. They openly admitted to possession with intent to sell."

"They won't do that if I'm around."

"Is offerin' people a job how you solve every problem? Huh?"

Finch pulled himself from Enzo's grasp. "Only the people who I think could be useful."

"Feh. These bums? They can't help you. They can barely help themselves."

"Hey there," Garret said. He held up a finger. "I have been alive, and a human, for *years* now. Same with Whisp."

Enzo sarcastically looked around. "Wow. You've done an amazing job. Almost making my argument for me."

"What's that supposed to mean?"

"That you weird body-stealing half-spirits are social pariahs for a reason." Enzo jabbed a finger at him, pointing with authority. "You're incompetent, you'll never get better, and you should've left well enough alone and just *stayed* spirits."

The inside of the tent got quiet. Finch immediately turned to face Kull. She wrung her hands with the same anxious energy as Whisp, and she refused to make eye contact. The color in her cheeks had faded, her gaze distant.

Finch knew what she was thinking—from her fear of messing up to her nightmares of never quite being human.

But Enzo was a cop at heart, who just spit facts as he saw them, regardless of how others would take them. He hadn't seen how much Kull had wanted this, or how much Kull had "researched" before taking her new role. Kull wanted this with every fiber of her being, and from Finch's experience, that was one of the prerequisites to greatness.

"They can do it," Finch stated, loud and with confidence.

When Enzo faced him, Finch glared.

The two men had a prolonged staring contest until Finch continued with, "They just need someone to help guide them. If they work for me, I can lend them a helping hand."

"How are they gonna work for you?" Enzo motioned to the bag of booze. "This is probably the least fantastical version of fantasy outside of fantasy football. The elves had to mix their fae magic in with the spirit's for a reason—they're weak."

"They're not necessarily weak."

"Their magic makes you see suits of cards differently. So what? How's that gonna help?"

"You could use a spirit of delusion to do all sorts of things, from minor illusions, to concealing your magical nature, to giving someone nightmares or—"

"The keyword is *minor*," Enzo snapped.

Kull stepped forward. "Adair has been helping me, and I'm doing amazingly as a human!"

Garret scratched at the waistband of his swim trunks as he looked her up and down. "Are you wearing someone else's shoes? And coat? I mean, I hate to hurt your case here, but you look like you just rolled out of a ditch."

Kull hugged herself and stepped away. Any confidence she had melted faster than an ice cube in a volcano.

And that was the last straw for Finch.

"I didn't ask for everyone's assessment," Finch said, his words on the edge of shouting. "Kull has only been a human for a handful of days. She's going to be fine, I can tell. And the two of *you*—" Finch gestured to Whisp and Garret, "—can be infinitely more than what you are right now, if you just give a damn."

Kull perked up a bit, her expression hopeful.

Whisp patted at her frizzy hair. "I've never met a warlock

who would h-help us without… us needing to make a pact." She held out her hand. "Is that what you want? I can, give you my magic… The powers of worry, doubt, anxiety, and dread."

"You're not *just* spirits anymore," Finch said, trying to calm his temper. "You're also humans now, and I'm in the business of helping humans. So, what's it going to be? Are you going to take my offer?"

Garret and Whisp exchanged hesitant glances.

"Wait." Kull leapt in front of Garret. "Don't work for Adair. Come work for *me*."

"You?" Garret tilted his head with all the curiosity of a golden retriever.

"I'm a super successful social media influencer!" Kull flashed a peace sign, smiled, and then winked. "I'm Fox-Pistol. Smash that like button and join my crew!"

Whisp lifted both eyebrows. "R-Really? I, well, don't know. We don't have any skills for, uh, social media people."

"You can be my bodyguards. Or something."

Enzo laughed. He tried to stifle it, but he couldn't. He coughed and stamped down his mirth. "Everyone here is insane," he murmured. "These lunatics can't help in a fight—they can't even rip up baby photos."

"I think this is a good idea," Finch stated.

If the half-spirits worked together, helping each other, they would feel more accomplished. Plus, they could watch each other's backs and stay out of trouble. Additionally, if Fox-Pistol could afford suites in high-class hotels and one million dollars' worth of gambling debt, she could *definitely* afford to take on two new hires, even if they weren't actually doing anything.

And Finch was impressed with Kull's willingness to step up to the plate. She didn't have to help them—Finch was already going to do that—but she came forward regardless.

"Okay," Garret stated. "Sounds like a plan." He held out a hand to shake. "Let's do this."

Kull shook it, a wide smile on her face.

And while Enzo didn't say anything, he crossed his arms and sighed, his expression conveying all the doubt he held in his thoughts. But then, after a deep breath, Enzo said, "Well, I hope this works. Legitimately."

"It will," Kull said, defiant. "It'll definitely work. Right, Adair?"

He nodded.

Again, her happiness clearly soared.

"Well, now that we know they will accept a job offer, it's time to go back," Finch stated. He was done with the tent, the smells, and strange noises coming from the encampment.

"We're going to have to do this again?" Kull frowned. "All this?"

"Next time, you'll just open with hiring them. It'll go faster—but we won't come back here again until we've solved everything else with Charlie. During our final run of the day, we'll pick these two up."

Whisp slowly furrowed her brow. "Wait... What?"

"Okay." Kull went to his side. "Let's do our best to solve everything."

When Finch activated his magic, all time stopped, coming to an utter standstill. Then all the color drained from the homeless encampment, leaving the world around him nothing more than a black-and-white photo. Once his surroundings bled away, becoming a void of white, Finch blinked.

He found himself back in the woodlands just on the outskirts of Oakland.

5:29 p.m.

Kull was on the ground, twigs in her red hair, dirt on her green dress. When she sat up, it was with purpose. She didn't look elated, or giggly—she was pensive. Serious. Finch hadn't been expecting that.

When she glanced up at him, with the last of the sunset catching on the strands of her hair, she had an otherworldly beauty, as though she were made of fire—or perhaps, her inner flame was so strong, it was seeping out into her visible aura.

"When I dress funny, people think I'm incompetent?" she asked, all business, no playfulness to her tone.

"Yeah," Finch muttered. He walked over, scooped her up into his arms, and held her tight.

Kull furrowed her brow. "But that's not fair. The clothes I'm wearing have nothing to do with my competence!"

"What clothing you wear is a choice," Finch stated. "And it's the first choice people will see. It's *not* fair that people will judge you over this one simple decision you made—but some people think they're a lot smarter than they really are. They'll jump to a hundred conclusions based on your appearance, thinking themselves clever the entire time they do so."

"Why didn't you tell me?" Kull whispered. She wrapped her arms around his neck. "Why did you let me do whatever I wanted?"

Finch darkly chuckled. "I can rewind time. Who cares if the homeless spirits thought you were weird? They don't think that anymore. They don't even know who you are. I figured I might as well just let you enjoy being *you* before I threw a bunch of disappointing reality in your face."

"Well, we should go to a clothing store—the nearest one. Right now. It should be a part of our new routine. I sit up, we go to your car, and then we get me some *real* clothes."

Kull didn't sound excited about this. She sounded determined. Like this was a task she needed to overcome in order to be better.

"It's not *that* important to wear certain clothes," Finch said, trying to downplay the severity of the situation.

"No, it is," Kull said, practically speaking into his chest. "In all her videos, Fox-Pistol is always wearing designer clothes. New clothes. Matching outfits. Beautiful swimsuits. When I was a spirit, I didn't understand. Now... I felt... *bad* when Garret made fun of me. I don't want to feel that way. I want to be... the best human ever."

Finch strode through the wooded area, crunching leaves and branches as he went. He didn't like the idea of Kull "growing up" so quickly, but he figured it was inevitable. Life was filled with expectations, responsibility, and social pressures. If Kull was ready for them, then he would help her with this, too.

"Adair," Kull whispered as they walked.

"Yeah?"

"Thank you for believing in me." She tightened her grip around his neck, hugging him.

"You never need to thank me. I wouldn't have said it unless I thought it was true."

————

Due to the rampant crime in Oakland, every store had a set of security guards outside. Finch and Kull headed into a *Ross —Dress for Less* that was also just on the outskirts of Oakland, and this place had two security guards outside *and* inside. *Ross* was known for its cheaper clothing, which wasn't really Fox-Pistol's style, but it was the closest place to the site of her death and would be a fast stop every time Finch rewound time, so this was what they had to do.

Kull bounded inside, her eyes wide and her smile finally returning.

The security guards were too busy looking at her "assets" to realize she didn't have any shoes on.

Finch gave them both glares, and then the guards turned their gazes to the sky, as though they hadn't blatantly been staring.

"Oh, look! The women's section." Kull ran over and gleefully grabbed a little black dress and then a pair of heels. "I need all this. And also panties. And maybe a coat? So I don't need to keep borrowing yours, Adair."

"Get whatever you want," he said. Then he poked at his phone. He hadn't gotten Enzo's phone number, or else he would've texted the man about why they were running a little late.

5:49 p.m.

As long as they got some clothes in roughly eleven minutes, he figured Enzo wouldn't mind so much.

Kull walked over to Finch, holding a whole outfit. A black dress, a denim jacket, and even some jewelry—a necklace and a few bracelets. She handed them to Finch, who reluctantly took them in his arms.

"Okay, serious question." Kull met his gaze. "Do panties need to match your dress? Or does it not matter?"

Several people in the nearby aisle snickered loud enough for Finch to hear. His face burned as he sighed.

"Don't ask me things like that," he said, trying not to sound angry or embarrassed, but failing.

"But what would a serious, competent, smokin' hot lady do?" Kull tapped her lower lip. "I want to be *perfect* and *amazing*. I don't want people to think I'm incompetent." She pointed at him. "My gut says everything needs to match."

"Please. Don't involve me in any of these decisions. As a matter of fact, don't discuss them aloud. Ever."

"Why?" She didn't ask the question with any mischief in her voice—just pure curiosity.

"Kull," Finch said through clenched teeth. "I'm trying my damnedest not to think of you as a hamburger. *Make it easy for me.* Just handle this on your own."

She giggled and then waved away his comment. But the gravity of his words quickly settled, and Kull's mirth faded away. "Wait—*you* think of hamburgers?"

Finch refused to reply.

Before Kull could ask yet another intrusive question, someone in the Ross shouted.

"You're *here?* That's impossible!"

The yell was so loud and abrasive, the other people in the Ross stopped what they were doing to see what the commotion was about.

A woman stared at Finch and Kull, her eyes wide, her motions jittery.

CHAPTER
TWENTY-NINE

The woman stormed forward, her heels clicking on the polished floor as she hurried toward Finch and Kull. Her brown hair was wavy and puffed in all directions, as though trying desperately to escape her scalp. Finch figured a copious amount of hairspray had been applied to allow her locks to defy gravity.

Long earrings hung from her ear, each adorned with a scarlet stone that glittered in the store's fluorescent lighting.

She wore a small black leather jacket and a lacy white top —but in such a way that left little to the imagination. Her pants were tight, black, and shiny, showcasing her long legs. If it weren't for the manic intensity gleaming in her eyes, Finch would've said she was strikingly attractive, but no one could be alluring when they looked like they might burn the whole building down.

She was pale, and the fluorescent lighting didn't do her favors, but there was something else about her—something Finch found odd.

"You're *here?*" the woman repeated as she neared, her gaze focusing solely on Kull. "But... But... That's not just..."

Kull half smiled and chuckled, but she sounded nervous. "Hello! Uh, sorry, I'm a little disoriented from all the partying I've been doing." She made a funny face and then waved her hand. "Do I... know you?"

The woman stopped dead in her tracks, her eyes going so wide they almost fell out of her skull. She seemed both confused and enraged, but then her expression softened. "You don't remember me?" she whispered.

Again, Kull nervously laughed. "Uh, no. I really am sorry. Who are you? Maybe that'll jog my memory."

"I..."

The woman touched her face, and her manic gaze fell to the floor. Finch watched her, his body tense. He hadn't realized how on edge he was until this moment, but something about the woman gave him the chills.

When she glanced back up, her expression had calmed down into something normal. She didn't look so frantic or angry anymore. Instead, she offered Kull a wide smile. "I'm your biggest fan, Fox-Pistol!"

"Oh." Kull nervously tapped her fingers together. "Really?"

"I can't believe you're *here*! In this Ross, of all places!"

"I just need to do some shopping," Kull awkwardly said. "Ya know. It's a normal thing. That people do."

"I understand. And I know you probably can't remember all your fans. My name is Heldi. Remember now?" She asked the question with a low and serious voice, her intensity returning for just a second.

Superfans could be scary, Finch realized.

"I'm so sorry, Heldi." Kull held out her hand. "How about I sign your cellphone for you? And maybe we can take a selfie together? To make up for my, uh, terrible memory."

Heldi smoothed her unreasonably sexy clothing. Then she reached into her pocket and withdrew a single, beaten up, cellphone. Then she also produced a pen. "Y-Yes. Here. Thank you so much, Fox-Pistol. This means the world."

Kull scribbled on the back of it and then posed next to the woman for a picture. Heldi slowly turned her gaze to Finch. "Are you... *with* Fox-Pistol?"

"Yeah," Finch said as he held out his hand. He figured he needed to take a picture to get this over with.

"You are?" The manic energy returned to Heldi's eyes. "B-But I thought Fox-Pistol was dating Waylon? Does she... have multiple side men?"

The phone slipped from her grasp.

Luckily, Finch lurched forward fast enough to snatch it out of the air. He stood straight and eyed the lady.

"We're not dating," Kull said, laughing much louder than before. "No, no, no. *No.* Uh, that's my *bodyguard*. Adair is super talented."

That statement seemed to calm Heldi all over again. She nodded, posed next to Kull, and then motioned for Finch to take the picture, all without saying a word. Finch snapped a couple and then handed the phone back to the woman. Heldi took it with an unsteady hand.

"You have a very handsome bodyguard," Heldi said, chuckling through her words.

Kull nodded. "Adair is super nice, too. Just amazing."

"*Enough*," Finch muttered under his breath.

Then Heldi glanced up to meet Finch's gaze. "Well, if you're not dating Fox-Pistol... Would you mind giving me your phone number? I'd love to chat with you."

"*What?*" was all Finch could bark out. He had been thrown for yet another loop, and he wasn't entirely sure what this woman's problem was. "No. You can't have my phone number."

Heldi took a deep breath. The manic energy returned as she blatantly struggled to find the words. "I... didn't mean to come across as too forward, I just don't meet many men who… really pique my interest like you."

Kull stepped back, so that she was out of Heldi's eyesight, and then silently pantomimed for Finch to hand over his cellphone number. But Finch ignored that.

"Listen," Finch said. "I'm flattered you want my number, but I'm not interested."

"I'm just not beautiful enough? *Is that it?*" Heldi's voice was practically venom.

The encounter was becoming an episode of Dr. Phil, right in the middle of the Ross, and Finch didn't understand how he had gotten here.

"It has nothing to do with your looks," Finch said through clenched teeth. "It's not you—it's me. Good luck out there."

Kull furrowed her brow, clearly not understanding.

Heldi, on the other hand, shook with visible outrage. She was silent for an awkwardly long period of time, seething. Then—without saying anything else—she turned on her heel and stormed toward the front of the Ross.

Finch and Kull both watched her go, never moving to follow. The woman was so strange, Finch was convinced she was an addict of more than one substance.

Only drugs could explain that behavior.

"Why didn't you give her your phone number?" Kull asked. "You really upset her."

"I didn't want to talk to her," Finch stated. "I thought I made that blatantly clear, but apparently I was too subtle."

"Don't you want to find someone to love?"

He sighed. "Is that why you were encouraging me to give my number to that woman?"

"Yes! What if you're soulmates? You'll never know unless you get to know her."

"Oh my god." Finch pinched the bridge of his nose. "I got

to know her enough. Trust me when I say I didn't just dodge a bullet, I dodged an RPG."

"Hmm. Okay. But she had—" Kull lowered her voice to a whisper, "—*magic*, so I thought you two would get along."

"She did?"

"She was wearing magic from a spirit of delusion." Kull grabbed another shirt off the rack and casually glanced it over. "At first, I thought she was going to say she knew the *real* me, but I guess she's just a fan of Fox-Pistol's."

Finch narrowed his eyes and then met Kull's gaze. "I didn't sense any magic on her."

"I'm *really* good at detecting magic." She tapped the tip of her nose. "So good. You can trust me."

"I do. But we've already spent way too much time here. Grab whatever clothing you want so we can go get Enzo."

———

Kull had the appearance of a pop singer.

She wore a denim-cropped jacket, a black cropped shirt that hugged her body and exposed her midriff, and jeans so tight they might as well have been painted on. None of it was luxury, but that didn't matter. Everyone they passed nearly broke their neck when they did a double take to get a good look at her—they obviously didn't mind the lack of designer logos.

Finch hadn't commented on her choices, because he wanted Kull to be as free as she desired to be, but he also couldn't look at her for longer than a few seconds, so he kept his attention glued to the road. It was just better that way.

Oakland was becoming so familiar, and the Friday night traffic so secondhand, that Finch almost didn't *need* to watch the road in order to make it to the hotel to pick up Enzo. He glided in and out of lanes without fear of getting stopped by the police, because he already knew the beat cops weren't patrolling this road just yet.

"Adair," Kull said.

He inhaled, kept his attention forward, and then exhaled. "Yes?"

"How come you don't ever leave your apartment to date people? When I loved my human family, and protected them over several generations, I was filled with happiness and purpose—so much happiness and purpose that it's all I've ever yearned for since then."

Finch listened, but didn't comment.

"It's so *amazing*." She blissfully sighed. "Why don't you want it?"

"Because."

"Because why?"

She just kept *pushing*. Finch tightened his grip on the steering wheel.

"Because love is like having hooks in your flesh," he said, callous, curt, and cold. "Someone *hooks* into you, and when they leave, they just *yank* the hooks right out, taking pieces of you with them."

It was Kull's turn to be quiet.

"You already know this." Finch glowered at the road. "Don't you remember how much it hurt when that family forgot about you? *Don't you?* Those were the hooks, Kull. That was when you lost pieces of yourself."

Still, she said nothing.

And Finch didn't want to glance over. After he calmed himself, he muttered, "I don't understand why you're so gung-ho to go through that all again. I mean, I'll help you find someone—I'll suggest what dates you should take, what words to say, what wedding venue to have—but I just don't understand. You could focus on other aspects of being human. Be a social media star. Travel around the world.

There are a hundred interesting things you can do with your time that won't leave you broken and bloody afterward."

"Oh," was all Kull said, her voice barely audible.

Immediately, Finch regretted saying anything. *This* was why he didn't want to give Kull advice.

He didn't want to infect her with the same darkness that clawed at his thoughts.

They drove in silence—painful silence—until they reached Oasis. Like before, Enzo was already waiting for them. The man hopped into the back of the vehicle the moment he could. Once positioned in the middle of the back seat, and once he and Kull had their Mark of Chronos, Enzo exhaled.

"Okay, so what's the plan?" he asked. "We know how the elves are doping people. Are we gonna mess with their operations? Or save Charlie? What's the next step?"

"We'll… go speak with Charlie," Finch said, only half listening. He panned his attention over the cab of his car, using the rearview mirror to keep track of everything.

Enzo glanced between Finch and Kull. "What's with you two? I'm away for five seconds and you're both acting like you just got into a fight."

Kull turned around in her seat and glared over the top of the headrest. She wasn't even wearing her seat belt, even though Finch was driving through the main streets of Oakland.

"Enzo," she said, "do you think love is like someone putting hooks in your body? And that when they leave, they just yank those hooks out? Taking pieces of you with them? Do you think that?"

Finch almost interjected, but he held back. He wanted to hear Enzo's answer.

Enzo mulled it over, but only for a short moment. "Yeah. I'd say that's a pretty accurate description of love."

"Really?" Kull's voice shook.

"Yeah. But I guess calling them hooks is a bit extreme. They're *connections*, kinda like power cords. When you love someone, and they're happy—you're happy. When they succeed—you succeed. It's the most empowering and fulfilling experience you can ever have, and it sure sucks to lose it, but even havin' it for a brief moment is worth all the risk."

Kull perked up again, her eyebrows rising.

"You should sit down and buckle up," Finch said with all the boredom of a high school teacher.

Kull followed his instructions, and once situated, she smiled at him. "Did you hear that, Adair?"

"I sure did," he sardonically replied.

"Was Kull trying to convince you to love someone?" Enzo scratched his chin.

"Some random druggie tried to get my phone number," Finch replied.

"Huh. Is that why you smell like death? That's all my werewolf nose has smelled since I entered this car. Everything is adding up now."

Finch rolled his eyes. "Enough inane distractions. Let's get Charlie before the last of my patience is whittled away."

CHAPTER
THIRTY

Finch parked just across from the Lake Merritt Grand Hotel. As everyone slid out of the vehicle, he turned to Kull. "Get them to take us to the high roller room. I'll do the rest."

"How are you going to save Charlie?" she asked.

"I'll think of something."

Enzo snorted and then laughed as he slammed the door. "I love how you just fly by the seat of your pants. Most detectives have a game plan. The successful ones, anyway."

"Did I ever fail the Oakland PD?" Finch lifted an eyebrow.

Enzo shrugged. "Well, maybe I shouldn't have seen how the sausage gets made, because I thought you two were just so brilliant you deduced all the correct conclusions like a modern-day Sherlock Holmes." He sarcastically ran a finger over the top of the car. "What's this? A bit of ash? The only place in the city with ash *this* color is over by the waterfront factories! *Quickly!* To the car to catch the killer!"

Kull snickered. "I bet Adair could do that, if he really wanted."

She walked around the front of the vehicle, and then

jumped in front of Enzo, showing off her pop singer outfit. She even did a little twirl, which caused Enzo to freeze up.

"Do you like my new clothes?" she asked.

"Uh…" Enzo took a step away from her, his back bumping into the car. "You look like a girl who might know the RAINN hotline number by heart."

Finch pinched the bridge of his nose and sighed. Now wasn't the time for cop jokes.

"Is that good?" Kull tilted her head. "Or bad?"

"The only woman whose outfit I'll comment on is my wife," Enzo stated.

"Oh." Kull deflated a bit. "Will you at least tell me if I look competent or not?"

Enzo choked back a laugh. "Oh, you look plenty competent."

Finch pointed at him. "*Don't.* No jokes. She's trying to be more confident. Just let her try on whatever outfits she wants, all right?"

"I didn't say a goddamn thing." He couldn't stop his laughter as he walked over to Finch.

Then as a trio, they headed into the hotel. Enzo managed to stifle his mirth, but only after Finch narrowed his eyes more than once. Together, they flanked Kull, who announced herself to the hotel staff just like before. The elven knight immediately led her to the elevator, and then up to the casino floors.

Finch kept his attention on the surroundings, and also on his phone.

6:18 p.m.

The shopping trip with Kull had set them back a bit—but it was only a small amount, and the hotel didn't seem noticeably different. By the time they reached the exclusive high roller room for people "in the know" about magic, it was nearly 6:20 p.m., but thankfully, both Charlie and Rad were exactly as they were before.

Finch caught sight of the fae soothsayer in the back of the room—the one who was meant to call out magic use to prevent cheating. Fortunately for Finch, he had already used his magic to rewind time. He wasn't actively using any magic *now*.

"Wow, what a great room that I've definitely never seen before," Kull said to the elf knight. "I love it."

"Uh, excellent," the man awkwardly replied, obviously suspicious.

Finch ignored that. He strode forward, despite the odd glances from elves in the room, and went straight to Charlie's side. Jay-W's wife glanced up as Finch reached her.

"Do I know you?" were the first words out of her mouth. She leaned back in her chair, defensive.

"My name is Adair Finch, and I'm a warlock for hire," he said.

The moment he said his name, several elves in the room gasped. It was a light, almost whisper gasp, because the elves never did anything with *oomph*, but Finch heard it nonetheless.

Charlie hardened her expression, her eyes searching his. "Does…"

"He doesn't know you're here," Finch replied. Judging by the relief on her face, his assumption of her question was correct. "But he thought you might be in trouble, so he sent me."

While that was half a lie, Finch figured it would work in his favor.

Charlie's face lit up, her features softening. "Jay sent you to help me?" she whispered.

"Yeah."

"This is an outrage," one of the elven knights hissed. He

grabbed Finch's elbow and attempted to yank it, but was too slow.

Enzo grabbed the knight by the shoulder and pulled him backward. Enzo's grip on the man's shoulder was so tight, he wrinkled the poor elf's suit.

"You *animal*," the elf said through clenched teeth.

Charlie frowned. "What's going on?"

"This man is auditionin' for an ass whoopin'," Enzo growled.

"*Adair Finch* is not allowed in here!" The elf didn't struggle much, but his voice had become irritatingly high pitched. "He isn't a guest of this hotel, and he made his way to this room under false pretenses!"

"He's with *me*," Charlie stated. She stood from her chair and placed a hand on her hip. In one quick motion her demeanor shifted to *boss bitch*. "Or should I leave your establishment and never return? We can make that happen."

The elves in the room exchanged nervous glances.

"Lady Liligale needs you to settle your debt," the dealer woman said. She gathered up the cards at the table and then retrieved a new deck. "You can pay now, or you can keep *attempting* to earn out what you owe us. But remember— Lady Liligale said she will only allow your debt to reach five million. Then we'll need to insist you settle up."

Finch stepped up to the end of the card table. "*I'll* earn out what she owes you."

"Y-You?" The dealer stared at him with wide eyes.

Kull softly clapped her hands. "Really? You will, Adair? I didn't know you were good at card games. You have to teach me."

Finch took Charlie's seat at the table. The woman stared down at him, nervous energy in her posture as she shifted her weight from one foot to the other. It was evident she didn't want to relinquish her control over the cards, but at the same time, a desperation in her expression told Finch she was scared.

She had been losing too much.

Perhaps Charlie was *great* at cards—Finch suspected it had to be the case—but since the elves were cheating, she had no hope of winning.

Finch wouldn't be tricked by them, however.

"Let's go," Finch said. "Deal me in."

"I don't think we can allow you to play for Mrs. Woolsy," the dealer said.

Finch tapped the black felt surface of the table. "If I lose more than three hands in a row, I'll *also* owe Lady Liligale five million. How does that sound?"

There were even more hesitant glances exchanged between all the fae who ran the shady hotel. A few of them whispered to one another. Once Enzo released the knight, the man smoothed his suit, rolled his eyes, and then pointed to the dealer.

"Allow him to play, *and don't let him leave this room.*" The knight pointed to the soothsayer. "If you're caught cheating, you'll owe us more than money, warlock."

Finch understood a threat on his life when he heard it.

"Let's play," he said.

Then Finch glanced at his phone.

6:19 p.m.

"What game?" the dealer asked.

Kull practically cartwheeled over to the table—that was how excited she was. With a smile wider than a car's windshield, she grabbed Finch's shoulder and playfully shook him.

"Play blackjack," she said. "I lost so much with that game. I want to see a master win back all the money!"

The elves in the room snapped their fingers. A knight

stepped between Kull and Finch and even pushed her back a few feet until she was right next to Enzo.

"You can't interfere with the players," the knight stated.

Kull crossed her arms. "Well, I'm still going to watch the game." Then she stomped a foot with a huff.

"What's the buy-in?" Finch asked.

"One hundred thousand," the dealer sweetly said. She moved a stack of ten grand chips over to Finch. "We will keep track of your winnings—and losses. Everything is recorded, and we're praised for our accuracy."

That was fine with Finch. One hundred grand would make this a little slow of a process, but if they played fast enough, it wouldn't take too long.

Blackjack was a simple game. The goal of the game was to beat the dealer's hand without going over twenty-one. Each player was dealt two cards, as was the dealer. Unlike with the players, one of the dealer's cards was played face up, so everyone could see. Each player could then take another randomly dealt card—or not. Once the players were done, the dealer would reveal their only face down card, and if their total was sixteen or below, they would draw until they had seventeen or higher.

If anyone went over twenty-one, they automatically lost —including the dealer.

It was one of the few player-friendly card games, and the rounds were fast.

Rad, the man who had been playing Charlie, remained at the table, even after all the drama. He tapped the felt with his fingers, indicating he wanted to be dealt in.

The elven dealer, with her slender hands and elegant motions, swiftly dealt Finch and Rad two cards.

Finch half glanced at his cards. A ten and five.

"Hit me," he said.

The dealer slid over a card. When Finch peeked at the

face, he rolled his eyes. All face cards were worth ten, and he had been dealt a queen. He showed his hand—a bust.

"What?" Kull asked with a gasp. "You lost? *But how*? Why? Adair shouldn't *lose*."

Enzo chuckled. "It's a game of luck. Calm down."

But Finch wasn't going to stick around. He activated his magic. Everyone froze in place, and all sounds instantly ended. Finch waited as the colors drained from the world, leaving it black and white, like an old movie.

Then the shapes melted, washing off into a white void.

When Finch blinked, he was back in the woods, on the outskirts of Oakland.

5:29 p.m.

Kull sat up, once again in her old green dress.

"How?" she balked. "How did you lose?" She plucked the twigs from her long hair. "I thought you would be *amazing* at that game!"

"I will be amazing at the game," Finch muttered. He walked over, scooped her up into his arms, and then smirked. "I just need a few tries at it."

———

Once Kull had a new outfit—a black cocktail dress and a tiara—they got Enzo and returned to the Lake Merritt Grand Hotel. He drew the Mark of Chronos on them, just like every time before, so they could remember everything once time was rewound. As if running through an entire evening of déjà vu, they went up to the casino floor and into the special high rollers room with Charlie and Rad.

Finch went to Charlie, offered to play on her behalf, and *basically* went through the same conversation—or at least what he could remember—in order to get back to the table.

The elf knight in charge of the room was just as disgruntled as ever.

"Allow him to play, *and don't let him leave this room.*" The elf knight pointed to the soothsayer. "If you're caught cheating, you'll owe us more than money, warlock."

"Yeah, yeah," Finch said as he took a seat at the card table. "I got it. Let's play."

6:18 p.m.

A little earlier than before, but not too much. Hopefully the cards would still be the same.

"What game?" the dealer asked.

Finch waited. Last time, Kull had jumped in to demand the game. This time, there was a long stretch of silence. Finch glanced over at her, and Kull met his gaze with confusion. Then she smiled.

"Oh! Right. This is my part." Kull cleared her throat and stepped forward. "Play blackjack, Adair! You can do it! I believe in you."

Finch sighed. He made a mental note to just recommend the game next time.

The same elven knight pushed Kull back over to Enzo. "You can't interfere with the players."

Kull sassily crossed her arms. "Well, I'm still going to watch the game." Then she stomped a foot with a huff, but was obviously holding back laughter.

"You look suspicious," Enzo growled. "Why don't you—"

Kull brought a finger up to his lips and pressed it against them. "Shh," she said with a wink.

"What's the buy-in?" Finch asked, ignoring their antics.

"One hundred thousand," the dealer sweetly said. She moved a stack of ten-grand chips over to Finch. "We will keep track of your winnings—and losses. Everything is recorded, and we're praised for our accuracy."

Then the elven dealer slid two cards each over to Finch and Rad, exactly like before.

Finch half glanced at his cards. A ten and five.

Just like last time.

"I'll stay," he said.

Rad tapped the table with his knuckles, and the elf tossed him a card—the ten. Rad groaned and showed the whole table he had busted.

"Wow." Kull excitedly fidgeted with her hands, beaming. "The perfect play, Adair!"

"Are you serious?" Enzo eyed her like she was embarrassing him.

But Kull didn't care. She clapped when the dealer revealed her hand, drew a card, and then quickly busted as well—leaving Finch the winner of that round.

"Winning once is easy," Charlie said. "But luck runs out for everyone."

The dealer removed the cards, gave Finch a new stack of chips, and then dealt cards for the next round.

He was given a six and four.

"Hit me," Finch said.

He was dealt a two.

Normally, a player might think and strategize, but Finch didn't have time for that shit.

"Hit me," he said, only two seconds after peeking at the face of his new card.

The dealer, her face almost contorting into a frown, dealt him another card.

A ten.

Finch had busted again. He sighed as he flipped them up for everyone to see.

"What?" Kull barked. "That's impossible! That's—"

But Finch didn't bother to listen to the faux outrage. He

activated his power by concentrating on Chronos's magic. The colors faded. The world melted. And once all the shapes were gone, he blinked and found himself on the outskirts of Oakland.

Kull sat up. "Wow. You almost had them."

He couldn't tell if she was being sarcastic or genuine. "Don't worry. It's just a matter of time."

"And the soothsayer can't see any of it?"

Finch picked her up and held her like a bride as he strode between the trees. "Nope. My magic is activated and takes me back to my mark in time. The soothsayer isn't here. And she can't tell anyone about my powers because she didn't remember when I rewound it before."

"This is…" Kull tightened her arms around his neck. "The perfect crime," she whispered.

Finch nodded. "That it is."

"Is this how you make your money? Just winning games of chance?"

"No—I don't use my powers to cheat honest and innocent people." Finch smirked. "But these elves aren't honest *or* innocent. Winning millions of dollars at their card tables is just payback."

Kull excitedly kicked her feet. "I can't wait until you win back all the money! It's going to be so hilarious to see the looks on their faces."

Finch agreed. He just had to memorize all the plays necessary to make that happen.

CHAPTER
THIRTY-ONE

What Finch didn't like was all the steps he had to take after rewinding time. They would stop at the Ross—avoid the crazy Fox-Pistol fan—pick up Enzo, draw the Mark of Chronos, and then drive back to the hotel.

Once situated at the card table, Finch could play through the card game like it was a scene in a play and he was the main actor. He reset the day over and over again, trying to perfect the sequence of events that would win him four million dollars the fastest. As long as he started the card game between 6:17 p.m. and 6:20 p.m. the cards were all the same.

He had to stay with the first hand.

Take one card and then stay with the second hand.

His third hand was a perfect twenty-one.

It was at this time that serving girls attempted to give him glasses of wine. Finch refused. He knew if he drank anything laced with the delusion spirit's magic, he wouldn't be able to play the game correctly.

He needed to hit twice and then stay with the fourth hand.

On the fifth hand, he was dealt a pair of sixes. He could split, and play off both cards as though he had two hands, but remembering a strategy like that would be complicated, so Finch never opted to do that.

On the sixth hand, Finch glanced at his cards and struggled to remember what to do with them.

"Sir?" the dealer asked him. "What would you like to do?"

"One second," he murmured. Finch closed his eyes and thought back to the hands he had played, treating everything like a game of memory. "I... want to hit," he finally said, almost like it was a question, and not a command.

"You know this casino uses four decks at a time to prevent people from countin' cards, right?" Rad asked. The man swept his shimmering black hair back with all the flair of someone in a shampoo commercial.

"I'm not counting cards," Finch snapped.

He was counting *something*, but it wasn't the deck the casino was using.

Still, the moment Rad had mentioned that, the dealer stuck the deck into an automatic shuffler mounted to the underside of the table.

Which had never happened before in previous versions of these plays. Sure, the dealer shuffled the deck every three games, but she hadn't done it *now*.

"Goddammit." Finch exhaled, pinched the bridge of his nose, and leaned his head back. All the strategies he knew for the next couple plays wouldn't work if the dealer shuffled the cards *now*.

But before he could rewind time, Kull waved her arms, drawing his attention.

"*Wait*," she said. Then she inched closer to the table. "You're going to give up, right?"

"Give up?" Rad shook his head. "The man has been doing amazingly. Five hands in a row is either great luck or notable skill. He shouldn't quit now."

Charlie, hovering close, nodded once. "If this warlock is going to win back my debt, he has a long way to go."

But Kull ignored them to say, "I want to try something first."

"Why?" Finch narrowed his eyes.

"We've done this like a dozen times, and I noticed Rad is drinking the *fanciest* drink here."

Rad glanced at the glass sitting on the edge of the card table. It was a crystal glass with ice, liquid, and a green olive. It was hardly fancy, but Finch understood why she was curious. Unlike Charlie, who had been drinking the wine, Rad had clearly been drinking a martini made with vodka and vermouth.

Kull leapt over to the card table and then picked up Rad's drink. "I've never tasted this before," she whispered as she brought it to her lips.

"What the?" Rad gawked at her, bewildered.

The elven knight attempted to intervene before she could take a sip, but Enzo grabbed the man's shoulder so tightly, he almost tore the man's suit. The elf hissed and tensed, his hand flaring with magic that smelled like wet soil.

Everyone in the room stood, as though this would become a battleground.

Kull took a sip of the martini. Then she gagged, coughed, and spit out the liquid right back into the glass. With the deepest of frowns, she replaced the glass on the edge of the card table, next to Rad.

"Blech!" Kull coughed again. "What's wrong with you? That tastes like misery."

Rad glanced at his soiled drink, and then back up at Kull.

To Finch's surprise, the man smirked. "Ya know, I just so happen to like a girl who knows how to spit things up."

The moment the words left his mouth, Kull took a step away from him. "Adair? Is this a hamburger situation?"

"Yes," Finch said with a groan.

Without hesitation, Kull slapped Rad across the face, the *smack* of her palm so loud, it could be heard from every corner of the high roller room. A red mark blossomed across Rad's cheek, and the card dealer immediately pressed some sort of button on the underside of the table.

"I'm *not* a hamburger," Kull shouted. Then she shook out her hand. "And that hurt a lot. Why? In all the movies I watched, it didn't hurt the people?"

Enzo laughed. So hard.

But Finch wasn't about to wait for the room to be swarming with redwood elves. He activated his magic, and the room froze. Then the color drained away. Then all the shapes. When Finch finally found himself back in the woodland outside Oakland, he didn't even need to glance at his phone to know it was 5:29 p.m. once again.

Kull sat up. She patted her dirty green dress and ripped the twigs from her hair. "Did you see that, Adair? That man thought of me like a hamburger."

"I was two feet away," Finch quipped. "I don't have bad eyesight yet." Then he picked her up, and held her close.

Kull glanced at her palm. "Adair…"

"Yeah?"

"If all men think of me like a hamburger, how am I supposed to find someone who loves me? And will remember me? And do all the things in life with me? I thought I first had to find someone who *didn't* want hamburgers."

Her questions were heartfelt and genuine, and even

though Finch wanted to ignore them, he knew he couldn't. Not this time.

After rolling his eyes, Finch said, "Listen—in a good relationship, you'll *want* the man to, uh, think of you like a hamburger. Sometimes."

"Really? Why?"

"Because you remember how good hamburgers are, right?" Finch continued to walk through the woods, his face heating. He would never think of a Shake Shack the same ever again.

"Hamburgers are so good," Kull said.

"Well, when you love someone, in a romantic way, you, er, two will have hamburgers… together."

Finch was certain a sex ed teacher from a run-down high school—the kind of teacher who was also the coach and occasionally the math teacher—would've done a better job explaining this, but he didn't really have a whole lot of options.

"And we'll both enjoy hamburgers together?" Kull furrowed her brow. "Is that what you're saying?"

"Yes. You understand, right? You don't need any further explanation?"

"Uh, I suppose…"

"Good."

Finch was almost back to the street. He needed to focus all his attention on blackjack, and he *definitely* didn't want to think of hamburgers now that he knew Rad could potentially mess up his winning streak.

———

Finch couldn't hesitate.

He had already done this twenty-two times.

Once he sat down at the card table, he pulled on his poker

face and hid all hint of emotion. He didn't even need to glance at his cards to know what play to make, but he did so anyway, to make it at least *seem* like he was playing the game normally and not cheating by manipulating time.

He had to stay with the first hand.

Take one card and then stay with the second hand.

His third hand was a perfect twenty-one.

He needed to hit twice and then stay with the fourth hand.

On the fifth hand, he took his sixes and stayed.

On the sixth hand, Finch hit and then stayed.

With the seventh, he sat out. He couldn't win that one. In order to avoid suspicion, he excused himself to go to the restroom.

On the eighth, ninth, tenth, and eleventh, he just had to stay in order to win. The dealer busted each time.

And that was when he had won over a million dollars—all in under thirty minutes.

The dealer tapped something on the underside of the table as she gathered up all the cards and began preparing for another hand. Finch kept his eye on the door, and after only thirty seconds, it opened to reveal Liligale, the Head of the Pacific Court.

The woman's black hair, laced with dark green highlights, was still coiled tightly into a bun. Her silver glasses shone under the beautiful lighting overhead, and she quickly made her way over to the card table, despite how tight her pencil skirt hugged her body.

Rad shuddered and leaned away from her when she approached.

It was clear Rad was part fae—his elegant features betrayed his heritage—but he wasn't a redwood elf. And redwood elves rarely got along with other fae, even if they all came from the same realm.

But Liligale didn't say anything to Rad. She turned her harsh gaze on Finch.

"Hello, Adair," she said in a cool and confident manner.

The door of the room opened again, and a dozen other elven knights strode into the room. They were quiet, and precise, each one clearly packing a side holster with a gun, but Finch wasn't worried.

Liligale wanted to intimidate him.

"My name is Liligale Vi'Thamis, Head of the Pacific Court," she said with the eloquent tone she'd had the first time they met. "What brings one of the most famous warlocks in the world to my establishment?"

Finch found it strange sometimes whenever he had to go through introductions more than once with someone, but this wasn't the first time. "A man can't play a few friendly games of blackjack in peace?"

Liligale turned her dark eyes to Enzo. "It is quite the insult that you brought your *dog* to this establishment."

"*What?*" Kull huffed and stepped in front of Enzo. "I hope you're ready to catch these hands because no one talks about my friends that way!"

With half a smile, Enzo placed a hand on her shoulder. "Settle down, champ. We don't need to use all our big guns. How about you take a seat, and I'll handle this one?"

Their height was so notably different, Kull had to stare up at him. "Okay, but I'm here to help if things go sideways."

"I appreciate that," Enzo replied, chuckling.

Finch remained seated at the card table. He tapped the felt with the tips of his fingers, eager to get this all over with. "I'm here to win back all Charlotte Woolsy's debt. I've already clawed back a fourth of it, and I was just about to suggest we up the ante so we don't waste our whole evening here."

Liligale glared at him through her half-moon glasses.

Then she glanced at his winning chips, the table, and then to the soothsayer in the back. The elf in charge of making sure no magic was being used just shrugged—Finch hadn't been using any magic during the games.

"I've been informed of your winning streak," Liligale said, her voice icy. "I came here to remind you we have strict punishments for those who… break the rules."

Finch leaned forward and lowered his voice. "I've gotta give you credit—it takes a lot of balls for *you* to accuse *me* of cheating." He held his gaze on hers, never blinking or hesitating.

For a prolonged moment, Liligale gave no indication she knew what Finch was talking about, but when the silence thickened between them, she stepped away. She was the Head of the Pacific Court, and the owner of this hotel. If anyone knew of the cheating, it was her.

And it would ruin her reputation, and her fine establishment, if her underhanded tactics ever came to light.

Liligale forced a smile and then motioned to the table. "I'll allow you to continue playing."

"Thank you," Finch said as he leaned back in his seat.

"But only for tonight. Once you're done—you're done. You won't be allowed back on these premises ever again. Do I make myself clear?"

"Very." With a halfhearted gesture to the table, he added, "But I'm only going to play two more rounds. Double or nothin' both times should allow me to pay off all Charlie's debt, I think."

In all the past versions of this day, she was five million in debt when she died, but that was after gambling all night. Four million was likely closer to what she owed *right now*.

Charlie hovered close. Never *so* close that the elven knights pulled her away, but close enough to witness all the action. The moment Finch made his proclamation, she sucked in air and held her breath.

Winning four million dollars in less than an hour would make any gambler jealous. However, casinos typically had table limits—they wouldn't allow bets to get *too* high.

"I can't believe this is happening," Charlie whispered.

Finch was certain the redwood elves wouldn't normally allow such high risks. But Liligale was right here, and if she approved this, no one would argue.

Liligale clenched and unclenched her fists. She eyed Finch, and then turned her attention to Enzo. "You can make your bets, Adair Finch, but this is twice you've disrespected me and my court. First, you bring an animal into my place of business, and secondly, you've clearly come here to take advantage of my hospitality."

Finch didn't argue. He remained quiet, and Liligale straightened her already stiff posture.

"I don't know why someone of your caliber would ever align themselves with the dogs of Level 22, but after tonight, I'm going to have to reevaluate our agreement with them." Liligale coyly smiled. "We *were* allowing them to conduct business inside the city limits of Oakland, but it's clear that was a mistake."

"*My lady,*" the soothsayer said with a gasp.

A deep and guttural growl drew everyone's attention.

Enzo was tense, black fur sprouting across his body, his teeth half fangs. "*You little piece of—*" he snarled.

CHAPTER
THIRTY-TWO

The elven knights drew their guns simultaneously, as though they had practiced to do that in sync. Enzo was on the verge of fully transforming, and his fingers were already sprouting claws.

He clearly cared for the other werewolves of Level 22. Enzo didn't want to see them harmed just because the elves were pissy about losing so much money. Especially since the elves were cheating, and had brought this all on themselves.

"Wait, wait!" Kull shouted. She leapt in front of Enzo and held out her arms. "Breathe. You need to take deep breaths. Remember what all those meditation guides said?"

Enzo hesitated, the muscles under his skin rippling as his body continued to slowly transform.

Kull stepped forward. This time around, she had picked a short skirt and a button-up blouse, but they were strangely schoolgirl in design. Finch hadn't been paying much attention when she had picked out the outfit, because she picked a new one every time, but it made the scene playing out before him all the stranger.

With a smile, Kull leaned against Enzo, and then carefully wrapped her arms around his midsection.

Finch heard someone gasp—who would dare touch a werewolf while it was transforming?—but that didn't stop Kull from holding on to Enzo. Fearing that Kull would get ripped to shreds, Finch stood from his chair so fast it fell backward and hit the carpeted floor.

"Picture those nice grassy fields," Kull whispered.

Enzo's breathing was ragged and hate-filled, but he never attacked her.

Obviously, Finch could rewind time, so he wasn't worried Kull would be permanently injured. He was, however, worried it would somehow take a toll on her friendship with Enzo. What if she became afraid of him?

Would it be best to just rewind time now?

But then Enzo would never get to practice keeping his anger in check…

"Your dog is unstable," Liligale stated. "If he so much as steps a foot out of line, we'll put him down."

"Don't listen to them," Kull said in a singsong tone. "Remember what Pornhub said? Think about your wife smiling."

Rad choked on his martini. Once he was done sputtering, he glanced at the card dealer. "Did she just say *Pornhub*?" he whispered. "I wasn't the only one who heard that, right?"

To literally everyone's apparent surprise, Enzo's breathing evened out. His fur smoothed, and once he took a deep inhale, his transformation halted. He gently patted Kull on the shoulder as he exhaled.

"I… I think…" Enzo rubbed the side of his face while he took another deep breath. "I think I need some fresh air."

As Kull smiled wider and tightened her grip around his torso, one of the elf knights fired. The *bang* was so loud, it was tantamount to a punch in the ear.

The bullet, a trigger-happy shot, went right through Enzo's skull, leaving blood splatters across the floor and far window. And since he wasn't fully a werewolf yet, Enzo's cursed magic couldn't help him. He hit the floor a second later, collapsing onto his side, two holes in his head, one small, one much larger.

Charlie screamed. Rad leapt from his seat and stumbled into the bar. The dealer ducked under the card table like they were about to experience an earthquake.

Kull, however, locked up, her arms out to the side, her body shivering.

"The beast was unstable," Liligale quickly and callously stated. "He wasn't to be trusted."

Finch *almost* burned everyone in the room alive. Instead, he forced himself to concentrate. He rewound time. The colors left him, the shapes melted—he couldn't get back to the wooded area outside of Oakland fast enough.

When he finally opened his eyes, and took a deep breath, he treasured the smell of the leaves and the soil.

"Goddamn elves," he muttered, his breath so hot it was steam and embers. His fire magic came from Ke-Koh the Ifrit of Rebellion, and since it was tied to his heart core, it was strengthened through strong emotions.

Finch held back the urge to burn down all the trees. While it would make him feel temporarily better, it wouldn't actually change anything.

"They shot him," Kull said. She sat up, brushed herself off, and then patted her fire-red hair. *"They shot him.* Adair, why did they do that?"

"They wanted to cause problems," he replied.

"Th-They did?"

Finch nodded as he walked over to her. Once she was comfortably in his arms, he sighed. "The moment Liligale knew I knew of her cheating, she wanted me gone. And the moment Enzo started to wolf out, she wanted to create a scene, no doubt in my mind, to justify attacking me, or discrediting my name, so I couldn't reveal she was a cheater."

Kull hugged him tight. "But Enzo was doing so well! He stopped transforming. *He stopped*. They didn't have any right to attack him. It's not fair!"

"Yeah, well, all this has taught me is I can't play cards with Enzo in the room, because Liligale and her knights will agitate him just to get out of the situation."

———

After Finch and Kull had purchased a new outfit at Ross—this time Kull wore black leggings and a pink T-shirt—they drove straight over to their normal rendezvous with Enzo. He stood outside, on the curb, right in front of the Oasis club, just like always.

But this time, his sweatpants and tank top were both slashed in multiple places, as though claws had been raked across them. When Finch parked, Enzo leapt into the back and slammed the door.

He said nothing.

Kull turned around to stare at him. "Oh no—what happened to your clothes?"

"I forgot my breathin' exercises," was all Enzo said, surprisingly calm.

"Are you... going to be okay seeing these elves again?" Finch asked.

"Nope." Enzo rotated his shoulders. "Definitely not."

His rage, while visibly hidden, did make him stink like only unchecked testosterone could. Finch slowly nodded and returned his attention to the road. It would be a mistake to take Enzo anywhere near the redwood elves in his current state.

Enzo cracked his knuckles. "If I see any of them again, I'm gonna rip their throat out with my fangs. And then carve out their chest with my claws and defecate in the cavity."

"Don't say that! You need to practice being calm." Kull smiled at him. "This is the perfect time to do that. We'll breathe, and focus on nice things, and this will all go away."

Enzo snorted. "We don't have time for that crap."

"Actually," Finch drawled, "we have all the time in the world."

As though he *wanted* to argue, Enzo opened his mouth. Then he closed it and sighed. "I keep forgettin' you're a time magician."

Kull winked at him. "That's right. So we *can* practice, okay? Lots of deep breaths. Tranquil music." She leaned around her seat, practically on the center console of the vehicle. "You did so well in the hotel! Those elves were totes aggressive, but you managed to hold it all together."

"Only because you were there, talking me off the edge," Enzo muttered.

"Still! That's one step closer. You got this. Believe in you. Adair believes in you. Soon, none of their words will affect you. Won't that be amazing?"

Kull's overwhelming optimism got Finch smiling. While Oakland was soaked in the darkness of night, the car seemed far brighter than even just a few moments ago.

"Why don't we take a short break?" Finch turned down a road toward a small mom-and-pop restaurant he knew of. "Kull, you haven't tried many desserts. I bet you're going to love the variety—some of humanity's finest work."

"Oh! Really?" Kull sat back in her seat and hopped up and down. "I'm so excited! What a fabulous idea."

———

Finch, Kull, and Enzo sat in the corner booth of an ice cream parlor named *Scoops & Smiles*. The interior was pale blue and white, with a checkered tile floor and 1950s memorabilia up on the walls. There was an old soda bar in the corner, and classic mugs for root beer floats hanging from pegs on the back wall.

While Oakland itself was a city filled with trash, covered in homeless encampments, and practically crumbling from neglect, Finch had almost forgotten all the small shops that still ran on hard work and love. First the pizza parlor, and now this place—there was a heart that still beat in Oakland, even if it was struggling to carry on.

Scoops & Smiles had opened decades ago, and the same couple had maintained it as though it were one of their children. All the tables were clean, all the desserts beautiful, and whenever they checked in on customers, they did so with genuine smiles.

Enzo sipped a soda, one arm up on the headrest of the booth. Finch stirred his chocolate shake, a fan of ice cream in general.

But Kull hadn't been able to make up her mind, so she ended up ordering a slice of cheesecake, apple pie à la mode, a banana split, a strawberry malt shake, and a rocky road sundae. Her side of the booth was so loaded with beautiful desserts, it was like she was living in a commercial for the store.

Kull took a bite of the banana split and almost melted in her seat. She made a *yuummm* noise and then used the same spoon to dig into the apple pie. She gobbled up a scoop of apples and let out an almost identical *yuummm*.

"We get it," Enzo muttered. "It's good."

Kull pointed at him with the tip of her spoon. "So good. Extra special good. I mean, milkshakes were already way up there for me, but these are way better." She took a bite of the cheesecake and immediately let out an even louder *YUUMMM*.

"You can't attack the elves." Finch stared across the booth table at Enzo. "No matter what they did to you in another timeline. You understand that, right?"

Enzo held up two fingers. "Twice, Adair. They've tried to kill me twice. I was good—I held back after the first time, because I thought it was mostly my fault. But this second time? It was all them. They *want* to kill me."

"You can't attack the elves."

"Yuuuummmmm," Kull said, even louder, obviously interjecting herself into the conversation. "Have you two tried malts before? So good!"

Enzo huffed and glanced away from the table, his attention on the far wall. He sucked down his soda until the bottle was empty, then he practically tossed it onto the table, causing a clatter.

"The whole point of you learning to calm yourself was so that you weren't prone to these types of outbursts," Finch stated.

"Maybe I can't do it." Enzo turned his glare back on him. "Maybe it's impossible for a wolf like me."

Kull held up a hand, coming between them. "Don't say that. You did really well!" Then she motioned to all her food. "And I know you can do it, because I do it all the time!"

"Do what?" Enzo asked. "You're not a wolf."

"I meant suppressing my nature to be more human. Look at all this food! Sometimes, my first thought is to drop it on the floor, or hide a piece under this booth cushion. Or what if I put this apple pie into my drink? So much mischief to get into."

Finch set his milkshake on the booth table. He hadn't known Kull was suppressing her spirit urges.

"But I don't do that because then all the humans would

think I'm weird." Kull licked her spoon clean. "So I know you can do it, Enzo. You're big and strong, and you can definitely put that lycanthropy curse in its place."

"I'll put it in a choke hold," Enzo quipped.

"That's more like it!" Then Kull turned her attention to Finch. "So, what would you say is the *best* dessert?"

Finch mulled over the question for a moment. Then he responded with, "Pavlova."

"Really? Do they have that here?"

"I doubt it. But maybe."

Kull pushed his shoulder. She was tucked at the far back of the booth, and couldn't escape unless Finch moved. He slid out, and Kull followed.

"I'll be right back," she said as she glanced at the register.

Once she was out of earshot, Enzo sighed. "Adair—just give it to me straight. Do you think I can get this under control?"

Finch hesitated. He wasn't certain about anything, and he most definitely wasn't an expert on werewolves, but stranger things had happened.

"You'll get it under control," he said, confident and firm. "You just have to practice. And don't worry—those elves are the perfect people to practice on. Even if you lose control, they probably deserved it."

Enzo snorted and laughed. He relaxed in the booth, a tired smile appearing on his face as he relaxed. "I hope so."

A tray hit the floor, and there was a clatter.

"Oh, sorry, miss!" someone said.

Both Enzo and Finch glanced over to see Kull and a young man, in his early thirties, standing over a mess on the floor. It seemed as though the man had dropped his tray near Kull. He wore a pair of jeans and a dark coat—an unassuming man who didn't seem clumsy.

"I'll help," Kull said as she bent over to gather up the spoon and a bowl.

The man went to grab the tray, and on the way up, his hand grazed her leggings-clad rump. It was quick, but the way Kull jolted into a standing position told Finch it hadn't been a feather touch.

"Oh, oops," the man said. "Sorry about that."

Finch hadn't even realized Enzo had exited the booth. Instead, he just caught sight of Enzo as he turned the man around by his shoulder and then grabbed the man's collar.

"You know what sexual assault gets you?" Enzo asked through clenched teeth. "*A whole lot of normal assault.*"

"W-Wait, wait!" the man shouted.

Kull held up a hand. "Take a deep breath! It's okay. I'm fine. Just breathe." She demonstrated by gulping down air and then exhaling.

After a long sigh, Enzo released the perv. He eyed the guy as he crept to the door of the ice cream parlor and then bolted out into the parking lot.

"It's okay to be angry in some situations," Enzo stated.

Kull held up a finger. "True, but that's for *after* you master your curse. Until then, every hamburger man is an *opportunity*." She used jazz hands when she spoke the last word.

Enzo rolled his eyes. "Ugh. Fine. Let's just get this over with."

CHAPTER
THIRTY-THREE

Before Finch rewound time, he allowed Kull to eat her pavlova. It turned out that Scoops & Smiles *did* have the rare dessert, which came as a shock. However, as they ate, Enzo sat on his side of the booth, obviously lost in thought. He kept his muscled arms crossed over his chest, his attention on nothing.

But then Enzo sat straight and glanced over at Finch. "Why does it take the two of you so long to come pick me up? Each time you rewind everything, it feels like it takes an eternity before you arrive."

"I marked the time while standing out in the wooded area just outside of Oakland," Finch said. "So when I rewind time, we always appear there."

"Explains the weird smells you sometimes have." Enzo snorted. "Why did you mark the time there?"

"That's where I died," Kull said matter-of-factly.

"What?"

Kull nodded. "Fox-Pistol died out in the woods. As soon as I inhabited her body, Finch marked the time."

As though this information jolted him out of his depression, Enzo leaned forward onto the table. "Wait. *Wait*. How long ago did Fox-Pistol die?"

"A handful of hours ago." Finch sighed. "I'd guess at least six, no more than twelve."

"And you haven't caught the killer?"

Finch shook his head. He thought over everything that had happened in the evening so far, putting all the facts in place. "I thought Charlie's death would be linked to Fox-Pistol's, but that turned out not to be the case. Apparently, there is a killer in Oakland who targets pretty women, but Charlie's death was unrelated. Since figuring that all out, the only lead I have left is Fox-Pistol's boyfriend, whom we've yet to find."

Not that they had been looking for him. Finch was more concerned about solving the Charlie situation before tackling the roaming Oakland killer.

Enzo slapped the surface of the table and smiled. "If she really died out in the woods, and you know the exact location, maybe this is a job for a bunch of wolves."

"What do you mean?" Kull asked, her eyebrows raised. She chewed more of her delicious pavlova, but she leaned closer to Enzo, clearly eager to learn more.

"I'll call up the guys at Level 22, and we'll sniff out the death site. Then we'll scour Oakland. There's at least fifteen of us at the club. If we spread out, we'll probably be able to find this killer in no time at all."

"And the wolves will just help us?" Finch asked. From his experience, packs of werewolves didn't typically help warlocks.

Enzo shrugged. "We might have to convince them, but I think we can do it."

"That'll probably be the fastest way to handle this."

Finch liked the idea, although he hadn't dealt much with werewolves in the past. He wasn't entirely certain what would be required to get their aid, but whatever it was, it was a small price to pay to catch a killer.

Or…

He would just get them to help, find the killer's hideout, and then rewind time so that they never remembered helping to begin with. That way, he wouldn't owe anyone anything.

Hopefully Enzo wouldn't mind.

"Oh, this was so good." Kull patted her tummy. "I'm glad humans have *so much* good food. I can't wait to see what else you all have."

"If you're done, I'm going to reset the day again," Finch said. "We'll finish helping Charlie, and then we'll go see our wolf buddies."

"Okay! Sounds like a plan."

Finch activated his magic. The ice cream parlor froze. The colors drained away. All the shapes fell into a white void —and then Finch was back in the woods, just outside Oakland.

5:29 p.m.

As Finch walked over to pick up Kull, she patted herself clean. Then she glanced up at him, her smile half gone.

"Adair, I thought you said you hadn't ever been in love."

He scooped her into his arms. "I haven't."

"But you said losing someone you loved felt like hooks being ripped from your body. How do you know that?"

"Love comes in many forms," he said with a groan. "Romantic, familial—I've lost people I loved. I wasn't *in love* with them."

"Like your brother," Kull said as she wrapped her arms around his neck.

Finch exhaled. He wanted nothing more than to change the subject. "Ya know, you don't need to focus so much on *love*. You don't need anyone else in order to live a full human life. You could focus on your career. Or develop a skill. Relying on someone could be a mistake—especially if they leave you."

But Kull just laughed.

Finch glanced down, his eyes narrowed in irritation. "What's so funny?"

"I didn't give up my immortality to do something as mundane as having a human career."

"You don't have to have a mundane career. You're already a Facebook star."

"YouTube," Kull corrected.

"Whatever. That's unique and special, right? You could pour yourself into that. Then you won't need anyone." Finch spoke the last statement in half a whisper, no emotion in the words.

Sometimes, he wished he could just go *far* back in time and do *everything* over. Maybe then he could've left Carter at home, and protected him, and…

And…

"Nothing is more special or precious than love," Kull finally said, dragging Finch out of his mire of thoughts. "It's one of the few things humans have that other creatures don't. And even among humans, real love is rare. Not everyone finds it. And it's my greatest dream to experience it."

Finch didn't have a counter for that.

Kull smiled. "I won't give that up because it became hard, or because I might find the wrong person a few times before I get to the right one."

He admired her tenacity. But Finch just couldn't imagine himself getting involved with someone. He could see having fun for a night, or maybe an occasional thing—but Finch didn't want any of the pains associated with a real relationship.

He was better off alone.

And at some level, he knew even *working* with others was a mistake. They were all a hassle. A potential tool to be used against him.

Heartaches waiting to happen.

As Finch traveled through the wooded area, Kull tugged on his coat. "Do you think I can go see all Fox-Pistol's friends while you finish up your card games? Maybe I can learn a bunch of fun human things from them. I mean, I've seen you play the exact same cards way too many times."

"All right," Finch said.

Kull excitedly clapped her hands. In a cute, genuinely happy way, she said, "Yay!"

"And if you run into trouble, just get me, okay?"

Kull poked the tip of his nose with her pointer finger. "Of course. I'll be there right away if anything bad happens." She ended her statement with a giggle, and Finch wondered if he was making a mistake.

―――――

Once they arrived at the Lake Merritt Grand Hotel, Kull leapt out of the vehicle with enough energy for three people. This time around, while at Ross, she had purchased a cocktail dress and stockings, and she definitely wore them well.

Maybe too well.

But Finch didn't want to think about that.

As he exited the vehicle, he glanced over at Enzo. *His* clothes weren't ripped this time around. Apparently, Enzo had gotten hold of his anger in the short time they had left him.

"Maybe you should go with Kull once she gets me into the high roller room," Finch muttered. "Keep an eye on her."

"I'd rather stick with you," Enzo stated. "So I can... learn to temper my anger when around those POS elves."

Finch decided not to argue. Instead, they traveled as a trio into the hotel, to the elevator, and all the way to the high roller room, just like the dozens of times before. An elf knight led the way, ushered them inside, and pointed out the table.

Finch walked over to Charlie, offered to win back her debts, and took her seat. Everything was exactly the same, except this time, Kull quietly let herself out of the room, intent on joining the rest of Fox-Pistol's crew for an evening of partying.

This would be the twenty-fourth time doing this, and Finch was determined to make it the last. He pushed all other thoughts out of his mind and focused on the game.

Finch had to stay with the first hand.

Then he had to take one card and stay with the second hand.

Third hand—a perfect twenty-one. Just like before.

Finch hit twice and then stayed with the fourth hand.

On the fifth hand, he took his sixes and stayed.

With his sixth hand, Finch hit and then stayed.

With the seventh, he sat out. The unwinnable hand.

On the eighth, ninth, tenth, and eleventh, the dealer busted each time.

Everything was playing out *exactly* as he remembered it. Each play, each card, each movement. Charlie hovered close; the dealer shuffled the cards at all the correct moments.

Then the dealer tapped something on the underside of the table. Finch kept his eye on the door until finally Liligale came to join them. Right on schedule.

Her knights funneled into the room, but unlike last time,

there were two less. Only *ten* elves joined them in the room, and Finch wondered why. Where had the other two knights gone?

Rad shuddered and leaned away from Liligale when she approached—just like before.

But Finch's attention went to Enzo. The werewolf watched the knights with an intense look in his eyes. He didn't move to attack, though. He didn't even seem that irritated. Enzo took even breaths, perhaps using the techniques Kull had discussed with him.

"Hello, Adair," Liligale said in a cool and confident manner. "My name is Liligale Vi'Thamis—"

"Head of the Pacific Court," Finch finished for her. "I know."

"Hm?" She straightened her thin-framed glasses. "I don't believe we've met. I would've remember talking to someone of your caliber."

"I'll never forget the first time we met, but I'll keep trying," Finch quipped. But before Liligale could process that cryptic statement, Finch added, "I'm here to win back all Charlotte Woolsy's debt."

Liligale glanced at his winning chips, the table, and then to the soothsayer in the back. The elf in charge of making sure no magic was being used just shrugged. No one could accuse Finch of cheating, because they'd never be able to figure it out.

"I've been informed of your winning streak," Liligale said, her voice icy. "I came here to remind you we have strict punishments for those who… break the rules."

Finch lifted an eyebrow. "People who live in glass houses shouldn't throw stones."

The statement clearly caught Liligale off guard. She slowly crossed her arms. "I see you brought a dog with you. I wasn't aware Adair Finch kept company with one of the three most disgusting things to walk this planet."

"Besides you, what're the other two things?"

Enzo stifled a laugh. He managed to choke it down, so perhaps it *could've* been a cough.

Liligale's face reddened as she lifted one eyebrow.

Finch knew he was pushing his luck, but he had already had this conversation, and now he didn't feel like being so serious.

Liligale was clearly not amused. The knights around the room reached for their sidearms. All of them were prepared for a bloodbath.

"It's a serious offense for a warlock to enter our territory and offer up such snide and childish remarks," Liligale whispered.

Even the card dealer felt the tension in the air. She scooted away from the table an inch or two, her eyes nervously darting over to the knights.

Finch held up a finger. "Listen, how about you allow me to play to win back Charlie's debt. Afterward, I'll apologize, and then I'll never step foot on this property ever again. I also won't investigate the losing odds at this establishment—which seem rather questionable. Do we have a deal?"

She was going to suggest that deal anyway, Finch just wanted to cut to the chase.

Liligale knitted her eyebrows, blatantly confused by his proposition. She probably thought it strange Finch had offered up the exact deal she was about to make. However, without a proper explanation—because the soothsayer still wasn't pointing out any magic use—Liligale moved on.

"I will accept these terms," Liligale whispered. "But it won't just be this hotel you're banned from—it will be all my territory. Everything the Pacific Court rules over."

That was the payment for insulting her to her face. Finch kept that in mind, for when he finally lived through this day.

If he wanted the satisfaction of mocking the queen-bee elf, he'd be barred from returning to most of Oakland.

Finch gave it serious consideration.

"Deal." Then he tapped the felt of the table. "Let's get these last two hands over with."

CHAPTER
THIRTY-FOUR

"This has been one of the most entertaining nights of my life," Rad said as he shifted closer to the card table.

"More entertaining than the nights where girls spit on you?" Finch quipped.

Rad's half-fae face paled. He held his breath, as though stupefied by Finch's comment. Once he managed to swallow some air, he murmured, "But how… how would you ever know that?"

"I'm Adair Finch. I know everything."

His own statement got him chuckling. It was beyond cocky, but after living through the same night for more than a month and a half, Finch didn't mind adding some spice to his interactions. Why not agitate the Head of the Pacific Court? Why not call out some rando's fetish? All the other elves in the room were snickering—they clearly thought it was funny.

"Wait," Rad whispered. "Now I remember. I *have* heard of you. Adair Finch is some sort of warlock for hire. A private investigator. You've never let a client down? Never failed a case?"

"That's right," Finch stated.

Liligale moved around the card table with the energy of a hungry shark. "Technically untrue, warlock. Or do you not count the death of your brother as a failure? It certainly sounds like a failure to me."

Her statement chilled the room. No more snickering. No more discussions.

Enzo took a step forward, and four of the elven knights crowded around him. He gritted his teeth and slunk backward, his eyes on Liligale.

Finch's chest hurt, like the words he *wanted* to use were clawing their way from his body. But he held back his rage and didn't give Liligale the satisfaction of seeing him upset. Instead, he smiled.

"My brother died so the people in Paris could live," Finch stated. "That might be a high price to pay, but given what was saved, it's no failure."

In his heart, Finch knew *he* had been the failure. If he had just done things differently, he could've saved Carter. But instead, he had fucked up. And then Carter was gone—and the hooks had taken their toll.

The card dealer hesitantly grabbed cards and tossed them out to both Finch and Rad. She went about it as quickly as professionally possible, her attention constantly shifting to Liligale. She was waiting for silent instructions, no doubt in Finch's mind.

"I met your brother once," Liligale said, the faux sweetness in her voice a dead giveaway of her vile intentions. She must've sensed how upset Finch had gotten at the mere mention of his dead brother, and now she was going to use that to her advantage.

Liligale wanted him to lose. She wanted Charlie's debt so

she could strong-arm Jay-W, and she definitely wanted Finch out of the picture.

Finch wasn't about to let any of that happen.

He glanced at his cards. A seven and four. A great hand, because all he needed was a ten to reach twenty-one. The probability of being dealt a ten was roughly thirty percent, but given whom he was dealing with, Finch knew hitting more than once would cause him to bust.

The dealer had one card showing—an eight. There was a good chance the house would end with eighteen, or perhaps even bust.

"Carter Finch was a talented warlock." Liligale continued to circle the table, her movements graceful, her tone grating. "Wasn't he married to a sweet little witch? His death must've really devastated her."

Finch tapped the table for another card. The dealer slid it over.

But he couldn't see it.

His thoughts immediately went to Carter—to his widowed wife, Jessica—and how Carter had been so eager to return home to see her.

Yes, Finch had seen true love. He had seen the way Carter and Jessie looked at each other. How they had their own little language made of gentle touches, small jokes, and reassuring smiles. How they had talked about their future together, even made grand plans, and spun wonderful dreams.

Whenever they were away from home, on a case for a client, Finch would wake to the sound of Carter's phone buzzing. Jessie always sent loving messages for Carter to see when he awoke. Never was Carter happier than when he rolled over to answer those messages.

But the hooks had taken their toll on Jessie, too.

For weeks after his death, she still sent those messages.

Every morning, like clockwork. Her hands shaking when

she typed out silly messages about her dreams, or cute things she saw. Like Carter would one day come back and see it all.

Finch knew her pain was his fault—which was why he had never reached out to her. Jessie had never blamed him, and had always remained optimistic, but Finch couldn't look her in the eyes.

"Sir?" the card dealer asked.

"Stay," Finch muttered.

He still hadn't glanced at his card. He had almost forgotten he was playing.

"*Adair*," Enzo called out. The elves around him tensed, but he didn't move or even begin to transform. "Focus, man. You got this."

Finch couldn't bring himself to answer.

Rad made his plays, but again, Finch barely saw what was happening. He hadn't thought of his brother's widowed wife in years. It hurt too much.

With a snort and half a growl, Enzo turned and headed for the door. The knights glanced at Liligale, silently asking what to do. She motioned to the werewolf, and four of the knights followed after the man as he left the high roller room.

Rad finally finished his plays and sighed something. Then the dealer went through her motions.

"The house busts," the dealer said.

It took a few seconds for Finch to absorb that. He pushed his cards away, aware he still needed to play one more game. Rad murmured something about winning, or wanting to win, but Finch ignored him.

He felt as though he were submerged underwater, the noises dulled and far off, his body heavy.

The dealer passed out two more cards to everyone. Then the dealer flipped over one of hers. Again, Finch didn't really see it. His mind was on other things. When he peeked at his own hand, he saw black and red, but none of the numbers.

What was the point of this, anyway?

It wasn't his job to help Charlie and Jay-W straighten out their lives. Finch gave serious thought to just leaving Oakland altogether.

The door to the high roller room burst open. Kull practically leapt into the room, somehow bringing light with her, as though the illumination from the hallway was now pouring in. Enzo and the four knights followed shortly afterward—the werewolf had obviously tracked her down.

"Adair?" Kull walked over, but was stopped by a knight in a dark suit before she reached Finch's side. Despite that, she continued. "Enzo told me everything. That weird elf is just big mad that you're winning so hard!"

"*What disrespect is this?*" Liligale asked from the other side of the card table.

"You heard me." Kull flipped some of her red hair over her shoulder. "I'm Fox-Pistol, and I calls it like I sees it." She flashed Finch one of her brightest smiles. "Don't listen to a thing she says, Adair. We have so many lives to save after this! Isn't that what Carter would want us to do?"

Finch ran a hand down his face, clearing his thoughts. If Carter were here, he would insist on helping everyone. And he, too, wouldn't have blamed Finch for what had happened. Finch knew that—it was just hard to see sometimes.

He glanced at his cards again. He saw the numbers and remembered what he was doing.

Nothing they did would prevent him from winning; they just didn't know that yet.

"Hit me," Finch stated.

The dealer tossed another card. He saw it, but his mind was elsewhere.

"I'll stay."

Kull grabbed Enzo's arm and shook it. "Adair is totes going to win!"

"Would you calm down?" Enzo growled.

"You said Adair needed some cheering on. Cheering requires *loudness*. I know, I've seen it in some commercials for a game about *Shadow Legends* or something."

Rad slammed the card table and turned in his chair until he was facing Kull. "Well, *Rad* needs some silence, hm? Anyone stop to think about Rad? No? I didn't think so." He peeked at his cards and grumbled, "Talkin' about dead brother and shit when I'm trying to play a high-stakes card game."

And although she had been as silent as the grave the whole game, Charlie shifted her weight before adding, "Well, whatever Adair needs is what *I* need, so you keep cheerin', girlie."

Liligale, without a single amused cell in her body, pointed to the door. "Remove these disrespectful animals. If they resist, you know what to do."

The knights of her court all tilted their heads in a slight bow before gathering around Enzo and Kull. Neither of them resisted, but Kull gave Finch two over-the-shoulder glances, as if to make sure he was okay.

Finch nodded to her.

He would be okay—he was focused again.

Kull gave him a thumbs up before she was dragged from the room.

"Hit me," Finch stated.

The dealer tossed him yet another card.

"I'll stay." He held his cards close and then took a deep breath. What had those meditation guides suggested? Something about picturing a grassy meadow.

Finch exhaled, and tried not to let his old wounds bleed him out.

Rad glanced at his cards several times. Then he tapped the table and got a new card. And another one. Then he tossed everything into the air in one dramatic go. *"Paska!"* he shouted.

Which was interesting. Finch only knew a little bit of Finnish, but he knew enough to know when someone was cursing. His half-fae friend was clearly from Finland.

When the dealer took her turn, she flipped over the cards with unsteady hands. Finch wondered why she would be so nervous, but he had a couple solid guesses. She'd probably be reprimanded if he won. However, unless she was going to use some sleight-of-hand trickery, the house could never win.

When the dealer flipped over another card, the house busted.

"Oh my god," Charlie shouted. She practically jumped into the air. "You did it! You lucky son of a bitch, you did it!" Without any warning, she wrapped her arms around Finch's neck and squeezed hard.

"Yeah," he croaked. "Woo."

Liligale glared daggers at the dealer, but didn't say a word to her. Instead, she sharked her way over to Finch, her movements stiff.

"Good game, warlock," she whispered. "You have exactly five minutes to leave my hotel—and this city. Let us pray to the northern forests we never see each other again."

He made a mental note of her declaration. Finch couldn't be banished from the whole city if he was going to do things like catch a killer and recruit a bunch of half-spirits. He would need more time. Which meant, whenever he did this for the final run, he'd need to make sure he didn't upset Liligale too much.

"I'm on my way out," Finch said as he got to his feet.

Charlie clung to his arm, giggling the whole way like a

child in a candy store. Together, they made their way to the door, and then exited into the hall, where Enzo and Kull were waiting. The knights sneered as they returned to their elven leader, none of them saying a word.

"I knew you could do it," Kull said, softly clapping her hands.

Charlie tightened her grip on Finch. "Thank you so much. *Thank you.*" She shook her head. "But how did my husband know? I... I never told him a thing. I was so careful."

"He doesn't know." Finch sighed. "I lied. Your husband hired me because he thinks you're cheating on him."

Charlie released Finch's arm in a heartbeat. "*What?* Jay said that? Of course he did. Ever since he put on all that weight, he's been a different—jealous—man."

"Why did you hide what you were doing?" Kull asked.

After a deep breath, Charlie fluffed her curly hair. "Oh, well... Jay didn't want me gambling anymore. I told him I could handle it, but he didn't like how much I lost last time. I, uh, ignored him. And gambled anyway."

Enzo rolled his eyes and groaned. "Oh. You're one of *those* types."

"Don't judge me," Charlie snapped. "I don't know what happened! Normally, I win some, I lose some. I never get too deep. But when I came here, things went south. Too fast. I couldn't tell Jay. He'd be upset—and I didn't want that."

"And then the elves started suggesting you give them property, is that right?" Finch asked.

Charlie grabbed Finch's arm, her hands unsteady. "I... couldn't tell Jay any of that. He'd be pissed. I just... I figured I could win my way out of the hole."

"This is textbook addicts' behavior," Enzo said matter-of-factly. "Satisfying their urges in secret. Not asking for help. Making the situation worse until the problem spirals out of control. You have a problem, lady."

Again, Charlie tightened her grip on Finch. She didn't argue this time.

Kull stared at Charlie's hands on Finch, and then let out a loud and anxious laugh. "Oh, well, it's all over now." She stepped forward, awkwardly wedged her way between Finch and Charlie and then waved. "Have fun seeing Jay-W. Don't go gambling again, okay?"

"What's gotten into you?" Finch moved away and patted his arm. "We need to take her back to Jay-W's place."

Kull tapped her lower lip. "Is it possible in under five minutes? I think it would be better if she just took herself."

"Once I know she's safe with Jay-W, I can rewind things, and we can solve the *last* of everything before leaving this dump of a city."

"Rewind?" Charlie whispered, her eyes narrowed.

"Never mind," Enzo snapped. "Let's do it. I want to get away from these redwood elves as quickly as possible."

CHAPTER
THIRTY-FIVE

They piled into Finch's Toyota and took off down the road to Jay-W's house. The drive through Oakland on a Friday night was a slow one, and they had used up their five minutes of the time only five blocks from the hotel.

Finch was hoping the elves would be understanding, but given Liligale's track record, he kept his eyes on the nearby buildings, waiting for some sort of surprise attack.

"You drive around in this old thing?" Charlie glanced around the inside of the car. She sat in the back, next to Enzo, her legs crossed and her posture stiff. "Jay would've called us a limo."

"I prefer to drive," Finch muttered.

Kull, in the front passenger's seat, turned around enough to stare into the back. "Charlie, how long have you been with Jay-W?"

"Almost twenty years." She shrugged. "We met in high school."

"And you love him?" Kull asked the question with a little *d'aww* in her voice.

Charlie couldn't seem to hold back a smile. "Jay is definitely my man." She flashed her ridiculously large wedding ring. "And he treats me like a queen."

"Okay, okay." Kull waved away her comments. "That's not important. What *is* important is whether or not you can tell me what love feels like. How will I know I've fallen in love, and someone has fallen for me? What am I looking for?"

"You're looking for someone who completes you." Charlie shrugged. "You're looking for someone who makes you your best and most interesting self when you're with them. Does that make sense?"

"*Best and most interesting self?*" Enzo repeated with a scoff. "Kull, don't listen to that new age garbage. You'll know you're in love because your happiness will be contingent on another's."

Kull furrowed her brow. "What does that mean?"

"It means you won't be happy unless they are. When their happiness and well-being mean more to you than your own. Love is about sacrifice, not about whatever nonsense she's talkin' about."

"It's not nonsense," Charlie snapped. She jabbed her finger into his arm, poking Enzo hard in his bicep. "What do you know about love, huh? Jay and I helped each other grow from nothin'."

"Don't touch me, woman," Enzo said through gritted teeth.

Charlie reached into her purse and pulled out a phone. She tapped at the screen with quick, furious pecks. "Let's see what the internet has to say. I bet it'll agree with me."

"I will confiscate your phone like I'm your teacher." Enzo shot her a cold glare.

With all the rebellious energy of an angsty teen, Charlie continued to tap away at the screen.

Kull sat back in her seat. When she glanced over at Finch,

she mouthed, *"No one can agree. Everyone always has a different answer."*

At this point, Finch did think it was amusing. How many definitions could one word have? He supposed he would find out, since Kull was so insistent on asking everyone.

A black SUV slammed into the side of Finch's Toyota with enough force to break the windows on the driver's side. Charlie screamed and, in the process of covering her head, dropped her phone.

While glass had cut up Finch's left hand, he never let go of the steering wheel. He kept the car in his lane, gently hit the brakes, and allowed the SUV to speed past him. Finch turned his car and positioned himself behind his attackers.

They were on Interstate-580, heading north, with four lanes of traffic. And even at night, California had a traffic problem. There were cars everywhere. If Finch wasn't careful, he could cause a pile up just trying to avoid someone else.

"What's going on?" Enzo shouted.

Kull pointed at the SUV. "It's the elves. I can smell their fae magic."

"Those sons of bitches."

Debris flew out of the SUV and splattered across Finch's cracked windshield.

No.

When he got a better look at it all, he realized it wasn't debris. The elves had thrown dirt and seeds. He knew they weren't harmless—he had dealt with redwood elves before—and he swerved his car to shake the seeds off.

But some of them clung to his vehicle.

They sprouted, their bright green roots wrapping around his windshield wipers and burying themselves in the hood of the Toyota.

"Goddammit," Finch muttered with a groan.

"Those are poisonous," Kull said, pointing at the seeds. "Can't you taste all that acrid magic? Gross."

"Pull up next to them," Enzo yelled. "I'll handle this myself."

Black fur sprouted across his rippling muscles. He growled, the sound coming from deep in his gut, claws exploding out of his fingertips. He had ears and an elongated snout before Finch could voice his plan.

"Calm down," Finch said.

He slowed and pulled onto the shoulder, but the SUV followed suit. Multiple cars on the interstate honked, and some of them even darted by. Only a few—smart and more alert individuals—moved away from Finch and his pursuers.

The seeds continued to grow, fueled by fae magic. The redwood elves were notorious for their growth magic. That was why their trees were so gigantic—no other fae knew how to make things grow like they did.

And within a matter of seconds, the plants that had erupted from the seeds were making their way into Finch's engine.

He suspected the villainous flora would stall the vehicle and even reach into the cab of the car and search for flesh. The poisonous plants fae kept would be dangerous to the touch. It seemed Liligale took her five-minute warning seriously.

Her foul play was enraging. Finch's heart beat faster—and hotter—than before. The plants would never survive his blaze, but would he endanger other people on the interstate with his magic?

Definitely.

Ke-Koh's fire wasn't subtle or nuanced. It was like a blast from a bomb.

Without warning, a whole flock of pigeons descended upon the interstate.

A couple dozen pigeons fluttered onto the hood of

Finch's car. Charlie screamed again, and Enzo growled loud enough to drown out all other noise. The birds weren't chased away. Finch tightened his grip on the steering wheel, but again, didn't swerve. He slowed, allowing the cars behind him time to realize what was going on.

"Kull?" Finch snapped.

She giggled. "Mischief magic."

The pigeons frantically pecked at the plants. They gobbled them up, including the seed casing, and in a few instances, grabbed the thin plant vines and attempted to fly away. The birds managed to rip away the largest of the vile plants and take to the sky, clearing most of Finch's vehicle.

More pigeons—*dozens* more—flew at the black SUV. They slammed into the side, into the windshield, into the mirrors —generally attacking the vehicle as though they were meth addicts and the SUV had the last stash of meth in the world.

The elves swerved, their tires screeching.

Finch took advantage of their panic. As soon as he could, he sped by the SUV, leaving them in the middle of the interstate with a cloud of pigeons swarming around them. The bird flock must've been too thick, because the SUV didn't react to Finch passing it.

The pigeons cooed at high-pitched frequencies, flapping their wings at feverish speeds as they attempted to get into the vehicle.

Enzo, now a full-blown werewolf, rested back in his seat. He took deep breaths, his fangs flashing. "Those elves…"

"It's okay," Kull said, turning to make eye contact with him. "We ditched them!"

"Thank you, Kull," Finch stated.

He preferred this outcome. He didn't like putting humans in danger, even if he could rewind time. There were just some things he couldn't un-see, and he wasn't yet so callous and jaded as to mind a pileup of bodies.

Finch thought about rewinding time right now, but he decided against it. The more information he gathered now, the more he would know what to do on the final iteration of this insane day.

Charlie exhaled and then smoothed her clothes with shaky hands. "I'm... I'm sorry about that." She turned her wide eyes to Enzo and gave him the once over. "Oh. I know you. You're the bartender at Level 22."

"Yeah," Enzo said with a growl. "Took you long enough."

"I've never seen you in human form before. You look good."

Enzo snorted. "Heh. Don't worry. We'll get you home. *And no more screamin'.* You're safe with us."

"Apparently." Charlie patted the back of Kull's seat. "Thank you. All of you. I don't know what I would've done if this was all left up to me."

Finch didn't mention anything, but he *knew* what would happen if it were all left to her.

———

It didn't take long before Finch pulled his car into Jay-W's underground garage.

The place could house two dozen vehicles, but currently, there were only fifteen parked here. Finch picked an empty spot and then stepped out of his Toyota.

His car was rather busted up, but all the plants were either shredded or gone.

Finch didn't dare touch what remained. He just rolled his eyes and headed to the elevator that would take them up to Jay-W's.

They all piled into the elevator, and Charlie visibly calmed down the moment the doors shut. She smiled and hummed as it went up and then *dinged*.

"Home sweet home." Charlie stepped out into the living room.

The gigantic space was everything Finch remembered. Famous artwork hung on the walls and over the massive fireplace. The couches were wide and luxurious.

And Lloyd, the gigantic thug in a suit, stood near the hallway entrance, his eyes huge as he reached for his sidearm. He stopped the moment he recognized Charlie.

"Little Boss!" he said, half gasping. "I didn't… think you'd be here tonight?" Then Lloyd glanced over at Kull. "Is that *Fox-Pistol?* The Fox-Pistol?" He comically rubbed his eyes and blinked several times.

"That's right!" Kull did a little twirl and then winked. "Remember to like and subscribe because you're gonna wanna see *this* face on the daily!"

"What are you doin' here?" Lloyd spoke as though he were talking to an angel.

Finch sighed and then stomped forward. Enzo, still in werewolf form, followed behind. Lloyd didn't seem shocked by that at all. He was part infernal, and Finch suspected Jay-W worked with werewolves on the regular. All the operations, and people, here were in the know. The supernatural didn't worry them.

Finch, Enzo, Charlie, and Kull strode down Jay-W's long hallway until they reached his office. The door was closed, but Lloyd quickly made his way past them in order to knock.

"Who is it?" Jay-W grunted from the other side.

"It's your wife, Boss," Lloyd said. "Should I let her in?"

"Of course you'll let me in." Charlie pushed by the man and walked into the office herself.

The office…

Jay-W sat beyond a grandiose desk, just like before. In one hand, Jay-W held a glass of brandy, but he almost dropped it when his wife bounded into the room.

"Charlotte?" he whispered.

Charlie hurried around the side of the desk and immediately threw her arms around his corpulent neck. She squeezed him tight. "Jay. You're so amazing. Thank you."

"W-What?" His fat face grew red, but he eventually returned his wife's embrace and gently rubbed her back. "Anythin' for you, babe."

Charlie kissed his cheek and then stood straight. "You hiring Adair Finch was the best decision you've made in a long time."

With a bewildered expression, Jay-W turned his icy blue eyes on Finch. He pursed his lips until the redness left him. "Explain," he demanded.

Finch held up his phone. "You were calling. I knew you wanted me to investigate your wife to see if she was cheating, so I went and found her. Turns out, she had a sizeable gambling debt. And no cheating."

"*What?*"

"Don't worry. I won it all back. She doesn't have a debt anymore."

Jay-W, still bewildered, allowed his mouth to hang open for a prolonged moment. "What?" he asked again.

"Then I brought her here." Finch pointed at the man. "The redwood elves want your waterfront properties. They were tricking Charlie into losing so they could hold the debt over your head. You've been officially warned."

Kull gave him finger guns. "Yeah! Officially warned! Pew pew."

It was all too much for Jay-W. He stared for a long moment, slowly absorbing the information like a small hill absorbs the melting snow from an avalanche.

"You owe me a hundred grand," Finch finally stated. "For bringing you back your wife, safe and sound."

Jay-W, a man of money and business dealings, snapped

out of his confusion the moment a bill came into the equation. "Now, you see here—I don't owe you jack shit. I didn't hire you. I never got a hold of you!"

That was true. In this loop of the day, Finch had never visited Jay-W to officially take the case. He exhaled, hating the fact he would *need* to factor this into his daily routine.

Then Charlie placed a hand on Jay-W's large shoulder. "Babe. Just pay him the money. He really did help me."

Jay-W turned his gargantuan chair until he was facing his wife. He didn't stand; he just remained seated as he cupped one of her hands with his. "This is business—I can't go lettin' people pick the price."

"I was four million in the hole. He played until I owed nothin'. A hundred grand is a drop in the bucket compared to that."

Jay-W caressed her knuckles. "And that's it? You were just gamblin'? With elves? Nothin' else?" He lifted his gaze to meet hers. "There weren't any pool boys? No side pieces?"

Charlie stroked the man's thinning hair and then leaned in to kiss him. The show of affection lasted longer than Finch wanted. At least fifteen seconds, which was fourteen seconds into *awkward*.

"Isn't that cute?" Kull smiled. "That's love, right?"

"Uh… It's something," Finch said under his breath.

"Will you point out when you see something genuinely loving?"

"Sure. If I see it, I'll let you know."

When Charlie finally stopped their kiss, she said, "I told you I'd never fool around behind your back."

"I told you not to gamble anymore," Jay-W grumbled.

"I learned my lesson." She used a finger to make a cross over her heart. "I won't go betting anything over a grand in the future."

With a frown, Jay-W eventually nodded. Then he glared

at Finch. "Fine. Whatever. I'll get you the money." With an aggressive point, he added, "But this also means you have to answer my got-damn calls in the future! Understood? That's a requirement to gettin' paid."

"Sure," Finch said. "We have a deal."

CHAPTER
THIRTY-SIX

Finch rewound time.

His payment from Jay-W vanished. His card games were undone. Charlie returned to the hotel, unaware of all the things he had done for her.

When Finch found himself in the woods outside Oakland, he took a deep breath and relaxed.

5:29 p.m.

The crunch of leaves and twigs caused Finch to glance up. Instead of waiting to be picked up, Kull had stood on her own. She walked over to Finch, grimacing with each step and uttering a little *ow*.

"What're you doing?" Finch quickly moved forward, but before he could grab her, Kull gave him a tight hug.

He was so stunned, they just stood in place for a long moment. The woods were cold, but the embrace was warm.

"Are you okay?" Kull squeezed him even tighter.

Finch pulled her arms off his body and frowned. "What's gotten into you? Don't hurt your feet. I'm completely fine." He showed her his hands, which were no longer cut up from the broken glass of his mangled car. "Everything returns to normal when I rewind time."

"I'm not talking about your injuries." Kull met his gaze, her eyebrows knitted. "Enzo told me what that elf said about your brother." In a voice barely louder than a whisper, she added, "I know it still bothers you. It still hurts."

After a deep inhale, Finch shook his head. "I'm okay. I was just… caught off guard. I wasn't expecting her to bring that up."

"Why *did* she bring it up?"

"To get an advantage." Finch scooped Kull up and held her. "I told you. She shot Enzo to make a scene. She tried to use my brother's death to shake me—Liligale would've done anything to see me fail."

Kull slowly nodded along with his words. Then her eyes went wide, and she stared with renewed intensity.

"What is it?" Finch asked.

"I think I understand people a little bit more now," she whispered. "You see, spirits are born of a certain feeling, and we announce who we are, and never pretend otherwise. But humans—and fae, too, I suppose—have ulterior motives. They hide things. They don't state their true desires or intentions."

Finch chuckled and then continued his way through the woods. That was true, he supposed. People did hide some of themselves.

"Like when Caleb told me I was the most important person. He lied! He said things to make me think we were in love, but he really just wanted to hook up." Kull puffed her cheeks in an adorable display of irritation. "And Liligale said and did all sorts of things to hide what she really wanted! I don't like that at all."

"A lot of humans will do that, with everything," Finch muttered. But then he snorted out a laugh. "Welcome to humanity! I hope you don't regret giving up your immortality to join us."

Kull giggled. Then she snuggled into Finch's hold. "These last few weeks have been the greatest of my life. Thank you, Adair."

"Don't thank me. I didn't make humanity. Trust me, I would've done a lot of things differently if I had."

Again, she giggled. "No, I was thanking you for being my human guardian. If I didn't have you, I probably would've ended up like those other half-spirits—living in a homeless encampment. You really had my back. Thank you."

Finch's face heated, and he shook his head as he replied, "Don't mention it."

———

After visiting the Ross, Finch drove to the location where he normally picked up Enzo and found the man standing on the curb, as usual. However, when Finch pulled the vehicle over to him, Enzo didn't jump in.

"Park," Enzo commanded. "Come inside. Meet the guys. We need to convince them to sniff around the death site as soon as possible."

With a heavy sigh, Finch did as Enzo instructed. He wasn't entirely sure how he was going to convince a pack of werewolves to help out with the case, but hopefully they would be good Samaritans all on their own.

Once he found a parking spot, Finch made his way to the front door of the massive building, figuring he'd need to go up to Level 22. Instead, Enzo was waiting for him, and motioned to a building down the road. Finch and Kull followed their werewolf pal until they made it to an upscale apartment building.

The sign on the side of the building read: **GULLY APARTMENTS.**

"Most of the guys who work at Level 22 live here," Enzo said as he punched in the code to get inside. "This place is friendly to people with *the curse*." He rolled his eyes and scoffed. "And the owners are a pair of witches. I think they're well over a hundred years old, but you can never tell. They always show up looking different each time. Sometimes older. Sometimes younger."

"Waxing crescent witches," Finch muttered.

Kull, who now wore jeans and a sporty tank top, gleefully leapt to the door of the apartment building. "Why don't *you* live here?"

Enzo shrugged. "These guys are younger than me. Not really my speed. And I like to be left alone."

"That's just like Adair."

"Hmm."

"We're going to meet *all* your werewolf friends?" Kull asked. "Right now?"

"Only the ones who aren't working." Enzo ushered them inside. "There's six of them. Frank, Mateo, Julian, Casey, Andre, and Leo. All good guys, but a little undisciplined, so don't make 'em angry, got it?"

Kull cringed and narrowed her eyes. "Oh. Right. They can wolf out if they get too angry. I almost forgot about that part."

"Most people don't willingly put themselves in a room with a bunch of wolves until they're one themselves. I'm surprised you two aren't a little more reticent."

Finch walked past the pair. "We'll be fine."

The main lobby of the Gully Apartments had high ceilings, and what Finch could only describe as "artful lighting." Different shades of blue and gold shone down from above, creating an elegant atmosphere, but not much illumination.

Finch hated it.

Kull entered and twirled in the lighting, her eyes wide. "Wow. So fancy."

"It's pretty nice," Enzo said with a shrug. "This way. Up the stairs to the second floor. There's a rec room that's shared. We're meeting the guys there. They should already be waiting."

"Why are they already waiting?" Kull headed to the stairs with a spring in her step. Finch understood why the man at the front lobby desk practically sprained something in his haste to glance up.

"I called them." Enzo waved to the receptionist. "They weren't doin' nothin' anyway."

The stairwell was brighter than the lobby, with carpeted steps and a clean railing. Once at the second story, Enzo opened the door and led them down the spacious hallway. Every door led to a rec room or a gym, each one in fairly decent condition.

Except for the claw marks.

Several of the workout benches were shredded as though a three-hundred-pound cat had sharpened its claws on them. Finch figured one of the wolves had probably gotten upset while lifting weights and raged on the machine.

Once they reached the last rec room, Enzo opened the door and went in first.

"*Heeeeyyyyy*," some guy said with all the enthusiasm of a college frat boy. "There he is!"

Finch and Kull entered afterward. The rec room was set up to watch sporting events. There were several couches, multiple chairs, and three giant TVs side by side. The table in the center of the room was large enough to hold dozens of snacks, and currently supported a mountain of chip bags.

The two mini fridges by the door were no doubt stocked full of beer.

Blinds were drawn on the two windows that looked out to the road.

The six werewolves were all in human form, and could've easily been mistaken for college football players. They lounged on the seats and couch, some with their feet up on the table.

They all wore similar clothes to Enzo—a tank top and sweatpants—though they were more colorful. One guy wore black, another had on a yellow jogging suit, and the others wore sweatpants with their favorite team's logo down one leg.

And just like Enzo, they were all in prime condition. The werewolf curse typically gave people extra energy, and the smart ones always burned it off in a gym.

None of them were quite as impressive as Enzo, however. He was probably the most disciplined of the bunch, given the demeanor of the group.

One man leapt off the couch—the one wearing red sweats.

"Enzo, you got a lot of nerve." The man waggled a finger. "You *quit* and then you call us here for a favor? That takes some serious balls."

Enzo shrugged. "Listen, Andre, this is important." He motioned with his head over to Finch. "Do you know who this is? It's Adair Finch, the most powerful warlock around."

Andre huffed and then rolled his eyes. "I don't care about that, man." Then he glared at Finch. "Is he why you quit? Huh? He gave you a better job? You're too good for us now?"

He spoke all the words with a playful tone, but even Finch could detect the building resentment. The guys in the room obviously liked Enzo—but they now had a beef with him.

"You know there's been killings around town." Enzo

crossed his arms. "Adair is trying to find the killer. I was hoping we could help him."

"Why?" Andre waved his hands like he was doing some pretend magic. "Can't the most powerful warlock just *hocus pocus* figure out who did it? Why does he need us?"

"He knows where someone was murdered just a few hours ago. We might be able to sniff out the killer."

Another one of the werewolves got off the couch—the one in the blue jogging suit—and he went straight to Finch. He was by far the tallest man in the room, and Finch had to tilt his head back to meet his gaze.

"I dunno," the man in blue muttered. "I think all I'm smelling is a little fear from our itty-bitty warlock." Then the werewolf inhaled and smirked.

The others in the room darkly chuckled.

But Finch knew the wolves didn't smell fear on him. He was holding back the urge to glance at his phone to see how long this was taking. The longer it took to convince them, the colder the trail would become. Did they really have time for a pissing contest? What was the fastest way to deal with this?

"Give it a rest, Mateo," Enzo said. "You're not as intimidating as you think you are."

Mateo opened his mouth like he was going to offer a retort, but then his attention snapped over to Kull. She had been standing back by the door, and slightly behind Finch. Once Mateo spotted her, his mind obviously ground to a halt.

Mateo shoved Finch to the side and strode over. Finch narrowed his eyes, brushed off his coat, and gave serious thought to starting something.

"Oh, hello," Mateo said, eyeing Kull. "What do we have here?"

She forced a smile and waved.

"You're so quiet." Mateo loomed over her.

"Thanks—you make me uncomfortable," Kull said in the most upbeat tone possible.

The other five werewolves all laughed. One of them grabbed a bag of chips from the table and hurled it at the back of Mateo's head.

"Pay attention," the guy shouted. "We're here to deal with Enzo's shit, not watch you strike out with the ladies. *Leave the poor girl alone.*"

Another guy scoffed. "Yeah, stop bein' so thirsty and focus."

Mateo stepped away from Kull, and then returned to the couch, his shoulders slumped. "I'm gonna be single forever," he muttered. That, too, garnered laughter from everyone around the room.

Finch glanced over at Kull, surprised she had been uncomfortable. She gave him a quick thumbs up, which he assumed meant she was okay to continue. Only once he was certain did he return his attention to Andre.

"What's it going to take for you all to help?" Finch asked. "Money?"

Andre shook his head. "We don't want your cash, warlock."

"Then what?"

Andre mulled over the question, clicking his tongue as he did so. Then he smiled. "You're the strongest warlock, huh? How about this—we'll help you out, but we want to know your weakness. A counter to your magic. Some way to shut you down."

"*What?*" Finch glared. "Why?"

"*Everyone* knows what werewolves are weak to."

"That's right," Mateo chimed in with a bark.

Andre shrugged. "You already know what it takes to hurt one of us, to kill all of us. You want us to help? Show a little trust. Show a little respect. Tell us what will shut down the great and powerful Adair Finch."

"No," Finch quickly stated.

On the one hand, he knew his weakness. It was the magic-eating god, Gixmoth, the one responsible for his brother's death. On the other hand, it would be impossible for these werewolves to use that monster's magic, so it was meaningless to tell them.

However, Finch intended to rewind the day, and wipe their memories of this event, so what did it hurt to tell them? He knew the answer to that—he couldn't tell the werewolves he had the power to rewind time, because then they would alter their actions, and perhaps even demand to keep their memories. Finch couldn't have that.

"If you're not going to tell us, we're not going to help you," Andre said matter-of-factly. "See? You don't trust us. You just want us to work for you like dogs."

Enzo stepped forward. "That's not true."

"*Yes, it is*. And if you were smart, you'd realize you're making a big mistake leaving *us* for *him*."

"Adair has been there for me," Enzo growled. "He's been helping me master this lycanthropy curse. I never would've brought him here unless I knew he was an ally."

"Bullshit." Andre pointed to the door. "You're a traitor. He's a douchebag. We have no interest in helping you."

Kull moved around Finch. "Wait!"

Andre narrowed his eyes at her, his lips curling up in a slight sneer. "What?"

"The killer is going around town, targeting innocent women," she said. "It's really sad, and I think it's important we stop whoever is doing it. Don't you think that's important?"

Finch found it interesting that Kull was determined. Then again, the killer had taken the real Fox-Pistol from the world.

Perhaps Kull just felt a duty to avenge her, as payment for the life Kull had inherited.

"That's why we have cops," Andre said. Then he tensed, his jaw clenched. "To catch murderers. And the cops don't trust us, either. So why are we going to risk getting into a tussle with a lunatic? Let humans deal with their own problems."

"Please reconsider."

"Nah." Andre turned away from her. "I made my conditions crystal clear. Speak up or get out."

Kull nervously fidgeted with her hair. Then she took a deep breath. "Okay. I'll tell you. Adair only has one weakness. And it's pussy."

The room was dead silent as that statement slowly soaked in.

Then everyone but Finch and Kull exploded into raucous laughter. Not normal laughter, like before—intense bellowing that could easily be heard outside the building.

"*That's so real,*" one of the werewolves said through wheezing laughs.

"That's *all* our weakness," another managed to choke out while gasping for air.

"*Aa-Ooo!*"

One of the wolves laughed so hard, and so long, he clearly wasn't breathing. He rolled off the couch and hit the floor, all while clutching his sides. Echoing guffaws filled the rec room, some of the wolves practically *hee-hawing* like donkeys.

Finch had never been so red in all his life.

He gave serious thought to rewinding time just to exit the situation.

Hell, he gave serious thought to jumping out the window, because years down the line, when he accidentally thought about this moment, the secondhand cringe would make him regret living.

Andre had tears streaming down his face as he braced his weight on his knees, doubled over. "That was so raw," he huffed out between laughs.

"They're tellin' it like it is!" another guy shouted, which only resulted in a fresh round of cackling.

Even Enzo couldn't help it. He bit his lip, but he was huffing out chuckles, unable to look Finch in the eyes.

Kull hesitantly smiled at him. "Ha, ha, funny, right?" she asked, her voice almost drowned out by all the mirth in the air.

"So funny," Finch deadpan replied.

Kull tapped the tips of her fingers together. "You'll forgive me?" Her face brightened with a coy smile. "I had this mischievous urge and I thought... it would be okay. Because they'll forget."

Finch's ears were still burning with embarrassment as he exhaled. "It's fine."

The werewolf on the floor still wasn't breathing. He was just dry heaving with uncontrollable laughter, his face purple.

"Okay," Andre said, gulping down air and rubbing the tears from his eyes. "Okay. That was good enough. We'll help you out."

CHAPTER
THIRTY-SEVEN

Finch drew the Mark of Chronos on Kull and Enzo and then drove to the woods outside Oakland. The six wolf-bros drove their own van, keeping close behind Finch the entire trek. It was an easy drive, but Finch worried about what order he would do everything in when he finally decided to finish this evening.

Enzo lounged across the whole back seat, smiling to himself. Occasionally, he would laugh once and then quiet back down. He was obviously still amused by Kull's statements back in the rec room.

"It wasn't *that* funny," Finch muttered.

"Says you." Enzo playfully punched the back of his seat. "You would've been laughin', too, if it had been someone else."

"I seriously doubt that."

Enzo sat straight, and his mirth disappeared. "Well, if you want us to be serious, why don't you tell me what happened back in the hotel, huh?"

"What're you talking about?" Finch snapped. He tightened

his grip on the steering wheel, keeping his attention on the road.

"You went dead behind the eyes when Liligale mentioned your brother and sister-in-law." Enzo leaned onto the back of Finch's seat. "You want to talk about it?"

"I do not," Finch stated.

"Maybe we should look on the internet to find guides on how to cope with grief."

Kull happily clapped her hands, her expression brighter than it had been the entire car ride. "I bet there will be *so many*. We can practice together."

"I don't need to cope with grief," Finch quickly said, hoping to shut this all down. "This was different. I'm… not ready to…"

"Face your sister-in-law," Kull whispered.

Finch sighed. "I don't want to think about her or my brother just yet. All I need is time."

"Says the man with literally infinite amounts of time," Enzo quipped. But instead of arguing the point, or forcing them to discuss the topic, Enzo just placed a hand on Finch's shoulder. "Listen, if you ever want to talk, I'm here."

"Me, too," Kull said. "We're your friends."

And while he wanted to say their words were just words, that wasn't the case. Finch nodded, and continued the drive.

He didn't want to talk, but it was nice to know they wanted to listen whenever he was ready.

———

Finch parked on the long road outside the city.

7:22 p.m.

It was dark out, but that didn't seem to bother the wolves. The six of them rolled out of their van, stretched their legs, and then turned to Finch. Andre stepped forward, a smirk on his face.

"This whole place stinks of death," he said. "Where, specifically, are we sniffing around?"

"This way." Finch pointed to the trees. He had walked the path from the murder site to his car over forty times now. He knew the way by heart.

As a group of nine, they all made their way off the road and between the trees. The crunch of dead leaves and dry twigs filled the air around them. The werewolf bros deeply inhaled every couple of steps, some of them with scrunched-up, confused expressions.

Kull stuck close to Finch and Enzo. She had shoes from Ross now, so Finch didn't need to carry her over the rough terrain. She didn't strike up a conversation or make any jokes. She only smiled whenever Finch glanced over.

They reached the murder scene in just a few minutes, and the instant the werewolves got close, they all stopped and tensed. Each of them sniffed around, all of them drawn to the exact location of Fox-Pistol's body when it had been dead.

Two of them transformed. At first, Finch was worried they had lost themselves to some sort of rage, but that wasn't the case. The wolves had assumed the more anthropomorphic shape in order to enhance their olfactory sense. They sniffed the leaves, the trees, the dirt, and even the bottom of Finch's shoes.

"Oh, somethin' messed up happened here," Andre said, his nose wrinkled in disgust.

Enzo knelt close to the ground and nodded. Unlike the others, who seemed fascinated and frantic, Enzo had the calculating look of a detective.

"There were at least five people here," Enzo muttered.

"Five?" Finch counted in his head and only came to four, and that was if Fox-Pistol was counted twice—once as herself, and once as Kull. "Me, Kull, and a man. Fox-Pistol's boyfriend."

"There was another woman here," Enzo stated.

Andre snapped his fingers and pointed. "Yes. Another woman. Dead, though. She was definitely dead."

Enzo nodded. "Yeah, that's the weird part. I smell two dead women, one woman who was alive, and two men."

That was news to Finch. He rubbed his chin, baffled.

"The good news is that the woman who was alive is… Kull." Enzo gestured to her. "She has a different scent now that she's a half-spirit. The scent of Fox-Pistol's body ends here."

So Enzo was counting her as two. That still left one dead woman unaccounted for.

And now Finch suspected it *was* Fox-Pistol's boyfriend who had done the killing. He *still* hadn't found the man, and he was the biggest missing link to this whole investigation. Was he some serial killer of women?

"Wait." Finch held up a hand. "Was the other woman dead before she got here? Or did she die here, like Fox-Pistol?"

"Dead before she got here," Andre stated.

Enzo nodded. "Yeah. A dead woman—who wasn't Kull—was here. Not for long. Only briefly."

Why would someone bring a dead body into the woods? Unless…

"Is she undead?" Finch whispered.

Enzo shrugged. "I can't tell. To my nose, the dead are dead. Does that make any sense? They all smell like corpses, whether they're reanimated or not."

Damn.

Finch cracked his knuckles, wondering if he would have to deal with some sort of monster. He hated most things undead, and fortunately, most of them burned fairly quickly.

It was one of the many reasons he had bonded with Ke-Koh, the Ifrit of Rebellion.

"Did the man die?" Finch asked.

Enzo shook his head. "No. He's alive. Maybe the murderer?"

"Well, we got a *lot* of smells here to work with." Andre straightened his sweatpants. "Me and the boys will follow some of these scents and search around, but it's going to take all night to get something solid."

"I appreciate you taking the time," Finch said. "While you do that, I'm going to speak to Fox-Pistol's crew. They know the man who was here—and perhaps I didn't question them hard enough about his location the last time I spoke with them."

———

8:01 p.m.

Somehow, Finch was back at the Lake Merritt Grand Hotel. He hated seeing the redwood elves, and even though none of them remembered him, he was starting to learn all their faces. Fortunately, in this loop of the day, Finch hadn't taken four million from them, so no one really cared that he was at the hotel.

All Finch's disrespect had been forgotten.

Enzo stayed close, his lips permanently downturned in a sneer while they were inside the hotel. He, too, didn't like returning to this place.

Kull bounded forward, straight for the elevator, and motioned for them to follow. They were bodyguards, and allowed to be here, which was how they went completely unbothered all the way to the top floor.

However, since Finch had rewound time, he knew Charlie would die at 9:40 p.m., which was unfortunate. He actually thought well of her, and didn't like the idea she was currently struggling at a card table because the elves were cheating.

Once they reached Fox-Pistol's suite, Kull knocked on the door.

It only took a moment before Louis answered. The twenty-something-year-old man stood before them, both his eyebrows lifting to his perfectly coiffed blond hair.

"*Samantha?*" He took her by the elbow and ushered her inside. "Where have you been? Why haven't you been answering your phone? We've been texting you constantly, and as your manager, you really should answer *my* texts, at the very least."

Louis was about to let the door shut, but Finch grabbed it and threw it open. Louis gave him the once-over and sneered. The man was as thin as a pipe, and was basically a scarecrow wearing an Armani suit, but somehow, he still appeared rather judgmental of Finch's overall appearance.

"These are my bodyguards," Kull said. "And also, they really need to know where Waylon is. You know—my boyfriend?"

Louis narrowed his eyes at her. "I know who Waylon is." Laughing while speaking, he added, "What kind of question was that, darling? Please. I know everyone."

"Do you know where he is, though?"

Louis shook his head. "Last I heard, he was with you. Why? Has something happened? Spill the tea."

"Uh… I think he might be lost."

Louis clicked his tongue in disappointment and then hurried deeper into the suite.

The accommodations were black, luxurious, and large enough for a grand party. The three couches, coffee table, and bar were all set up as though they were expecting at least fifty people to arrive shortly. Drinks were set out in fine glasses, and food was present on several large trays.

A woman in a skintight red dress sat on the nearest couch, her inky black hair pulled up in an elegant bun that showed off her slender neck. She had almost as much head-turning beauty as Kull, but her eyes held an icy intensity that added *menace* to her demeanor.

Harper.

Finch couldn't forget her.

Once Harper spotted Kull, she flew off the couch and rushed to her side.

"Samantha? What's going on?" Harper patted Kull down, shaking her head in disbelief. "What are you wearing? Grunge?"

"Do you know where Waylon is?" Kull asked, ignoring all Harper's demands. "Or maybe where he would go if, let's say, we had a fight?"

Harper's eyes went so wide they almost popped right out of her skull. "*You had a fight?* I knew it. *I knew it.*" She snapped her fingers and pointed at Kull. "I told you. He is a piece of shit. But you wouldn't listen."

"Uh…" Kull rubbed the back of her neck and forced a single laugh. "Yeah. But where would he go? Do you know?"

"Don't chase him." Harper exhaled with all the drama of a daytime soap opera. "You give a man all the power if you chase him. You shouldn't even care he's gone, got it? Let's just party so hard tonight. You should hook up with as many guys as you can—totally forget him."

Finch stepped around Kull and positioned himself in front of Harper. He was done playing games. The fact no one knew what was going on only grated on his nerves.

"I'm a detective with the Oakland PD," Finch stated. "Waylon is a potential suspect in a chain of serial murders. If you have any information on his whereabouts, I'd appreciate your cooperation."

"Serial murders? What makes someone a serial murderer?"

"The unlawful killing of two or more victims by the same offender in separate events," Enzo rattled off like he was a dictionary.

Finch pointed to him. "Correct."

Harper rolled her eyes. "Well, I'm not Waylon's keeper. I'm—"

"If you don't have information," Finch said, half-shouting, "we'll be on our way. I don't need any of your superfluous guff."

Harper frowned and then smoothed her dress. She gave Finch the once-over, a coy smile on her face. "Oh. Wow. You're so no-nonsense. I like that." She practically purred the last sentence.

And in that moment, Finch realized he didn't understand young twenty-somethings.

What is this?

Hadn't Harper hated him the last time they were interacting? Now she was staring up at him through her eyelashes, batting them in a playful way. He just... frowned.

Harper placed a hand on his shoulder. "I've known Waylon for a few years, if you have any questions. Why don't you sit down?"

Finch didn't move. "Does Waylon live in Oakland?" he asked, maintaining his no-nonsense demeanor.

"No. Waylon lives in LA."

Which meant he probably wasn't the killer. It was nearly a six-hour drive to get from LA to the Bay Area, or an irritating plane flight. It wasn't impossible; it just wasn't likely. The majority of serial killers stuck to well-known hunting grounds. It was the safety of familiarity that typically gave them the final boost to commit their heinous acts.

"Does Waylon have financial troubles?" Finch asked.

The number one reason for serial murders was financial gain.

Harper shook her head. "Uh, no. What kind of detective are you? Haven't you seen his videos? He has all sorts of sponsors."

"I'm also his manager," Louis chimed, snapping his fingers twice. "All my clients are ballers."

If Waylon wasn't the killer, he had at least been *there in the woods* with the killer. He and Fox-Pistol had gone off together, alone, for a romantic evening. Apparently, that meant getting out of their vehicle and walking off the road, likely to hook up, though Finch was just guessing. At that point, when Waylon and Fox-Pistol were out in the woods, what had happened? Someone had come up and killed Fox-Pistol? But what had Waylon done afterward?

The wolves had said Waylon was alive.

Perhaps Waylon had hired someone to kill her?

CHAPTER
THIRTY-EIGHT

"Did Waylon and Samantha get along?" Finch asked. "Or were they currently fighting over something?"

Harper *tsked* and then rolled her eyes. "I wish."

Then perhaps Waylon was motivated by bizarre fetishes? Carnal desire was the second-most common motive for all serial killings. Perhaps he had wanted Fox-Pistol dead because he was a necrophiliac. That would also explain the second dead woman at the scene of the murder.

"Is Waylon known to be a sexual deviant?" Finch crossed his arms, trying to rule out all motives.

Louis half laughed. "Oh, my giddy aunt! We should be *filming this.* Can you imagine? The title of the video should be —*My Boyfriend Was Accused of Being a Seggs Deviant.* Everyone would be losing their minds in the comment section."

"Samantha, get over here." Harper waved over Kull. "I'll film it on my phone. It'll be gritty that way. This'll be gold to splice into the party weekend video. And it'll be perfect if you break up with Waylon. We can even say he was creepin' you out, being inappropriate. Perfect, perfect, perfect."

Kull stepped close to Finch and then stiffened her posture. Harper grabbed her phone off the couch and pointed it at them, filming from only a foot or two away. Then she rolled her other hand.

"Okay, okay. Say it again. Ask the question again."

Except for Finch and Enzo, everyone in the room waited with bated breath. Harper kept the phone up, smirking as she angled it just right.

After a deep inhale, Finch asked, "Is Waylon known to be a sexual deviant?"

"*This can't be real*," Harper shrieked. "Waylon is being investigated by the cops! He hasn't shown up to the party. He's probably on the run."

Kull turned around, her eyes wide. She appeared genuinely nervous, and fidgeted with locks of her hair.

"Okay, I got the shot." Harper lowered her camera and shrugged. "I think we can totally make this work. If we splice it together with a few other little things that make Waylon seem predatory, this video will get some of your highest view counts ever."

"Well, but we don't know that Waylon is predatory," Kull muttered. She forced a single laugh and then added, "Why would we lie about this?"

"People fake videos all the time." Harper tossed her phone back onto the couch.

"They do?"

"Don't act surprised. We do it all the time."

Kull pointed to herself. "*I do?* Me?"

Harper placed a hand on her hip. "What do you think pretending to play video games is? Why do we pay Justin to play *Call of Duty* for you? Wouldn't that be *fake?* What's gotten into you, Samantha?"

"I just…" Kull patted her hair, her gaze drifting to the floor. "I… lie?"

Louis waved his hands and sighed. "Don't get weird on me. People fake videos all the time. You think Kobe Bryant jumped over that car? Nope. Fake. Remember when that YouTuber SweetTop got attacked by a SWAT team? Those were just his friends. Fake again."

"I have ulterior motives? What are they?" Kull furrowed her brow.

"Views," Enzo interjected with a grunt. "Fox-Pistol wants views on her videos. So she does whatever she can to get them."

It took a moment for this to sink into Kull's thoughts. She stood still and silent for several seconds, her expression pensive. Both Harper and Louis exchanged baffled glances.

When Kull finally turned to Finch, her bottom lip was quavering. "Wow. You're right, Adair. Humans have ulterior motives for everything."

He stepped closer and lowered his voice. "I was just jaded when I said *everything*," he whispered. "But this is why you have to get to know people. Some humans are trustworthy, and some are not."

"I see…"

Harper sauntered over and then stepped between Kull and Finch. She kept her gaze locked on Finch's as she said, "So, I really like your whole vibe. Why don't you stay for the party?" Harper poked the center of his chest with her pointer finger. "You look like you could use a little relaxing."

Finch brushed her finger away. "I just told you I was in the middle of an investigation. What part of that makes you think I have time to party?"

"Oh, c'mon, it can wait." Harper grabbed the belt loop on his pants and playfully tugged. "A real man would stay to party."

"You've obviously never met a real man."

Finch jerked out of her grip and then headed for the door. He was done here.

"What're you, some sort of forty-year-old virgin?" Harper shouted after him.

But Finch didn't reply. His level of giving-a-damn was zero.

Plus, no one had bothered to answer his last question. Fortunately, he literally had infinite time. If he wanted, he could search all Oakland and eventually find Waylon. The man couldn't have gone too far—he was on a tether. Every time Finch rewound things, he would be jerked right back into position.

When Kull went to join Finch, Louis sputtered something.

"Where are you going?" he managed to finally get out.

"To look for Waylon," Kull replied. "He's my boyfriend. I'll be back. Probably."

"But…"

Enzo's phone buzzed as he walked over to join Finch. "Yeah?" Enzo said, answering the call. "Andre—you find anything?" He smiled. "Good. We'll be right there."

––––––––

Finch drove his car to the east side of Oakland. Kull sat in the back, and Enzo sat in the front passenger's seat. The trip was an easy one, since East Oakland was the bad side of town. Not a lot of people hung out during the evening hours —unless they wanted to get mugged. Everyone stayed indoors. Except for the homeless, who kept to their massive underpass encampments.

Enzo practically bounced in his seat. "I think we've got him."

"Why's that?" Finch asked.

"A wolf with a pack always gets its prey."

Kull didn't contribute to the conversation. She rested her head on the glass of her window and stared out into the darkness.

"Is everything okay, Kull?" Finch asked.

"Hm," she replied.

Enzo snapped his fingers and then pointed at her. "Hey. Do we need to look up motivational techniques to get you happy again?"

After a sigh, Kull tucked some of her red hair behind her ear. She continued to gaze into the gloom, her attention drawn to nothing in particular. "Is there a motivational post to help me get used to lying?"

"What?" Enzo was so buff, it was difficult to turn all the way in his seat, but he managed to face her. "What're you talkin' about?"

"I'm Fox-Pistol now, so I guess I have to make a bunch of fake videos." Kull leaned more of her weight on the window, like she wanted to be absorbed by the darkness outside. "I thought... Fox-Pistol was well liked by humans because she was so amazing and cool. Now I've come to realize it's all fake. Like Caleb's love. Like Liligale's politeness. Maybe all humanity is just hamburgers, being eaten by ever larger hamburgers, in a chain where every human is out to consume what they can before they die."

Enzo turned his intense glower over to Finch. "What is this girl talkin' about? *Explain.*"

While Finch kept half his attention on the road, he said, "Kull, there are a lot of people who aren't like Caleb, Liligale, and Harper. Most humans are basically good. Remember James? Remember why you wanted to give up being a spirit in the first place?"

The mention of James immediately infused Kull with some life. She sat straight up, her eyes twinkling. Then she grabbed the back of Finch's seat and leaned against it. "He was such a beautiful artist. He never used people."

"There are lots of people like James."

Kull slowly nodded. "Like you," she whispered. "Like Bree. Like Liam. Like Enzo."

"Right."

Realization dawned across Enzo's face. "Ah. Okay. I know how to fix your problem."

"How?" Kull asked.

"It's your social media page, right? You can do whatever you want with it. If you don't want to make fake videos... Don't. Go straight from here on out."

Kull practically leapt out of the back in order to give Enzo a hug. She made a delighted *squee* noise as she wrapped her arms around his neck. It was then that Finch realized she wasn't wearing a seat belt. He decided to let that slide.

"It *is* my YouTube channel!" Kull smiled wide, holding on to Enzo with all her might. "I'll definitely make changes. I'll learn how to play video games! *Oh!* Or maybe I can do charity. No, wait! *Prank videos.* So mischievous!"

"That's a good idea," Finch said. "Prank videos."

"You like them? *Then I'll definitely do it!*"

Technically, Finch didn't like prank videos, he just wanted to make sure Kull would be happy. If she made mischievous videos, he knew that deep down, she would continue to love life, and that was a prize all its own.

Enzo patted Kull's arm. "Great. Right. Whatever. I'm sure it'll be amazing."

"You two are the best!" Kull then tapped her lower lip. "I just need to learn how to do all those new things while also in a hot tub."

The resulting bewilderment on Enzo's face was meme-worthy.

But before Finch could join in on the conversation, he spotted Andre near the upcoming stop sign. Finch pulled his Toyota to the curb, and then parked. The dank streets around them were filled with graffiti and smelled of old booze. When Finch stepped out of his vehicle, he quickly made his way over to the werewolf.

"What's the news?" Finch asked.

He glanced around. They were in a residential district, with several tall apartment buildings, some of which were condemned. Finch could guess why—once a meth lab was found in a building, the owners typically had to renovate, which required everyone to leave.

"The scent led me straight over there," Andre said, pointing to the apartment building on the opposite corner.

A chain-link fence surrounded the entire property. A sign hanging on the side read: **WOOLSY PROPERTY MANAGEMENT.**

That was the name of Jay-W's business.

Andre motioned to the security guard walking along the fence. He was a heavyset man with bright copper hair receding so far back, it was well past his ears. He had a tiny goatee, and wore a dark uniform that included a bulletproof vest.

The security guard glanced at his wrist several times, poking a screen on his Apple Watch. When he caught sight of Andre, and then everyone else, he flipped the group the bird. Not the friendliest person.

"I would've kept searching, but the security guard stopped me," Andre said.

Enzo scoffed. "How did that meatball stop you?"

"He threatened to call the cops."

"Oh." Enzo crossed his arms. "Fair enough."

Andre shrugged. "Yeah, I don't mind helping you find your killer, but I'm not about to endanger our pack, or get the boss irritated with me. You can take it from here, right? You can somehow… sneak in? Or something?"

Finch focused on the front door of the building. Boards had been nailed across it, along with most of the windows.

"You're certain someone is in there?" Finch asked.

"The scent of the man and the dead woman both led here." Andre shrugged. "Technically, the scent of the dead woman goes *all over* the city. The rest of the boys are searching now, but the man's scent just… ends. Right at that building."

"Damn."

If the dead woman was moving around without anyone else, this was likely the doing of a vampire or some other crazy undead monster. Finch ran a hand down his face, hating this but determined.

He had fought many undead monstrosities in his prime.

"How are we going to get past the security guard?" Kull tilted her head. "Are we gonna fight him? Or trick him?" She made a karate chop motion. "Knock him out?"

Finch pulled his phone out of his pocket and called Jay-W. The phone only rang once before the man picked up.

"Adair?" Jay-W barked. "Where are you? I told you that I have a job for you and—"

"And you want me to investigate your wife," Finch interjected.

Jay-W sputtered to a halt. Once he gathered his thoughts, he said, "Got-damn, you're good. How'd you know? *Where are you?* Get over to my place right now."

"I already found your wife."

"You… You did?" Jay-W hesitated for a long moment. "Where is she?"

"Do you know the condemned apartment building you

own on the corner of Webb and Henry? The one with the gray paint?"

"Yeah, yeah. Druggies were ripping copper wires out of the walls, and one lady was hoarding things so bad, we couldn't open her door. It needs to be cleaned out. What about it?"

"Your wife is sleeping with the security guard who patrols the place," Finch stated.

Kull's eyebrows rose. "Huh?"

Jay-W hung up. He didn't say goodbye. He didn't ask any further questions. He just ended the conversation.

Two seconds later, the security guard stopped and pulled a cellphone out of his front pant pocket. He answered with a smile, but that quickly vanished.

Jay-W's tirade was so cacophonous, Finch could hear it from across the street. The security guard blubbered something, tried to explain, but it was clear Jay-W wasn't going to stop until all the air was drained from his lungs.

And even then, Jay-W would still find a way to yell at the man, even while suffocating.

The security guard paced, his hands unsteady. After only thirty seconds, he hung up his phone, shoved it into his pocket, and then ran for his car. No other guard came to relieve him—he was just leaving as fast as humanly possible.

No doubt Jay-W had threatened his life more than once.

"The security guard is gone," Finch said.

Andre watched as the security guard peeled out in his haste to leave. "Wow. That was interesting."

"That poor man," Kull murmured.

Finch felt a little bad—but not much. He would rewind this day, and the man would remember none of this. Everything would be okay. Finch just needed to check the inside of the apartment building.

"Why didn't you just ask Jay-W if we can go inside?" Kull asked.

"Because he would've insisted I come to see him. But I knew if he thought the guard was messing around with his wife, he wouldn't care about me anymore." Finch shrugged. "This was just the fastest solution to our problem."

Andre sniffed the air. "Okay. Let's go inside. I still got the scent."

CHAPTER
THIRTY-NINE

ndre and Enzo effortlessly ripped off the wooden boards covering one of the windows. The glass was shattered, and the room within covered in mold. A stench of decay wafted out, and Finch held back a gag. The darkness within was both literal and metaphorical. He knew he wasn't going to like what they would find.

"This place is icky," Kull whispered.

"You can wait out here." Finch motioned to the other side of the street. "We'll be right back."

She shook her head. "No. I'm with you. I'm the best one at detecting magic, remember? You might need my skills."

Finch nodded. "All right. Just stick close."

Enzo and Andre slipped in through the window. Finch and Kull followed afterward. Using the light on his phone, Enzo took point. He went for the door, slowly opened it inward, and then glanced into the next room.

When Finch entered the diseased corpse of a kitchen, he almost vomited. He grabbed the collar of his shirt and pulled it over his mouth, his eyes watering.

Food had been left in the sink and on the tiled floor, most

of which was writhing with insects. The yellow grime that coated the walls told Finch whoever had lived in this apartment had been a heavy smoker. He tried to focus on his job, and not all the biohazards swarming around him.

As a group, they exited the apartment and found themselves in a long hallway.

"Can you still smell the man?" Finch asked.

He didn't understand how the werewolves could stand breathing in a place like this. Their olfactory sense was much stronger. Finch would've died if he had ten times the nose power.

"Yeah, I smell him," Andre said. He motioned to a door in the hall. "It goes there."

Enzo nodded. "I got the scent, too. Let's go."

They crept along, Enzo's light their only source of illumination. If ever there was a time to film a horror movie, it was right now.

When they reached apartment 2A, Enzo tried the handle. It was locked.

"Stand back, I'll break it down," he whispered.

Finch shook his head. He stepped forward and visualized the lock undoing itself. He was still technically bonded with Kull, which gave him access to her mischief magic. The instant Finch touched the handle, it sprang open.

"There," Finch said.

Enzo tried the door a second time, but it slammed into something on the other side, and barely opened a few inches. With a huff, he slammed his shoulder into the door, and it slid in a few more inches, giving them a foot of space to wedge themselves through.

Enzo shone his light around as he entered, his face twisting in disgust. Finch went in second, and quickly shared the same expression.

The apartment was a cavern of chaos.

Piles of newspapers and magazines created extra walls in the already tiny space. Broken appliances, stacks of chairs, and fourteen coffee tables had been hoarded with the frantic energy of a mind seeking solace in *things* rather than *thoughts*.

As Enzo went into the living room, he flashed his light over a mattress that had been gutted for its meager contents. Nearby, the hollowed-out television sets and dismantled radios spoke of a desperation that was not confined to collecting but extended into destruction.

Whoever had lived here—or did live here—was not well in the head.

"Stay vigilant," Finch whispered.

Enzo darkly chuckled. "And here I was just getting comfortable."

Andre braved the rubbish and sniffed the air. He pointed to a door. "There."

They all kept close as they walked over yellowed papers, fast food wrappers, and a dozen toilet seat lids. When Enzo opened the door, he held his breath.

An overpowering wall of *rot* and *decay* washed over Finch. He couldn't breathe. He shook his head, held his breath, and stepped inside.

It had once been a master bedroom.

Now it was a graveyard.

Finch only glanced around the room for a moment, but he counted seven bodies. They were all men, their corpses shoved up against the wall like a pile of dirty laundry. When Finch took a second look, he noted some were more decayed than others.

But they all had the same injuries. Their faces had been torn open and ripped apart, to the point there was no skin left.

Each of the bodies had holes in their stomachs, with all their insides missing. No other parts of their body seemed harmed, except for what the maggots had done in order to drill out of their hosts.

All of them were still fully clothed, though their shirts were pulled up to expose the hole in their guts. Two of them wore suits, one wore a casual T-shirt and shorts, and the others were so rotted and decaying, it was difficult to make out their outfits. Finch couldn't see any similarities between them, other than the fact they were men.

The faces, though—they had been clawed off so thoroughly, the skulls were damaged.

Kull stepped in, and then immediately jumped back out of the room. "Oh, no."

Finch couldn't bring himself to speak.

"Adair," Enzo said through a strained cough. He pointed his light at a man at the far end of the room.

Unlike the other bodies, this one *wasn't* crawling with bugs.

It was also actively bleeding.

However, like all the corpses, the face of the man had been annihilated. There was nothing left from one ear to the other.

Finch knelt next to the man and touched his throat. Still warm. He had likely died within the last two hours. Someone had dragged him here, and then torn into his face.

It was 8:32 p.m.

Why would someone do this?

In Finch's experience, injuries to the face meant this was personal. Whoever had killed this man—killed all these men —had wanted to be close, and wanted them to suffer. It wasn't an efficient killing. It wasn't quick. It wasn't pleasant.

"Adair," Kull said, coughing. She forced herself to step into the bedroom. The carpet crunched with her footfalls. The dried blood had made everything crusty. "That's Waylon. That's... I recognize him."

Finch turned his gaze to the man's shirt. It had Fox-Pistol's logo on it.

Waylon had been murdered.

"What the dipstick is going on?" Andre asked, breathless. He refused to go too deep into room, his body trembling. "I'm out. Whatever this is—I'm not dealing with it."

That was fine. Finch had other plans.

He rewound time. First, because he needed to breathe, and he didn't want to smell the rot mixed with profound sadness any longer. Second, because if this was Waylon, Finch needed to know if he could save him.

Everything froze.

The colors drained away, leaving everything black and white.

And then the shapes around him melted until all was a void of white.

Finch blinked and found himself back in the woods just outside of Oakland.

5:29 p.m.

Kull sat up like she had been jolted to life. "Adair! What... What are we going to do?"

"We're going to save him," Finch said, thankful he had never marked the time to some point later.

He ran over, scooped up Kull into his arms, and then jogged back to the road. His heart hammered as he thought back to the corpse room.

Why?

It still didn't make much sense to him. Wasn't the killer after women? Why was there a room full of men?

"Are we going to stop whoever did this?" Kull whispered.

"Fuck yes we are," Finch said through huffs.

———

Finch drove like a bat out of hell straight for the abandoned apartment building. He had wanted to pick up Enzo, but he wasn't certain how much time he had before Waylon was killed. His primary goal was making it to the scene of the crime before the man died.

Which meant they couldn't stop at the Ross.

Once Finch arrived at the correct four-way intersection, he was surprised to see Enzo was already there, dressed in his tank top and sweats. He waved as both Finch and Kull stepped out of the Toyota.

"How did you get here?" Finch asked.

"Uber." Enzo shrugged. "Believe it or not, I've lived in Oakland for years now, and I know how to get around the city."

Finch snorted back a laugh. "Fair. I'm glad you came—we might have to fight something. It's always good to have backup."

"What about the meatball?" Enzo jutted his thumb over at the security guard.

The balding red-haired man paced along the length of the fence, occasionally glancing over at them with a squint.

"What about him? We *want* the cops to show up." Finch crossed the street. Kull and Enzo hurried after him.

As soon as he made it to the chain-link fence, Finch climbed over.

"Hey!" the security guard shouted. "You're not supposed to be here! This is private property. I'm going to call the cops!"

"Good." Finch brushed off his pants. "Tell them it's an emergency. Someone has been murdered."

Enzo and Kull both made their way over next. Once they joined Finch, everyone went to the same window as before and tore off the wood boards. The security guard watched them for a prolonged moment, as though he couldn't decide on the correct course of action.

Finally, the guard pulled out his phone and spoke to someone, but Finch didn't hear much of the conversation. He leapt into the death-filled building and hurried his way through the first apartment.

Once in the hallway, he dashed down to apartment 2A. Finch relied his own phone's light to guide the way.

Using Kull's mischief magic, he opened the door. Then Enzo slammed into it, opening it a bit further, and they all piled inside. Finch already knew about the nauseating smell, so it was easier to stomach this time around. He had only one thought on his mind, and it was getting to Waylon before it was too late.

Finch burst into the master bedroom, his attention snapping to Waylon. The young man was unconscious on the dirty, crusty floor—his face still intact.

"He's alive," Finch managed to say before his throat closed up in disgust.

"Thank all the good spirits," Kull said from outside the door. "Is the monster here?"

Finch flashed his light around. While there were still six bodies, all actively decaying, there was no one else.

The undead monster wasn't here.

But clearly the monster would be here *soon*. Waylon would die in the next hour or so. If Finch knew the exact time of death, it would be easier to catch the beast.

Finch crossed the room and then knelt next to Waylon. The man's eyelids moved, and Finch suspected he would wake soon.

With cautious movements, Kull made her way into the room. When she got close to Waylon, she frowned. "He's been put to sleep with a witch's brew. Poor guy."

Enzo snorted and rubbed the side of his nose. "What kind of magic is in this room?"

"Cursed magic. The curse of the undead…"

There were many types of curse magics, all stemming from different sources. The undead curses had been with humanity since the dawn of civilization. The type of undead a person became depended on which of the individual's magical cores had been corrupted.

If someone's *crown* was infected with the undead curse, they became a lich, a corpse infused with the magic of the underworld. If the *eyes* became infected, an individual became a shade, a slippery cadaver that could hide from sight. If the *heart* was infected, the person would become a revenant, a beast that grew more powerful with sorrow. If their *soul* was infected, the person transformed into a draugr, a type of zombie that needed to feast on the flesh of the living in order to keep from going insane. And if the *loins* were infected, the person would ultimately transform into a vampire, the monsters who loved draining blood from their thralls more than anything else.

And, in theory, if all a person's magical cores became infected, they became a grim reaper, but Finch had never actually seen that happen in real life, he had only heard rumors.

Which of the undead fit this situation? Which was the killer?

He wasn't entirely certain, but Finch quickly ruled out vampire. Too much blood had been spilled out on the floor.

As Finch shook Waylon, his phone buzzed. Since Finch was holding it in his hand, using it as a light, he saw the screen flare to life with the ID of the caller.

Jay-W.

Why was he calling? He hadn't called at this time in any other timeline.

Finch hesitantly answered. "Hello?"

"*Finally.*" Jay-W grunted. "Where the hell are you? I told you to get to my place hours ago." After a short pause, Jay-W practically yelled, "*Are you at one of my apartment buildings?*"

"Yeah, I'm at one of your apartments. The one that was condemned before some sort of hoarder moved in here. How did you know that?"

"My security guard outside called me!"

Finch rolled his eyes. "I told him to call the cops."

"The police? On my properties? *Never.* I told my guys to call me straight away if anything weird happened, and Rudy told me some detective-lookin' thug came breaking into my apartment, and I knew it was you, Adair. What're you doin', huh?"

"Does some sort of undead creature live in the apartment?" Finch wanted to find this monster no matter what.

"Not that I know of. Are you sayin' there are squatters in my building? *Get rid of them!* Damn squatters make everythin' so damn complicated. Freeloadin' lunatics."

Right as Finch was about to ask another question, a *thump* echoed throughout the apartment hallway. It was hushed somewhat by the walls and the mountains of trash, but Finch heard it all the same. And he knew it was the killer.

He hung up.

The time? 6:14 p.m.

His phone buzzed again, but Finch didn't care.

Both Enzo and Kull heard the thump, too, and they tensed, their eyes wide.

"What's the plan?" Enzo whispered.

"We wait for the monster to come to us," Finch replied.

CHAPTER
FORTY

Finch, Enzo, and Kull stood in the corner behind the bedroom door, listening to the rustling of newspapers and rubbish as someone made their way through the apartment. Whoever this was, they weren't a friend of Jay-W—he clearly didn't want anyone living inside the apartment building. They were Waylon's killer.

No one had their phone light on, but slivers from the streetlamp outside the master bedroom window managed to pour in through the cracks between boards. Finch could see rough shapes, and the outlines of the corpses, but not much else.

The most difficult part of waiting was the foul odor.

Finch would give anything to rip his nose clean from his body.

Waylon, still unconscious, remained on the floor at the back of the master bedroom, his chest rising and falling evenly.

When the door finally squeaked open, the temperature went from eighty to forty like it saw a cop hiding around the bend. Someone stumbled into the room, their steps shaky, their breathing ragged.

Breathing...

Finch knew what kind of undead it was immediately.

A draugr.

Technically, draugrs in all ways appeared to be alive as long as they occasionally feasted on the flesh of living humans. And each of these bodies were missing their internal organs. If the draugr ever stopped eating for too long a time, they would fully transform into a mindless zombie, and act like one straight from a George A. Romero movie.

Which meant draugrs were the only "undead" that still needed air.

Once the monster was fully in the master bedroom, Enzo rushed at the door. He slammed it shut, trapping the beast inside with them.

Finch switched on his phone light and shone it over the killer.

A woman.

But even stranger than that—Finch recognized her.

Her wavy brown hair was puffed in all directions. She wore a small black leather jacket, lacy white top, glittering red earrings, and her pants were tight, ebony, and shiny, showcasing her long legs.

But it was the frantic desperation in her eyes that Finch recognized the most. This was the same woman who had confronted him in the Ross—the one who had claimed to be a Fox-Pistol fan.

"Heldi?" Kull asked. She stepped forward, her eyes wide. "What're you doing here?"

"*Ahh!*"

Heldi screeched so loudly, it rattled the window. She backed away, her eyes perfectly spherical, her hands unsteady. When she took in air, she was gulping it down by the bucketful.

"How…" Heldi's lip quavered. "How…? This is impossible."

"Wait," Kull whispered.

She must have put it all together.

Finch stepped forward. "Heldi. You're done. Put your hands on top of your head, and we don't have to hurt you."

Heldi forced a laugh. It was the insane kind of cackle that only the delusional ever uttered. With a twisted smile, she shook her head. "What is this? *What is this?* I killed her. Fox-Pistol is dead. I… She can't… This is impossible."

Finch recalled Heldi's reactions in the Ross. The woman had been *spooked* to see Fox-Pistol purchasing clothes. It all made sense now. Heldi had killed Fox-Pistol only a few hours earlier. Why wouldn't Heldi be distressed once she found Fox-Pistol walking around afterward?

"What're you doing to Waylon?" Kull asked. "What's going on, Heldi? I thought you said you were a fan of Fox-Pistol—I mean, of me."

"*Shut up!*" Heldi backed away, inching closer to Waylon's unconscious body.

Finch readied himself to leap forward. He wouldn't allow the woman to hurt Waylon, not when he finally understood she was the madman they had been searching for. However, he was curious to hear the woman's explanation for her murderous pastime.

Enzo stayed close to the door, his eyes locked on Waylon. He, too, was concerned about having another potential body on their hands.

"What's going on?" Kull whispered. "Maybe I can help you."

Heldi dragged her fingernails down her left cheek,

leaving red lines on her flesh. "Help me? *You're a dumb bitch, and I hate you.*"

"What? I—I don't understand."

"All you *slutty, pretty girls*, who think you own the world. I hate all of you. Men used to think I was attractive, but then girls like you came along..." Heldi laughed again, the sound grating. "My husband left me. All the men at the clubs just wanted to use me. Then I got cursed. *It was all a sign.*"

Kull panned her gaze over the bodies stashed against the wall. Their faces had been torn away, but everything else remained.

And once Finch heard that rabid tirade, he understood what was happening. Driven insane either through actual mental illness or the draugr curse, this woman was obsessed with obtaining the men who dated beautiful ladies.

Heldi wanted the men for herself. She probably killed the women, and then kidnapped the men and brought them here. Perhaps she was going to ask Waylon to date her—and the moment Waylon refused, because she was clearly deranged, Heldi would kill him, too.

That was why several women had been found dead around Oakland, but no men. All the men were probably recorded as missing, since their bodies were all obviously stashed here in the master bedroom.

That was also why Heldi had been desperate to get Finch's number at the Ross. The moment she thought Finch had been dating Fox-Pistol, her derangement started anew.

"Once you made your YouTube video announcing you'd come to Oakland, I knew I'd have my chance to kill the sluttiest of them all," Heldi said. She cackled, obviously pleased with herself. Then she frowned, ending her mirth. "But... you're alive again."

"Stay behind me," Finch commanded, pulling Kull behind him.

Draugr were known for their strength and speed. They weren't humans anymore, even if the curse hadn't fully taken them.

Then something horrifying happened. The bodies around the room stirred. They leapt from the floor, lunging as though they had only been pretending to be dead.

And with screams that would haunt Finch's nightmares, they moved much faster than Finch had ever seen before.

Two grabbed Enzo's ankles. Two clawed their way up Finch's leg. The last ones went for Kull, but she fled into the corner of the room, keeping her back to the wall.

They weren't draugr. They were zombie puppets, controlled by the main draugr herself. Finch cursed himself for not taking into account all the powers Heldi had at her disposal.

"I love it when psychopaths pick *fuck around, and find out*," Enzo shouted, smiling.

His werewolf form practically burst outward from his body, his black fur and ears appearing in a rippling explosion over his muscles. Claws shot from his fingers, and his feet became canine in nature. When Enzo's skull finally finished reshaping itself and sprouting fangs, he crunched his teeth down on the nearest body, crushing its shoulder in one impressive bite.

Finch drew on the magic of his heart core, summoning forth Ke-Koh's flames. The fire erupted from his palms at the same time one of the bodies dug its teeth into Finch's shin. He yelled out, and then evoked a torrent of fire so bright, and so hot, it momentarily lit up the whole master bedroom.

To Finch's surprise, the embers and heat spread. The air was thick. Dust helped carry fire.

And it spread. The carpet and walls caught the tiny embers and immediately started to fuel them.

Fortunately, the undead were quite weak to fire. The

monster Finch had burned was already a crispy piece of toast after a mere sampling of Ke-Koh's power.

The second corpse jumped up to its feet and flung itself onto Finch. After a moment of struggling, Finch stumbled backward. He blasted the monster with more of his fire, filling the room with an inferno in a matter of seconds—but also torching the other body in the process.

Enzo tore apart another corpse, his werewolf form overpowering the corpses. His claws shredded the flesh, his fangs capable of breaking bone. When he had picked up the attacking body, he had been able to rend one arm off with a single devastating pull.

Finch turned to fight off the cadaver lunging for Kull. He stepped forward, kicked it into the wall, and used more flames, though his eyes were hurting from all the heat, and the room was quickly filling with black smoke.

"*Die!*" Heldi hissed.

On instinct, Finch threw up an arm to defend himself, but to his surprise, he wasn't the target.

Heldi had lunged at Kull. With superhuman speed and strength, she slammed Kull into the wall and then dug her fingernails into Kull's shoulders, drawing blood. Heldi didn't stop applying pressure until her fingers were submerged in Kull's flesh to the first knuckle joint.

Kull's screams sent Finch into a panicked rage.

He *had* been in control of his fire, but when he wheeled around on his heel, flames were streaming off him from the sheer rage. This whole apartment building would burn.

Finch grabbed Heldi by the arm, his palms glowing bright with red-hot flames. He burned straight through her flesh, down to the bone, like she was cotton candy and he was water, leaving her with only a single functioning arm.

"*No!*" Heldi refused to let go of Kull. "It's not fair! *Not fair!*

I shouldn't have been cursed! My whole life was destroyed! I deserve love! Fame! It should all be *mine!*"

Finch swiped at her back, and his hand seared through her shirt and then through her flesh. Before he managed to char her spine, Heldi finally undid her grip on Kull and jumped at Finch. She tackled him to the floor, her strength so phenomenal that she knocked the air straight out of his lungs.

Once on top of him, she drilled her fingers into his shoulder, and then snapped her teeth as she attempted to bite his nose clean from his face.

With his vision tunneling, Finch grabbed her neck.

"I'll kill you," she screamed. *"And then I'll—"*

Finch burned straight through her throat, then her spine, until she was effectively decapitated through immolation. Her head practically hit him in the face as it left her body. It was then that Finch took special note of her earrings.

What had Liligale said? The undead were hiding from the elves using red gemstones that hid their curse?

Finch ground his teeth. Why was every magical being in this city so difficult?

When Finch attempted to get a deep breath, his throat was irritated by the embers and ash.

He rolled to his side, forced himself to stand, and then turned to Kull. "Are you all right?"

With blood soaking her clothing, Kull hurried to his side. Her attention was only on Finch's minor injury. She coughed back the smoke and touched the portion of him that was wounded.

"Are you infected with the curse?"

Finch shook his head. "You can only be infected by a draugr who has completely turned. She could still speak— I'm fine." He grabbed her wrist. "Are you?"

Kull nodded. Then she forced a smile. "We spirits are tough."

"We need to move," Enzo shouted. He stood at the other end of the room with Waylon in his massive furred arms. He was full wolf, his eyes drilling into Finch. The flames were crawling up the walls now, and spreading across the ceiling.

Finch gestured to the window.

Without the need for further instruction, Enzo ran for the window and lunged. He smashed through the glass and even broke through the wooden boards on the other side. Then the werewolf tumbled across the ground and leapt to his feet as though nothing had even happened.

Waylon was uninjured.

Coughing back the ever-growing smoke, Finch pulled Kull over to the window. He helped her out, and then followed afterward.

Once outside, in the crisp evening air, Finch wheezed up all the smoke that had gotten into his lungs. He patted his chest, and then stared at Waylon. The man hadn't woken up.

"What's wrong with him?" Enzo asked.

Finch shook his head. "If it's a witch's brew, he'll be asleep until it wears off. I suspect that'll be in an hour or two."

"What's the plan? Bring him to the hospital?"

"No. The plan is to wait until he wakes so I can question him. Then I draw the Mark of Chronos on the both of you, and we rewind time."

Enzo's wolf ears went ever straighter. "*What?*"

"Trust me. I need to do everything perfectly, but that'll only work if I know for certain this nightmare will end with this."

Kull held her injuries. Despite the obvious pain she was in, she still smiled. "I like it. Let's do that."

Enzo snorted. "Fine. We'll do it your way."

CHAPTER
FORTY-ONE

The apartment building had been a fire hazard.

The Oakland firefighters swarmed the place more thoroughly than bees in a flower field. They brought trucks from every corner of the city, and despite the fact California was in the midst of a fifteen-year drought, they hosed the flames with everything they had.

Finch, Kull, and Enzo waited with Waylon in Finch's vehicle. The man was curled up in the back seat next to Enzo, sleeping peacefully. Kull sat in the front, fidgeting with the radio and playing on Finch's phone.

And while Kull had been wounded, Finch temporarily bandaged her with supplies he kept in his trunk. He had his own varieties of brews, one of which dulled pain rather nicely.

About an hour into the waiting, Waylon finally opened his eyes, blinking several times before fully sitting up.

"What's going on?" he asked.

The man was young—in his mid-twenties at the latest—and his face was as smooth as the day he was born. He had a distinct jaw line, and his eyes were bright green, both of which likely made him popular with the ladies. His sandy blond hair was matted with blood, and his clothes streaked with ash, but he didn't seem to notice any of that.

"Samantha?" he asked, turning his attention to Kull. "What's happenin'?"

Kull scooted closer to the center of the vehicle. She was about to answer, when Finch held up a hand, cutting her off.

"I'm a detective with the Oakland PD," he said. "What's the last thing you remember?"

Waylon rubbed his temples. His eyes focused and unfocused as he panned his gaze around the vehicle. Thankfully, Enzo was no longer in his werewolf form, but the muscled man *did* have crimson smears across his tank top that made him look like a murdering lunatic.

"I was with Samantha," Waylon murmured.

"Yes. And?"

"We were hookin' up in the woods."

Which explained why she never had underwear. Finch sighed and rolled his eyes. "And then what?"

Waylon scrunched his eyes shut. Then he took a deep breath. When he opened his eyes again, he seemed sleepy. "I don't remember. Now I'm here. What happened?"

Although Finch didn't have Heldi to question further, he suspicions were likely correct. Heldi, jealous of women in happy relationships and not cursed by the draugr, went around killing the prettiest of ladies in order to steal their men. Once alone with them in her disgusting apartment bedroom, she would wake them, ask them to be with her, and kill them if they refused.

Heldi had been eating the insides of the men, staving off the draugr curse with their flesh.

Fox-Pistol, who apparently had a gigantic fan base from all over, was caught by the monster and killed. And then her boyfriend was abducted. If Kull hadn't taken her body, Fox-Pistol's story would've ended there.

"Is anyone gonna answer me?" Waylon asked.

"What's the plan?" Enzo asked, ignoring the man. He then crossed his arms and sneered. "We gonna bring him to the hospital? Or what?"

Finch shook his head. "I have everything I need. Now I just need to execute everything in the proper order."

"Really?" Kull's eyebrows went for her hairline. "You know how you're going to do everything perfectly in one day? Does it involve me getting real clothes? Because I think I know what I want now."

Finch exhaled. "Yes. We'll get you clothes."

"What should I do when you rewind time?" Enzo asked.

"I want you to head straight to the apartment. You know who the killer is now. I was hoping you'd call your cop friends in the Oakland PD, and collect the dead bodies in the apartment room. Then you'll follow Heldi, see if she has any other hideaways, and wait for me. We'll capture her together once all the evidence is gathered."

Waylon's eyes got larger and larger. "Did you say rewinding time and… bodies?" he whispered.

But before the man could ask any other inane questions, Finch did just that. He rewound time. The colors drained. The shapes melted. And when he blinked, he found himself on the outskirts of Oakland.

But it was no time to relax.

5:29 p.m.

Finch dashed over to Kull just as she sat up. However, unlike before, where she always seemed happy to see him and eager to get into his arms, she currently wore a frown, her eyebrows knitted.

"Adair," she whispered.

He scooped her up, and then lifted an eyebrow. "What is it? Everything okay?"

"Isn't it sad, what happened with Heldi?"

"Of course. No one wants to be murdered," Finch quipped.

Kull shook her head. "No. I mean she just wanted someone to love her. Right? Just like me? That was what was happening?"

"It wasn't like you at all." Finch hurried toward the road, jogging as much as he could while carrying a full-grown adult woman. "Heldi clearly gave up hope, wallowed in envy and bitterness, and frankly, is deranged. She says things like she deserves love, but what she deserves is a psychiatrist."

Kull wrapped her arms around Finch's neck, her fingers twisting into the fabric of his coat. For a long moment, while he ran, she was quiet.

"What if I become like her?" Kull pressed her face into his collarbone. "What if I can't find someone to love me? What if I give up hope and then also wallow in sadness?"

While Finch mulled over how he wanted to handle this final day, he said, "You won't ever become like her. First, you never give up hope, even when you probably should. Second, I've got your back. You're not going to wallow in bitterness, because I'll be there to pull you back up. Any time of the day, through any problem."

Kull relaxed her grip on his clothing, her smile so wide he could feel it on his shoulder, even through his clothes. "Thank you, Adair. For everything."

———

If anyone had been watching Finch on this particular day, they would think he had the worst kind of ADHD.

Finch left the wooded area with Kull in his arms. He ran

to his vehicle, and sped all the way to the condemned apartment, where he met Enzo and a single police officer. Together, they broke into the building and saved the unconscious Waylon.

The officer then called in backup to clear out the bodies, and identify all the victims. Waylon was taken straight to the hospital. While he had no injuries, it was probably for the best. Finch didn't have time to watch over him.

Finch left the scene and drove like a crazy person over to the Lake Merritt Grand Hotel. With Kull leading the way, Finch entered the high roller room exactly at 6:17 p.m., which allowed him to play blackjack just as he had memorized.

He offered to win back Charlie's debt *without* being snarky.

And he also accepted a glass of wine. Not to drink it, but to covertly pour some of it into a water bottle, to take with him.

Finch won each round just as he had before, until Charlie's four-million-dollar debt was completely wiped from the books. Liligale banned him from the hotel, but Finch barely hung around to hear her condescending speech. Instead, he hurried Charlie out of the hotel, and sped all the way over to Jay-W's.

He escorted Charlie into Jay-W's study, collected one hundred thousand dollars, and then left.

Then Finch took Kull to go shopping for the perfect outfit. Which was ironic, because once she had a full-length dress, heels, and accessories, they went straight to the homeless encampment. Finch prayed the smell wouldn't cling to her new clothes, but he didn't give it much more thought than that.

Instead, Finch allowed Kull to hire the two half-spirits to help her with her prank videos. They both had magic, though it had waned compared to when they had been *full* spirits. Still, with their powers combined, Finch was certain no other human YouTube channel could compete.

Then Enzo called. With all the evidence secured, and Heldi spotted in a normal apartment building not too far from the condemned one, it was time to apprehend her.

And since the spirits insisted on packing their things, Finch left with Kull. They'd be back Saturday morning, to which the spirits agreed.

Driving with all the reckless frenzy of a drunken teen who had just gotten dumped, Finch quickly arrived on the scene to help Enzo and the Oakland PD. Since Waylon was no longer in danger, there was no one for Heldi to hold hostage.

Three police cars were outside the apartment complex, as well as most of the inhabitants. It was 9:01 p.m. by the time Finch stepped out of his vehicle and approached Enzo. The werewolf was speaking with one of the detectives, but stopped once Finch and Kull were close.

"Adair," Enzo said. "This is Detective Elisa Ramirez. She's the one in charge of the supernatural division for the city. I worked with her for several years before I got cursed."

Finch glanced over and tensed.

She had the same reddish skin as the redwood elves, and for half a second, Finch was afraid he'd have to deal with the fae's nonsense all over again. However, the moment he realized she wasn't one of the fae, he relaxed. Her features— her long black hair, and sharp chin—were actually Native American.

She stood with confidence and wore civilian clothing, which was quite common for detectives. Her red jacket, jeans, and black shirt made her seem more like a hip party girl than a cop, but it was her steady stance and harsh look that told Finch she was more than capable.

"Nice to meet you, Detective Ramirez," he said.

She lifted an eyebrow. "You're *the* Adair Finch? I was led to believe you had died."

"I got better," Finch quipped.

That garnered a snort and laugh from the detective. But she regained her seriousness. "Enzo informed me of everything."

That statement didn't sit well with Finch. He waited, his breath held. If Enzo had told her about his ability to rewind time, Finch would need to restart the day. He didn't want normal mortals knowing his abilities. He couldn't really hide it from spirits or other creatures made of pure magic, since many of them could speak to Chronos himself, but mortals generally didn't know the extent of Finch's power.

And that was by design.

"He said you got into town and found the dead body," Detective Ramirez said. "He said you followed the trail to the condemned property, and since you know the owner, were allowed inside to investigate. Is that all true?"

"That's exactly correct," Kull said, interjecting herself into the conversation.

She looked completely out of place. While everyone else wore practical clothing, she wore a black dress that went to her ankles, with a slit up the side almost to her hip. She also wore a belt on the outside of the dress—which was completely and utterly useless since it wasn't holding anything up.

Kull's high heels were also some of the most club-height shoes Finch had ever seen. At least she walked in them with confidence, but it was still strange to see just outside an active police investigation.

"Who is this?" Detective Ramirez asked.

Finch sighed. "My assistant."

The look she gave him was the same Enzo had given him the first time the man heard that explanation.

"She's a half-spirit," Finch continued. "And she's the one who helped me follow the magic trail to the bodies." In order to move the conversation on, he gestured to the apartment. "If you want, I can go in and subdue the draugr. I have plenty of experience with the undead."

"No need," the detective replied, confident. "My boys will handle it from here. We have a warlock on staff who is in possession of a chain from a chain demon. You familiar with them?"

Oh, Finch was very familiar.

Chain demons were some of the worst creatures to deal with. They could render individuals helpless by causing paralysis. The chains of the chain demon were the most potent. Even just tapping someone with it would cause them to lock up and fall to the floor, unable to move.

Shouts from the apartment building drew Finch's attention. Several cops poured out the front door, two of them hauling Heldi by her underarms. She was completely limp and unable to move, even though her eyes were half open.

"There she is," Detective Ramirez said. "Looks like we're going to wrap this up before it gets too late."

Finch held up a hand. "Wait. While you're still here…" He reached into his coat and pulled out his water bottle half filled with red wine. Even though she looked confused, Finch handed it over to the detective. "This is wine they're serving over at the Lake Merritt Grand Hotel. If you have your warlocks or witches analyze this, you'll see it causes delusions in anyone who drinks it."

Detective Ramirez spun the bottle in her hand, examining the liquid. "You mean the hotel and casino run by the redwood elves?"

"They're cheating," Finch stated. "Robbing good people of their money in subtle ways. I'd definitely suggest you send a team over there tonight or tomorrow, before they realize I took some of their wine home with me."

In this time loop, Finch never made promises *not* to tell the cops about the rampant cheating. And he really disliked Liligale and all her knights. Now that he had taken her half-spirit of delusion, and informed the police, he was hoping the elves would lose most of their clientele.

"Wait, didn't you just get into town?" The detective glanced up to meet Finch's gaze. "Enzo said you arrived at six."

"That's right."

"And you tracked down a murderer—while also collecting evidence of a casino's cheating?"

"I also made sure two homeless half-spirits got jobs and disproved a woman's infidelity to her husband," Finch muttered.

"But... you've only been here a few hours. How did you—"

"I'm *the* Adair Finch," he quipped. "And if you don't mind, I need to go because there's still a few things I want to get done tonight."

CHAPTER
FORTY-TWO

n this final version of the day, Finch took Enzo and Kull to one of his favorite restaurants.

Outback Steakhouse.

It wasn't the fanciest. As a matter of fact, most people considered it tacky. The restaurant had the theming of an Australian steakhouse, with all the puns of a forty-year-old father. They served *kookaburra wings*, a *bloomin' onion*, *shrimp on the barbie*, and a *Sheila filet*.

But the first time Finch and his brother, Carter, had finished a big job, they had celebrated at Outback Steakhouse, and since then, Finch had always considered it a comforting space.

For years he had avoided it, though. Even remembering how much his brother loved the bloomin' onion was too much. But now, with Enzo and Kull, it felt happier again. Warm and inviting. Nostalgic.

Once seated at the table, Finch scrolled through the call history on his phone. He went to the missed calls and stared at the "Jessica Finch" name that lingered there. She had called again.

He took a deep breath, envisioned some peaceful green fields, and then tapped the name. He didn't call her. Instead, he opened up the messages.

He wrote:

> Sorry I missed your calls. It's been difficult lately, but I've gotten some help. If you want to talk, I'll be free tomorrow.

Then Finch tucked his phone away, determined to make things right.

"I'm gonna get a full rack of ribs," Enzo said as he set down the menu.

The entire inside of the restaurant was covered in Australian knickknacks. Everything from boomerangs to pictures of kangaroos plastered the walls. It made Finch smile.

Kull set her menu down as well. "I'm going to get the outback burger."

"You're going to get a hamburger?" Finch asked, genuinely surprised. "I thought you said you weren't ever going to eat those again?"

She nodded. "I did say that. But I think I was just overreacting. People like hamburgers for a reason. They're good. And while some people like them a little *too* much, to the point they'll lie just to get them, that doesn't mean it was the hamburger's fault." Kull smiled wide. "Hamburgers are beautiful."

Enzo glanced between Kull and Finch. "We are talking about the food, right?"

Ignoring that comment, Finch chuckled. "I'm glad your bad experiences didn't sour you to hamburgers."

Kull stared at him with striking blue-gray eyes—always reminding him of the ocean. "I think if I find the right person, hamburgers will be amazing."

"Oh, we're definitely not talking about the food," Enzo murmured, shaking his head.

Finch cleared his throat and set his own menu down. "So, uh, are you still going to be an Twitter star?"

"YouTube," Kull corrected. "And Instagram. And Twitch."

"Right. You're still going to do that? Make some pranks? Or something?"

"I think once Waylon gets out of the hospital, I'm going to meet up with Harper and Louis, and I'm going to be Fox-Pistol. By myself. For a few weeks. Is that okay?"

"Why are you asking me?"

Kull shrugged. "I just want to make sure that if I don't like it, I can come work at your agency. Or if something bad happens, I can call you?"

Finch nodded. "You can always call me."

"Well, after a few weeks, I'm going to return to tell you all about it. I want to level up as a human, and get even better and better, and really impress you!"

"You don't need to impress me."

Kull pointed at him. "I want to. *You*, specifically. You'll see. I'll be the best human ever, and you'll have to acknowledge it. And if you ever need my magic, you *have* to call me. Understand, mister?"

Again, Finch nodded. But the brief mention of the agency reminded him of something. Finch reached into his coat and pulled out the small yellow envelope Jay-W had given him. It was stuffed with bills, but that was how Jay-W did most of his business—in cold, hard cash.

"Here." Finch pushed the thick envelope over to Enzo. "A year's pay."

Enzo stared at the fat envelope a moment before taking it. After a long exhale, he opened it up and counted it all. His gaze seemed distant as he closed it tight.

"After this, do you mind if we stop somewhere?" Enzo whispered. "I think… I'd like to see someone."

————

Finch pulled up to a quaint home at the northern end of Oakland. The suburbs were nicer here, though it was clear most families in the neighborhood weren't even middle class. The houses were old, but well loved, and most of them used chain-link fences to portion off their yards.

Enzo stared at the house before them, his mouth set in a frown. It was night, but the white paint on the building was so new, it practically glowed in the moonlight, giving the house an ethereal feel.

"This is where your wife lives?" Kull whispered.

"Ex-wife." Enzo sighed. "She remarried."

"O-Oh. Because she thinks you're dead?"

"That's right."

The inside of Finch's car was silent for a long moment. Eventually, Enzo leaned against the back of the driver's seat, his breathing heavy. "Adair, can you mark the time here?"

"Yes," Finch stated.

He glanced down at his phone.

11:23 p.m.

"You sure you want to do this now?" Finch asked. "We could wait until tomorrow morning."

"Aiysha's new husband works evenings. He's a security guard. I figured…" Enzo swallowed hard. Then he shook his head. "I figured Zuri would be asleep. I don't know if I can see them both at the same time. This way it'll just be her."

Finch marked the time. Then he pulled out his Sharpie pen and drew the Mark of Chronos on both Kull and Enzo, so they'd remember everything about to transpire.

Enzo slipped out of the car. He didn't bother shutting the

door. Instead, he just strode toward the house, never glancing back, never looking away. He opened the chain-link gate and then made his way up the path to the door.

He knocked, as softly as he could while still being heard.

Then Enzo waited.

Silence filled the street. Finch and Kull said nothing.

When the door finally opened, it revealed a beautiful woman in her mid-thirties. She had short, wavy hair, dark eyes that somehow shone in the moonlight, and the athletic frame of someone who loved the outdoors.

Aiysha wore a white shirt and pajama pants, but somehow made it seem elegant.

The moment it dawned on her who was at the front door, her eyes went wide.

"Elijah?" she said, half gasping. "*Elijah?*"

He held out his arms, and Aiysha flew into him with a bear hug, her arms wrapped around his torso as tightly as possible. She held on to his tank top as tears immediately poured from her eyes. Aiysha's lips quavered, her words failing her.

Enzo held her tenderly, running one hand over her hair, his other arm around her back. Tears also streamed down his face, falling onto her shoulders.

"I think about you every day," he said, his voice strained. The raw emotion in his voice threatened to steal his words as well. "You and Zuri are the best things that ever happened to me. You two are my happiness. You're the only things that keep me sane when everything goes wrong."

"*Elijah…*" was all Aiysha was able to utter. She just sobbed into him, holding ever tighter.

Enzo squeezed her back, his chin shaking. "I'm sorry. I've got to go."

"*Go?*" Aiysha snapped her gaze upward to meet his. "You can't *go*. Don't go, Elijah!"

"I don't want to. But I have to. I just wanted one last chance to hold you. It's selfish. I'm so sorry."

Aiysha let him go and attempted to wipe the tears from her face. They continued to stream from her eyes, soaking her cheeks. "Don't go," she said. "Don't leave me again, Elijah!"

Enzo couldn't respond. He placed a hand over his eyes, the pain of the moment clearly seeping in.

And Finch understood why Enzo had both wanted and dreaded this moment.

So he rewound time.

Everything froze in place. And then the colors all swept away, until the world was black and white. Finally, the shapes dissolved until Finch was in a void of white.

He blinked, and Enzo was back inside his vehicle.

11:23 p.m.

His sobbing filled the cab.

Finch and Kull said nothing. They waited in the car together, content to admire the night sky while Enzo cried.

Finch wasn't entirely certain how to make this better. He knew why werewolves left their families. And he had seen firsthand what could happen if Enzo lost control of the lycanthropy curse. But still, he hoped in his heart he could help Enzo become the first ever werewolf who had full control over himself. Perhaps then, he could return to Aiysha, and say those things for real.

Eventually, the car became silent again.

After a deep and ragged breath, Enzo said, "Thank you. I just wanted to tell her one last time."

"We could always come back." Finch glanced at him in the rearview mirror.

Enzo half smiled. "Maybe when Zuri is older. Just so I can tell her I'm so proud of her."

"Whatever you want."

Then Enzo opened the back door and stepped out.

He walked across the street with purpose, a determined look on his face. When Enzo made it to the front door, he pulled out the fat envelope of cash, and placed it in a potted plant in such a way that someone exiting would see it, but the world wouldn't.

And then Enzo left it there.

"I don't understand," Kull whispered, watching intently from the passenger seat. "Why would he do that?"

Finch rubbed his eyes. "Because that's true love."

THANK YOU SO MUCH FOR READING!

Please consider leaving a review—any and all feedback is much appreciated!

Adair's Finch's story continues in *24-Hour Warlock*!

To find out more about Shami Stovall and Adair Finch, take a look at her website:
https://sastovallauthor.com/newsletter/

To help Shami Stovall (and see advanced chapters ahead of time, including Chronos Warlock) take a look at her Patreon:
https://www.patreon.com/shamistovall

ABOUT THE AUTHOR

Shami Stovall is a multi-award-winning author of fantasy and science fiction. Before that, she taught history and criminal law at the college level and loved every second. When she's not reading fascinating articles and books about ancient China or the Byzantine Empire, Stovall can be found playing way too many video games, especially RPGs and tactics simulators.

Shami loves John, reading, video games, and writing about herself in the third person.

If you want to contact her, you can do so at the following locations:

Website: https://sastovallauthor.com
Email: s.adelle.s@gmail.com

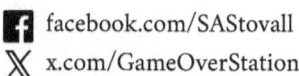

facebook.com/SAStovall
x.com/GameOverStation